Fervent Charity

together by fate
bound by friendship

PAULETTE
CALLEN

Table of Contents

In memory of my grandmother, Pauline Sirien Magnus, who told me the stories, and Cindy Poulson, who allowed me to re-tell her those stories on a bus ride to New Jersey.

And for Greg.

This book is dedicated to the horses—all of them. Throughout history, we have used them and abused them. We still do. They have served us with devotion and deserve better than being forced to race and to pull carriages through city traffic. They deserve better than being hunted down in their wild herds because we think the land can't support so many of them, while what the earth can't support is so many of *us*. They deserve better than to be slaughtered for food. My grandmother loved horses and knew them well. She passed this love on to me, perhaps through blood, perhaps through her stories. I am only here on this planet as the person I am because a horse named Dolly saved her life when she was a tot. In gratitude, I offer up this Buddhist metta practice for them.

May all horses be happy and free from suffering and fear.

May all horses be healthy and free from illness and injury.

May all horses be safe and free from harm.

May all horses live with ease.

God knows, they deserve it.

Acknowledgments

I am grateful to many friends who have supported and encouraged me during the writing of this book: particularly Patty and Jimmy Short and Gayle Nilson. Thank you, my anchor and my engine—the Every-Other-Monday-Night-Brilliant-Writers' Workshop: Harriet Mendlowitz, Mary Burns, Suzanne Heath, Jon Fried, Gary Reed. Thank you, Doris Hess, Bruce Bryant, and Carol Johnsen for your creative jumpstarts; Jim Nilson for insights and information about local South Dakota lore; Bill Morris for showing me which end of a gun is which; and Valerie K. Angeli for telling me about horses. Thank you, Tony Guest of I.S.W.D. and Roger Broadway of Roger Broadway Ent., Ltd. for answering my questions about well drilling in the late nineteenth century. And many more thanks are due to Ylva Publishing, who picked up the reins after they were dropped.

And above all things have fervent charity among yourselves: for charity shall cover the multitude of sins.

– I Peter 4:8 –
King James Bible

Prologue: November 1899

WALKING WAS EASIER ONCE THEY were out on the frozen lake where ankle-deep waves of snow alternated with strips of unevenly powdered opaque ice—its bumps and ridges attested to the struggle: Crow Kills did not go meekly to its winter rest.

The blizzard had swept the ice, banking tons of snow along the shoreline and in the trees. Only one who knew about the cabin and recognized the particularities of the two barren cottonwoods projecting through the highest drift like old bony hands grabbing at the sky would know that a human dwelling was there.

The man stopped.

The boy said, "There is no smoke."

Little Bull, chief of the Red Sand Tribe of the Dakotah Sioux, and his son Leonard unstrapped the shovels they'd carried on their backs and began to dig. In spite of the cold, both were sweating when they finally reached the door and made an opening wide enough to step into. Little Bull pulled at the door, then pried it open with his shovel. Not wanting to break the door, he pulled it slowly; its creaking shattered the frozen silence like the cry of an injured crow, until the opening was wide enough for him to squeeze through. In the dark, the cold cut deeper. Leonard slipped in behind him. The only light was the little that came in with them.

When his eyes adjusted to the dark, Little Bull went to the old woman seated at the table. He took her hands in his. She seemed lifeless, but he did not feel himself in the presence of death. "Make the fire, Son."

Little Bull half carried, half dragged the old woman to the bed in the corner, covered her with blankets and began to rub her hands and feet.

Chapter 1: April 1900

Lena Kaiser gave birth on the dining room table presided over by the horse doctor while her husband lay passed out on the living room floor. Will Kaiser had come home drunk to find his wife in labor and had stayed ambulatory just long enough to make it to Gudierian's Harness and Tack Shop and back.

She would have been more comfortable on the floor, or standing up clutching the back of a chair, which is how they found her, but Harlan Gudierian made her lie down on the table so he would not strain his back while he fished around inside her.

Between waves of pain, Lena cried out for Gustie, for Alvinia, for her mother, but her mother was dead and Lena feared that she soon would be too.

The screen door opened a crack. Kermit Torgerson stuck his head in, turned tail, and ran all the way home. "Ma! Something bad is happening at Kaiser's."

He gulped a deep breath. "Mrs. Kaiser is hollering something awful."

"Is Doc Moody there?" Alvinia wiped her floury hands on a dish towel.

"I didn't see him. All I saw was Mr. Gudierian."

"Gudierian?" Alvinia fairly roared the name as she tore off her apron and flung it across a chair. "Go find Doc Moody and don't come back till you've got him."

"Yes, Mama." The boy hit the screen door running. It banged shut behind him.

Eight of Alvinia's ten children were gathered around the table. "Vernon, are Brownie and Popper still hitched to the wagon?"

"Yes, Mama."

"Bring them around for me, Son. Alice, get my bag. You and Betty are coming with me. Lavonne, stay here with the little ones and tell Daddy where we are when he comes home for dinner. Boil up the potatoes and don't let the roast dry out. We probably won't be home till late. Malverne—you run now and get Mary Kaiser and then go to the depot. Tell Willie to telegraph Joe Gruba in Wheat Lake for Gustie. Tell him Mrs. Kaiser is having her baby. Tell him Will Kaiser will pay him for it tomorrow."

Eldon and Ira, the two youngest boys, watched wide-eyed as chairs scraped the floor and their older siblings scrambled to obey their mother. Kirstin, still in her highchair, banged her tin cup loudly so as to be part of the excitement.

Alvinia Torgerson was a large, pretty-faced woman, strong and light on her feet. As soon as her last instruction was given, she was out the door, her midwife's bag in hand, followed by her two eldest

4

daughters. Betty took the reins and galloped the team toward the south of town.

The Torgerson women entered Lena's house quietly. Alvinia paused in the doorway between kitchen and dining room, surveying the scene. Lena's still, small form was lying on the table, covered by the tablecloth. Beside her lay a bloody newborn still connected to the afterbirth. Gudierian's hands and arms were bloody as a butcher's, and his eyes flicked back and forth in panic. When they came to rest on Alvinia, they widened in fear, then closed in relief. He stepped aside.

Only Lena's lips moved as Alvinia lifted the tablecloth. She saw more blood, way too much. "Get me some ice, Alice."

Lena tried to speak, but Alvinia hushed her. "Don't you worry now, Lena. From here on in, me and my girls've got you. We've got you."

Alvinia tied and cut the umbilical cord and then handed the baby over to Betty. Alice hammered furiously at a chunk of ice she had pulled out of Lena's ice box. Alvinia filled a basin with hot water from the cook stove's reservoir. The two sisters exchanged glances. Their mother's nose and ears had turned bright red, and her pale blue eyes had darkened two shades. Alvinia was in a rage. They did not often see her like this. They maintained a respectful silence.

Alvinia carried her basin back into the dining room where Harlan Gudierian still stood, his bloody arms hanging limply at his side. "Harlan, get out of here." She jerked her head toward Will Kaiser's sprawled figure. "Take him with you. You can clean up outside at the well."

5

"He's too heavy. I can't lift him." Harlan was bigger than Will, but the excess was in fat, not muscle, and much of it, it seemed to Betty and Alice, was in his head. No one ever talked back to Alvinia.

"Then drag him!"

"Where to?"

"I don't give a tinker's damn where to! Leave him in the barn or get Sheriff Sully to throw him in jail where he belongs—and you with him!"

Harlan Gudierian shuffled into the living room and began to study the physics of moving Will Kaiser.

The infant squawked.

"Is she all right, Betty?"

"Fine, Mama. Just fine."

"Lena, you hear that?" Alvinia removed the bloody tablecloth and began cutting away Lena's dress. "Your baby's all right. You have a little girl."

Mary Kaiser, Lena's sister-in-law, arrived, stepping over Will as Harlan Gudierian dragged him by his feet out the front door. She hardly took notice—she had stepped over Will Kaiser before, almost everyone in town had once or twice—but when she saw Lena looking more dead than alive, she gasped, "Oh, dear Mother of God! Tell me what to do, Alvinia."

"Rip up a sheet into squares about yay big." By the time Mary had torn a sheet, Alice had pounded the ice into a snow-like consistency. Alvinia made small pockets of crushed ice from the squares of cloth and packed Lena's womb to stanch the bleeding. Rivulets of tears streamed from the outside corners of Lena's eyes. She whispered, "Stuffed like a chicken."

"Now, you hush." Alvinia dabbed the tears away with a piece of leftover sheet and touched Lena's cheek soothingly with the palm of her plump hand.

She and Mary washed Lena carefully and patted her dry. Mary found her nightgown and they slipped it over her head. "It's all we can do. Let's get her to bed."

Alvinia lifted Lena in her arms and carried her into the bedroom. They tucked her under thick covers.

Lena whispered, "I want my baby."

Betty brought the infant, clean and wrapped in a soft blanket, and placed her in Lena's arms.

The wind swirled through the branches of naked cottonwoods, laid low the stiff brown slough grasses, ran its unhindered course over fallow fields, and raised the gooseflesh on Will Kaiser's naked torso as he washed himself in the icy stream of well water. The morning was too cold for an outdoor bath. He had come to with a fuzzy, throbbing head and unsteady gait, but when Will rattled the screen door of his own house, Alvinia would not let him in. Before he turned away, he asked, "Is Lena doing okay?"

"Barely. No thanks to you." Alvinia shut the door in his face.

Giving up on the thin pump stream, Will plunged his head up to his shoulders into the horse trough and then gripped the rim of the trough and shook himself like a dog. Water flew out of his hair and ears.

The screen door flapped shut behind him. He cocked his head to see out of his good eye the tall, slender woman approaching him on his right. The

7

shrill sun glinted off her glasses. Over one arm was draped a clean shirt and a towel and in her hand she held a cup. In her other hand she carried a pot of steaming coffee.

She came to his side and without a word offered him the towel. Now he remembered passing her black mare stalled next to his gelding in the barn. As he dried himself he said, "'lo, Gus. Alvinia wouldn't let me in."

"I overheard. I was in the bedroom with Lena."

"Lena all right?"

Gustie sucked her lower lip. "I think she will be." She sensed he was afraid to ask the next question. She reassured him, "The baby is fine. You have a daughter."

Will held the towel to his face. When he finally lowered his hands, Gustie took the towel and gave him the shirt.

"How long you been here?" he asked.

"Since just before dawn. Alvinia and the girls have been here all night. So was Mary, but when I got here, she went home to fix Walter's breakfast."

"Doc ever show up?"

"This morning. He'd been out at the Grode place. He gave Lena something for pain. He'll be back this evening."

Will's large hands were clumsy with the buttons of his shirt. He left the bottom two undone and tucked the shirt into his trousers. "I really did it this time, didn't I?"

"I'm afraid so." Gustie poured coffee into a cup and gave it to him. She set the pot down on the overturned washtub next to the trough and perched on the rim of the trough. Will, still unsteady in spite of the icy water and bracing wind, sat down heavily on the tub. He ran his fingers through his wet hair, smoothing it down with the palms of his hands. He winced and felt for a tender spot on the back of his head. "How'd I get this bump on my head?"

"Harlan dragged you out of the house yesterday. I guess you got knocked around some."

Will took a sip of his coffee and winced again. "This is *your* coffee." He gave Gustie a lean smile. "You could stand a pitchfork in it."

Gustie nodded and grinned back. The wind had loosened strands from the mass of brown hair piled on top of her head and was whipping them across her face. She tried to tuck them back under her hairpins.

"You don't look so hot," he said, taking another sip.

"I was at Crow Kills. I rode all night to get here."

"Figured." He nodded.

She countered with, "You look like something mucked out of the barn."

"Feel like it." Then, his voice husky with misery, he asked, "What am I going to do?"

She considered him sadly. In spite of everything, Gustie liked Will Kaiser. She casually plucked a bit of lint off the dark fabric of her split skirt. "My grandfather used to drink himself sick. He was a good man, otherwise. I wish I could have done something for him. But I was a child then." Gustie's eyes met Will's for a moment. His hands were shaking so badly he couldn't pour himself a second cup of coffee. She did it for him.

The sound of the door opening and closing and girls' voices carried to them over the wind as Alvinia and her daughters came out of the house. Will didn't look up. Gustie watched them climb into their wagon. This time, Alvinia took the reins, driving the team in a circle stopping in front of Gustie and Will. Her face bore the strain of the long night, but her rage was still in full flare. She looked down on him. "Will Kaiser, a woman is not a horse. But a man can sure be a horse's ass." She snapped the reins over the rumps of her horses and the wagon jumped behind the team.

Will raised his head and watched them go.

"Alvinia saved Lena's life, Will."

"Yup. I know." He drained his cup and shook out the dregs on the grass.

Gustie stood. "Let's go in and introduce you to your daughter."

The sun, bright and climbing, had little warming effect on the chilly April wind that scudded across the prairie and rattled the shutters on Mary Kaiser's house. Winter clung to the earth in dull patches of snow and ice and could still rise again in force, unmindful even of the bells of Easter.

Mary sat alone in her chair by the window, looking out. She kissed the crucifix and made the sign of the cross: *In the name of the Father and of the Son and of the Holy Ghost. Amen.*

Her fingers traveled the rosary, the string of beads as familiar as the road home. She sat like this every day, praying with devotion, but today she prayed with a special intention. Mary had had her share of attending at bedsides, but yesterday, seeing her sister-in-law lying still, white-lipped, and helpless, had shaken her. She offered up today's Rosary for the wellbeing of Lena and her baby.

I believe in God the Father Almighty, Maker of heaven and earth and in Jesus Christ, his only son, our Lord, who was conceived by the Holy Ghost, born of the Virgin Mary, suffered under Pontius Pilate, was crucified, dead and buried. He descended into hell... The wooden beads soothed her hand as the words soothed her heart...*on the third day He rose again from the dead; He ascended into heaven, sitteth at the right hand of God, the Father Almighty; from thence He shall come to judge the quick and the dead.*

After all these years of faithfulness, Mary's fingers moved as nimbly as her babka's had. Even toward the end, hardly able to do anything else, her eyes closed, her lips just trembling the prayers, her grandmother's skeletal fingers could still play out the beads fluently. In her grandmother's final hour, the child Mary whispered, "Let the Rosary take you to heaven, Babka." And it did. *I believe in the Holy Ghost, the Holy Catholic Church, the Communion of Saints, the forgiveness of sins, the resurrection of the body and life everlasting. Amen.*

Someday, she thought, the Rosary would do the same for her; but now it was Mary's anchor to life, her sustenance, and, along with the two rose bushes outside her house, her connection to her beloved grandmother. *Our Father, which art in Heaven, hallowed be Thy Name; Thy kingdom come...* Mary spun the words out in her mind. The repetition was not meaningless. The sense of each word, of each prayer, was planted deeply in her heart and flowered in their continuous flow, like Babka's roses transforming sunlight into blush and fragrance. *Hail Mary, full of grace, the Lord is with thee. Blessed art thou among women, and blessed is the fruit of thy womb, Jesus.* Mary nodded her head on the sacred name as her prayers and thoughts continued, uninterrupted. She could see the rose bushes through the window— twiggy stumps covered with straw and tarpaulin, and in her mind's eye could see their summer plumage— the one bearing crimson blossoms; the other, mauve which aged through the summer to magenta. These same two bushes had survived the journey with Mary's grandparents from Poland, bloomed in prairie earth, and again survived freezing winters, drought, and a blight of grasshoppers that utterly consumed everything else. Babka had covered the two bushes, and without sleep fought the swarming plague for three days with broom and fire.

The wheat was lost, and the garden. Only the roses were saved, and Babka's family decided she was crazy. Little Mary knew that Babka was as sane as all the saints. *Holy Mary, Mother of God, pray for us sinners, now, and at the hour of our death. Amen.*

A few years after Babka's death, the roses survived another transplanting when she married Walter Kaiser and moved to town. Mary nurtured them, worried over them, and loved them like children. *Glory be to the Father, and to the Son, and to the Holy Ghost. As it was in the beginning, is now, and ever shall be, world without end. Amen.*

Mary moved into the next decade of the Rosary and hoped for a wind that would carry warmer weather,

weather with no mean surprises, when she could carefully remove the bed of straw that had sheltered her roses all winter and work some sheep manure into the soil. Sheep manure was not as readily plentiful as horse or cow dung but it was better, Babka insisted on that. So Walter rode far from his rounds as a well driller to find farmers that raised a sheep or two, collecting manure for his wife's roses.

Mary's devotion to her religion, to her roses, and to the memory of her grandmother sprang from one root. The child who traversed the swamp to look after Babka, learned to tend the roses, say the Rosary, and pay devotion to the Blessed Mother—all from this old Polish woman who wore bangle earrings and treasured flowers more than food.

Hail Mary, full of grace...

Mary brought her soup or bread, emptied her chamber pot, washed her bowl, and brushed her hair. On warm days, before Babka became too sick to leave her bed, they sat outside between the rose bushes. Later, Mary sat on the bed with her, and they did the beads and said the prayers. The sound of the words, over and over, like the lapping of waves, transported them—above the smells of sickness and old age, the urine-soaked rags, the unwashed body, the hunger that seemed always to gnaw at them—to a place where death seemed like an invitation to something better. *Holy Mary, Mother of God, pray for us sinners, now, and at the hour of our death. Amen.*

Mary told Gustie how she crossed the slough. "It was Babka's good luck that it never got too deep. The water was never above my knees. Mostly it was just mud squishing around my ankles. I liked it best in

the winter, though, when I could walk on the ice."
Besides Walter, Gustie was the only person who knew
about her babka. Augusta Roemer was the only friend
Mary had ever had.

Hail Mary, full of Grace...

"When Babka died, I took her rosary and her
prayer book. It's in Polish. I can't read it." *Holy Mary,
Mother of God, pray for us...* "Babka said that flowers
bring life. When she first came to this country as a
girl, she said, the prairie was quiet. There was just
the tall grass—grass as high as a pony's back—and
the wind. All grass, no trees...no birds except during
migrations. Everybody said it was the grain crops
and then the trees that brought the insects and birds
and the life to the prairie, but Babka said it was the
flowers. Only flowers, with their color and perfume,
could do that."

Chapter 2: May 1900

ALVINIA WAS FAVORED WITH LIGHT blue eyes and corn silk hair, traits she had given to each of her children. She was sixteen when she gave birth to Betty, her first child. Leaving her comfortable Minnesota home at fifteen to traipse off with Carl Torgerson had been a reckless and foolish thing to do, and Alvinia had not regretted it for a moment. Carl had been the hired man on her father's farm and five years her senior. When her parents found out that Alvinia and Carl had gotten married at the city hall, they carried on so, that the newlyweds started west, with Carl working whenever he could. It took them two years and two children to get as far as Charity, South Dakota. Elef Erdahl, the butcher, hired Carl and, more or less, adopted the young family as his own. When Elef, an old bachelor, died, he left his business to Carl who made the most of it.

Carl Torgerson was a man with no education who had been taught to read and write by his young wife. He was an orphan who treasured his family, a man with no prospects who had turned a modest butcher business into a prospering enterprise. The first in Charity to avail himself of electricity for profit, he installed freezers, which he rented out to people to keep their meat. With his freezers came ice cream. In the last year, he had added on to his establishment a comfortable parlor where people could enjoy a hot cup of coffee and a cold dish of ice cream served up by one of the smiling Torgerson children.

Alvinia had seen in this quiet, unremarkable looking man, a vein of gold. He had never told her he loved her. But she felt loved. His reticence complemented her ebullience, and their children fell in between their two extremes of temperament. Alvinia was also aware of how simply lucky she had been. Every young woman marries a man in whom she has high hopes. Not every man is able to fulfill those hopes as well as Carl had.

Lena, nursing her baby in the chair across the room from Alvinia, was a case in point. Will was a hard-working man. And a hard-drinking man. Lena had certainly not bargained for that when she married him. But things happen and people change. An accident at a drilling site lost him an eye in the same year that an altercation with his brother Oscar robbed him of the hearing in one ear. Those two disabilities coming upon him all at once started him on the drink. He hadn't been able to leave it alone for long since.

Lena's home was tiny. Alvinia, used to larger spaces, felt like she was in a doll's house. Lena's immaculate housekeeping and her skill with a needle didn't conceal her poverty. Will made a decent living, but most of his money ended up with Leroy, the local tavern keeper. To Leroy's credit, he threw Will out more often than he invited him to stay.

But Alvinia and Lena were discussing Betty, not their husbands. Lena was saying, "Betty is a sensible girl."

"I know, but she's so taken with this boy..." Alvinia shook her head and watched Kirstin happily thumping the floor with chubby hands and feet.

"You don't think she'll get herself in a family way, do you?"

Alvinia was silent.

"Well, if that's what you're worried about, you'd better let them get married. 'Better to marry than to burn.' Martin Luther said that. And he ran off with a nun! Ha!" Lena caressed the infant's forehead with her finger. "If you don't give them your blessing, Alvinia, they'll just run off like you and Carl did. Come to think of it, you two haven't done so badly."

"This is different." Alvinia's lips clamped together in a hard line.

"Wirkus's have that farm. It'll be Pauly's one day."

"Farm! Half of it's a slough and the other half's a rock patch. They barely scratch a living out of that place. And they're Catholic! I don't want Betty leaving our church."

"Maybe Pauly will join ours."

"You know that won't happen. You know how the Catholics are."

"You should watch how he treats her," Lena added, trying to be helpful. Then she said, "The two of them might make something of that place."

"I don't want her marrying a polack and living on a rock patch, Lena! She's a beautiful girl. She was first in her class. She can do better. We hoped to send her on to do something with her music, but we just couldn't manage it." Alvinia's voice broke, and she busied herself with reaching into a voluminous pocket and taking out a ball of red yarn, which she passed down to Kirstin. The ball became a fascinating point of interest to the child who stopped abusing Lena's floorboards. "So, Lena, how are you getting along?"

"I'm sure grateful for your girls, Alvinia. I don't know what I'd do without them. Wish I could do something for them."

"There's nothing they need doing. So, don't you worry about it."

"They've been doing all my washing and ironing and cleaning my house...that must mean more work for you at home. You don't have them to help you. I feel bad."

"Now you listen. Carl and I came here with not two pennies to rub together. People helped us all along the way. That's the way it is. Or if it isn't, it should be. And I have Malverne and Lavonne at home who are good help to me."

"Mary has been here every day, too, to make sure I get a little nap in the afternoon. She's turned out to be a real brick." Lena felt a lump rising in her throat so she changed the subject. "What do you hear from Severn?"

18

"Got a letter yesterday." Alvinia puffed with pride at the mention of her oldest son. "He's too busy to be homesick. Doc Moody did a wonderful thing for Severn, getting him a scholarship."

"He'll make a good doctor. He has a nice way about him."

Lena felt sorry for Alvinia that someone hadn't been able to give Betty the same kind of help to go off and study music that Doc Moody had given to Severn. But Betty already played the piano like nobody's business, so she did all right.

The baby had her fill. Lena tucked her breast inside her dress and did up her buttons.

Alvinia held out her arms. "Give me that chicken and you have your dinner."

"Can I fix you something?"

"No. I ate with Carl at the shop before I came over."

"Then just have a piece of pie with me and a cup of coffee so I don't have to eat by myself."

"Never turn down a piece of your pie, Lena. But you know you don't have to bake. I'll be happy to send..."

"Oh, fiddlesticks! I can bake a few pies. I'm not as lazy as all that!"

Alvinia followed Lena into the kitchen with Gracia in her arms and Kirstin toddling after, still clutching her ball of yarn.

Lena dished up a slice of apple pie for Alvinia, home-made bread covered with clotted soured cream and sugar for herself, and a black coffee for them both. "Now, what can I get for you, Precious?" Lena bent down and touched Kirstin's nose with her finger.

"She can have some of my pie." Alvinia settled in comfortably with Gracia in one arm and Kirstin leaning into her knee. She gave Kirstin the first bite of pie off her fork. "I saw Oscar and Nyla at the shop this morning," Alvinia said. "They were picking up a couple packages of meat. Nyla sure looks tough." She enjoyed the next forkful of pie herself. "What do you put in your pies, Lena? They are always better than mine."

"They are no better than yours. You always like something better when you didn't have to make it yourself. I know I do. Except for Ma's cooking."

"Is Nyla sick?"

"I think Ma is just working her to death. And she doesn't have the gumption to say no."

"I see them going in and out over at Gertrude's. They're not still living there, are they?"

"You bet they are! Ma whines whenever Nyla says she wants to go home, and Oscar doesn't mind because he's got two women waiting on him now instead of just one. He's something, that one! He doesn't care how much extra work it is for Nyla in that big house or that she might not want to live with her mother-in-law."

"Well, Gertrude is what? In her seventies? She needs somebody to look after her."

"Fiddlesticks!" Lena spat out in disgust. "There's nothing wrong with that old battleax that a good swift kick in the bloomers couldn't fix."

Alvinia stifled a laugh behind her hand. Anybody who knew Lena knew that she was not fond of her mother-in-law, Gertrude Kaiser.

"Will looks in on her and so do Mary and Walter. I go over once in a while, not so often now since Gracia was born, and she sure doesn't hurt herself getting over here to see her only grandchild. I'd go over there more often if I knew she gave a snap about Gracia, but she doesn't. Walter told me that she said to him and Mary once that she wasn't taking care of any more babies. That she'd brought up four and that was enough. The idea! That I would want her to take care of my baby! I've never asked her and I never would.

"I felt sorry for her after Pa was killed, but she's so kind of hard like. She's not easy to be nice to. But she's Will's mother..." Lena shrugged and took a big bite of her cream-soaked bread. "I feel bad for Nyla, but she's going to be stuck as long as she doesn't put her foot down. That's what I had to do with Will. Oh, he's good to his mother and there's nothing wrong in that. But we're not going to run over there every time she has a pain. Especially since I know she's strong as an ox." Lena did a good job of eating and talking at the same time. She finished her bread and cream, cut a slice of pie for herself, and continued.

"She can just sit over there being a sour puss with that sour-puss Oscar. I don't know how Mary stands to be around them but she goes over every day." Lena remembered finding her mother-in-law, alone, swathed in black taffeta, sitting like a fat spider in the web of her cluttered house the day that Pa's body had been found in the barn. For a while, Lena even suspected her, like a spider, of killing her mate. It turned out that she hadn't, but the nasty old thing had sat there, rocking back and forth, mewling about Will having done it. Lena had never forgotten how quick she had been to throw Will to the dogs. She had not forgotten and she had not forgiven. Ma Kaiser had remained in her widow's weeds and tried to draw her children in and had succeeded in entrapping Oscar and Nyla. Lena didn't care about Oscar one way or the other, and when she thought of Nyla, she just shuddered. Better Nyla than herself.

Alvinia had heard Lena go on about her in-laws before, especially her mother-in-law, and she sympathized. Even though Gertrude had always been, as Lena said, cold and stand-offish, after old man Kaiser's death, Alvinia, as Gertrude's nearest neighbor, had extended herself, visiting her with gifts of food, produce from her garden, and a little conversation. She was always received with an irritability that bordered on suspicion, even hostility. Alvinia gave up her neighborly overtures.

Gracia had fallen asleep in Alvinia's arms. She carried her back to the living room and laid her in her cradle, covered her up with the crocheted blanket that Lena had made, and took Kirstin by the hand.

"I think I'll get back. See what kind of trouble my chicks have gotten into. Thank you for the pie, Lena." Smiling, Alvinia wagged her finger at Lena. "I still think you put something in your pies that I don't."

Lena just shook her head and laughed. "Thank you for stopping by." She chucked Kirsten under the chin. "Bye now, Precious."

"I'll be sending one of my chicks over to check on you. Lena, you say something now if you need anything. You hear me?"

"I will, Alvinia. I will."

"And say hello to Gustie for me. I haven't seen much of her lately."

"I'll do that. Bye bye now."

Say hello to Gustie. Well, that was nice of Alvinia, since Lena knew Alvinia didn't care a lot for Gustie, but Gustie was Lena's friend so she made allowances.

Lena Kaiser and Augusta Roemer were about as different from one another as two women could be. Yet, they shared a love of horses and a sense of humor that flared up out of nowhere over trifles, and for awhile, they had also shared a condition unusual for women of their age: childlessness. After Gracia was born, however, things had not been the same between them. Lena was busy now with the baby, and while Gustie helped her with shopping and a bit of cleaning when she was in Charity, she was spending at least half of her time on the reservation, something Lena still couldn't understand. Lena didn't like Indians. *No matter what you do for them*, she thought, *they always end up back in a tipi.* Of course, allowances could be made for Jordis, who had a college education. But that just proved Lena's point. Jordis, with her college education, was where? Living in a shack with an old Indian woman back on the reservation and succeeding apparently in dragging Gustie down with her. Lena tried to shake such thoughts out of her head, but they stuck there. She couldn't help it, even though Jordis had suffered on Lena's behalf. Well, she reasoned, that wasn't really true. Gustie had come in just in time to save Lena's life and Jordis had just got in the way. Technically, Jordis had suffered for Gustie, not Lena. And no matter what, she didn't like Gustie spending so much time out there with the Indians. It didn't look right.

She heard a squeak from the living room. Gracia was awake again already. She put a spoonful of pie in her mouth and savored it. Yes, her pies were better than anybody else's. It was the tablespoon of whiskey that she sprinkled over the layer of sugar that did the trick. She licked her lips and went to pick up her baby.

Chapter 3: June 1900

THE PRAIRIE WAS IN ONE of its bad moods: the heavens grumbled and shot forth an occasional thin slice of lighting the way a cat flashes a claw. Gustie liked weather and preferred stormy to fair. It was more interesting. But she had learned not to challenge or take casually the prairie's temperament. Dakota winters brought death to the careless, the unfortunate, and the foolhardy; lightning killed and started fires; summer storms spawned deadly tornadoes. As with capricious cats, one rarely knew if the weather would actually bite or slink off to reappear docile and caressing.

With Biddie tucked in at Koenig's livery stable, Gustie relaxed in the cozy comfort of Olna's Kitchen. The smells of baking rolls and pies, roasting chicken, and the continuously brewing coffee made Charity's one cafe a pleasant place to be on a dark afternoon.

Gustie pulled aside the blue-checked window curtain. The sidewalk was deserted. Across the street a dim light glowed behind the window of the Stone County Gazette. The shadowy forms of Arnold and Janelle Prieb moved within. The train whistle announced the arrival of the east-bound freight train. Arnold and Janelle paused to listen. Moments later, a light flickered behind the smaller window next door. Emil Mundt, Charity's postmaster, was getting ready for the first mailbag of the day.

Gustie sipped her coffee and waited. Jack Mohs came trotting up the street with the mailbag slung over his shoulder. He dropped it off with Emil, pausing for only a moment's greeting as he did every morning but Sunday, and sprinted back to the depot for his next assignment.

The street was again deserted. The sound of the departing train whistle lingered, caught in the thickening storm-dark air.

Suddenly, Mary Kaiser filled the frame of the window. Head down against the rising wind, and staying close to the buildings, she made her way north. She stopped, startled to see eyes looking at her through the glass. Gustie smiled quickly and Mary's face relaxed. She turned around and walked the few steps back to the door of the cafe. The bell on the door jingled as she came in. Cold and wind had heightened the color in her cheeks; the light rain beginning to fall had coated her skin, making her complexion dewy.

Mary Kaiser was remarkably beautiful. Gustie wondered if anyone else noticed. "Mary, what are you doing out on such a day?"

26

She pulled off her headscarf, sat down at Gustie's table, and smoothed her black hair away from her face. Her dark eyes were bright. Beauty was seldom spoken of here, where people considered a clean house, a kind heart, and well behaved children greater assets in a woman. "I stopped by Lena's this morning. She was up all night with the baby. I watched Gracia so she could rest awhile. I'm trying to get home before the storm hits." She asked Gustie with some alarm, "You're not going to try to make it home are you?"

"No, I'm waiting it out here."

A crack of thunder made them both jump. Mary laughed shyly. "Maybe I'll wait with you."

"Good. You can join me for dinner. I haven't ordered yet. Is Gracia all right?"

"Oh, she's fine. A little restless. She was sleeping when I left."

They made small talk over roast chicken, mashed potatoes, and carrots. Gustie and Mary had become friends when together they had cared for Lena during an illness that had been precipitated by a family tragedy. Mary had surprised Gustie with her efficiency and willingness to help in an almost unbearable situation, when neither of Lena's sisters could help, or her other sister-in-law, Nyla, would. Gustie knew better than anyone the worth of the woman sitting across from her. While Mary possessed none of Lena's confidence and seemed unaware of her appealing physical presence, her sweetness and beauty were disarming. Gustie could not fathom what she was doing married to Walter Kaiser, who, Gustie thought, resembled a creature crossed between a frog and a banty rooster.

"Mary, are you happy?" While Gustie had often turned the question over in her mind, she was appalled to hear it come out of her mouth.

Mary swallowed a mouthful of pie and looked at Gustie with laughing eyes. She reached across the table and took Gustie's hand. "Oh, Gustie, I like you so much."

"You do?" Gustie had been prepared for *Mind your own business.* "Why?"

"Because you asked, and not because you're nosy. Nobody else has ever cared whether I'm happy or not. At least not enough to try to find out."

"Well, are you?"

"I'm not miserable. And for me, that's a blessing. Walter has..." Gustie sensed Mary had never put her feelings into words before. "Walter has...allowed me... to not live in misery."

Mary described a childhood that was little else but wretchedness. Her parents had been unsuited to life on the frontier, cursed each year by bad luck and illness. Of six children, Mary was the sole survivor. "I still remember the smells of sickness and dirt. The barn was never kept clean." Here she had paused for a long time. "There is nothing worse smelling than a dirty pig barn, Gustie, unless it's a dying woman who hasn't bathed in years."

Gustie, deeply moved, wiped her mouth with a napkin and considered her friend, who was so unaware of how like a rose she really was, having sprouted from a dung heap.

Mary continued, "I was fifteen when Walter came to our place. He'd made some deal with my pa to drill us a well in exchange for some pigs. Then...let's see...

Walter was twenty. He was good-natured. Laughed and talked a lot. Didn't bother him that nobody talked back. He didn't seem to notice the squalor of our place. Although, by that time I was older and doing better at keeping things up. Babka was dead and so was my mother. So all I had to do for was my pa and me. But Pa didn't care what I did, really. Walter came every day for a few weeks. He had a hard time getting to water. The old well was dried up and I was carrying water from the creek. Finally, he did find water, and after he finished the well, he told Pa that he'd take me instead of the pigs. So my pa said, 'You willin', Mary?' I said I was. Pa was glad. He couldn't spare the pigs." Mary smiled ruefully and stirred cream and sugar into her coffee.

"It's not as bad as it sounds. Without saying much Walter and I had a sort of agreement. I'd never seen many men besides my pa and some of the old farmers who came over once in awhile, mostly for a buryin'. Walter was the only young man I'd ever met. He had a good team of horses that were well fed. He had his equipment and a new buggy. He told me he'd build us a house anywhere I liked. I picked the place close to the church so I can go to Mass every day no matter what the weather. He told me I could have whatever I wanted. He needed a woman in his home to do for him because he didn't want to live with his ma and pa anymore, and if the work was too hard for me, he said I could bring a girl in to help me. I never did. I like taking care of my own things.

"He has always been as good as his word. I have everything I want. My house is beautiful, Gustie. I have real lace curtains. I have two sets of china

29

and crystal glasses that came all the way from St. Paul. He even moved Babka's roses for me." Her voice trembled. "I have flowers planted all around. Mostly roses, but some peonies, and tulips for the spring. Marigolds for the fall. Come and visit me sometime, Gustie."

"I will, Mary. I certainly will."

"Lena doesn't like me. I know she doesn't. Because I'm Polish and Catholic. Not a good combination if you marry into a German Lutheran family. Oh, it's fine to marry a German if you're Norwegian—like Lena did— but not if you're Polish. But mostly she thinks I'm weak. She didn't have it easy as a girl either, but Lena was strong. She got away and worked, went out on her own. Did you know that when she was fourteen, she rode the train Sunday evenings to Argus to work, and came back Saturday mornings? I could never do that. I could never do what you did, coming out here to a strange place on your own. You and Lena are both brave and strong. I'm not. I need Walter to take care of me. Lena looks down on me for that."

"Why? She has Will."

"That was a love match. From the first. They were crazy about each other. They still are when he's not drinking.

"Walter is...he's not a drinker. He's not mean like Oscar. He is..." Mary lifted her eyebrows, smiled enigmatically, and sipped her sweet coffee.

Chapter 4: July 1900

O WEN BRAATEN, THE NEW INDIAN agent, had restored
the Agency in Wheat Lake to a place where the
Dakotah could not only get their fair share of
annuities, but also buy or trade for food and goods.
Gustie and Jordis had come in with Dorcas's morning
catch of fish to trade for coffee. Gustie also purchased
sugar, flour, and canned goods for Dorcas to tide her
over until the next disbursement of annuities.

Jordis was inside, in conversation with Owen,
while Gustie loaded their parcels onto her wagon.
In an effort to shield her horse from the July sun,
she had left the mare and wagon in the alley in the
L-shape formed by the back of the agency building
and its storehouse.

In the heat of summer, Gustie made these trips
back and forth between Charity and Crow Kills at
night. On this day, she wanted to be on the road to
Charity by sundown. She had to be there tomorrow,

because she had promised to help Alvinia and Mary prepare for the open house after Gracia's baptism. The baptism wasn't till the end of the month, but they all agreed that Gertrude Kaiser's house needed a lot of work. This was too important a day to just throw something together slap-dash. They wanted to do it right, in a way that Lena would have done herself if she'd been strong enough.

Tomorrow Gustie also had an appointment with Pard Batie, her lawyer, to finalize the purchase of her house. By the town's good graces, she had been allowed to live on land abandoned by a homesteader, but it was time to make her position more secure.

She was about to lead Biddie and the wagon around to the front of the building when she heard a shuffling behind her. She turned to see Jack Frye in his usual state—drunk and dirty. In spite of his unfocused whiskey stare, his expression was menacing. He blocked her exit from the alley.

Gustie did not feel afraid even though Jack Frye had reason to wish her ill. "Mr. Frye, you are in my way."

"Mr. Frye, you are in my way," he mocked. "You're in my way."

My Christ, how I hate drunks. She was impatient to be out of this alley and away from his stench. "Move aside, please, Mr. Frye."

"Move aside, please, Mr. Frye." He mimicked her again. "Move aside." His spindly arms and legs bobbed in puppet-like motions. "I still have lots of friends in this town," he slurred. "Lotsa friends." His voice cracked. "Good friends, and nobody here likes what you did, taking the Indians' part against me.

32

You don't have any friends here." He pointed a grubby finger at her then swung his arm wide.

"No one has given you a job, then, among all your good friends?" The sun poured itself out, dry and hot, and Gustie felt itchy and irritable. "You're still spending your days in the saloon?"

"I have something put by. I can afford to take my time," he boasted.

"Yes, you must still have profits from the years you cheated the Indians out of what is rightfully theirs."

"Nuthin is rightfully theirs! They didn't work for nuthin!" He jerked and bobbed in emphasis. "Things is given to them for doin' nuthin!"

Behind him, Jordis materialized. Like a cat who has, at long last, cornered a bug, her eyes gleamed, a smile twitched on her lips. Gustie thought of warning Jack Frye but too late.

Jordis grabbed the back of his collar and pulled as she kicked one leg out from under him. He landed hard on his back. Her right foot came down on his chest and she leaned in heavily on her knee. She had smoothly drawn the long blade from her boot, and he already felt the point of it in the hollow of his throat. His eyes bulged. Spittle drooled out the corners of his mouth.

Gustie could barely hear Jordis, but Jack Frye could most certainly hear, "I am going to kill you." He croaked with fear. She continued, her voice velvet. "Nobody will miss you. I'll give your body to Shoonkatoh to feed the hungry spirit."

He cried, inarticulate whining.

Pure pleasure shone in Jordis's eyes. She had told Gustie once that she wanted to kill Jack Frye.

Only Chief Little Bull had prevented her from doing so, while he tried to get rid of Frye legally. As Indian agent, Frye had cheated and insulted the Dakotah for years. The fact that a few letters from a white woman to some influential friends back east had accomplished what the Indians themselves had been unable to do, rankled some of them. Others were simply relieved that he was gone and did not care how. Jordis, Gustie suspected, was one of the rankled.

Gustie recognized naked hatred on Jordis' face. And cruelty. "Don't, Jordis." She said it quietly. Jordis was not hers to command, but she felt a need to diffuse what might be boiling over in the scene before her.

"She doesn't want me to kill you." Jordis played the point of her knife back and forth across Frye's throat.

"Listen to her, Miss," he blubbered.

"Be grateful to Miss Roemer. She has saved your filthy life—today."

Jordis straightened up, sheathed her knife, and climbed into the wagon seat without another glance at Jack Frye. Whimpering, he rose part-way to his feet, and, like a tipsy spider, scrabbled away.

Not until they were on the road to Crow Kills did Gustie ask, "If I hadn't been there, would you have killed him?"

"If you hadn't been there, he would not have stopped in that alley."

The sun floated high above the horizon in the late afternoon sky. Dark would be a long time coming. Usually, these lingering evenings of summer—these periods to leave taking—passed too quickly. But

34

today, Gustie felt the need to be away, to be alone with the rhythm of Biddie's hooves on the road and the less quaint throbbing of thoughts in her head.

Jack Frye was a pathetic, mean-spirited, but now harmless man. Stripped of his job at the agency he was just a poor snake with its fangs pulled out left writhing in the dust. The sight of Jordis playing with him had disturbed Gustie.

Gustie wished she had brought a hat. Lena was forever telling her she had to wear a hat in the sun. When she left Philadelphia, she had also left her three aunts behind—three women who had tried in vain to dress her in corsets and lace and teach her the ways of a society lady. Now, she had Lena who tried to teach her the ways of a woman who wished to keep the trappings, at least, of a civilized life in the middle of what really seemed at times to be nowhere. Lena's advice often had more to do with life, death, and health than with appearance. This time she wished she had listened. Her skin felt scorched.

The hum of insects, the occasional chirp of a lazy, sun-soaked bird, and the muffled rolling of wheels on the dirt trail were the only sounds for about half a mile until Jordis spoke.

"What?" Gustie stared at her.

"Tell me about your father," Jordis repeated.

Gustie was taken by surprise. At that moment, her father was far from her thoughts.

"He must be a powerful man to persuade the United States government to do so quickly what we could not get them to do at all. Father Flagstad and a number of other whites around here even wrote on our behalf. They got nowhere."

"He's not powerful. He's...influential. He knows powerful people."

"Same thing."

"He's a judge—I told you that. He's retired now. I told you that too..."

"That is all you told me. I did not know you had a father till he wrote to you last May."

"I didn't want to get anyone's hopes up in case he wasn't able to help. Dorcas knew I wrote." Gustie brushed an insect away from her hair. "My father and I aren't close."

"What is he like?"

"He's..." Gustie thought how to describe her father in a word or two. "Self-possessed."

"What was he like with you?"

Gustie tilted her head in a dismissive gesture. She had no words for that.

"Was he unkind to you?"

"Unkind?"

"Some white men hit their children. Did he beat you?"

"No! He never beat me! What an idea! He indulged me. I had whatever I wanted. Did as I pleased."

The wagon rolled along the dirt track with a subtle rattle of its old parts. Gustie felt Jordis's waiting like a soft but strong hand pushing her forward. "It's just that, I couldn't...*see* him."

Jordis cocked her head and waited.

"When I was a child, I thought of him as a kind of magus, a wizard who could summon a fine mist around himself. I could never quite see through it. I could never really see *him*. When I was fifteen I went to court and slipped in the back and watched him preside over the case of a man who had robbed a store. It was a revelation. The shadow, or the mist that hung around him as my father wasn't there. As a judge he was clear, distinct. I could feel that everyone in the courtroom respected him. The lawyers seemed to be afraid of him, in fact. He ran a strict court, but he was merciful. I went back to watch him many times. After the verdict and before sentencing, he always asked the accused person to come to the bench and tell him why he had done what he had just been convicted of. What was interesting is that sometimes the stories they told him were different from what they had said in the witness box. I remember the case of a robber—he'd been hungry. That's all. Just hungry. My father sentenced him to some prison time, mostly I suspected, because there he would be fed regularly. One of the clerks told me that Judge Roemer would probably see to it that the fellow found some kind of work when he got out. I realized then that my father was a good man. We weren't Quakers, but behind his back, people referred to him, fondly, I think, as the Quaker Judge. I don't know if he ever knew about that."

"What did he say when he saw you in his courtroom?" asked Jordis.

"He never saw me."

Jordis remained still.

Gustie continued. "After I had seen him in court, I had this fancy that I should go out and break a law, get myself arrested and tried in his court. Then he would have to see me. I staged it all in my mind, very dramatically. The accused will please rise, he would say at my sentencing. And I would rise and step

37

forward. And then he would ask as he asked every person, 'Explain to me sir, explain to me madam, why you did what you did.' And I would say—'in order to see my father, Your Honor.' Well, I could be ridiculous in my own head, sometimes."

"You were not ridiculous, Gustie."

All at once Gustie felt defensive of her father. "He was better on paper." An unreadable expression took over Jordis's face. "He used to travel—when I was a girl—and he would write to me. In his letters, he was almost warm. Sometimes, even witty." The trail passed slowly beneath them. "I used to think it was because he had wanted a son and that in letters he could forget that the child he was writing to was a daughter. Then, at times I thought maybe he would have been happier with the sort of daughter he could have covered in ribbons and lace—I was never that. But when he was with me, he didn't..." Gustie trailed off. "...I really don't know why..."

"Did you ever ask him?"

"No."

"Why not?"

Gustie answered, articulating something as certain and unchangeable as the law of gravity. "I could never have asked him such a question. I doubt if I could even now."

Jordis looked straight ahead. An "mmm" sounded in the back of her throat, reminding Gustie of Dorcas. All she lacked was the old woman's squint that signaled she had just figured something out.

"Mmm...what?"

Jordis replied, "It explains why, when you are not happy with me, you do not say so."

38

Gustie was getting more and more annoyed. She didn't know why. "I'm not unhappy with you very often."

"You were just now."

Gustie shifted the reins into her left hand and rubbed her right palm on her skirt.

"You did not like what I did to Jack Frye," Jordis persisted.

"It's not for me to tell you how to treat him. He cheated you, not me."

"No, but you can say you did not like it. You did not like what I did."

"No," Gustie admitted.

Jordis nodded.

A muskrat waddled onto the road ahead of them. Gustie reined Biddie to a stop. They sat for a while, unmindful that the animal had already disappeared into the weeds on the other side of the road. The black mare tossed her head to rid herself of a fly. Gustie felt like something was about to burst inside her. She tapped the horse's rump with the reins and they once again moved forward.

"Why did you not like it?"

Gustie exhaled in audible irritation, "Because it was unbecoming!"

Jordis remained still. Only her eyes shifted sideways to look at Gustie. A smile began to take over her face until she laughed out loud. "You are a true Philadelphian, Augusta!"

"I'm not," Gustie said, still irritated and more so with Jordis's laughter.

"Oh, you are." Jordis's laughter subsided into a chuckle. She lightly caressed Gustie's cheek with the

back of her hand. "You are a lady. A fine lady at that."
She was no longer teasing.

"I'm sorry," Gustie was embarrassed, but now
smiling herself, still feeling strangely disturbed.

Jordis asked, "Tell me more about your father."

"Why do you want to know about him?"

"Because I think he is important to you. I want to
know about the things that are important to you."

Gustie had never gotten used to Jordis's directness.

"What did he do to make you leave Philadelphia?"

"Nothing. He just didn't do anything to make me
stay." The hot breath of the prairie now carried the
cooler scent of Crow Kills—its fishy, intensely green
smell. Gustie thought with relief how they would soon
be at Dorcas's cabin where she could have a dip in
the lake before supper and then take her solitary
night ride back to Charity. But Jordis took the reins
from Gustie and gently drew them back. The horse
stopped. Gustie, aware of the endless patience in this
woman and knowing they would sit there all day if
she didn't say something, began, "Clare's brother,
Peter, was making her life miserable. She needed to
get away from him. He would never have given her any
peace. He made our association known to everyone in
the most lurid and obscene terms. He stirred up a
scandal that had social repercussions for my aunts
and, possibly—I never really knew—professional ones
for my father. At the least, my family must have been
disappointed in me, and at the worst—humiliated.
But no one *said* anything. Not to me or in my defense.
Clare and I decided to leave Philadelphia. It was the
only way for her to escape her brother and for me to
get out from under all that stifling politeness.

"I went to my father's study. I think I was hoping he would ask me to stay. Tell me that we would weather this thing, fight it out. I thought he could have done something to put an end to Peter's nonsense if he had wanted to." Gustie kept her eyes straight ahead and waved away a fly. Surprised at how sharp the pain of this memory still was, she said, forcing her voice to remain unbroken, "When I told him we were leaving, all he said was, 'You are certainly of an age to do as you please.'"

She took back the reins and urged the mare forward again. As the wagon trail curved up a slight incline, they began to see the tops of the cottonwood trees that formed a patchy fringe around the lake. "Then he said, 'I'll have Fitszimmons'—that's our banker—'draw up an arrangement. You'll need money…' I didn't let him finish. Something about the way he said that made me furious. I told him I didn't want his money." As they rounded the curve over the top of the rise, Crow Kills appeared, coolly mirroring the blue sky, shining like a mirage in the heat.

"It was the only time I ever showed him much feeling. I stomped out of his study. Slammed that big oak door behind me. Clare and I left the next day. That was the last time I saw him or communicated with him until I wrote him last November asking for a favor and for money."

"How did you know he would help?"

"I knew he would try. It's the kind of thing he can do. Respond to a letter. From a distance."

The land surrounding Crow Kills could not rightly be called hilly. Ridges of varying sizes, grown over with wheat grass and buffalo grass, looked like the backs of great muskrats lying about the lake. The wind blew and parted the grasses one way and then another in a lazy kaleidoscope of color from brown to tan, and closer to the lake, from green to yellow green.

"What else do you think about your father?"

"I think he only wanted a wife. He didn't want a child. And then he had both. And then, the wrong one died."

They passed on their right a small mound, at the head of which grew a young cottonwood, transplanted there as a sapling by Gustie herself to mark Clare's grave. Gustie would water it before she left. It had lived through four Dakota winters, but this was the driest summer Gustie had known since coming to this place. She did not want it to perish from thirst. If Dorcas or Jordis ever thought she was addled carrying buckets and buckets of lake water to pour into the ground at the foot of this tree, they never said a word. It was important to Gustie to keep the tree alive.

Lena had been this happy twice before in her life. The first time was her wedding day. The second had been the day she was sure that she was pregnant, before she had had a chance to think about the self-inflicted tragedies of the Kaiser family and been flooded with misgivings about bringing a child into such a bunch. Gustie had told her she shouldn't think about the Kaisers, that she was making her own family. From that moment on, Lena had rejoiced in her condition, dreaming about and planning for Gracia's baptism day, where after the service, the whole town would come to see her baby and congratulate her and Will on the start of their family. Now she knew that this *was* their family. Doc Moody had told her that there would be no more children. All the more reason to make the most of this day. Even though she and Will didn't have much, she would have served coffee and pie, cleaned her house till it shone and worn her blue dress, and Gracia would have been in her long white lace baptismal gown that she had begun to sew as soon as she found herself with child. But after Gracia's birth, Lena was slow to heal, slow to get her strength back. She couldn't handle more than one pie. She couldn't even clean her own house yet. The baptism couldn't wait.

In passing, she had mentioned her disappointment to Mary Kaiser who had rushed to Alvinia and Gustie with a plan to give Lena what she had dreamed of. They both readily agreed to give Lena back this day, and Lena would be forever grateful, even though she hadn't been sure about having it in Ma Kaiser's house. Alvinia had made a good case for it. "Now Lena, you'll need a big place because everyone will drop by. And it's next door to me so I can go back and forth and still keep an eye on my chicks while we fix things up. It also might cheer Gertrude up to see some happy faces. You said yourself, Oscar and Nyla are sour pusses."

"She's never come to see her own grandchild but once." Lena didn't care one way or the other if Ma Kaiser was cheered up.

Mary said, "Well, you know Ma isn't good with things like that."

"She might not even let us use her house." Lena scowled. "There's been no love lost between the two of us, I can tell you."

"She'll let us use the house," said Mary. "I'll take care of that. I think she'll like it, too. Yes. I think she will."

Lena grumbled, "But that house is not clean. It's so dark and dreary, like."

Mary assured her, "Nyla and I'll clean it up nicely."

"I'm not the best cook, but I can swing a mop," offered Gustie.

"Everything will be nice." Alvinia patted Lena's hand. "I promise, Lena."

"Well..."

Alvinia put an end to the discussion by declaring that Lena wasn't the only woman in Charity who could bake a decent pie or clean a house, for goodness sake. Lena was worried all the same.

When the day dawned with a bright sun in a cloudless sky, Lena didn't care if the open house was not perfect. Her baby was perfect and nothing else mattered. Even though she was feeling better than she had in a long time, her friends hadn't let her do anything. Not a blame thing. Just get yourself dressed and show up, they told her.

Gethsemane Church was full. At the end of the opening liturgy, Pastor Erickson called up the new parents and godparents to the front of the church. Lena and Will walked up the center aisle behind Alvinia and Carl. Will hadn't been to church since his pa's funeral. He was cleaned up, handsome, and looked happy to be there. Lena was proud of him. He hadn't had a drink since the day Gracia was born. As they approached the smiling pastor waiting for them beside the wooden baptismal font, Lena was light-headed with joy.

Alvinia held Gracia while Lena and Will watched. The minister began to intone the words, "Suffer the little children to come unto me and forbid them not..." Lena mouthed the words along with him. Then he cupped his hand and dipped into the water three times—for the Father, the Son, and the Holy Ghost—pouring each handful on Gracia's head. She didn't cry. Gracia never cried.

They returned to their seats for the sermon and the closing hymns, all but Alvinia who slipped away to the house where Gustie, Mary, and Nyla had been busy since early morning. The four of them had spent two weeks cleaning Gertrude's house. The old lady had glowered a bit, but not complained. Mary had a knack for smoothing the old bird's feathers.

Anxiety fluttered briefly in Lena's breast as she entered the house of her mother-in-law. She was met by the aroma of coffee, fresh and strong, and under that, instead of the stale slop-pail sourness that she expected, was the pungency of strong soap and furniture polish, just enough to put a tang in the air.

As she progressed deeper into the house, the fluttering moth of anxiety in her breast transformed into a butterfly. All of Ma's dark, thick drapes had been taken down and the windows hung with crisp, sheer white curtains. Bright July sun drenched every room. The mess was gone; even some furniture was missing, leaving space to walk around and room to breathe. The usually dingy antimacassars had been laundered, bleached, and starched.

Even Ma herself had been scrubbed and starched for the occasion and seemed the better for it. Lena wondered what they had done to get her to clean up. She suppressed a giggle at her image of a naked Ma Kaiser being thrown into a hot washtub, yowling like a cat.

The dining room table was covered with a snowy white tablecloth. In the center were fresh flowers in a glass vase, Mary's vase. At one end, a stack of Ma's heavy cream-colored dishes stood like sentinels over an array of matching cups and saucers and Ma's German silverware, polished for the occasion. The huge table was also set with the coffee urn, milk jug, cream pitcher, an assortment of pies, cakes, cookies, bread and butter, and sliced ham.

In the living room, Gustie was arranging more flowers. She wore gray silk, a finer piece of work Lena had never seen. The dress was simple, but, a seamstress herself, Lena recognized the fabric and the cut as being not something she had picked up around here. *Why you couldn't even get a pattern for such a dress around here. My!* The drape of the silk softened Gustie's tall slender frame, and its color matched her eyes.

Lena just stood in the middle of the living room and gaped. Of course, the wallpaper was still dreary and short of stripping the walls, nothing could be done with it. Even so, the place seemed like a different house. "Who did all this work? Oh, my!"

"We all did," answered Alvinia, pleased with Lena's reaction.

"Nyla did the curtains," Mary was eager to point out.

46

Nyla stood by in a green print dress that looked like it might have been new for the occasion but still did nothing to improve her lumpish figure or her sallow complexion. Oscar had probably let her buy only what was on sale at O'Grady's. Lena thought, *Too bad they didn't have a sale on shoes.*

"Took me three days to do those curtains." Nyla seemed more pleased than put out. It was hard to tell with Nyla.

Lena had known that they would do their best. She had had no idea just how fine their best would turn out to be. She swallowed and blinked back a tear or two. Then she said, "The curtains look swell, Nyla. The whole place looks just swell! Oh, my, look at the floors! I've never seen a shine on these floors. What did you do? And the rugs. They actually have colors..." The carpets had been beaten to within an inch of their threadbare lives by the Torgerson children and aired for several days. Alvinia thought it a blessing there had been no rain. They'd have disintegrated had they gotten wet.

People were already starting to arrive. Lena put Gracia down in her cradle and took a seat in the big overstuffed chair they had moved to the center of the living room: Lena's place of honor.

Betty, Alice, and Alvinia kept the kitchen flowing with refills to the coffee urn, the milk jug, and the cake and pie plates. Mary and Gustie welcomed guests and made sure Lena's plate was full and her coffee cup refreshed. The more that was eaten, the more the table was laden with fried chicken, cold beef tongue, potato salad, lefse, more donuts, cookies, pies and cakes, krumkake and rosettes, for nobody came empty handed. The people of Charity also had good appetites. Ma Kaiser stayed at the sink, washing dishes in the hot water kept in abundant supply by Malvern and Lavonne Torgerson. Both Lena and Mary tried to get her to come out of the kitchen and let someone else take over, but she just grumbled in German and kept on washing. They finally gave up.

Besides food, people brought gifts. Mary and Walter presented Lena with a silver baby cup engraved with Gracia's name and birth date. From Alvinia and Carl, she got the matching silver spoon. Gustie's gift was a hand-tooled leather bound book of fairy tales and children's poems illustrated with intricate woodcuts. Lena, never having owned any book except her mother's Norwegian Bible, was moved to tears, a frequent happening during the day as she unwrapped hand-made baby blankets, bonnets and dresses, removed the bow on a highchair that Morgan O'Grady carried in on his shoulder, and opened a plain white envelope containing the paperwork for a savings account in Gracia's name with a balance of five dollars from Lester Evenson, president of the Farmers and Merchants Bank.

The most spectacular gift of the day was a quilt. Lena's friends, the women from her church, and many others had each contributed a quilt square; the ladies of the Ruth and Esther Circle had put the quilt together.

Each piece was unique, reflecting the skill and interests of its maker. Charity's women had plied their needles rendering every kind of flower and leaf in every color and stitch. There were sheaves of wheat, shocks of corn, trees and flying geese; red birds, blue birds, robins and a swan; the silhouette of Gethsemane Church done in appliqué; and one square that looked like rich brocade but was many tiny pieces of fabric from her husband's old silk ties, stitched together in a miniature patchwork design by Edwina Moody. The center piece, embroidered by Solveig Erickson, the minister's wife, was the Twenty-Third Psalm, in its entirety, in the tiniest, most perfect chain stitch Lena had ever seen. The quilt was a wonder, designed beautifully and made well, to carry Gracia through childhood and go with her to her own house to swaddle her own children. Gustie and Mary spread it out on the table in the living room. Even the men took time to marvel at its detail, and even though the initials of the maker were in the corner of each piece, people enjoyed trying to guess who had fashioned which square.

Gustie found Lena lingering over one piece in particular—the most unusual and deceptively simple in design. "I just love this one. I wonder who made it?" Lena couldn't place the initials JMR.

Gustie looked over her shoulder. "Which one?"

"This one." Lena fingered the outline of a horse against a background of light brown material. The horse was worked in a feathery stitch that resembled light brushstrokes in shades of blue, orange, yellow, and black, intermingled so that they gave a kaleidoscopic effect, changing depending on the angle from which it was viewed and the play of the light.

Gustie broke into a radiant smile. "Oh! I know who made that."

"You do?"

"Yes."

"Well, who, then?"

"Jordis."

"Oh. My!" Lena was once again teary-eyed. It had been that kind of day. However, between the tears and the chatter, the laughter and good wishes, something had disturbed Lena. She had seen something. A moment of observation had opened a door, which closed again before she could get her mind around it. She was left with a feeling of unease, and it was maddening that she retained the feeling but not the memory of what had triggered it. *Probably nothing,* she thought. *It's just this house.* The place might be clean and uncluttered, but it was still Ma's house, and things had happened here, leaving their haunts in the walls and the floors and no amount of scrubbing and airing and letting in the light would get rid of them. Nothing but a match would do that. Lena pushed the unease to the back of her mind and visited with her neighbors.

The women tended to gather in the living room around Lena, while the men, after paying their respects to mother and child and filling up their plates, ended up outside, where more tables and chairs had been arranged. Will stayed out there most of the day, and Lena hoped and prayed that nobody had brought any whiskey to pass around. Who in this town didn't know Will's problem with the bottle?

She needn't have worried, because Alvinia had spoken to Carl, who had in turn dropped a word here and there among the men that no one was to let Will Kaiser near a drop of whiskey. Alvinia had been stern in her warnings. Nothing and no one were to mar this day for Lena. Hadn't she been through enough in the last couple years? Alvinia also made it known to Carl, who somehow got the news to Harlan Gudierian, that the horse doctor was not welcome. Maybe it wasn't fair, Alvinia conceded. Harlan had been asked to attend Lena that day of Gracia's birth, and maybe he had done his best...but Lena couldn't stand the sight of him and really, neither could Alvinia. Fair or not, he should stay home.

Twice during the day, Lena withdrew to nurse Gracia in the spare bedroom upstairs. The first time, she was joined by Alvinia. She tried again to express her thanks, but Alvinia cut her off. "We had a lot of fun doing this, Lena. I didn't know Mary Kaiser well before, but I have to say she worked like a trooper—on her hands and knees on the floors and then pulling out all of Ma Kaiser's tablecloths and finding not one that wasn't frayed or didn't have a stain or hole, so she brought over her own. She brought her own flower vases and some pretty bowls and cake plates. I never knew she had such lovely things! Gustie was no slouch either. She brought us groceries and a jar of floor wax and another one of furniture polish and she worked right alongside us. I never saw such work and we all were laughing all the time. Why, I even saw Nyla smile once."

"No!"

"Yes, I did!"

"Well, the place does look fine. What did you do with all the mess?"

"The boys took a lot to the attic. And if you look under the beds and in the closets up here you'll find things." Alvinia lowered her voice, though they were the only people on the second floor. "Some things,

Nyla and Mary just got rid of. They say by the time Gertrude looks for it she won't remember what all she had. What she doesn't find, she won't miss. Walter pitched in and helped a little, but Oscar didn't do much. Just sat around and watched. He can't do much I guess with only one arm."

"Ho! That man can do plenty with one arm if he wants to! He has a good well business going, though he needs a hired hand to help him."

They enjoyed their conversation in the quiet bedroom, away for the moment from the rest of the people milling around downstairs. Lena sat propped up on pillows against the bedstead, one leg folded under her and the other dangling over the side, Gracia lying in the crook of her left arm, which was supported by a pillow. This was the most comfortable way, she had found, to nurse Gracia, who was a slow feeder. Lena didn't mind.

Alvinia sat a little distance from her on the bed, taking up a good space, her blue and white striped skirts puffing out all about her. Her face, with its pale eyebrows, blond lashes and pug nose was given definition by wide-set eyes and a wide, well shaped mouth that smiled often, revealing large white teeth. Good teeth seemed to be a Torgerson family trait. Today, her daughters had plaited her thick yellow hair, starting the braids forward in the French way and pinning them at the back of her head in a neat coil. Lena had always thought her such a pretty woman. As comfortable as Lena was with her friend, she knew she was not to be trifled with. Lena had heard about Alvinia's rage on the day Gracia had been born. Mary said that for a month, the only men in Stone County who weren't afraid to talk to her were Doc Moody, and, maybe, Carl. She was still cool with Will and absolutely had no time and never would for Harlan Gudierian.

Alvinia had saved her life, all right, and there was nothing Lena could ever do to repay her. "You'd have done the same for me," Alvinia had said once, off-handedly, when Lena had tried to at least properly thank her.

"I couldn't have carried you into the bedroom."

They had both laughed out loud.

They were laughing now, about Axel Kranhold, the head of the town council, and his wife—both of whom put on airs as though they didn't live in the same prairie town and step in the same horse manure on the streets as everyone else did; about Mathilda Langager who bragged and bragged about a son who was worthless, dumb as a post, and would likely never amount to a hill of beans. But it was gentle laughter, the kind you reserve for family eccentricities, because these very people were downstairs, had contributed their food for the occasion, and fashioned their squares for the quilt that Lena would cherish and would teach Gracia to cherish her whole life long.

It felt good to laugh. It felt good to feel good, to be in her best dress, to be surrounded by her neighbors and her friends, to be holding her own baby at her breast. It felt good to be completely happy.

The second time Lena went up to attend to Gracia, she found herself alone in the same bedroom. She had just changed Gracia's diaper when she heard two sets of heavy footsteps coming up the stairs. They stopped at the bedroom door next to the one she was in. That was Oscar and Nyla's room. Through the open door of the spare room, she heard Nyla's voice, petulant and cutting. "Did she turn you down again?" Lena peeked out through the space left between the door and the frame, where the door swung open on its hinges. She saw Oscar with his hand on Nyla's arm. He squeezed it and made her grimace with pain, and then he pushed her ahead of him through the door. As it closed behind them she heard Nyla again, this time plaintively. "No, Oscar..." If she pressed her ear to their door, Lena knew what she would hear, but she didn't want to. Anyway, what could she do?

Lena went back into the room, gathered up her baby, and walked down the hall, passing the closed door of Oscar and Nyla's room as quickly as possible. When she got to the landing above the stairs, she stood for a moment, looking down into the living room. There it struck her. Nyla's face, her accusation—*did she turn you down again?*—the hard look of ungratified lust in Oscar's eyes. Now she remembered what she had seen. Another similar look. Oscar had been sitting by himself in the corner of the living room where he had an open sight line into the dining room. His eyes were hard, with a glittery cast, like the eyes perhaps of a snake eyeing a mouse. But worse. Snakes just got hungry like everybody else. This was more than simple hunger. Troubled by his expression, Lena followed his gaze into the dining room. The only person there at the time was Mary gathering empty plates and used silverware and keeping the table fresh and tidy. She was wearing a white blouse with three-quarter sleeves of netting. Tiers of silky fabric trimmed the bodice and stirred fluidly in the gentle breeze flowing through the open dining room window. Her blue skirt, though not tight, fit her well. Lena always noticed Mary's beautiful clothing, but today she noticed Mary. A few strands of her curly black hair had escaped the loose bun at the nape of her neck and softly framed her face, which was flawless and with high color. Lena looked back at Oscar whose attention was now on a farmer next to him. They were talking about the well business. She thought she might have imagined what she had seen and then forgot it altogether except for the nasty feeling it had left behind. Until now. Lena saw now why Oscar was keeping himself and Nyla in Ma's house, instead of going back to their own house a few miles out of town, not because of his devotion to his mother, but because Mary visited Ma every day. And every day, Oscar was there.

Chapter 5: August 1900

GLEEVIE PRUITT DOWNED HIS THIRD whiskey at Leroy's Tavern and complained about that good looking squaw living outside of town there and how she was too goddam uppity for a woman, never mind a goddam squaw.

Leroy tendered him some advice. "Leave that alone, Gleeve."

Gleevie was a drifter. He'd only been in Charity a month or so, and Leroy, while not much interested in managing other people's affairs beyond sending a man home while he could still walk or before he started breaking the furniture if that was the direction he was inclined to when he got a snoot-full, was alarmed by what he heard in Gleevie's voice—a rawness, and a recklessness born of ignorance. Leroy at least could try to relieve him of a little ignorance.

"Leave that alone," Leroy said again, his voice laden with meaning. *He who has ears, let him hear.* Leroy was a church-going man.

Gleevie needed a shave and wasn't in any case careful about personal hygiene, even when he was sober. This was his second afternoon running spent in the tavern. Something was wearing on him and it wasn't soap and water. "She ain't livin' out there just foolin' with them horses and makin' a livin' without gettin' somethin' on the side."

"Now where'd you get a notion like that?" Leroy polished the top of his bar in rhythmic circles.

"No wheres. I just figured it out," Gleevie boasted, full of his own brilliance. "I don't want nuthin for nuthin. I'm willin' to pay, but I'm goin' to get me a little, that's all."

"Don't look for trouble. Go on now. Sober up and forget about it." Leroy refused to sell him another drink, so Gleevie left the tavern, swaying as he went.

Leroy motioned Hank Ackerman over. "I think you should go tell Dennis that thresher that's been hanging around here is looking for trouble."

"You worried about the squaw?" Hank asked.

"Nope." Leroy made more circles with his bar rag. The surface of his bar gleamed. "I expect she can take care of herself."

"Yup. I expect she can." Hank took a swallow of beer.

"Don't know about Pruitt though."

"Nope, don't expect he knows his ass from a hole in the ground or his own shit from shinola." Hank downed the last of his beer and left the tavern in a leisurely search for Sheriff Sully.

Gleeve Pruitt was no man's fool. He'd been smart enough to leave Arkansas and too smart to go south where there was nothing but cotton fields—no fit work for a white man. No, he went north and hired on to a ranch in Nebraska, but the work was too hard, and he was too good to spend his time eating dust and staring up the butt holes of cows, so he went on farther north. He got to the Dakotas in time to hire on to threshing crews and made enough money to keep going and to stop for a drink when he needed one. He had decided to hang around because, while the work was harder than he'd expected and the money not as good as he deserved, the food was good on the farms where he worked, he didn't have to work in the rain, and he could leave whenever he wanted to and move on to the next crew, which is what he'd done two days ago when the foreman caught him napping in the hayloft when he was supposed to be working and fired him. Didn't matter. There was another crew a few miles east and he'd hire on there. When the oats were harvested there would be wheat, barley and then corn to pick. But he was too smart to work for dirt farmers any longer than he had to. Gold would be his fortune in the Black Hills. It was only August. There were three months of work left in this place, and by that time he'd have enough money to winter in Lead and get work in the mine. He'd heard that a single fella with money in his pocket could have a lot of fun out there. In the meantime, there was some fun to be had in these parts too if you were man enough to find it.

Jordis was raking out Moon's stall when the mare whickered from the corral outside. Then she heard hoof beats. It wasn't Gustie returning because Moon wouldn't sound off for Gustie, and she'd have heard the rattle of the spring wagon. She didn't rush out to see who it was. The barn door was wide open so anyone looking would know where to find her. She finished spreading straw on the floor of the stall. The straw shone bright gold where the sun struck it in narrow shafts through the window. She turned around. A strange man was silhouetted in the opening to the barn. She waited for him to speak.

When he did, it took her a moment to figure out what he had on his mind. She burst out laughing.

He came closer.

She said, through her laughter, "Go away. You've come to the wrong place for that."

"I ain't goin' nowhere. I'll pay you what you're worth. You should be glad to get it."

"Are you crazy?" She closed the door to the stall and brushed her hands against her split skirt.

He took another step closer and pulled some crinkled bills out of his pocket so she could see them. Then he unbuttoned his pants.

Jordis still looked at him in disbelief. "You are crazy." Then she got a whiff of him. "You're drunk, that's for sure."

His pants began a slow slide down his hips. He hooked a finger through a belt loop to keep them from falling all the way down and impeding his forward progress. He came to within three feet of Jordis and then it was she who closed the distance between them. In a motion too fast for his bleary vision, she produced a long knife and he felt the point of it in his gut and her strong hand twisting his shirt tight at his throat.

"You wouldn't use that," he said, his bravado now being choked out of him.

"I would just as soon kill you as smell you, White Man."

It was the way she said 'White Man,' like it was the first cut of the knife in his belly, that chilled the whiskey right out of his blood. He snickered and tried to back up, as if it had all been a joke. She wouldn't let him.

Then she did. He backed up, turned and started for the door. As he got to it, he saw propped up against the wall, a pitchfork. He grabbed it, turned around, half yelled, half choked, "No squaw does me like this!"

He lunged, the pitchfork ahead of him like a jousting spear. Then he had one leg shot out from under him.

Dennis Sully, Sheriff of Stone County, stood just outside, holstering his pistol. Gleevie howled from the barn floor. "You shot me! Owwww! Goddam! Goddam! You shot me!"

Dennis walked in and lifted Gleevie's leg up to view the damage. He let the leg drop and Gleevie howled some more. "I got you in the meat. In six months, you won't even limp. Now get the hell out of here. And I mean out of Charity. If I see you around here again you won't get out of jail till you're an old man." Gleevie struggled to his feet and, cursing all the way, hopped and hobbled out of the barn.

Jordis did not look pleased to see Dennis. "I could have handled him."

"I know. But if the stupid sonofabitch was going to get himself killed today, I thought it was better I did it."

She didn't like it but had to accept that if Gleeve Pruitt was killed by an Indian, he was just a poor white man in his cups. If the sheriff shot him, he was a drunk who probably needed killing. "I assume you meant to hit him just there."

"Yup. Woulda rather hit him some other place, but his back was to me. His ass was too big a target. Didn't seem sporting."

They heard groaning and complaining as Gleevie mounted his horse, then the soft clopping of hooves fading into the afternoon.

"Who is he?" Jordis slipped her knife back into her boot.

"His name is Gleeve Pruitt. He come through about a month ago to get work on the threshin' crews. But he seems to spend more time at Leroy's than in the fields. Anyway, if I see him hanging around Charity again, I will lock him up."

Jordis picked up the pitchfork and put it back against the wall. "You want some pie?"

"What kind you got?"

"Apple and rhubarb. Lena baked this week."

"Lena's pies." The sheriff smiled. "Well, maybe I'll have a little of each."

"Come on to the house. Gustie should be home soon. I'll make some coffee." Jordis led the way out. Emerging from the dim interior of the barn, her eyes quickly adjusted to the bright afternoon, and she saw Dennis's horse Fever. He was lathered. Dennis had taken the threat to Jordis seriously. Then she smiled. No, he'd taken the threat to Gleeve Pruitt seriously. A solitary bird sounded his musical notes against the faint percussive buzz and ratchet of insects that drifted off the surrounding prairie in the drowsy dry August heat. "Why don't you stay for supper? You can turn him out in the pasture," she nodded to the saddle horse. "He can drink from the trough."

"Poor Jordis." Gustie smiled over her coffee cup. They had just finished a satisfying cold supper of smoked fish, potato salad, pickles, bread and butter, during which Jordis and Dennis had related the details of Gleeve Pruitt's visit. "No one will let you kill anybody."

Dennis raised his eyebrows.

"We had a run-in with Jack Frye a few weeks ago," Gustie explained. "She didn't get to do anything to him either but scare the living daylights out of him." Gustie got up and refilled their cups.

Dennis chuckled. "I'd 'a liked to seen that."

"Gustie intervened on his behalf," said Jordis without amusement. "Otherwise I would have turned him into fish food."

"Well, pity the poor fish. And none of 'em would 'a been fit to eat after, so I guess Gustie did a public service." Dennis stirred cream and sugar into his coffee. "This is sure better'n Fritz's coffee. Course, his is better'n mine. You want me to talk to Frye? Give him a warning?"

"I don't think that will be necessary." Gustie said it dryly, a smile in her gray eyes. She collected the supper plates and brought the pies and fresh plates to the table. Jordis cut wedges and served. To Dennis, she gave a slice of each.

Dennis felt comfortable in this house. The place was clean and shiny but not fussy, and he felt he could stretch his legs and lean back and breathe. Which he did. "What'd he do exactly?"

"Nothing," was Gustie's answer.

Jordis disagreed. "He was blocking your way out of the alley. He was threatening you."

"I didn't feel threatened. Just annoyed."

"He was being disrespectful."

"He wasn't dangerous," said Gustie.

"He has been. He has never paid for what he did to us. You do know that, Dennis?"

"Yeah. I know it." He ran a squarish hand over the top of his bald head before applying himself to his dessert. "I know life ain't fair. Not one damn bit." He took in the floor-to-ceiling shelf of books that covered almost half of one wall. Gustie had been a school teacher. The same bunch of fools who paid his salary had fired her from the section school. He'd only heard about it after it was done. He couldn't have prevented it had he known, but it still stuck in his craw. Gustie seemed to have fared none the worse for it though. In fact, she'd gone from being as poor as a flea on a mangy dog to being well off. Rumor had it she'd inherited some money from someone back east, but nobody knew for sure, and Dennis had never asked because it wasn't any of his business. He was glad she was doing well. It was hard to see good people, dependent on the whims of weather and luck, scratch out a living. And Gustie had been generous. He knew that for a fact, too. She didn't call attention to herself and, as far as her being friendly with Indians, he couldn't see anything wrong with that either. And Jordis was a full blood, smart as a person gets, and a looker. He understood Gleeve Pruitt's desire. Just didn't hold with his methods.

Chapter 6: September 1900

GUSTIE LIKED HOW AUTUMN DESCENDED gently over the prairie, without the fanfare that attended its arrival in the east, where trees and foliage ignited with color. Here, with few trees, the signs were subtler: birds flying in clouds or Vs overhead; a drying and thinning of the air; a growing crispness in the breezes drifting down from the north; the crops going from green to gold, or, in the case of flax, blue; the hay bales dotting the fields and then suddenly disappearing into barns; the people working from dawn to dark to bring in the harvest; the smells of cooking, canning, preserving wafting from every house.

Today, on the Red Sand, the smoke from the fires mingled with the fog and drifted low, collecting in pockets, stirred by the running feet of children and dogs. The dogs, kicked away from the stew pots by the old women, received their morsels from the children who streaked from fire to fire and were fed by everyone.

Old men smoked, laughed and told stories of the buffalo days when they ranged far—even crossing the Big Muddy—to hunt and count coup against their enemies. Good days! Young men listened to the old ones or gathered to play plumb stones and gamble. Women, young and old, prepared food, tended babies and visited. The fires were kept smoky to discourage mosquitoes. A few men who could intimidate, either by physical presence or moral force, patrolled the grounds looking severe. Chief Little Bull had directed, "You find anyone drinking..." and finished his sentence with a jerk of his head, which signified a cold dunk in the lake, the trail home, or both.

On this day, the people of the Red Sand were celebrating the wedding of Sarah LaBourteaux and Clayton Nighthawk. The LaBourteaux family had been among the earliest Christian converts on the Red Sand, which, by the luck of the draw and the whim of the United States government, made them Episcopalians. Whether church members or not, almost everyone turned out for this happy event. A wedding was an opportunity to visit, an occasion for a feast.

Jordis and Gustie had traveled from Crow Kills to Shoonkatoh, where the mission church rose up in two stories of unadorned yellowish brick, starkly perpendicular to the subtle undulations of remarkably flat land—Gustie in her spring wagon drawn by her black mare and Jordis on Moon, the white horse that was nearly as much a part of her as her own limbs.

The fog was now merely dew on the grass. A white, glacier-like cloud loomed high up from the horizon filling half the sky. The sun was in the other half and daybright remained undiminished.

Blankets were spread in front of the church and covered with pots and pans, utensils, tobacco, new blankets, moccasins, even a saddle—items that would later in the day be part of a give-away from the bride's family. Beyond these were two wood tables laden with food. Gustie pulled her wagon in close to the tables, and as she and Jordis unloaded their contributions to the feast, Father Flagstad came flying towards them, his cassock flapping and his long arms gesticulating. "Miss Augusta! Miss Jordis! Bring your wagon...come this way...we've got some sick folks here who need to get to Wheat Lake and you're all hitched up and ready to go." Jordis and Gustie followed him around the church.

Father Flagstad, the Episcopal priest, was tall and gangly. His red hair ascended to a frisson above a hairline that had long ago receded from a freckled expanse of forehead. His nose sloped thinly down to a point. Though only in his early thirties, his skin was dry and lined from exposure to the elements. As he spoke excitedly, tiny flecks of saliva collected on his thin lips. "They pulled in on three wheels, the whole family looking worn to the bone and starving. The little ones are sick." His protruding eyes darted back and forth behind spectacles that continuously slid down his nose. "The missus is sick too. She won't say so. Says she's just tired. But to my eyes she is not a well woman. We've gotten out of them so far only their names—Ina and Reuben Lesner—but nothing else. Don't know where they're going or where they came from."

In spite of his unprepossessing appearance and his unhinged sort of gait, Father Flagstad emanated kindness and self-assurance. He had come to the Red Sand several years ago, a widower with two sons. He had built his own house and dug his own well, with help from his parishioners and even the Catholic priest in Wheat Lake. As far as Gustie knew, he was well thought of by the Dakotah.

Gustie observed Ina Lesner sitting on the ground leaning against a cottonwood tree. Her fair skin was sallow and stretched thin over the bones of her face. Her oily hair was twisted into a messy knot on the top of her head. She held a rosary. Her two children, not as emaciated as she was, were covered by a thin blanket and lay with their heads on her lap. Their faces were rosy with fever.

This poor family, stumbling onto an Indian reservation sick in body and soul, struck a sorrowful chord in Gustie. She turned to say something to Jordis, but she was already attending the Lesners' horses, who were sagging and spotted with sores.

Winnie Little Bull and Carrie Red Standing Horse knelt on either side of Ina Lesner and her children. Winnie had a dish of stew and Carrie a bowl of water. Sluggish flies began to buzz around the boy. Carrie brushed them away. Cradling his head in one of her long slender hands, she bathed his face with cool water. *Where is Dorcas?* Gustie wondered. She expected to find her here busy with her herbs and medicines.

Gustie identified Reuben Lesner at once, pitifully shabby, as thin as his wife, looking dazed and helpless among the men who circled his dilapidated wagon, shaking their heads and muttering in discouraging tones.

Dakotah youngsters gathered in open curiosity around the strangers. Carrie's youngest, Louise, tall for her age and slender like her mother, reached out and touched the colorful rag doll that the Lesner girl clutched in her hand. In contrast to the drab aura that enveloped the Lesners and their few possessions, the many-colored doll spoke eloquently of a loving mother garnering scraps after the quilting and the mending were done, and of hours with her needle fashioning a treasure from almost nothing.

Ina Lesner instructed her daughter softly, "Give her the doll, Angela. I'll make you another one. I promise." The girl handed her doll to Louise who smiled at her, bolted, and ran to show off her new plaything. Mrs. Lesner turned her head toward Winnie. Her voice sounded like one dry sheet of paper slipping off another. "I wish we had something more to give you."

Gustie knew better than anyone that the generosity of the Dakotah people was without parallel; no repayment was expected. Winnie smiled and offered the woman a chunk of bread soaked in broth. Gustie fingered the piece of antler she wore on a leather thong around her neck, a gift from Dorcas, and wiggled her toes inside the moccasins that Carrie made for her. Among people who had little, gifts meant a great deal.

Jordis unhitched the Lesners' team. As Reuben Lesner watched her lead his horses away toward the lake, Chief Little Bull reassured him, "Don't worry. She will take care of them like they are her relatives."

Father Flagstad bent over Mrs. Lesner. "Miss Roemer will take you in to Wheat Lake to the doctor. It's not far. Red Standing Horse will follow with your things in his wagon."

She nodded gratefully and was helped to her feet. Her husband left the men contemplating his rig to help her into the back of Gustie's wagon. When she was settled, Little Bull picked up her son and Red Standing Horse her daughter, and the two men carried them to their mother's lap. In the arms of these big men, the Lesner children appeared like drab dolls themselves. Reuben Lesner climbed in beside his family.

The priest continued, "We can't fix your wagon here. Besides that broken wheel, you've got a cracked axle. We'll haul it into the blacksmith in town tomorrow."

"I have no money," Reuben Lesner said.

"Well, the smithy's a good Episcopalian," Father Flagstad smiled, exposing his crooked teeth, "and he owes me a favor. There's nothing to worry about. I'll be looking in on you. We have a Catholic parish in Wheat Lake. I'll see that Father Gregory knows you're there, too."

Ina Lesner nodded and in her papery voice said, "God bless you." She closed her eyes.

Winnie made final adjustments to their blankets while Carrie smiled up at Gustie perched on her wagon seat. "You'll miss the wedding," she said.

Behind them, the Lesners' few worldly goods were transferred to Red Standing Horse's box wagon. Above, a small cloud calved from the glacial cloud and, borne on the high air currents over Shoonkatoh, cast a shadow over the brooding lake. A sudden wind lifted Biddie's mane and ruffled Gustie's hair. She pulled away from the feast site, leaving behind the sounds of barking dogs, iron spoons scraping the sides of iron pots, and people talking about hunting and fishing, old times, the plenitude of the gifts, and the beauty of the bride.

The sound of two wagons pulling up in front of his small office at the end of Wheat Lake's Main Street brought Doctor Clark Llewellyn outside. A handsome, slender young man, the doctor looked slight in the presence of Red Standing Horse, who stood over six feet tall and weighed nearly three hundred pounds.

The first thing Gustie remembered hearing about the doctor, a newcomer to the Dakotas, was that he was afraid of horses.

The locals laughed at this man who had to depend so entirely upon an animal that made him sweat. Still, the doctor accomplished his rounds with good humor, both on the reservation and off and looked forward to the day when he could afford a motor car.

Clark Llewellyn was fresh out of medical school and single. Hoping to ignite a spark between him and her eldest daughter, Alvinia Torgerson had already invited him to dinner, but Betty was in love with her poor farm boy. Alvinia had not considered the evening a waste, however, since Alice was almost seventeen, and Betty could still change her mind.

Doctor Llewellyn asked Red Standing Horse after the health of Carrie and the children, greeted Gustie and then followed her around the back of her wagon to meet his new patients. A grim look crossed his face, but he covered it briskly. "Right, then. Let's get them inside."

The second room of the doctor's modest office had four narrow beds. They laid the children in one of them and Mrs. Lesner in another. "You can bunk in here with your family, Mr. Lesner," the doctor invited.

Reuben Lesner nodded gratefully, took his hat off and sat gingerly on the edge of the extra bed, his hat in his hands. Doctor Llewellyn's offer could have been simply a kindness, suspecting the man had no money for a room, but Gustie wasn't sure. She was no physician, but, to her eyes, Reuben Lesner was not looking particularly well either.

"Have they had something to eat?"

"They were given stew and bread. I don't know if they were able to eat much," Gustie replied.

Red Standing Horse unloaded the Lesners' belongings, piled them under the eaves and headed back to the mission while Gustie helped the doctor settle them in. The entire family was immediately asleep. She wondered how long it had been since they had lain in real beds.

Doctor Llewellyn walked Gustie outside. She asked, "Any idea what's wrong with them?"

"Besides malnutrition and exhaustion, I'm not sure. I don't like the looks of that boy. On your way out of town, could you stop by the Tollefsons? Ask Mrs. Tollefson to come around. She acts as my nurse. Good she is too."

Gustie smiled at the lilt of Welsh music in the doctor's speech. No, he would not remain a bachelor for long, not while Alvinia had marriageable daughters.

How eager people were to marry! The rhythm of Biddie's hooves on the dirt road reminded Gustie of waking up a few nights ago to what she thought was the sound of hoof beats. Once her eyes were open, however, and staring into the darkness, listening, all she could hear was the regular thumping of her own heart. She threw back the quilt, lit the lantern, put on her glasses, and picked up the pocket watch lying on her nightstand. It said two o'clock.

She pulled on some warm clothes, tucked her hair up under her old conductor's cap, and took the lantern outside. A damp wind eddied around her, licking the glass lamp, unable to consume its small fire.

When she opened the barn door the amiable mare whickered her customary greeting even though Gustie was four hours earlier than usual. Gustie led her out of the barn and over to the fence. She hung the lantern on the post, unsnapped the lead rope and re-attached it on either side of the halter for reins, and giving herself a leg up on the slats of the fence, mounted Biddie's bare back. On the dark road to Charity, low cloud cover meant she had to trust her own good night vision and the mare's instincts to keep to the road.

She nudged the horse into a fast walk. The worst that could happen was that she would get to Charity, the feeling of urgency that had drawn her out on this blustery night would dissipate, and she could go home and back to bed. No one but Biddie would know of their wild goose chase. They covered nearly three miles when the mare stopped suddenly and snorted.

Gustie heard panting sounds of grief and exhaustion before she was able to discern a figure in the road.

The panting stopped as fear of an unknown horse and rider clutched the woman who stood before her. Gustie hastily uttered reassurance into the night. "Lena, it's me. Gustie."

"Oh!" A cry of relief. "Oh, what are you doing out here?"

"I guess I've come for you. Hand up the baby and get on behind me. I'll take you home."

"Not my home."

"No. Mine."

"All right, then."

Lena, with Gustie's help, pulled herself easily onto the mare's back. She wrapped her arms around Gustie's waist and leaned her head into Gustie's back. Holding the baby in the crook of her arm and the reins loosely in her other hand, Gustie turned Biddie toward home.

"Lena, we're here."

"Oh."

Gustie thought that Lena must have dozed even while holding her tight around the middle. She gave her a second to clear her head.

Lena slipped off the horse and reached up for Gracia, who had not wakened even while being passed from one set of arms to another and back again.

Inside, with the lanterns lit, Gustie could see that, while Lena had been out with little enough between herself and the night air, Gracia was bundled snugly in warm blankets. Gustie pulled the trundle bed out from under her own bed and rolled it into the main room, which was warmer than the bedroom. She took the baby out of Lena's arms once again and laid her down on the bed.

Gustie poured milk into a saucepan. "When did you eat last?"

"I don't know. I had supper, I guess. Will didn't come home till about ten or eleven...so drunk and mean...he doesn't usually come home at all when he's like that. He was mad about something...something happened during the day... I don't know what...that set him off, you know. He broke some dishes and then came after me."

Gustie was aghast. "Did he hurt you?"

"I didn't let him catch me! I grabbed the baby and ran out. I've been walking and walking, but I couldn't go all night, and I was afraid to go home yet. So I started out here."

When the milk was warm, Gustie poured it into a bowl and put a loaf of bread on the table in front of Lena. Lena tore the bread, put the pieces into the warm milk and ate with shaking hands.

"Why didn't you go to Alvinia's or Mary's? You wouldn't have had so far to walk."

Lena frowned. "They already know enough about me."

"Then, you should have come here right away. Whether I am here or not, you know the place is never locked."

Lena nodded almost imperceptibly and pushed the empty bowl away from her. With the side of one hand she shepherded breadcrumbs into the palm of the other and dusted them into the empty bowl.

As Gustie helped her take off her shoes and lie down next to her daughter, Lena asked her sleepily,

"What were you doing out there in the middle of the night for heaven sakes?"

Before Gustie could think of an answer, Lena was asleep. She pulled the blanket over her and went back outside to bed down her horse, again.

The next morning, after Gustie and Lena had finished their breakfast, Will appeared, cleaned up and sober. Only his blood shot and puffy eyes gave away his night of drinking. He had driven out in a borrowed rig. Gustie recognized it as belonging to Harlan Gudierian.

Gustie sat at the window holding Gracia in her lap and watched Will and Lena outside performing their ritual of contrition and forgiveness. In fifteen minutes, Lena came back in to collect her daughter.

"You're not going to be warm enough." Gustie gave Lena her wool coat. "Don't get a chill on the way back. You were lucky not to catch your death last night."

Lena looked lost in Gustie's coat. Buttoning it up obediently, she said, "Thank you Gustie. You're a brick."

The Spittoon, Wheat Lake's only saloon, lived up to its name. It was dark and dirty and smelled of stale tobacco—smoked and spat, sour beer and whiskey, and worse. And it was, more or less, home to Jack Frye. Losing his job as Indian agent meant that he also lost his dwelling—the back room of the agency building. Since then, he had slept in the bunkhouse next to the livery stables—a place for itinerant workers and those who were so down on their luck they couldn't even afford the modest cost of a room in Mattie Olson's hotel.

For a nickel one could rent a narrow bed in the bunkhouse for a week. No bedding—most men just unrolled their own bedroll on top of the straw mattress—Jack lay on the mattress and covered himself up with an old horse blanket he'd stolen from the stable. The bunkhouse was hot in the summer and cold in the winter. But it was better than sleeping in the rain or in a snowdrift. One pot-bellied stove in the middle of it served to heat up the bunks nearest to it in the worst months of the year. But in the worst months of the year, no harvesting was done and few people traveled. So, in the winter, Jack Frye mostly had the place to himself. Now, however, he had to share it with about fifteen other men whose presence he mostly ignored, and they tried to ignore him. They weren't generally interested in drinking with him or listening to his woes. They had troubles of their own. He found one exception—someone who had limped in with a bottle of cheap whiskey (though the rules of the bunkhouse, clearly posted for anyone to see, were no drinking or spitting allowed on the premises) and drank it up in a cloud of curses.

"Shut up," Jack told him loudly. "Can't a man get some shut-eye?"

The man threw his empty bottle at Jack, missing him widely. The bottle landed on the floor at the foot of his cot and broke.

"Now you're going to pick that up," Jack snarled. "A man could cut himself on that."

"Pick it up yourself, you old shit."

Jack Frye wasn't drunk at the moment. He had been lying on his bed, clad only in his grimy long-johns, dozing and contemplating the possibilities in the day ahead. Taking the insults of a young punk wasn't one of them. He shot off his cot with a speed no one could have predicted and flung himself on top of this snappy young dog and began punching him in the face. Gleeve, who was drunk and taken by surprise, didn't react. Jack hauled him over to where the broken pieces of bottle lay and threw him on his knees. "Now you pick up them pieces before I whip ya again."

Gleeve hesitated. His head was foggy from drink and the punches. Jack punched him again, this time hitting his shoulder.

Gleeve picked up the three pieces of bottle, got to his feet and limped out of the bunkhouse.

Jack didn't think about the man again till the following afternoon when he was hunkered down in his usual corner of the Spittoon, rolling a cigarette, and he noticed the same fella. In the dim saloon light, he recognized him by his limp. The fella ordered a glass of cheap whiskey and started drinking, leaning on the bar. The more he drank, the louder was his voice till Jack could plainly hear him complaining about being shot for no good reason for just having fun with a squaw. A good lookin' squaw, as they go, with the damndest thing by god—a knife in her boot, but that could only add to the fun, but for the interference of a sheriff who should know whose side to be on. Jack perked up his ears, then got up, stubbed his cigarette out on the floor with his foot, and strolled to the bar.

"Naw, she don't live in Charity," Jack amiably corrected the man he had so thoroughly pummeled just the day before. "Snuce, hit me again."

Snuce was the bartender and the owner of the Spittoon. He got his name from the tobacco invariably pouched in his lower lip, and the dribble of brown always seeping out of the corner of his mouth. Nobody remembered anymore what his real name was.

Snuce poured Jack another drink and slid it toward him.

"Well, that's where I got shot," said Gleeve, eyeing Jack from under his hat and thinking he should know him from somewhere.

Even in barroom light, Jack could see that the man's face was swollen and purple. He congratulated himself on a good job.

"She was right there in the barn," insisted Gleeve Pruitt, "and Charity's where I seen her all week, buyin' oats in the livery stable big as you please, and buyin' stuff at that O'Grady place with money and they was waitin' on her like she was good as any white woman."

"Yeah, she goes there sometimes. But she lives out here on the reservation. That one is trouble. How's that eye? I popped you a good one, huh? Not bad for an old shit, huh? No hard feelings?" Jack stuck out his hand. Gleeve hesitated while he put it all together in his mind, his black eye, his bruised face, his calling the old man a shit before having the old guy's fists in his face. He put out his hand cautiously. Jack gave it one good shake, took his fresh shot of whiskey, and went on, "You think she done you something? You should hear what she and that skinny old maid she's with all the time done me. You should hear. Boy."

Gleeve was all ears.

As Carrie had predicted, the wedding ceremony was over by the time Gustie got back to Shoonkatoh. She wandered the mission grounds among the multitude of strange faces, and though she was greeted with friendly smiles, she felt out of place. She saw the bride and groom and decided it was time to pay her respects, then find the people she knew.

The young couple was seated on a blanket surrounded by well-wishers. Sarah LaBourteaux, now Mrs. Clayton Nighthawk, wore a dark blue dress with white cowrie shells sewn in rows across the bodice. A belt of white shells trailed down from her waist, and a silver cross hung on a silver chain below a dentillium shell choker necklace. Clayton, in rawhide trousers and a tanned leather shirt, looked happy and shyer than his bride. Gustie made her way quietly to stand before them. "May you have a long and wonderful life together," she said as she presented her gift, a china bowl with a garland of flowers painted around the rim. Sarah smiled and ran her finger around the bowl's smooth, delicate surface.

Gustie left them to look for Jordis. She found her at Little Bull and Winnie's fire playing with Deborah. The Lesners' two horses were tethered nearby, their sores anointed with yellow salve.

Gustie reported what there was to tell about the Lesners. She took the baby from Jordis into her lap. Deborah gurgled contentedly.

Gustie remembered the baby's naming ceremony. Father Flagstad had performed a baptism according to the rites of his church, but afterward, Gustie and Jordis participated in another ceremony, during which they gave the child a secret name. An old Sioux custom held that it was good luck for a child to be given a name by a two-spirit person. The day was precious in Gustie's memory, unlike Gracia's baptism day, which would also stay in Gustie's memory, but shrouded in forebodings. For, as much as they had tried to make that day happy for Lena, their efforts still tasted like pretty frosting on a stale cake.

One event in particular cast a shadow. In the late afternoon, when only a few people remained sitting around the living room, sipping coffee, reviewing the gifts and listening to the Larson sisters, Minna and Kate, explain the story behind their quilt designs, Lena, though tired, was still basking in the glory of this once-in-a-lifetime occasion. Gustie, knowing that Lena had had few such days in her life, hoped they could make it last as long as possible. She slipped out of the living room taking some empty plates with her to the kitchen. She intended to brew fresh coffee, but the stove had gone out and the match tin was empty. While she was in the pantry, scanning the shelves for a box of matches, she heard someone come into the kitchen. It was probably Mary. She would, no doubt, know exactly where Gertrude kept matches. Gustie stopped at the entrance to the pantry, Mary and Oscar were at the sink. Rather, Mary was at the sink and Oscar approached her from behind. Gustie watched in silence, shielded by the pantry door. Oscar's right arm went around Mary. His hand, outspread, paw-like, pressed below her pelvic bone drawing her in close to him. Gustie heard his ragged intake of breath and saw Mary stiffen. She could see them both in profile. Mary looked like a doe in the grasp of a predator.

Gustie was about to step out and put an end to this scene. If necessary, she would borrow a page from Lena's book and hit him over the head with a cast iron skillet. She'd seen Lena do that to Jack Frye once. It had been extremely effective. But then Mary collected herself and side-stepped out of Oscar's one-armed embrace. She turned to face him. Gustie held her breath.

"Don't ever touch me again, Oscar," Mary said in a low and even voice.

He gave out a deep snuffle of derision. "I know Walter's problem." He reached out his hand as if to lay it on her breast. She backed up. "We could..." he began huskily.

"I don't like you, Oscar. I don't want you near me. If you ever touch me again, I will tell Walter."

"What's he going to do?" He smiled.

"Shoot your other arm off."

His face went slack, expressionless, and he quickly left the kitchen. Gustie felt that now wasn't the time to reveal herself. Mary had handled the situation. Gustie didn't want to embarrass her, so she withdrew silently into the pantry. Walter had shot Oscar's arm off when they were youngsters. Lena told Gustie the story. "It was no accident. Oscar probably had it coming one way or another. And Walter has a temper and not much sense. So whatever Oscar did, it was enough for Walter to shoot him. I wish he'd shot him in the head."

"Lena!"

"Well, I do! I know it's not the Christian thing, but there it is. Oscar is mean. He's never been anything else and he isn't getting any lovelier as he gets older.

Somebody is going to have to shoot him before long.
If I thought I could do it and get away with it, by jinx,
I would!"

Gustie never mentioned what she had seen in the
kitchen to Lena, to Mary, or to anyone. But for some
reason, it haunted her.

She kissed Deborah on the forehead. "She gets
sweeter every day, Winnie." Then she asked, "Where's
Dorcas?"

Jordis answered, "Down by the lake."

As Gustie moved off to find her, she stopped and
looked back for a moment, observing Jordis from a
distance: tall and strong with dark skin and straight
black hair held back from her face with the silver
combs Gustie had given her last Christmas. One of
Jordis's charms was that she did not know she was
beautiful. She was silk and velvet to Gustie's paper
and straw; starlight to Gustie's candle flame. *She will
age like a tree. She will get stronger, tougher, have
more substance, will bear more... I will wither like a
shrub.* Gustie was not much concerned with her own
aging. Jordis turned to see Gustie looking at her and
flashed her a smile. *When she smiles, her demeanor
rivals the night sky with a full white moon lighting the
prairie, softly reflecting upon water and the backs of
playing rabbits.* Three children interrupted Gustie's
reverie running by with something that flared bright
and colorful in the sun. The Lesner doll.

Shoonkatoh Lake was nothing like Crow Kills
where Dorcas lived. Shoonkatoh was bigger, cold at
all times of the year, and, in places, its depth had
never been sounded. Shoonkatoh rested in the heart
of the Red Sand reservation, and most Dakotah lived

in proximity to it. There were other lakes on the Red Sand besides Shoonkatoh and Crow Kills, but in Gustie's opinion, Crow Kills was the most beautiful; Shoonkatoh the most forbidding. People drowned in Shoonkatoh with enough regularity to give credence to some Indians' belief that a hungry spirit lived in its depths. Mostly whites drowned there, people who did not respect its numinous quality. Gustie had experienced too much of the mystery and awesome power of this prairie land to discount anything. Even lakes with hungry spirits.

She approached Dorcas from behind, making enough noise so as not to startle her when she stepped alongside. The old woman turned. A moment passed before the faraway look on her ancient face was replaced by a bright smile for her adopted granddaughter.

Dorcas Many Roads could have been anywhere between seventy and eighty-five years old. When Gustie first encountered her, Dorcas had had an ageless vitality. But, last winter, Little Bull and Leonard found her in her cold cabin, nearly frozen, seated with her bundle of precious mementos spread out on the table before her. The cabin had been well stocked with firewood and food. No one knew what had happened to cause her to let the fire go out. The chief and his son started the fire, wrapped her in blankets, and dripped warm soup down her throat.

In a few days she gained strength. Little Bull took her to live with his family. Then, Jordis insisted on caring for her. Gustie made the trip to Crow Kills often, bringing supplies to supplement their government annuities. Many people on the Red Sand visited Dorcas. She did not want for company. But some vital spark in her had gone out.

"Wondered if you'd show up," the old woman said.

"Afraid not to. Special summons from the chief. I drove the Lesners into Wheat Lake. Just got back."

Dorcas's smile faded. She turned her face back toward the lake.

"I thought I'd see you up there, with them."

"Can't help them," Dorcas said cryptically. Her eyes still fixed on something over the lake, she said, "We should have the drum today."

"What do you mean, Grandmother?" She waited to see if Dorcas would elaborate. Then she asked, "Have you had anything to eat? Come back with me."

As they moved up from the shoreline, Dorcas stumbled and Gustie put an arm around her to steady her. The old woman was less substantial than she used to be. Age was leeching her ample flesh; Dorcas was wizening from the inside out.

Father Flagstad spied them from a distance and sailed, once again, toward Gustie, calling, "Miss Augusta!" A long arm waved in the air to make sure he had her attention. She stopped and waited for him. "Hello, Mrs. Many Roads. Nice to see you here today." Dorcas muttered something like "Um hm," which tickled Gustie. With some non-Indians, Dorcas pretended to a poor grasp of English. This clergyman, for all his good intentions, would never be treated to Dorcas's wit and wisdom.

"Miss Augusta, what did Dr. Llewellyn have to say about the Lesner family?"

"He wants to observe them. He believes they are seriously ill, especially the boy. But we could see that."

The priest looked thoughtful. "Well, I'll go to town tomorrow and see them. I'll bring Father Gregory with me. He's the Catholic—" Someone called to him from the church door. "That's Leo LaBourteaux, Sarah's uncle. He's building a pulpit in the church so I don't have to preach from a packing crate. I've got to go." The priest turned and called, "Matt! Tim!!" He looked and listened, his head craned like an awkward, thin prairie bird. Then he shrugged and looked back at Gustie. "If you see my boys, tell them I could use some help in there." He took off in a fluttering of vestments.

The day continued to smile upon the Red Sand as Gustie accompanied Dorcas back to Little Bull's family. The clouds were now just puffs in the sky. Cooking fires blazed, pots boiled, meats were stewing or roasting on spits. Elders rose to talk against the background music of playing children. Gifts were exchanged. Carrie Red Standing Horse gave Gustie a new pair of winter moccasins that she had beaded and sewn herself.

As Gustie ate, she glimpsed off to her left the two Flagstad boys, their frizzy thatches of red hair easy to spot among the black-haired boys with whom they played a game with sticks and a hoop. They appeared to be enjoying themselves so much, Gustie didn't feel like disturbing them. She finished a bowl of stew and a piece of fry bread and noticed that Dorcas was unusually quiet and not eating. She was about to say something when she saw two older women with a black dog between them come around the corner of a wagon. They each had hold of a rope. The other end of each rope was in a noose around the dog's neck. She knew that the Sioux ate dog meat. She supposed that this dog was meant for slaughter. A nasty foreboding scrabbled across Gustie's heart.

The women walked away from each other and began to pull. The dog was lifted up, paddling the air with his front legs. His eyes rolled. Foam bubbled around his mouth as he fought, uselessly, the tightening noose. One woman was now on her knees leaning back hard while the other, still on her feet, bent forward and pulled. Laughter broke out among those who watched when the standing woman slipped on the slick grass and fell. The noose loosened and the dog flopped down on the ground, twitching and gasping for air. The fallen woman got up and the choking began again. Gustie felt her blood pounding till her fingertips throbbed. She looked up. Jordis stood beside her but faced away from the scene. Little Bull glanced up, grinned at the huffing and puffing of the two heavyset women pulling at their ropes and went back to his conversation with Red Standing Horse.

Jordis's long knife was at hand. Gustie grabbed it, surprising Jordis who looked down and laughed until she saw the terrible look in Gustie's eyes. Without a word, Gustie went to the dog, gripped his muzzle, met his tortured eyes with her own, and with a single stoke, cut his throat. Arterial blood warmed her hands, spurted up her arms, over the front of her clothing and spattered her glasses. The force of the animal's heart kept the blood pumping even after he went limp. She let him go and strode down to

Shoonkatoh. She dropped to her knees in the shallow water. With shaking hands she cleaned her glasses first, then rinsed her face and arms, and let the water seep up the bloodied fabric of her clothing.

Gustie was still trembling when she looked up, a bright tear of rage in each eye. She said to Jordis who had come after her, "My Christ! Why not kill the animal quickly?"

Jordis did not answer.

Gustie rinsed the blade clean.

The dog's blood dispersed slowly in the water. From a shallow cavern beneath the mossy outcropping of the embankment, a cloud of leeches appeared undulating toward the cloud of blood. Gustie hastily removed herself from the lake. The bloodsuckers were another reason she didn't like Shoonkatoh. She watched them swimming, blindly searching for a host on which to feed.

The wind felt raw now as Gustie shivered in her wet clothes.

Gustie held the knife out to Jordis who slipped it back into her boot. They faced each other.

Jordis said, "I think we should leave now. You better get dry."

The realization of what she had just done chilled her more deeply than Shoonkatoh's bitter wind, and in the silence between them, what Jordis did not say echoed across the lake. Gustie had transgressed a tradition, insulted her hosts. She had, in short, behaved like an arrogant and ignorant *wasichu*, the very sort of person she despised. And yet, if some wave in time washed the moment up before her again, she would do the same thing. Because it was not killing that outraged her, but the inflicting of fear and pain.

Jordis brushed her fingertips across her lips. Her eyes rested on the thinning cloud of leeches, and Gustie could almost hear, falling all around them, the broken shards of their dream. They had come a long way through bad times to find each other and tentatively claim a place to call home. But the Red Sand would never be that place, at least not for Gustie. Not now.

"Let's go then," Jordis said again.

Gustie said, "You don't have to." The rest of what she would say swirled around them, unspoken, in the cold wind. *This transgression is mine. These are your people. This place is your home. You can stay.*

Jordis never displayed her affection for Gustie in front of others. Now she took Gustie's hand and walked beside her up the embankment and back through the people who sat quietly by their fires. No one smiled now. Even the children were still and followed them with solemn eyes. Dorcas had disappeared. Little Bull watched them sadly. As Gustie and Jordis passed, Winnie got up with Deborah in her arms and joined them and so did Carrie. The four women walked together to the far side of the church where the horses stood out of the wind.

Jordis took the reins of her white mare. "Can Leonard stay with Dorcas for a while?"

Winnie nodded.

Gustie, unable to speak, leaned in to kiss Deborah, holding her baby cheek close to her own for a moment, and then turned away. Jordis was already on Moon's back. Winnie and Carrie walked back to their families.

88

When Gustie went to the back of the wagon for a blanket, she emitted a soft, startled moan. Jordis walked Moon around to see. There, in the center of the wagon bed, was Gustie's wedding gift to Sarah and Clayton Nighthawk.

Gustie climbed up into the wagon seat, wrapped herself in the blanket, and let the bowl rest in her lap.

They rode slowly for a short time, bearing west. Jordis turned around to check on Gustie, who had not spoken a word since they left the lake shore. The reins were slack in her hands, the returned gift heavy in her lap, her eyes raised only enough to stare dully at Biddie's rump. Jordis turned the white mare around, leaned over and plucked the bowl out of Gustie's lap. She pressed Moon's sides with her knees and the horse trotted forward to where Shoonkatoh looped out before them. She raised the bowl and threw it with a strong backhand. The porcelain with its painted flowers sailed in a high arc and came down far out on the water, indistinguishable from the white caps prancing across the surface of the lake.

Gustie could hear the lake—the continuous in-and-out slip of water over smooth stones and across the soft tissue of water-logged, moss laden tree roots. Crow Kills breathing.

Jordis had made a smoky fire to warm them, cook their coffee, and ward off mosquitoes. Gustie had changed into her split skirt, blouse and one of Jordis's flannel shirts and washed her bloody clothes, draping them on a willow branch to dry.

A crescent moon was visible in the night sky. Gustie and Jordis sat close together by the fire.

"Are you warm?" Jordis asked.

"Warm enough."

They sipped hot coffee.

"What did I do today?"

"Something a Dakotah would not do." Jordis gazed over the rim of her cup into the fire. "I know what you saw." She folded her legs and sat her cup on the ground and glanced at Gustie who stared at the sparks that flew from a sheaf of wet grass. "You saw an animal being tortured. That was an accident. If the old grandmother had not fallen, the dog would have lost consciousness in a few seconds and died of strangulation in a few more, and no mark would have been left on its body. The dog is treated differently from game or cattle because it shares the fire, food, and in freezing weather, the tipi. It is treated with more respect—killed in a more sacred manner. No knife or weapon is used on it. Its skin is not broken before death. The suffocation happens after the blood is cut off to the brain and the animal is unconscious. It really is the most painless way to kill, when it is done right."

"When it's done right," Gustie echoed with emphasis.

"Indians do not perfectly fulfill all their traditions any more than white Christians do."

Gustie was suitably chastised and didn't answer. Jordis continued kindly, laying her hand on Gustie's cheek. "I know why you killed the dog. So do they. They are not unreasonable people. But you have to understand how it feels to them."

90

"Like I did not respect them."

"Yes."

"Is that how you feel?"

Jordis poked the fire with a green stick. The smoke began to rise again. "I interfered with Indians trying to kill Moon, and I knew at the time what they were doing and why. I did not just interfere, I fought them."

Gustie remembered the story of how Jordis had seen Indians, not of the Red Sand, chase a white man on a white horse. The man had been responsible for the death of one of their children. He escaped by jumping from his horse to the train pulling out of the Wheat Lake station. They had been full of rage and grief, craving some justice, and since they couldn't kill him, were set to kill his horse. Jordis stepped in, drew her knife and fought two of their young men before they gave up, disheartened and not wanting to fight a girl. They left and that was how Jordis got Moon.

"I know why you did what you did. Little Bull knows too, although he could not walk with you. But Winnie and Carrie did. They are your friends."

"Will they...suffer for what they did?"

"Suffer?"

"I mean, will they be reprimanded or shunned..."

Jordis laughed, delighted with the idea. "I would like to see someone try to reprimand Winnie or Carrie! Even their husbands! And, no...they will not be shunned. They are too respected. Too many people depend on them. Do not worry about them. First thing in the morning, you and I should go back to Charity."

"What about Dorcas?"

"Leonard will stay with her."

"I thought you wanted to be the one to take care of her."

"I do. But, after this, my being with her all the time might keep some people from visiting her. That would not be a good thing."

"You said Winnie and Carrie would not be shunned," Gustie said. "Why would they shun you?"

The darkness gathered around them. The firelight played on the smooth, sharply chiseled planes of Jordis's face. She said softly, "I am different."

Gustie never tired of looking at her exotically beautiful face.

"When I came back from the east I had no place to go. My mother was dead, her people scattered. Dorcas...everyone on the Red Sand welcomed me. But I had been with whites too long."

Stars appeared and suddenly brightened, leaving the little moon only a modest place in the heavens.

Jordis continued, "Little Bull and Winnie have tried to connect me to the others. But they cannot give me what I lost. And what I lost was not just the language. I lost everything but this." She brought a long finger down hard across the dark skin of her forearm. "I do not belong in white society either." She stirred the fire one more time, then threw the stick into the blaze. The fire hissed. "I turned out to be a poor investment. They never got out of me what they wanted. I did not embrace their ways, their church. Only their language. They stole me from my mother then pushed me far out on a limb, and the line they tossed me I would not grab. So here I am. Living on fish and berries and Dorcas's fry bread, riding Moon between Shoonkatoh, Crow Kills, and Charity. I take care of Dorcas knowing Little Bull and Winnie could do as well or better. But I owe her my life and taking care of her is the only worthwhile thing I do. I am one of the most educated, useless people in the state. To whites I will always be just an Indian. An Indian with an education, but still not quite as useful as cow shit."

Gustie lost her mouthful of coffee, mostly through her nose. Jordis grinned. Gustie wiped her dripping face with her sleeve. "Well, today I've insulted the only people who have ever been unfailingly kind to me, and I have taken from you the only thing that made your life worthwhile. My work here is done."

They both laughed and kept laughing until they sat with their arms around each other staring into the fire. Gustie could smell the sage in Jordis's hair, and hear, in the spaces left by frogs and crickets, the whisper of bat wings overhead.

Chapter 7: October 1900

"COME ON, LADIES." A LEAD rope in each hand, Gustie led the two mares out of the barn. The black nuzzled her neck and she responded with an affectionate cheek.

The grass was stiff with nearly frozen night rain. The only sound was the gentle plop-plopping of water from the eaves of her house and barn. As she passed through the barn door, a big drop landed on her shoulder like someone wanting her attention.

The sun rose and the world lightened in spite of thick cloud cover. In the east, above the horizon where the clouds thinned, lay a brilliant sash of orange, like prairie fire.

October. The Dakotah called it *Falling Leaves Moon*. This was also the time when insects lost their vigor and the broad-winged black and orange butterflies drifted through the air in a final, sad and majestic dance of death; when honking lines of low-flying geese swept

94

overhead on their way to warmth and sun; when the prairie began to doze and the sound of wind gained ascendancy over all other sounds as they receded into the stillness of winter.

Gustie turned the horses loose in the fenced pasture behind her house. Biddie trotted her dignified way around the perimeter of the enclosure, while Moon leapt like a filly and pranced in the opposite direction. The two mares came together and stood side by side, tossing their heads taking in all the scents carried on the early morning air. Gustie caught her breath. What a lovely picture they made!

Gustie brought in her cream jug. She started the coffee, tapped through the thin crystallization of water that topped the cream and spooned a generous portion of thick yellow stuff into her coffee cup. The aroma of boiling coffee permeated the house.

Before she could enjoy her first sip, she heard the thudding of hooves outside. Besides Jordis, Gustie's only regular callers were Iver with his deliveries, and Mary or Lena and Will, but their horses were all shod. This was an Indian horse. Had Moon jumped the fence? Gustie opened the door and dropped her gaze to Leonard, Little Bull's son. Behind him, his father's horse Swallow foamed sweat, his head held low.

"Leonard! Come in here. What's the matter?"

"Jordis." The boy seemed dazed and cold.

Gustie turned toward the bedroom. Jordis was standing in the doorway, still in her nightgown.

"My father wants Jordis to come. There's a sickness on the reservation."

Jordis whirled to get dressed.

Gustie went down on her knees in front of Leonard to be eye to eye with the boy who was small for his thirteen years. "What kind of sickness?" Gustie placed her cup of hot coffee in his hands.

"People are dying. They have fevers."

"Did your father send for Dr. Llewellyn?"

Leonard nodded. Gustie urged him to sip the coffee. He did.

"Does the doctor know what kind of sickness? Did he give it a name?"

"Father says it's the rotting face."

"Rotting face? What...?"

Behind her, Jordis said, "Smallpox." Gustie heard a moan and realized she had made it herself. She looked over her shoulder.

Grim and silent as stone, Jordis was tucking her shirt into her split skirt.

Gustie grasped Leonard fiercely by his shoulders nearly spilling his coffee. "Leonard, have you been vaccinated?"

"I... I don't know..."

Gustie took away the cup and set it on the floor. She pulled Leonard's poncho over his head, fumbled with his buttons, pulled his shirt down over his bare shoulders, and examined each of his arms in turn. There, on his left arm was the light puckery oval. "You have been vaccinated, Leonard. You won't get sick." As Gustie helped him back on with his shirt, she said, "Surely, most of the people on the reservation have been vaccinated. Little Bull would have seen to that. Wouldn't he?"

Jordis was buttoning her wool shirt. Gustie knew that she bore the scar—a smallpox vaccination being the only legacy of good from the mission school that still haunted her memory, the only scar from her time there that did not still hurt. Gustie asked again, "Wouldn't he?"

Jordis said, "The chief does not give orders. He cannot make people do what they will not do. He serves. He does not rule."

The terror that had subsided for a moment filled Gustie once more. She said to Jordis, "I'll follow you in the wagon. I'll tell Doc Moody and pick up some supplies." She stood up, unable to get enough air into her lungs, though she tried. Leonard took back the cup and drank the thickly creamed coffee.

After a moment, Jordis said, "I'm going to take the train. The morning freight is due here in a few minutes. Willie will find a place for Moon and me in a boxcar." They embraced fiercely. Then Jordis was gone.

Gustie poured more coffee and again loaded it with cream for Little Bull's oldest son, the joy of the chief's heart, the future chief of the Red Sand Dakotah, if they had a future. She fried him some eggs and put a loaf of bread on the table along with bowls of butter and jam.

"Leonard, you eat. I'll take care of Swallow."

Gustie led the exhausted stallion inside the barn, toweled him down and covered him with a blanket. Then she hitched Biddie to her wagon.

When she went back inside, only the heel of the bread remained. "I'm going into town and then I'm going to head out to the Red Sand. I want you to get in bed and sleep. When you wake up you can go out and fix some hot bran and molasses for Swallow. You'll find what you need in the bin against the wall in the barn. There's plenty of food here for you for at least a week. Make yourself at home. Don't come back to the reservation until you are rested. Promise?"

The boy nodded.

"I have a friend who will look in on you. Her name is Mary. You'll like her."

Gustie had never seen the smallpox, but she had seen its ravages on the survivors—the deep scars that pitted the faces of rich and poor alike. She kept Biddie at a steady pace and tried to keep her own fears and dread from rising any higher. She felt ready to suffocate, even as the cool October wind hit her squarely in the face. She pulled her conductor's cap down and lifted the collar of her coat.

Just this morning, the dawn had warned her of fire, but she hadn't recognized the omen. Even if she had, she couldn't have predicted this. *The invisible fire*...so named by those who'd seen it, because the victim's skin bubbled and burned as if on fire from within. The Indian name, rotting face, was more apt, more descriptive of the raw agonies that lasted for days, even weeks, before the sufferer was released unto merciful death. Gustie did not believe she was ready to confront such a horror.

She had kept the fear at bay while propelled by her sense of urgency and purpose. First she had gone to Doc Moody's thinking she would be rousing him from his bed. But he was up, packing his last bag and on his way to Gethsemane Church. Mrs. Moody was already there, he said, setting up a temporary surgery. He had received a telegram late yesterday from Dr. Llewellyn. As soon as the young Welshman had diagnosed smallpox, he had telegraphed the surrounding towns as a warning and a cry for help. The sheriff, his deputy and members of the town council were already knocking on doors and posting signs all over town. Every person, without exception, was to come to Gethsemane to be checked and vaccinated if they weren't already.

Doc Moody had nothing to give Gustie. He said he didn't know if he would have enough vaccine to handle all the unvaccinated in town until the train came in later in the day. He hoped the vaccine he'd sent for from St. Paul would be on it. Dr. Llewellyn's supply would be on the same train. It would be unloaded in Wheat Lake. As soon as the population of Charity was vaccinated, he would come out to the reservation to help. Before she could leave, he made Gustie roll up her sleeve and show him her own scar.

Next, Gustie went to Mary Kaiser's. When Mary opened the door, she looked surprised to see Gustie; she had already been visited by Sheriff Sully. She was dressed and ready to go to Gethsemane. She had been vaccinated. She was going early to see if she could help Mrs. Moody.

Gustie said, "Mary, I need you to check on Leonard, Chief Little Bull's son. He's at my place. He rode all night to get here and tell Jordis. He's sleeping now, but if you could look in on him I'd be grateful."

Mary responded, "Well, he can't stay out there by himself. I'll bring him back here."

Gustie had discovered the hard way the invisible wall that separated the whites from the Indians in

Charity. Once, Dorcas and Jordis, forced to stay overnight in Charity, were invited to sleep in someone's barn. No one else, not even Dorcas or Jordis, had reacted with outrage. Only Gustie. She looked at Mary with alarm. Leonard was better off alone in her house than here in Mary's barn, if that's what she had in mind. Mary read her face.

"Oh fiddle! I'll tuck him up in our extra room. He'll be snug as a bug. Don't worry." Mary laughed. "You go on now. Gustie?"

"Yes?"

"Take care of yourself now."

"I will. Thank you, Mary."

Gustie's next stop was O'Grady's store. Both Kenneth O'Grady and his son Morgan were there already. They didn't always open this early. "Have you heard?"

From behind the counter, Kenneth nodded and peered over his glasses. He was, as usual, poring over his account book.

"I'm going out there. I need some things." Gustie felt strangely disoriented, almost wringing her hands. With all she had been through, this was brand new. "I don't know what would be useful, really. Food, blankets..." she trailed off. Kenneth nodded to Morgan who disappeared into their stock room. She heard him carry something out the side door to her wagon and come back for more. She turned to the senior O'Grady. "I can't wait till the bank opens, Kenneth. Could I charge these things, please?" Gustie had never charged anything before, though she knew most of Charity's residents did.

Kenneth shook his head gravely. She heard the door bang again as Morgan came back for yet another load for her wagon. Kenneth said, "Nope. Fraid not."

Gustie's heart sank. She had given Kenneth good business since she had come into her inheritance. She didn't know what to do. She didn't feel anger, just a huge lump of despair lodged in her throat. She would have to wait then till the bank opened. Almost three hours from now.

"Oh, Kenneth..."

She was about to plead with him when he said, "Your money's no good here today, Miss Augusta. On the house. Take what you need."

The lump in her throat dissolved and tears filled her eyes. She nodded her thanks and walked briskly to the door. He called after her. "Hey, your friend still have a sweet tooth?"

She turned around in time to catch a brown bag of candies sailing through the air in her direction. When she bought her supplies to take out to the reservation, she had never failed to add a bag of candy for Dorcas. He remembered.

"Thank you, Kenneth." He nodded, pushed his glasses up his nose and went back to his account book.

Gustie traveled south to her last stop. She couldn't leave town without seeing Lena. Like everyone else, Lena had been awakened before dawn. Fritz Mulkey had ridden like Paul Revere, knocking on doors south of the tracks. Will was already on his way to Gethsemane. Lena was dressed and Gracia was in her highchair.

In few words, Gustie explained that Jordis was already on her way to the reservation. Mary was going to look after Leonard, and Gustie was taking her wagon-load of supplies out now. She shed a few tears when she told how Kenneth knew what she needed and had given it freely. Lena looked at the back of the wagon where cartons of canned goods were neatly stacked next to bundles wrapped in brown paper that looked to be sheets and blankets. There were bags of flour and salt, sugar and coffee, a pail of eggs and another of butter.

Lena ran in and brought out several jars of her rhubarb sauce. She placed them in among the parcels so they wouldn't get banged around. Then she looked at Gustie. "I'll bet you didn't have a thing to eat this morning."

"I've got to get going..."

"You can take something with you. You've got a minute for that. Come in the kitchen. It's cold out here. You won't help anybody by going hungry yourself."

Gustie followed her inside.

Lena poured her a cup of coffee, dosed it with cream, and then went to her cupboard and spread slices of bread with butter and jam, which she wrapped in a dish towel. She took half a roast chicken out of her ice box and wrapped that up in newspaper. Gustie swallowed the last of her coffee gratefully.

Together, they went out to the wagon where Lena placed the food under the seat. "There. Just reach down when you're hungry. You don't have to stop. Wait a minute." She rummaged in the back of the wagon for one of the jars of sauce and put that with the rest of Gustie's food. "You take care now, you hear me?" Then, uncharacteristically, Lena threw her arms around Gustie and gave her a ferocious hug.

The sun, higher in the sky, was gradually warming the air and Gustie took her hat off. She reached down and brought the paper-wrapped chicken up from the floor and laid it out on the seat beside her. She ate slowly until there was nothing left but bones. By now they were at Dryback Grade. She stopped Biddie and let her drink. She cupped handfuls of the lake water to her own mouth and drank deeply. Then they went on their way. As she got closer to the reservation her fear rose and fell in waves. Fear of what awaited her; fear, she had to admit, of a cold welcome. She had not been included in Little Bull's request to return to the reservation. Well, she sniffed, a little like Lena, she thought and laughed at how she had taken on this characteristic of her friend, they would just have to deal with it. She was going to help whether they liked it or not. She would bring them her supplies and try to not get in the way.

Chapter 8: November 1900

CLOUDY NIGHT BLANKETED SHOONKATOH AS Gustie stood on the shore. Behind her, the mission with its campfires and the lanterns glowing dimly through the windows of the church and rectory shone like a mirage of light in a desert of darkness. The light, dampened by opaque night, shed no illumination outside its own tiny sphere. Facing Shoonkatoh, without starlight, without the risen moon, water, night, and her own soul were one darkness.

The smallpox had savaged the reservation and departed, Gustie had to think, fully sated; nearly half of the population of the Red Sand had perished.

The mission churchyard gleamed with new white crosses. Fresh burial mounds scarred the reservation. Embers still glowed from burnt houses and tipis.

Through it all Gustie had shed no tears. Once, she vomited when, first to enter a tipi, she found a family in a pile where they had fallen and died, being eaten by their dogs.

104

After that, the homes of the dead and dying all blended into one confused nightmare. Gustie could not remember where they found the grandmother rocking a baby's corpse, the rest of her family dead in their beds, or whether it was Shoonkatoh or Crow Kills where a woman had run to the shallows seeking a cool refuge, finding cold death instead...or where it was, exactly...behind which cabin, they had found a boy, the only survivor of his family, hungrily gnawing on a maggoty calf's head.

What Gustie had expected—the sick, covered with pustules, moaning in death agonies—she did not find. She had traveled to the farthest reaches of the Red Sand and had been met time and time again with the silence of the dead. Winnie had prepared the church to receive the sick, but none of her beds were ever occupied by anyone suffering from smallpox. "The dead don't need much," she said, sadly eyeing the stacks of donated blankets, canned goods, and clothes that lined the walls of the sanctuary. The beds had been used only by the people who had come to the reservation to help.

They had gone out in small groups. Little Bull, Father Flagstad, Gustie, and Dr. Llewellyn in one; Jordis, Mary Kaiser, Sheriff Sully, and Doc Moody in another. They returned to the mission where they rested, ate a decent meal, got fresh horses, supplies, and were joined by others, including Father Gregory the Catholic priest and the four nursing sisters he had sent for from the Yankton convent, re-grouped and went out again.

They were grateful when they found the living. Those who did not have the mark of the pox lived through at another time or the scar of the physician's needle were vaccinated. This was not always easily done. Often Little Bull and Father Flagstad had to talk them into it. Earnestly. Pleadingly.

They found people with swollen bodies, already comatose whom they knew would be dead by morning. If they were members of his church, Father Flagstad performed the proper rituals; if not, he simply prayed silently. They were buried on the return trip and their homes torched. At one time, Gustie looked behind her and it seemed to her that the whole northeast quarter of the Red Sand was burning.

They slept in the open, or, when it rained, in the homes of the dead and the dying. They ate out of cans, went unwashed in dirty clothing day after day. They were in a race, trying to move faster than the rotting face. For, if they found people before they were stricken, they could save them. One night, Gustie at last asked the question that had been on her mind. "Why weren't they vaccinated before? All of them?"

Little Bull silently stared into the campfire. Father Flagstad answered. "Miss Augusta, you must understand that the white man has given the Indian many things—most of which have turned out to be a curse. One of the few things we offered that would have been a blessing, they were afraid to take."

They all watched the fire until Father Flagstad wrapped himself in his blanket and curled up and went to sleep.

Gustie said, "I seem to ask the wrong questions."

Little Bull lay down and pulled up his own blanket. "Some people don't even ask. Get some sleep."

Of all the sights and sounds, the one Gustie would never forget, even if all else dimmed across time, was that of Little Bull exchanging his usual denim blues for his ceremonial buckskins and his father's war bonnet, carrying his sheaf of sacred eagle feathers out onto the open prairie. She watched the chief of the Red Sand Dakotah raise the sheaf high above his head and listened as he chanted the death song of his ancestors.

But in the midst of the nightmare, flourished bright little astonishments:

Mary Kaiser arriving in a large wagon, Leonard perched in the back atop bundles of bedding, clothing, and food she had gathered by going from door to door in Charity, Doc Moody at her side (he had succeeded in vaccinating everyone in Charity in fewer than eight hours). Next to Doc Moody, driving a pair of Walter's Percherons, sat Sheriff Sully, his saddle horse and Swallow were tied to the back of the wagon.

Father Flagstad bearing the strain of those weeks with dignity and sadness. Only once did she see him break down and weep—when they found Sarah and Clayton Nighthawk. Sarah was propped up against straw pillows with Clayton's head in her lap. Clayton had died of the pox. Sarah had shot herself.

The devotion and sheer stamina of Little Bull and of Red Standing Horse who traveled the length and breadth of the reservation, making sure the living were vaccinated, the dead buried and all contaminants burned, and gathering in to the care of their wives at the mission, the orphans, of which there turned out to be about forty, children who had been inoculated at the mission school, children who had watched their parents and grandparents and younger siblings die.

And the greatest astonishment of all—Jordis, who became Little Bull's right hand, chief by proxy in his absence, since he could not be all places. She held the dying in her arms and spoke softly to them and gave them water and closed their eyes in death and helped to dig their graves. She soothed the fears of the well, showed them her own scar and lightly caressed their arms as Dr. Moody or Dr. Llewellyn or one of the nuns outraged small ovals of their flesh to save their bodies. A vitality she had never used had been stored within her, earning interest, and she drew upon it now. She glowed with purpose. She transcended her own grief and left her rage like an old skin on the prairie to disintegrate in the wind.

And Gustie marveled, too, at the way life continued to stream around them, like a river flowing around and filling in the spaces behind rocks and boulders after an avalanche:

Father Flagstad and Jordis, as well as the chief and Red Standing Horse, taking their rifles with them to bring back waterfowl and rabbits to add to the provisions necessary to feed the increasing number of people who began to gather at the mission.

Dorcas at her fishing pole.

The children who fished, washed dishes, carried water, and who, when their chores were done, played raucous games running wildly all around the mission grounds.

Owen Braaten, the Indian agent, who was not adept at hunting or fishing or much else, dug the graves in the churchyard and filled them in, and made the trips back and forth to Wheat Lake to pick up mail and supplies that arrived daily in answer to his many telegrams to government agencies and surrounding communities. He quietly made himself useful and was, along with another, observed by Jordis, casting wistful, if not lustful, glances in the direction of Mary Kaiser.

It happened one evening toward the end of the nightmare, when many of the helpers as well as those who were merely taking refuge were gathered at long tables made from boards laid across saw horses in front of the church. Mary was one of the women bringing the food from the rectory kitchen to the tables. Jordis whispered to Gustie, "Owen Braaten and Dr. Llewellyn are looking at Mary Kaiser like she's the main dish."

"Jordis!" Gustie kicked her under the table.

"Look at them!"

"They're young, new to this country, considering their prospects," Gustie whispered back and tried to keep from smiling.

"She's married!"

"Jordis, I think there's some Philadelphia in you, too." Under the table, Jordis kicked her back.

When Mary finally took a place at the table, it was safely between Dennis Sully and Father Gregory—the law to her right and the church to her left—what could be safer?

The air grew colder, though not cold enough to snow. Gustie pulled her coat tighter at the throat and hoped it wouldn't rain. Rain would be worse than snow.

The night blotted out detail. Gustie felt disembodied. She could not even see her own hands clasped before her as she turned to walk along the shore, occasionally wetting her feet before correcting her course again to the left, to dry sand. In its unlovely voice, a cricket sang on, determined to sound the last note before the winter freeze, which was late in coming.

She sensed them and stopped. Then she heard the gentle thudding, the disturbance of water and their breathing as they came nearer. She remained still, feeling them all around her. Once, blinded not by darkness but by snow, she had found herself surrounded by creatures that, she was assured later, could not possibly have been there. She did not assume now that she was surrounded by flesh and blood, even though she heard them, felt them, smelled them. She was not afraid.

A vein of lightning illuminated the landscape with a blue-white shimmer. She knew then that they were real. She was surrounded by the horses of the dead. Dozens of them. In one flash she could only get a sense of many, not how many, the paints and piebalds, and grays, blacks and browns and the one magnificent white—Moon.

"Jordis?"

"Here."

In another flash she again caught sight of the white mare, and when the darkness flowed around her again she made her way around the flank of one horse, ducked under the arched neck of another and was at the mare's side. She found Jordis's hand and held on. Jordis had been absent from the mission, out on her own for three days. "Little Bull told me you stayed out to get the horses."

"I could not leave them to fend for themselves with winter coming on," said Jordis.

Gustie said, "There is no corral here."

"We'll tether a few, the rest will stay close by."

"What are you going to do with them?"

"They belong to the tribe. People who need them will take them. Leonard and I can look after them in the meantime."

What will I do? Gustie didn't say it and only held tighter onto Jordis's hand, not eager to return to the mission, now as populous as a village. They had begun to gather, people who had lost one or more members of their family, whose homes and possessions had been put to the fire, who had nothing and would start over with the things donated. The pots boiled, the church was slept in, prayed in, and sung in; and Matthew Flagstad pounded the rickety, out-of-tune piano in accompaniment to the liturgy and hymns sung by the faithful in gratitude for surviving and in grief for the dead. Holding Jordis's hand, Gustie relished the night, the company of her beloved, and the warm comfort of horses. Her tranquility came to an end when thin voices called to her from out of the darkness, "Miss Gustie! Miss Gustie!"

"Here, Matt, Tim. Over here."

"Dorcas Many Roads is taken sick. We've been looking for you."

Gustie let go of Jordis's hand and began to run. Jordis squeezed the sides of her mount and Moon broke away from the herd and took her up the bank. They ran toward the light, Jordis passing Gustie and flying ahead of her on the white horse.

Dorcas, she was told, lay on a pallet in the church. As Gustie made her way through the crowd, Dr. Llewellyn came out, his stethoscope around his neck. "It's not the smallpox. But she's not good."

"What's wrong with her then?"

"Miss Gustie, all the strain of the past month... has taken its toll."

"That's it? Strain?" Gustie found herself angry with this young doctor, as if he were at fault for Dorcas's age, for her collapse.

"And old age. She is a very old woman."

Jordis came out of the church and announced, "She wants to be taken back to Crow Kills. Now."

"Carry me outside, Granddaughters. I do not want to die in here. Is the drum here? I want to hear the drum."

They had made the journey from Shoonkatoh to Crow Kills in the pitch black of a moonless night—and, Little Bull had said—by the seat of their pants and their horses' whiskers. When they finally reached the cabin and carried Dorcas to her bed, they made a fire in the stove and another outside where they put the coffee on to boil.

Dorcas had begun asking for the drum as soon as they carried her out of the church. Leonard rode Swallow, Little Bull drove Gustie's wagon with Gustie and Jordis in the wagon bed holding Dorcas across their laps. Red Standing Horse rode out in the opposite direction, thinking that he would bring back old Jimmy Saul, too, because, although White Eagle had the only decent drum on the reservation, he couldn't sing. Jimmy Saul was the best singer and knew the old songs.

By the light of one dim lantern, Jordis and Gustie had taken turns throughout the night sitting inside the cabin with Dorcas, while outside one of them sipped coffee with Little Bull and Leonard. Nobody talked much. Winnie and Carrie remained at the mission to care for the orphans and their own children. At first light, Dorcas had insisted on being taken outside, asking again for the drum.

"The drum is coming, Grandmother."

Dawn came, cloudless and cold. The sun itself seemed without heat. Gustie worried that Dorcas would die of chill if they took her outside. She wanted her to stay in the cabin where they could maintain the fire in the stove and keep her warm. Jordis disagreed firmly, "No. This is what she wants. Let's take her out."

They laid her on a soft pallet of blankets facing west, with Crow Kills on her right, the prairie sweeping away to her left. They covered her with more blankets and wrapped her shawl snugly around her head and neck, and waited. Feather, Jordis's gray cat, appeared and tucked himself under Dorcas's blankets. She seemed content.

All her life, Gustie felt like she was in some kind of free-fall, with no place and nothing to hang on to. It was only upon waking up in Dorcas's cabin that she felt like she had landed. There, in that tiny, one-room cabin with only two cowhides on the wall for insulation and decoration, that queasy, falling-through-space feeling had left her. When she was broken in body and spirit, Dorcas Many Roads had literally picked her up off the prairie and put her back together again. Dorcas was the nearest thing to a mother she had had. Her mother had died when she was small, and Gustie had been raised by a warm and loving woman who always carefully acknowledged the barrier between them; who never forgot her place as housekeeper; who, as the hired help, could never embrace her employer's child with the fullness Gustie craved. Recognizing no barriers, Dorcas had cradled Gustie in her arms, sung to her and let her cry, had cleaned her up and fed her. For the last three years, whenever she had felt herself unraveling, Gustie had come back to this old woman to eat her stew, drink her coffee, and listen to her stories about the buffalo days, nourished by her warm, often silent presence, clinging to her like the motherless child she was. For her part, all she could ever do for Dorcas was make sure her shelves were never empty and that she had a comfortable bed and a rocking chair for her tiny porch.

"I am not a blood relative either," Jordis said to her once. "You are as much her granddaughter as I am." And, at the time, it had felt true. Dorcas had given her a new name, Woman Who Sees the Deer, and a piece of polished antler on a leather cord that she wore around her neck. But it wasn't true, much as Gustie would have liked it to be. Gustie was white. She felt this land deep in her bones and could lay claim to a patch of it by virtue of having buried a loved

114

one here, but still, her ties were more wished for than real, and she had demonstrated that painfully when she killed the dog. Dorcas had never mentioned that incident, and Gustie had been afraid to ask her how she felt about it.

Little Bull replaced Gustie at Dorcas's side. Leonard puttered around the campfire, keeping the flames high and hot on this bitterly cold day. Gustie went by herself to sit alone under the trees behind the cabin. She sat on the cold ground, her knees drawn up, her head in her hands.

Gustie knew that this day was the beginning of the sad last act of a two-month-long tragedy. Survivors of the plague, already burdened with the loss of friends and family, now began to appear, paying their respects to a tribal grandmother whom they would mourn because they loved her and because she was one of the last of the old ones. With her passing would go one of the last living memories of the days before contact with the *wasichu*. She remembered when the deer were plentiful and the buffalo herds were so large you could walk for many days and never see the end of them. Dorcas's first contact with whites had been her first experience of death without honor, disease unaffected by her healing plants. She remembered the days before the Black Robes, when the Sioux danced for all occasions, when their singing rang out over the prairies and plains, when the drum was the living heart of a village and seldom silent.

On her deathbed, she longed to hear the drum, to hear the old songs. *Where was Red Standing Horse?*

Gustie was the first to see them as they came around the trees from the east, Red Standing Horse on his big roan, White Eagle riding a shabby mule harnessed to a travois that appeared to bear the drum as well as some other bundles. Behind them, on their own swaybacked ponies were Jimmy Saul and Clarence Cut Bow, another singer of old songs. Gustie followed them back around the house and watched them set up in the shelter of the trees where they would be somewhat protected from the wind that cut across the prairie like a scythe.

Now Jordis also worried that Dorcas was too exposed to the elements. As if in answer to her worries, Jimmy unrolled from the travois some poles and steer hides and left them in a jumble at her feet. She smiled.

"What's all this?" Gustie asked.

"A windbreak."

Jordis pounded the stakes and propped up the short poles fashioning a sort of three-quarter, miniature tipi around Dorcas sheltering her from the direct blast of the wind, but not cutting off completely her view of the sky and open ground.

And so the drumming began and continued with White Eagle taking very few breaks, and Jimmy Saul and Clarence Cut Bow singing in the high-pitched Sioux style that had so startled Gustie when she first heard it and that now relieved the aching in her breast as she sat vigil with the others at Dorcas's deathbed. For now, Gustie could hang on to the sound. She felt better.

Dorcas seemed to rally with the singing. She asked to sit up. "Will someone dance? I want to see the buff'lo dance." This was not a dance anyone had done in a long time. They no longer had the buffalo masks and headdresses they used to wear, but, to keep the dance alive, Little Bull had learned it from his father and taught it to his son, and Clarence could do it, old as he was; the three danced, imitating the buffalo. Other men joined them and Little Bull returned to sit with Dorcas.

Gustie watched and listened. She couldn't tell if the singing was just vocalizations, or actual words. She asked Little Bull.

He nodded, "This one has words," and paused to listen a few moments to the singing then he translated for Gustie,

"In the north...
the wind blows...
they are walking...
the hail beats...
...they are walking...

It is an old song," he added.

Gustie shivered. She could almost believe this song had the power to summon the shaggy walkers— while they lived. But there were no more beasts to answer the call of the Sioux.

Dorcas's eyes sometimes closed. She did not sleep. She was probably, Gustie thought, letting her mind wander back over happier times. So Gustie was surprised when the old woman's eyes opened and focused directly upon her. "Grandmother? Can I get you something?" Gustie asked.

"Little Bull, go away." Dorcas's voice was labored.

The chief rose and ambled over toward the singers. The dancers dispersed. The drum and the buffalo song continued.

Last words? Is that what they were going to hear? Gustie didn't want to hear any last words. She wanted Dorcas to rest, and regain her strength, and for things to go back to the way they used to be.

"You know how we used to do the sun dance?"

Jordis nodded. "Yes, Grandmother."

Would she request a sun dance? Gustie knew enough to know that the sun dance was a bare-chested, if not close-to-naked dance done in warm weather, not in the spiteful cold of late November.

Jordis answered. "You have told me, Grandmother. I will not forget."

Dorcas motioned with her chin toward Gustie. "Tell her, like I told you."

"In the full moon of July," Jordis began, "the sacred tree was chosen, cut and brought to the dancing circle. A man, if he had a special sacrifice to make, or if he had made a promise in battle, would stand up in front of all the people. His chest was pierced through in two places." Jordis touched the two places on her own body, reminding Gustie of the two points of the cross made by Catholics. "Pointed willow sticks were pushed through and ropes were tied to the ends, the ropes that hung down from the sacred tree in the center. He had to pull back on these ropes, hard and dance until the willow sticks broke through his flesh. He suffered. He suffered in the heat, from the pain, from exhaustion, and from staring into the sun, for he danced in a circle always facing the sun, looking straight into the sun."

118

Dorcas moved her hand slightly to rest on the piece of blanket rolled up at her side. Her eyes opened full upon Gustie once more. "Have you seen him yet?"

"Who?"

"The buff'lo."

"No... I..."

"You see the deer, still?"

Gustie saw a white-tailed deer occasionally. No one else ever saw them. She was told that the deer had been wiped out of this part of the country along with the buffalo. She didn't understand it, but she had gotten used to it. Anyway, she no longer mentioned it, and the visions had faded. She got impressions, glimpses in the periphery of her vision of deer leaping, skimming over the prairie with their graceful running stride. She answered truthfully, "Sometimes. Not like before."

The old woman nodded. The small hope that had flickered in her eyes faded and she closed them. "Thought you might see buff'lo spirit too. We are calling him. You tell me if you see him."

"I'll tell you."

Gustie joined Little Bull again at the fire. Neither of them felt the urge to speak.

Jimmy Saul's voice now rose alone, in a plaintive song that was clearly different from the buffalo song.

Gustie said, "That's a different song."

"Yes." Little Bull listened and translated the words for her as he had done before.

"From the north
a dry wind
blows cold

like the breath
of the dead."

"Is it old, too?" Gustie asked.

"I do not think so. I have never heard it before."

The drum never stopped. The singing was intermittent, the songs and the singers changed; sometimes Jimmy Saul, sometimes Jimmy and Clarence, and from time to time others joined in or replaced them. Gustie thought it was only the drum that kept the survivors on their feet, the earth spinning, and the sky from falling.

People continued to come to the half-moon tipi, as Jordis had begun to call it, and Gustie once more retreated. Alone, she walked far out on the prairie. With all that Dorcas had given her, Gustie had never given back more than a few trifles.

Not expecting to see anything, Gustie scanned the horizon. No birds remained, no insects. Behind her, the cottonwoods were barren of leaves. There was nothing now to stir the prairie, nothing to resist the wind. Only rabbits and the occasional raccoon would venture out of warm burrows and not till dusk. Right now the marriage of wind and earth was a sterile union. Gustie stared into the distance, wishing she could have given Dorcas something. Then she realized that she could. She threw the shawl back off her head, spun around and ran all the way back to the half-moon tipi.

Gustie knelt close to Dorcas. "I saw him, Grandmother! The buffalo bull. He's come back! He came up over the rise and stood there with his big shoulders high. He lowered his head at me. His nostrils blew hot steam. His horns were new moons curved around his head. His coat was shaggy and silver in the sunlight, like the edge of a thundercloud. He was like thunder, Grandmother. He roared like thunder."

The old woman smiled, gave a tiny nod of her head, and relaxed visibly. Then Gustie walked out alone again leaving Jordis holding Dorcas's hand when she died.

Gustie, inured to the cold wind, stayed out on the prairie and waited for Jordis, who eventually came to her and wrapped herself in Gustie's arms and wept.

They buried Dorcas a short distance from Clare Madigan on the rise, looking down over the cabin and the lake and looked over by the cottonwood Gustie had planted there. "We will plant another in the spring," said Jordis.

Dorcas had never accepted the white man's religion, so Little Bull said an Indian prayer over her grave. He began a traditional Sioux prayer in his own language, then stopped, and out of deference for Jordis and Gustie, began again in English:

"Oh Great Spirit
Whose Voice I hear in the Winds
And whose breath gives life to all the world,
Hear me. I am small and weak and need your strength and wisdom.
Let me walk in beauty and make my eyes ever behold the red and purple sunset.
Make my hands respect the things you have taught my people.

Let me learn the lessons you have hidden in every leaf and rock.

I seek strength not to be greater than my brother but to fight my greatest enemy—myself.

Make me always ready to come to you with clean hands and straight eyes.

So when life fades as the fading sunset my spirit may come to you without shame."

Jimmy Saul and Clarence Cut Bow chanted more prayers in Dakotah and then they moved the drum to the mission church to drum for the living and the dead. Father Flagstad did not mind. Drums, pianos out of tune, what did it matter?

Chapter 9: December 1900

J ORDIS KNELT AT WATER'S EDGE and stared into the cold, glassy surface of Crow Kills, her face reflected clearly in the green-tinted water. *My face. I do not recognize it. It is an Indian face. But I am not Indian. I am not white, though I speak their language, have read their books, and survived their schools. I do not think like an Indian or act like a wasichu. I am neither wolf nor dog.*

Three winters had passed since she cut her hair. The plaints of hair, now long again, flowed through her hands like water. *The only thing about me that is truly Indian. My hair has no thoughts, does not feel. My hair has only to grow. Three plaits of hair I hold tight in my hands: one for Gustie; one for Dorcas; one for me. I lay one plait over the other: Gustie, Dorcas, me and pull them tight. Gustie, Dorcas, me...pull them tight till I reach the end of the black water and bind them like three rivers come together.*

Her braid tied securely, she looked up at the sky, suddenly black. The December sky. The Trees Popping Moon sky. *The Milky Way is the path of souls, but Dorcas Many Roads has a year before she will walk there.* At the moment of her death, Jordis took a lock of Dorcas's hair. She placed it in her memory bundle. This act placed her grandmother's soul in her keeping. *No one left to teach me the traditional way of soul keeping, so I honor her presence as I am able. I know only that I must bring food offerings; that I must walk and talk and do all things with respect. I have to stop swearing.*

Lena wished she had never agreed to come. She carried Gracia, who was cocooned in a blanket with just her nose and eyes peeking out under her red knit cap. Lena's own boots, she had lined with pieces of an old felt hat she had found at Ma's. To Ma it was just something she never used but couldn't throw or give away. So Lena took it and Ma was none the wiser. In front of her, breaking a path through the ankle-deep snow, Will carried the highchair and her pie box. Lena squinted against the winter glare and stayed fixed on Will's broad back.

This Christmas Day was the first family dinner since Pa's death, and if Lena knew anything, it would probably be the last. Holidays with this bunch were dismal in a good year. The death of the family patriarch had not had a sweetening effect on anybody.

Mary had suggested it as a kindness to Ma, so the old battleax wouldn't be alone at Christmas— so she'd be surrounded by her boys on Christmas.

Fiddlesticks! Ma Kaiser didn't give a snap about her boys except for what they might do for her. She cared less for her daughters-in-law—not Mary, who did the most for her mother-in-law, nor Nyla who did her share, that's for sure; certainly not Lena who'd done plenty before she'd had her baby, but now her own family came first. Ma didn't even seem to care much for her one and only grandchild. The woman was cold as a mackerel. Lena cast a squinty eye up into the crystalline blue. Not a cloud, not a haze on the horizon. No excuse to leave early on account of the weather.

The Kaiser house loomed before them. The front step creaked under their weight. They were inside. The only good thing was that Gracia was too young to know what she was missing. Next year, Lena would insist on having their Christmas dinner at home. She would decorate the house with red paper ribbons and popcorn on a string. During the year she would save up for a few candles to light. She would bring out the angel that her grandmother had made out of white sheeting and scraps of lace from her wedding dress. The house would be festive, and only happy people would be allowed to enter it. Let one day of the year be totally happy and magical for a child. That's all she would ask. Next year.

This year, there was nothing for it but to put on a good face and make the best of the next few hours. That's all she had agreed to give to this sorry event.

Mary greeted them, smiling and flushed from the warm kitchen. A white apron covered her dress from neck to hem.

"Something sure smells good, Mary." Will grinned as he stamped the snow off his feet on the entry rug.

"I've got a duck roasting in there, with stuffing, and Nyla is doing the potatoes."

Well, sniffed Lena, *what's to do with a potato? You peel it, you boil it, you mash it. What an accomplishment!* But it was one less thing Mary had to do, so it was something at that.

Mary took the highchair and the pie box while they got out of their winter wrappings. "What a pretty girl you are today," she crooned to Gracia, as she led them into the warmth of the kitchen.

"Hello, Ma. Merry Christmas to you," Lena greeted her mother-in-law. "Merry Christmas, Nyla."

Nyla nodded and tried to smile, "Merry Christmas."

Gertrude Kaiser responded in mumbled German. Lena understood German, though she was no good at speaking it. She thought she heard, "Oh, yes, another Christmas," as if the holidays were a burden; or perhaps it was just a lament on the passage of time.

Lena softened. "Gracia, there's Grandma." The baby gurgled. The old woman did not look up from her work. Lena came up beside her to see what she was doing. Gertrude stood at the kitchen table, toiling over a floured board. Her sleeves were rolled up and flour coated her hands and wrists. She was kneading and shaping rolls. She had a row of them along the side of the board. When she finished the one she was working on she placed it on line with the others, then took another from the row and started kneading it again, as if she wasn't satisfied with the job she had done the first time. She worked the roll of dough into more flour. The dough had a gray cast to it.

126

Lena went over to the sink where Mary was rinsing a few dishes. "How long has she been doing that?"

"All morning. She had the dough mixed when I got here."

"What time was that?"

"Five-thirty."

"Oh, for Pete's sake! The dough is...it looks dirty!"

Mary shrugged. "She's done other things, and then gone back to the rolls."

Lena looked aghast at her sister-in-law. "What other things?"

Mary covered her mouth with the back of one of her wet hands to stifle a giggle. Lena buried her face in Gracia's wool sweater to do the same. They turned their backs on their mother-in-law and, as quietly as possible, choked on their laughter. Mary got out, but barely, "I told Walter...not to eat...the rolls." They had to stifle another torrent of giggling.

Mary got control of herself and went back to washing a couple of dishes. Ma looked around at Lena still snuffling into her baby's sweater. Lena held up her hand. "I just swallowed wrong. I'll be okay."

"Ma," Mary said, "you better put your rolls in the oven now. Dinner will be ready in about twenty minutes.

Ma sighed and dropped each wad of dough on a greased tin and carried it to the stove. Mary took it from her and slid it into the oven.

"Why don't you go rest now, Ma. Go sit with the boys. We can finish up here."

From the living room, Lena heard Walter's voice sounding like pouring gravel. Oscar's responses were bearish grunts. She heard nothing from Will. He was probably reading the paper. That's what he did to stay out of arguments.

The house, Lena noticed, was cluttered almost as badly as before the baptism. Gertrude was unhappy unless she was hemmed in by junk. None of it worth a blame thing either, to look at or in usefulness, except maybe to line an old boot.

Since Ma was too cheap to have more than one stove lit at a time, the living room was cold. Lena looked at Nyla, quietly mashing her big pot of potatoes. The poor woman must freeze at night upstairs or be crushed under all the quilts needed to keep her warm. Lena always felt sorry for Nyla, but it was hard to know how to help her. She couldn't remember ever having a conversation with her that was longer than a single sentence uttered by each of them.

Fortunately, a lot of the warm kitchen air found its way into the dining room. Lena claimed the chair closest to the kitchen door and set up Gracia's highchair next to her. The rest of them could sit where they pleased, but she wasn't going to have her baby be cold because Ma was a tightwad.

Lena secured Gracia in her chair and left her some colored paper on the tray to play with. Lena made these folded paper trinkets from paper scraps that Kenneth O'Grady saved for her.

When Lena came back into the kitchen, Nyla was still hard at mashing potatoes. *Good grief! She's going to turn them into soup.*

"Well, what can I do, Mary?"

"Everything's done. Just bring it to the table."

They carried in bowls of vegetables: Mary's canned beans from her garden, mashed turnips, and candied squash; a dish of pickles, a ham, the roast duck, and a bowl of stuffing on the side. Mary was as good a cook as Lena, maybe better, Lena had to admit. But Lena had it all over her with her pies. She had it all over everybody with her pies. Nyla finally finished the potatoes and carried them in along with a bowl of pickled herring. Butter, salt, and pepper were already set, and—Lena breathed a sigh of relief—a loaf of Mary's wholesome, snowy-white bread.

Walter rattled on and on. He always seemed to have the hardest ground, the most rocks, and the worst time collecting his money from the farmers. No one had it as rough or worked as hard as he did. Will just shook his head and laughed, and Oscar didn't seem to pay attention. The talk irked Lena, who knew Will worked as hard as anybody, with worse equipment. Pa Kaiser had seen fit to leave most of his good machinery and tools to Walter and Oscar, neither of whom was inclined to share with a brother.

When Mary called them to the table, Walter at least took his soggy cigar stub out of his mouth. Oscar claimed the chair at the head of the table. He wore his permanent scowl, and she noted that he was getting jowly. His hair had started to turn an iron gray at the temples. They had all been handsome boys. Will was the only one who still was. Not just because he was the youngest, but because he still did all his own work. Oscar always had one, sometimes two, hired men. He never did any of the hard lifting or pulling. Walter, the shortest and stockiest, was also doing less and less of the hard work.

Even so, strength was relative; they were strong men, with big powerful hands. Even Oscar, if you put him in a contest with, say Lester Evenson, the banker or Pard Batie the lawyer, would win with one arm and not get winded.

Lena took her place by the highchair, Ma sat at the opposite end of the table from Oscar, and Nyla and Will, Walter and Mary found their chairs in between.

Lena said, "Mary, do you want to say grace?"

"You go ahead, Lena." Mary smiled and bowed her head.

Lena folded her hands, closed her eyes and said, "Bless this food which we are about to receive, in Jesus' name, Amen."

Only Mary responded with her own *Amen*. Oscar reached for the duck and Walter the ham. They each cut off portions for themselves and passed the dishes on. Soon everyone had a full plate and the conversation picked up where it had left off in the living room.

Walter: "The winter sure is dry."

Oscar: "In '92 it was dryer."

Will: "A little more snow would be a good thing, though. Don't feel right, so little snow in the winter."

Walter: "Might mean a drought and we don't need that."

Will: "No, we don't need that."

Oscar: "Drought would have to last more than one summer before it affects me."

Will: "Well, sure. One summer you could still find water, but you wouldn't get paid for doin' it."

Lena asked, "Nyla, I haven't seen you it seems like in such a long time. How do you...?"

Oscar interrupted her: "Did you ever get paid for that job you did for the Lauterbauers?"

Walter: "It took 'em three years. But I got all my money."

Oscar: "I heard you had to take the last payment in a side of beef."

Walter: "Where'd you hear that?"

Will: "That's still payment. You gotta have beef."

The men continued in the same vein, and Lena gave up trying to bring the women into the conversation. She at least could occupy herself with feeding Gracia, who played with her mashed potatoes and milk-soaked bread, getting more food in her hair than in her mouth. Mary and Nyla ate in silence.

When the meal was over, Mary said, "Why don't you go take it easy now, Ma, in the front room with the boys? We'll clean up."

"I'll just finish my pie," the old lady said. She had eaten well, if more slowly than the others, and had just started picking at her slice of apple pie.

Lena said to Nyla, who looked more tired and put-upon than usual, "You go sit down now and relax. You helped do the cooking, the least I can do is clean up."

Lena knew it was no use to tell Mary to relax, but at least Mary was good company, though she was quiet when the men were around.

They discreetly threw Ma's rolls away. No one had eaten any. They put the left-overs in the ice box except for what Lena said she would take home—a little ham and stuffing for Will's supper.

The men went into the living room, and Lena heard Nyla's heavy foot falls on the stairs. She had looked so tired. She was probably going up there to get some sleep. Lena looked up. The vent from the kitchen to the upstairs was open. Maybe it would be warm enough up there, now, for her to get a better sleep than she was used to.

Mary said, "Oh, there's no hot water. I forgot to fill the kettle before we sat down."

"Well, put the kettle on and let's just visit awhile. Shut the door. Gracia seems to be wearing more potatoes than she ate. I'll nurse her a few minutes and then she'll take her nap."

Mary paused in the doorway to look at Gertrude Kaiser sitting by herself at the table eating her pie, before she shut the door. "I'm worried about Ma. She's not herself."

"Well, you know, Mary, she lost part of her mind when Pa died. I told you how I found her that day while you and Walter and Oscar were at the funeral home, she was sitting in that rocker, just rocking and whining and not making much sense, not that she ever did."

Lena adjusted her daughter comfortably in her lap and the child began to suckle. "I used to think she was just being ornery-like and didn't want to tell me things, like it wasn't my business, but she's Will's mother and I wanted to know all I could about Will, and I wanted to tell Gracia something about her grandparents, something good if I could come up with anything. So I asked her one day, oh a long time ago, when Will and I were first married, I asked her about Berlin. You know she came here when she was eighteen but she grew up in Berlin. That's a city. Not like anything we have out here. Not like anything I'll ever see. But I thought it must have been a change for her, you know, coming out here from a big city, so I asked her and she didn't remember. How can you not remember eighteen years of your life? Nothing. I said, well, what was the weather like there? What kind of a house did you live in? What did your Pa do for a living? She just didn't remember anything and I thought she just didn't want to tell me, but lately I think she really didn't remember. I asked her things about Will, when he was a little boy. Things like what he liked to do and the kind of mischief he used to get into, and she didn't remember that either. She told me something once about her sister when they were kids and that's the only thing I ever got out of her. I wanted my Pa to tell me about Oslo and he told me something but he was only there a couple days before he got on the boat. So he didn't know much. He grew up on a little farm in the country that sounded just like what we were living on." Lena shrugged.

"I came over here once—it was I guess about six in the evening. I had made an extra loaf of bread and was bringing it to her, and she was sitting at the table here waiting to eat, and there was another place set. I said, 'Ma, who's coming to supper?' I thought it was nice she was going to have company besides Oscar and Nyla, and she said she was waiting for Pa. And I sat down—right here—and I said, 'Now Ma, you know Pa isn't coming back. You were at his funeral. He was killed out there in the barn and then you pulled the barn down. You remember that, now, don't you?' And she said to me, 'Oh, no, he'll be here. He's just over at Julia's. They're doing the books, and he'll be home for supper.'"

Lena did such a good imitation of Gertrude's wheezy voice that Mary smiled in spite of her obvious sympathy for her mother-in-law.

Lena went on in her own voice, "And I said, 'Ma! Pay Attention! Julia's gone too! Ma, Julia's dead and gone. They are both dead and gone.' She gave me the spooks."

Mary nodded. "I know, Lena. Once in awhile she... slips. She's done that with me, too. I feel sorry for her. She is so...alone. It wasn't so long ago she could really put the fear into her sons."

"I remember the day she smacked the living daylights out of Walter." Lena laughed and Mary joined her.

"He had that coming, I'm afraid," Mary said.

Lena was surprised. She had seldom heard Mary utter an opinion about anything, and never her husband. "Well I guess I feel sorry for her too, sometimes. I guess."

They hadn't heard anything from the living room since they had closed the kitchen door. Gracia had fallen asleep in Lena's arms and she was just buttoning up the last button on her bodice when Walter pushed the door open, startling them both. "Let's go home, Mary."

He looked mad as a country goose. Expecting Mary to rise and get her coat to follow him, Lena said, "That's fine, Mary. I'll clean up here."

"No. I'm not going to let you clean up all this alone."

"Nyla's here," Walter said, as if that settled matters.

"Nyla's not feeling well. She's upstairs lying down. I'll be home later, Walter. You go on ahead."

He looked at her with a slightly open mouth. He didn't say anything, just grabbed his coat and hat from the entry where he had hung it and stomped out.

"Well, it was a matter of time," Lena said. "Those boys can't stand each other for long."

"I wonder what happened?"

"It won't matter what happened. They'll each have their own version and swear to it. So it doesn't matter. She's sound asleep. I'll just put her down here and we can do the dishes."

"Let me help you." Mary pulled two chairs over and placed them next to the one Lena had just been sitting on. She put the chairs against the wall with the backs to the outside so the child could not roll off. Then she put some coats down for a soft bed and laid Gracia down gently and covered her with another coat.

Mary opened the kitchen door. Ma was still at the kitchen table. She went to the old woman's side and placed her hand gently on her shoulder. "Ma? Why don't you go into the other room and spend some time with the boys. I'll bring you a cup of coffee."

"Is there any pie? Didn't Lena bring pie?"

"Yes, Ma, there's pie. I'll bring you some."

Mary had always been a good, kind woman, but she was different somehow since she'd come back from the reservation. She seemed to hold her own place in the world with more ease, more authority. She was less invisible. Lena credited Gustie with that. Gustie had her own way about her and treated everybody the same. She had treated Mary like anybody else. People in Charity, including the Kaisers, including Lena herself, she admitted with shame, had treated

Mary as an empty trinket, an unlikely appendage of Walter, more than his cigar, less than his Percherons.

Lena looked into the living room and found Will dozing upright in the overstuffed chair and Oscar absent. Lena presumed he had gone upstairs. She went back to the kitchen and started the dishes.

When Mary returned, after serving Ma her second piece of pie, Lena said, "See, what I mean? Spooks! And no wonder she's big as a house. She eats. Then she forgets she eats and she eats again. She can do that all day. For Pete's sake."

Dear Miss Augusta,

This letter is not to alarm you. Your father is well. That is, he is not ill. But he has expressed a desire to see you again, a desire he would never communicate to you directly, and he would, I am confident in saying, be most displeased to know that I am writing to you. However, I have served your family for more than a generation and feel a responsibility to speak on his behalf; an old man myself, I know the dispositions of other old men: how pride can stiffen with joints, and stubbornness get in the way of sense and family feeling.

The judge is failing in the way of the old, as I am myself. I have retired, by the way. All my duties at the bank are now under the able administration of my former junior associate, Atlee. I am content to keep the polish high on my collection of old coins and take leisurely visits with dear friends, your father being among them. I believe a visit from you though, however

*brief, would afford him a measure of peace that he
lacks in his old age.*

*Your most dutiful servant and affectionate friend,
Albert Fitszimmons*

Gustie folded the letter and slipped it back into
her pocket. She rested her chin in her hand and
stared out the window at Moon and Biddie munching
hay in the pasture, the sun bright on their backs.
A soft dusting of snow covered the earth and made
everything sparkle.

She had read the letter so many times she had it
memorized, but she still liked the feel of the heavy
white paper in her hand and the sight of Fitz's artful
penmanship. This letter was the first thing to inspire
even a twinge of homesickness since she had come to
South Dakota, and now she was drenched in thoughts
of home.

She could feel the cool peeling hide on the massive
slanting trunk of the sycamore that stood directly in
front of the red brick, ivy-cloaked house in which she
grew up. Next door, the curtains trembled from the
fish-belly white hand of Hannebelle Rush, who kept
watch on the comings and goings of her neighbors.

She stepped again into the foyer, onto the black
and white tiles that Oksana kept at a high gloss and
entered the kitchen where walnut table and chairs,
cabinets and counters gleamed under her incessant
polishing. Gustie and Oksana had taken their lunches
together there on most days, because the judge never
came home, if he came home at all, before dinner.

She watched her aunts in their constant flock of
three, flutter into the parlor. The Weird Sisters she

called them, but never to their faces, and the only
time she had ever seen her father throw back his head
in a hearty laugh was the first time she had slipped
and it came out of her mouth when she was thirteen
that the Weird Sisters were coming to lunch and
she would prefer to be out in the garden, reading by
herself. He had said it was an apt description as they
had a tendency to stir the pot. They were his sisters
and he knew them well: Louisa, Margaret, Edith, nee
Roemer, now Hartigan, Pryor and Willing respectively.
They had in common their widowhood and Louisa's
money—since she had married into the most—and an
unconditional devotion to their elder brother, but
they were nothing alike in looks or manner.

Louisa, the eldest, was tall, slender, cool as
a knife edge, and always striking in elegant blues,
which brought out her keen eyes, porcelain skin,
and platinum hair. The last time they had all been
together, Louisa had flowed around her brother like
cool water, coming to rest at his left side, towering over
his seated figure. Her right hand hovered lightly above
his right shoulder, and like a white bird skimming the
surface of a pond, moved across his back to alight
for a moment on his left shoulder before flying to her
bosom to worry a pearl button.

Margaret, the middle sister, the one always
adorned in a froth of peach or pink and trailing
shawls and scarves and feathers was an anomaly in
Philadelphia. In a town that did not care for show,
Margaret glittered and wanted Gustie to do the same:
"...now dear, you must wear blue, a blue with the
merest *hint* of gray. Too much gray and you'll go flat.
Some accents of ecru and powder blue, perhaps a bit

of pale yellow about the face would be quite becoming. Softness, softness, softness! That is what you must strive for as you approach a certain age. And, dear, those glasses! Why must you wear them?"

"I need them to see, Aunt Margaret."

"But my dear, what is there, really, to see? It is more important that you be seen."

Edith was the youngest, the dark one, and no amount of corseting disguised the fact that she was thicker and shorter than her sisters. Gravity had not been kind and black did not become her, but she refused to wear anything else, because she was in mourning for Abraham Lincoln and had been since she was sixteen and witnessed his catafalque being pulled through the streets of Philadelphia by a team of exquisitely matched black horses. When she was upset she became a squeaking, shuddering little engine of distress, which manifested most frequently over her niece, who disappointed and mystified her in a multitude of ways.

The only thing Gustie would ever buy for herself was a book. She refused to attend any of Philadelphia's societal functions, invitations to which the Weird Sisters assiduously obtained for her. She wore most of the clothes they bought her but refused the corsets. It wasn't that Gustie won her battles with her aunts, she just refused to enter the fray, but she admired their indefatigability. They never gave up. Till the day she up and left them. Gustie smiled. Affection for her aunts had increased with the time and distance between them.

Gustie missed Oksana Chapek, the Roemer's housekeeper, the woman who had spent the most time with her as a child. If Gustie had any warmth in her own soul, the seeds had been planted there by Oksana.

Not a few seeds had been scattered and watered by Michael Flynn. He had tended the Roemer garden since Magnus had first brought his new bride Philippa to live in the house. Michael Flynn seemed as much a part of the garden as the roots creeping out gnarled and knobby from the base of the ancient oak that had reigned over the northeast corner of their city plot since before William Penn and his band of Quakers had laid out the grid for the city of brotherly love. Nothing much grew in the shade of this tree, but felling such a venerable old native was unthinkable. Instead, when Gustie was a child, Michael and she had fashioned a village under its branches. "My own Lilliput" she had named it. They made miniature houses and laid tiny paths with flat stones and buttons. They built a bridge over a small creek they dug out and lined with more stones and pieces of glass and mirror, and when it rained, it filled up with water and shimmered in the slanting rays of the afternoon sun. They populated their village with a motley assortment of figurines of people and animals. When Gustie had gotten too old to play with her Lilliput, Michael kept it up, and when she was again old enough to take an interest, the village was as if she had never left it. The creek was deeper and retained more water so the grackles and sparrows that haunted the garden preferred it to the iron birdbath. "It's my little hobby, now you see," Michael said. "I had to replace a couple of the houses, did ye notice that, girl? They were crumblin' away lookin' more like Ireland every day and gettin' depressin'" Before she left, she had placed in her village square the tiny porcelain figure of a dancer. She wondered if Paddy O'Ryan, the fat and shabby squirrel that Michael fussed and fretted over was still there to knock it down and perhaps steal it as he had some of her other trinkets. She hoped he was.

She thought of the house, full of sturdy old furniture, its cupboards and mantels laden with Grandmother Caine's pewter, how it had seemed at times to sigh like a dowager who had had a good life but regrets it wasn't the one she wanted. The symphonic whisper that started in the back rooms and echoed down the square added to the whisperings and sighings of the other old homes throughout the city—the sound of subtle, inexorable disintegration. Trees grew and rubbed their branches against the houses while their roots tried the foundations. Ivy clung to the outsides like a garment that feeds upon its wearer. The whole city sprouted moss from every shaded patch, whether on walls or underfoot. Buildings, steps and stairs leaned and sagged. The very stones were being worn away by moss and vine and the feet of men and horses. It had not been difficult to leave a place where even the light seemed old.

Gustie thought of her father and the worn strip of Persian carpet that provided silent passage down a twilight length of hallway to its end where a dark wood door loomed. Even now, her hand remembered the feel of the etched brass doorknob as she turned it. Garden air drifted through the open French doors diluting the mustiness of old books and leather upholstery. Judge Magnus August Roemer was behind his desk, which was, Clare had observed dryly, the size of Iowa.

Stepping into that room, even as an adult, Gustie often felt like a small white flag in a gale.

The judge was never the same after Philippa died. Gustie had heard that refrain from various people all her life. She remembered little of her father before the death of her mother, and she remembered nothing of her mother except for a feeling of sweetness that filled her whenever she heard a piano played well. Gustie had tried to learn to play but had no aptitude for it. Even though no one in the family could play it, no one dreamed of getting rid of Philippa's baby grand that still inhabited the parlor. It stood there now, Gustie knew, as she watched a small whirlwind pick up a shovelful of snow. The snow devil careened madly around the pasture eventually wearing itself out in a fall of crystals.

The father Gustie had grown up with was a man irrevocably changed by grief. And while she was never afraid of him, she had often found him easier to avoid than to confront. Now she wished she'd had more courage. No—more *will* to confront him, to draw him out. She had left the sighing house, that old city, her eccentric aunts, and Michael and Oksana in anger. Anger at him. Comparing her memories to the view outside her window, she realized that he could have asked her to stay and she would never have come to this place. Clare would still have died, only instead of her dying free of her mean-spirited brother and content at last under the expanse of blue prairie sky, she'd have breathed her last breath in her own dark house or worse, in a hospital surrounded by strangers, and her brother would have seen to it that Gustie was not allowed at her side.

If Gustie had not left Philadelphia, she would have still lost Clare but would not have found the friends she had now. She wouldn't have calluses on her hands from doing her own house and barn work. She wouldn't be strong from carrying endless buckets of water for laundry and baths. She wouldn't know the exhilaration of running to an outhouse on a cold wet morning instead of treading down a carpeted hall to a water closet where, with a pull of a velvet cord, fresh water swirled into a blue-flowered porcelain bowl. She wouldn't have learned to catch a fish, clean it and cook it. She wouldn't have learned to ride a horse. And she wouldn't know the love of the woman whose hand now rested on her shoulder.

They both gazed out through the window at the horizon where a dullness was beginning to encroach on the brilliant sky. There was still a little time for the horses to enjoy the pasture before they brought them into the barn out of the snow that was clearly on its way. Such a place! Where you could see the weather brewing at the rim of the earth, where the trees were young and the light on a clear day was always like the first morning of creation. She had never been sorry she came and she had no desire now to leave.

"I think you should go back." Jordis's voice was gentle but firm, as it always was when she offered an opinion that Gustie hadn't asked for.

Gustie took a deep breath. "Why?"

"It would be good for you."

"It was good for me to *leave*."

"You are not going back to stay."

"Why, then?"

"That letter."

"What about it?"

"You have worn it out reading it."

"You notice everything. It's annoying."

Jordis laughed softly. Then, she said, "Go back and find out why you cannot put that letter away."

Chapter 10: January 1901

GUSTIE DIDN'T OFTEN MEET THOSE eyes, but today they looked back at her with more clarity and humor than they used to from the mirror in her room in her father's house. There, she had had a full-length mirror. Here she had only a small, cloudy rectangle that framed her dimly from the waist up. Still, it was enough to see the scars: a splash of scar tissue on her chest, and the matting of twisted tissue along the insides of her wrists. Few people saw the extent of her scarification. Jordis, of course. And Dorcas, who had treated the wounds. Lena had only glimpsed the bandages and inquired about the cause of her injury. She described a clumsy fall from her wagon, which hadn't been such a great lie. While getting used to life in South Dakota, she had suffered plenty of bruising mishaps.

This was Gustie's biggest secret—the one she kept from everyone—even Jordis. How hard it had been.

Digging Clare's grave (she remembered every shovel-full of dirt) had left her hands bloody, her muscles on fire, her body ill and spirit broken. After she recovered and took up residence in her house, she had had to learn, from scratch, how to live.

Every ounce of water that she drank or used to wash herself or her clothes or water her horse had to be brought up from the ground by strenuous effort at the hand pump in the yard and carried, one bucket at a time. To heat the water for baths or laundry, or even a pot of coffee, to warm her house, or to iron her clothes, she had to light a fire; the coal had to be carried in and ash carried out.

The labor was hard and mistakes cost her in cuts, bruises, scalds, and burns. She became adept at bandaging her own wounds before she acquired the skills to avoid them.

Going anywhere involved a long walk, or hitching the horse to the wagon. She learned to ride, not only because Biddie could travel faster without having to pull the wagon, but also because, once she learned how, it was easier to saddle her than hitch her, and she found that she enjoyed riding. She thanked God for Biddie and for the Swede in Wisconsin who, when Gustie explained she wanted to buy a gentle horse, had led the tall black mare out of the stable. Biddie had been forgiving of her mistakes.

Worse than the labor and the self-inflicted wounds were some of the creatures she had encountered, if only during the warmer months.

The first time she'd lifted the square of floorboard that had been cut to fit neatly over the hole in her kitchen floor where she stored vegetables, mice had poured up and out, skittering in all directions. Gustie dropped the lid with a clatter and screamed. There was no one to hear her, for which she was grateful. She shook for half an hour, gasping and whimpering in horror and revulsion, fighting tears of humiliation and helplessness. Finally, with a half sob, half laugh she said out loud, "They're only mice." Every nerve had been frazzled, but she had learned that day that edibles had to be kept in sealed crockery containers. Will lined her cold cellar with tin, and while she still saw a mouse or two, she never again had to face an entire congregation.

She found ants and spiders, earthworms and white grub worms and creatures she couldn't name at all. With each surprise first encounter, she screamed and had to overcome her fear and aversion by sheer force of will. She had no choice. And she learned with time and experience, that none of these creatures would or could inflict any harm on her. All of her injuries were the result of her own ineptitude. After a year or so, she was able to live her life with fewer bandages and less screaming.

Gustie could now look at herself with satisfaction. In Philadelphia, the women of her class did not have muscles. Nor did they have calluses on their hands. Gustie had both.

In her father's house, an army of people, most of whose names she never knew, came and went in order that not a speck of dirt should come to a complete rest on any surface. The one exception was her father's study. He did not allow Oksana and her "hoards and minions," as he called them, access as often as she would have liked. There were people who

147

cleaned and waxed the floors, people who beat the rugs, laundresses and wielders of the hot irons. The windows were without smudge or streak. The water in the vases of the fresh flowers was always clear enough to drink. All the copper and metal fittings of doors, windows, fireplace, and light fixtures gleamed. The house was warm from coal that came in and ash that was carried out without Gustie's ever having seen a spot of coal dust.

And, while all of these people had deferred to her with curtseys and tipped hats, murmuring a deferential "Miss Roemer," it was Oksana who actually managed the keeping of the house. Gustie would have learned had she stayed. But she didn't.

She wished she had paid attention.

For laundry, how much soap was enough, and how did one boil the linens? How did one cook a meal with more than two dishes and get them ready to serve at the same time? How did one strike a balance between cooked well enough to eat and burnt?

Gustie saw shiny floors wherever she went. She knew she'd never again have one of her own. All she could manage was a mop and a broom, which she found useful for sweeping out more than Oksana would have dreamed of. Like the small garden snake she found one day placidly curled in the middle of her living room, soaking in a warm pool of sun. She almost hated to disturb it, but she didn't see herself with a snake as a permanent houseguest. She had realized on that day she was a fully initiated resident of the prairie, because, without a sound or a twitch, she gently shepherded the small reptile outside with her broom.

She still liked best to clean her barn. Physically strenuous, this chore involved no fussiness. She shoveled and raked and spread the straw and carried the hay and the oats and the water. She groomed her horse, whom she had grown to love, and oiled the tack. She never got tired of it, and she never got burnt, scratched or scalded. What was more, she found the mice in the barn less disturbing than the ones in the house.

Two things had driven other people out of this country or out of their minds, the space and the quiet; but, except in the winter, the prairie wasn't silent. There were birds and the continual buzz of insects, and around creeks and lakes, bullfrogs that could wake the dead; even so, it was a different, softer voice than the city. Gradually a quiet spaciousness had opened up inside her, and not once had she missed the city's constant thrum. She welcomed winter when she was free to immerse herself in her books, which she did not have time to do in the summer. She, thus, learned to ride the rhythms of the seasons. She felt that this place had welcomed her home and rewarded her for learning how to live her new life.

"Remember, oh, most gracious Virgin Mary, that never was it known that anyone that fled to thy protection, implored thy help or sought thy intercession was left unaided. Inspired by this confidence I come to thee, oh Virgin of Virgins, my mother. To thee I come, before thee I stand, sinful and sorrowful, oh Mother of the Word Incarnate, despise not my petition but in thy mercy hear and answer me. Amen."

Mary Kaiser finished praying the *Memorare* and, trembling, brought the crucifix to her lips. "Oh, Mother of God, what am I to do?"

She sat staring at the rosary draped over her hand. She could not let Walter find her like this.

The wind rattled the windows and whipped a tree branch against the side of the house.

Mary put her boots on and her coat. She tied a wool scarf around her head, tucked the rosary beads in her palm as she pulled on mittens, and left her house. Her face, wet with tears, burned in the icy wind.

She needed to talk to someone. Not her priest. She was afraid of Father Nicolay. She had never made a confession to him of her sin. A sin unconfessed was a double sin.

She walked south for twenty minutes, shielding her face as best she could. Then she took the road east out of town, laboring, head down against the wind in ankle-to-calf-deep snow. After fifteen minutes, she stopped, and turning her back to the freezing blast, covered her mouth with her hands and wept in frustration. She wanted desperately to talk to Gustie. But she would surely die getting there. Maybe that was the thing to do. Walk into the freezing wind, lie down, fall asleep. Wasn't cold a merciful killer? No, she didn't have the courage for that. She didn't have the courage for anything. She stifled a cry with her mittens and headed toward Lena's house.

"Good night, Mary, you're half frozen!" Lena ushered her sister-in-law into her kitchen and made her sit down. "Let me fix you some warm milk. What in blazes are you doing out on a day like this?"

January was a dangerous month. So were the other eleven, but for different reasons. Lena could understand Gustie, a newcomer, trotting out half dressed in the cold, but not Mary. Mary was born here. She poured milk into a saucepan and placed it on the stove, her irritation bristling. "What were you thinking, going out on a day like today, Mary?"

"I started to go to Gustie's. But I couldn't make it." Mary was cold beyond shivering.

"Why did you try to walk? For heaven sakes! Walter can't have his team out on a day like today? Why didn't you hitch up your buggy?"

"I can't handle those big horses. The Percherons, they're too much for me."

"Well, Walter should get you a nice horse you can handle. Why doesn't he?"

"I've never asked for one."

"Well, if you're going to take it into your head to go wandering around in this weather you better ask him. Believe me, if we could afford another horse I'd have one. A nice little brown mare all my own. You bet your life I would."

Lena poured the warmed milk into a cup. Mary could hardly hold the cup in her hands. Lena helped her. "Now tell me what in Sam Hill is the matter."

Alvinia recognized the set of Lena's jaw. It meant no good news. Mary Kaiser, right behind her, looked bloodless. They stamped the snow off their feet in the entryway, and Alvinia swooped Gracia up in her ample arms. "How's my beautiful girl? You're getting soooo big." She cooed and bounced the baby while Lena helped Mary off with her coat and then took off her own. Alvinia called for her second eldest daughter, who appeared from the next room holding Kirstin by the hand. "Honey, look who's here."

Alice, shorter and plumper than Betty, was, of all her siblings, most like Alvinia in looks and temperament. She greeted the two Mrs. Kaisers and took the baby. "Gracia can stay with you and Kirstin in the front room," Alvinia said, then assured Lena, "The stove is hot in there. It's nice and warm."

Lena asked, "Where is everybody?"

"The boys were outside chasing around like jackrabbits. But it's so cold I made them go to the locker. They can work off all that steam helping their dad. Malvern and Lavonne stayed over last night with Annie Erickson's girl. I don't suppose I'll see them till after dinner. Betty's working at Olna's and Kermit's out cleaning the barn." Alvinia shut the door to the living room, poured coffee for all, placed a plate of fresh donuts on the table, and sat down.

Reassured that they were now alone, Lena began, "We've got trouble, Alvinia." She shook her head and sucked the tip of her forefinger. "Mary came to me, but I don't know the best thing to do."

Alvinia braced herself.

Mary sat very still. Alvinia thought she must be in shock. "Has something happened to Walter?" she asked.

"Not yet," said Lena. And since she could not stand the silence waiting for Mary to speak for herself, she blurted it out. "She's pregnant."

152

This should have been happy news. Was Mary sick?

Lena explained. "Walter's not the father."

Alvinia took a noisy breath and leaned back in her chair. Then a hard look came over her and she bent forward again. Taking Mary firmly by the hand and peering into her face, she asked, "Were you raped?"

Mary's reply was quick and definite, if softly spoken. "Oh, no."

"She wouldn't tell me who the father is. She's set on protecting him, I guess."

Alvinia let go of Mary's hand and settled back. Her judgmental nature was tempered by her mother's words: *When you find somebody lying wounded in the road, stop the bleeding. Ask questions and lay blame later.* It was clear from Mary's demeanor that she was, indeed, bleeding to death.

"Well, it's her business and beside the point. Does Walter know?"

Lena shook her head.

"Can't you just tell him you're expecting? Won't he assume it's his?"

Mary hung her head and Lena threw up her hand letting it fall back into her lap. "He will know it's not his. They haven't slept in the same bedroom in years."

"Well, there's only one thing you can do, Mary. Sleep with your husband and the sooner the better. Yours won't be the first premature baby in Stone County. Somebody have one of these donuts." Alvinia took one herself, dunked it in her coffee and ate it.

Lena brightened. She should have thought of that. That's why people came to Alvinia. She was practical.

Mary whispered something unintelligible.

"What?" Lena was beginning to get angry. She didn't know why.

Alvinia brushed donut crumbs off her bosom and moved her chair around the table so she could put her arm on the back of Mary's chair in a kind of embrace but without touching her. "However you feel about your husband, you have to think of..."

Mary shook her head.

"What's the matter?" Alvinia coaxed, the same way she would have spoken to one of her younger daughters. "Tell us, Mary."

Mary uttered, just above a whisper, "Walter can't... function...like that."

Alvinia stared at Lena. "Oh, this gets worse and worse."

Ha! Lena thought. *And he struts around like a little rooster! He puts on a good show, that's all. Some cock of the walk he is. Wait'll I tell Will.* Then she realized with disappointment, she couldn't tell anybody.

Alvinia's face took on the expression of someone looking for the next stepping-stone across a treacherous river. She found it. "Mary, now listen to me. Is it possible..." she paused, testing the stability of the stone against the strength of the water, "a man without children—who can't ever have one, apparently—isn't it possible that Walter would accept this child as his own? No one but the two of you would know otherwise. You wouldn't tell him Lena and I know. To save his pride, you know."

Mary's answer was a heartbreaking smile. "Oh, you know the Kaisers," she glanced at Lena, "Except for Will and Lena—they don't love children."

154

Lena chilled. She knew things about the Kaisers that Alvinia did not. She knew what Mary said was horribly true.

The waters seemed to rise around Mary. She shrank before their eyes. "She's been out walking in this cold all morning," Lena said. "She's all in."

For the moment the river seemed impassable. Alvinia tried to be cheerful and patted Mary's hand. "Now, we'll think of something. Sure we will."

She and Lena led Mary upstairs and made her lie down. The upstairs was heated only by warm air rising through the vents from the living room below. Lena and Alvinia helped Mary remove her shoes and undo the top three buttons of her dress. They covered her with quilts, and Mary fell asleep immediately. When the three women had passed through the living room, Alice had watched them with bright curiosity. On their way back, without Mary, she asked, "Mama?"

"Mrs. Kaiser is not feeling well. She's taking a nap in your room."

"What's the matter with her?"

"Just never you mind. Keep the little ones back here. I'll bring you some cocoa. If Gracia needs changing, Kirstin's old diapers are in the chest in the closet."

"I know where they are, Mama," Alice said, somewhat crossly. She hated being treated like one of the younger children.

Alvinia stirred up some cocoa and sugar and a quarter cup of water in a big pot on the stove while Lena thought out loud. "Will and I can't take her. What would be the use? She needs to be away from this town." She brought a loose fist down on her knee.

"Gee whiz, I wish I knew somebody in California! Do you know anybody in California?"

A small laugh escaped Alvinia. "No, I don't know anybody in California."

The chocolate mixture bubbled. Alvinia stirred it smooth, then poured in two quarts of milk and stirred some more while Lena continued. "My sisters won't have her. When the Lord said 'Ye who is without sin cast the first stone'—hmph—if my sisters had been in that crowd he'd have had to duck all right! They're so high and mighty. Anyway, Ragna would plead too poor even though they've got money socked away. Don't think I don't know it!" Lena waggled her finger at Alvinia for emphasis. "They let their children go without decent clothes on their backs so they can hoard it for their old age. They're going to have something to answer for, believe you me! And Ella won't because she can't do a blame thing on her own. If Ragna sniffs a cat, Ella sneezes." Lena sighed loudly from deep in her chest and brought the flat of her hand down on the table with finality. "No, Gustie's the one."

Alvinia looked skeptical and continued to stir.

"I know you don't think much of Gustie, but..." Lena made thoughtful little circles on the table top with her finger.

"I don't dislike Gustie..." Alvinia wasn't sure how she felt about Gustie. To her, Lena's friend was still mostly an unknown entity. Gustie had always been helpful and friendly, but Alvinia liked to have things and people clear in her mind, and she just couldn't get Gustie sharply in focus. "But...do you think she would help Mary?"

"You don't know Gustie, Alvinia."

"Not like you do, no. But she doesn't have much room in that little house of hers. And it's right here. Just outside of town, really. Not that far away."

"It's still better than being smack dab in town where she is under the noses of the Kaisers and everybody else who've never cared about Mary except to boast that they've eaten cake off her nice china plate in one breath and in the next one, criticized her for having it. Why shouldn't she have nice things? Well, I don't know." Lena rearranged her cup and saucer, then moved the donut plate slightly to the left as if she were straightening a picture. "I don't think they'd stay in the Charity house anyway. Jordis has some kind of place out at the Red Sand where she lived with her grandmother. I saw it once but was never inside it. It doesn't look like much, that's for sure. But Gustie is comfortable enough there, so it can't be too bad. Maybe they can make room for Mary out there. No, all we have is Gustie."

"Where is she now? Here or out there?"

"Here, I think."

"Well, let's find out." Alvinia left the stove to stick her head out of the door and yell, "Kermit!"

He came to the door and Alvinia let him into the porch. His boots and pants were mucky from the barn. He wore a short barn coat, a knit cap, mittens and muffler around his neck. "Yeah, Ma?"

"Saddle up Brownie and go out to Gustie's. Tell her we need her to ride back with you now."

"What's the matter?"

"Never you mind, Sir. And if she's not there—wait a minute—" Alvinia rustled around in a cabinet drawer and found a piece of envelope. She scribbled on it, folded it once and handed it out to the boy. "That's private, Son. If she's not there, leave it stuck in her door where she'll see it first thing."

"Sure, Ma." He stuffed it into the pocket of his jacket.

"Now, if she's not there, you leave the note and you go to the depot and have Willie telegraph Joe Gruba and tell him to get Gustie and send her home. Now. She can hitch a ride on the train and be here this afternoon. And if he wants to know why, just tell him you don't know. Because you don't. And keep your face covered so you don't get frost-bite."

Kermit grinned at his mother and went back to the barn to saddle the horse.

Lena and Alvinia had just finished all but the last donut when Kermit came in with Gustie. Handing him a cup of cocoa, his mother said, "Put Brownie and Gustie's horse in the barn and then go help your father."

"Aw, Ma! I was gonna—"

"Don't argue with me, Son. Just go."

Gustie quietly unwrapped her woolen scarf and took off her coat. Alvinia took them from her and hung them on the coat tree in the corner of the kitchen.

"Hot cocoa, Gustie?"

"That would be very nice." Gustie didn't ask why they had summoned her. She wiped the condensation off her glasses and sat next to Lena. She took the cup she was handed, sipped, and waited.

Alvinia took the chair on the other side of Lena who began by saying, "We're sure glad you were in town, Gustie. Mary's upstairs."

Alvinia chimed in, "Sleeping, poor thing. She's limp as a dishrag. Eat that last donut."

Gustie left Lena and Alvinia in the kitchen. Having finished the cocoa they were now starting a fresh pot of coffee. She greeted Alice who was ready to burst from curiosity but who said only, "Hello, Miss Gustie." She stood at the bottom of the narrow stairway for a moment, her mind full of the news she had just been given, and of the scenes from Mary's time at the mission, including Jordis's kick under the table. Well, as Alvinia had said, all that was nobody's business and beside the point, because what mattered now was how she could help. Gustie already had an idea. She climbed the stairs and opened the door to the bedroom where Mary lay, a fragile thing among the folds of the quilts. The room was cold and Gustie pulled her wool sweater closer around her as she sat gingerly on the edge of the bed.

Mary's eyes opened, but she made no further movement.

"Hello, Mary."

"Gustie." Her voice sounded from far away. "What are you doing here?" Mary looked to Gustie like a wounded dove.

"Alvinia and Lena sent for me."

Mary's eyes fluttered closed and she sighed, so softly, had Gustie not been sitting close to her, she wouldn't have heard it.

"How would you like to live with me for awhile?"

Mary did not answer. Only her eyelids moved sluggishly, as if she were about to drift back to sleep. Gustie waited.

Finally, Mary said softly, "I'll bring shame on you, Gustie."

Gustie almost laughed, but smiled instead. "Oh, Mary, bringing shame on me would be like carrying water to Shoonkatoh."

Mary looked at her blankly.

Gustie continued. "I have an idea." She reached into her pocket and brought out her letter from Alfred Fitszimmons. She gave it to Mary who pulled herself up to a sitting position to read it. She looked at Gustie questioningly.

"I've been trying to decide whether or not I should go back home for a visit. I'm thinking now that maybe I should and that maybe you could come with me."

Mary seemed bewildered.

"Do you want to, Mary?" Gustie waited to see if Mary would say anything. She did not. "Where is Walter right now?"

"With Will in Argus. They're buying some equipment...or something."

"You've got to tell him."

Mary shook her head.

"Are you afraid of him?"

"I just can't face him, Gustie." She began to weep.

Gustie sat back a little and took a moment to consider. "Then, Will and Lena will have to do it."

Mary shook her head again.

"Someone has to. You can't just disappear. Walter needs to know—not where you've gone, but why. He'd look for you, wouldn't he? If you just disappeared?"

"I don't know." Mary wiped her eyes with the edge of the sheet.

"You really don't know?"

"No."

"I'm not asking you to confide in me, Mary, but does the father of the baby know?"

Mary shook her head.

"If he did, is there a chance that the two of you could go away together?"

"In the eyes of God I'm married to Walter. I can't erase one sin by committing another."

Oh nonsense. Go with the man you love and be happy, Gustie thought. That's what she would have done. That is what she had done once. Left everything to be with the person she loved. But Mary wasn't Gustie.

"We need to decide what to do. Do you feel like getting up now and coming downstairs?"

Mary nodded.

Chapter 11: ~~February~~ 1901

ACOMMOTION ENSUED ON THE BACK porch as Alvinia's family stamped snow off their feet, hung up coats, pulled off boots, and came tearing into the kitchen from their pre-breakfast rough-housing in the snow. Her husband came in last and sat down at the head of the table.

Alvinia served up hot oatmeal and cold milk and listened as her children chattered in anticipation of seeing their big sister off at the depot and their afternoon visit to the Peterson farm, where they would have a pony to play with, sheep, a haystack, and an endless number of things to fill a town-raised child with delight. Alvinia and Carl had planned this excursion on this particular afternoon ostensibly to deliver some supplies to the elderly Petersons, but, in fact, it was a diversion on the day Betty left them for her trip with Mary and Gustie to Philadelphia.

162

The warm kitchen bounced with late-winter sun and children. Mismatched china plates and home-woven rag rugs added splashes of color to the old wood hues that predominated in this big house. Alvinia looked down the table at her young ones in varying sizes, all blond headed and blue eyed—her children matched even if her china did not. Their voices receded into ambient sound as Alvinia let her gaze rest upon her husband. The glint of sun on his hair could still stir her up inside. A soft smile settled on her face. Carl Torgerson was the reason Alvinia believed in God.

They had discussed sending her so far away before they brought it up with Betty herself. Carl was not as set against Pauly Wirkus as a husband for Betty as was Alvinia, nor would he be the one to stand in the way of broadening his daughter's horizons. "Only if she's willing to go, Mother. I won't push the girl." Alvinia promised not to push.

Carl took his watch out of his pocket. "Well, it's time."

"Yes," said Alvinia.

They met each other's eyes across the table. Neither of them moved. Betty stood up and said softly, "I'll go get my bag."

All the young Torgersons were once again excitedly donning their winter coats and boots and knit mufflers, mittens, and hats. Betty came downstairs looking so sophisticated in her new traveling suit that Alvinia felt a lump rise in her throat. She corrected herself sharply. *We'll have none of that. This was, after all, my idea. The girl doesn't even really want to go.*

Lena and Will and Mary and Walter were already at the depot. They looked relieved to see the Torgersons. Pauly Wirkus was conspicuous by his absence. He and Betty had already said their goodbyes. None of them had arrived too early. Nobody wanted this to be a long parting. For Walter's sake, the women had concocted a fiction that Betty was going east as a pre-wedding gift from her parents to buy her trousseau, and Mary was accompanying her as chaperon. Gustie was boarding the train at Wheat Lake to make the journey with them to visit her family in Philadelphia. The story was plausible enough, if one did not think about it too hard.

The train pulled into the station in a roar of smoke and steam. Will and Lena hugged Mary while Walter took her suitcase to the baggage car. Willie Mohs took Betty's bag from Carl so he could stay with his family. Sheriff Sully trotted by on his saddle horse and called out, "You need help there, Willie?"

"No, thanks, Sheriff."

Dennis gave a quick nod of his head and paused a moment to watch them saying their farewells. Will noticed him and hollered over the heads of the others, "Mornin' Denny!" The sheriff gave a salute against his hat and turned on up the street.

In a tremulous voice, Mary said to Will, "You'll look at my roses once in awhile?" Walter was not good with growing things. Will was.

"You bet. By the time you get back, they'll be bloomin' like a house afire. Don't you worry."

"You know where to sit, honey, so Gustie can find you?" Alvinia made a business of adjusting the collar, which was perfect, on Betty's coat.

"Yes, Mama, the second car from the front."

Betty extricated herself from her younger siblings to hug Alice who stood mutely biting her lower lip. Then she embraced her father and mother. Carl said huskily, "Now you telegraph if you need anything."

Alvinia said, "A letter every day, now, if you have time."

Betty nodded and turned toward Mary. She put her arm around her, mothering the older woman onto the train as Alvinia watched, her back stiff and straight, every inch of her proud of this daughter they had raised.

The train roared out of the station and was gone, leaving prairie silence like a vacuum pulling at their eardrums. Everyone remained still, suspended in a moment of loss. Then Carl said, "What say we all go to the shop for coffee and ice cream? On the house!" The Torgerson children, who would normally have been ecstatic at sweets so soon after breakfast, held on to each other's mittened hands and slogged quietly through the snow behind their parents.

Lena, Will, and Walter followed, Will attempting to cheer up his brother. "Yup, they're going to have a nice visit with Gustie. Don't you worry about that."

Walter, who had come to the station without the ever-present cigar in his mouth, took one out of his coat pocket, chewed on it, lit it and listened to his brother's small talk. "Yup, they got good traveling weather, that's for sure. You wouldn't get me on a train in the heat. No sir."

Alvinia said to her husband, "You go on ahead. I left something back at the house. I'll be right along."

Carl nodded and watched his wife walk away, knowing that she never forgot anything in her life.

Alvinia entered her house and without removing her boots or her coat proceeded upstairs to her daughters' bedroom. Now, Alice would have a room all to herself.

Alvinia sat down on Betty's bed, grabbed the pillow that her daughter's head had rested upon only the night before, clutched it to her bosom, lay her cheek against it, and inhaled raggedly.

She had sent her girl off on a course of discovery, to "see something of the world before settling down on that little rock patch." And now, she was not afraid that her first-born would not discover anything of value in Philadelphia, but that she would. Alvinia sobbed hard into the pillow.

The brittle cold amplified every small squeak and rattle of the wagon as it rolled along the narrow trail of impacted snow. The snow was not deep for this time of year, and Red Standing Horse kept the roads, such as they were on the Red Sand, open by dragging a log behind his mules after light snowfalls. This worked only until the first big snow, then everyone took to shovels and snowshoes. This winter had been relatively mild so far. The bitter wind that cut their faces was the only indication that this was, indeed, February. Gustie pulled her cloak tighter around her face and ears and squinted against the sun. Jordis held the reins as Biddie pulled them ever closer to yet another leave-taking. They had been separated often, and often for weeks, even months at a time, but never, since they met, at such a distance. This time, the separation felt different.

"You'll be all right while I'm gone?" Gustie asked.

"Of course," Jordis answered.

A green shawl covered Jordis's head. Gustie reached out to tuck the end of it snugly under the neck of her army-blanket poncho. "Will you miss me?"

"I'll try to remember to miss you, Augusta."

"That's all one can ask." Of course, for almost a month, they had discussed every aspect of Gustie's going. Her last-minute qualms felt childish. The snow provided a quieter cushion than the naked dirt road. She closed her eyes and imagined they were on a sleigh—a sleigh that was sailing north and west over the snow in the opposite direction of the Wheat Lake depot.

"You'll write to me," Jordis said.

From her happy sleigh ride, Gustie murmured, "I'll try to remember to write to you."

"That's all one can ask."

Gustie opened her eyes and saw that the wisp of smile that had been on Jordis's face was gone. She laid a gloved hand over Jordis's mittened hands and tugged gently on the reins. Biddie stopped. Gustie put her other arm around Jordis and pulled her close. They rested cheek to cheek, not speaking for several moments—enough time for them to not say the things that each already knew filled the heart of the other. Then Jordis, without looking at Gustie, straightened and clucked Biddie back into motion.

At the depot, the train was just chuffing up its engine prior to being on its way. Gustie climbed down and took her bag from the back of the wagon. As she came around the front, she caressed the mare's neck and said, "Take good care of her."

Jordis answered, "You know I will."

Gustie looked up. "I'm talking to Biddie."

Jordis smiled.

In his bow-legged, one-leg-shorter-than-the-other gait, Joe Gruba trotted toward them, waving a hand over his head. "Hi there, Miss Jordis!"

"Hi, Joe."

He took Gustie's bag and his short legs did double time to her long stride to the second car. He held her bag up to her saying, "You have a nice trip now, Miss Augusta. A real nice trip."

"Thank you, Joe, I will." She hoped she would, as she took her bag and a deep breath. The locomotive shuddered under her feet and began its head-long plunge eastward.

When Will and Lena stepped out of Walter's house that night, the stars blazed in a quiet sky. A thin layer of snow sparkled over Charity like sugar on a cookie.

Lena pointed up. "Look, Will. The dipper!"

"Yup." He scanned the sky. "You warm enough, Duchy?"

"I'm fine."

He stopped and she stopped with him. He kept his eyes upward, but she knew his mind was back with his brother. Lena felt bad for Will right now and even harbored a small pang for Walter, although she had never liked him. She also felt a tickle of exhilaration. Never having lied before, she had had no idea how good at it she would be. Her first lie was to Will. Mary had come to her, she said, excited about going to Philadelphia with Betty and Gustie. Alvinia wouldn't let Betty go without Mary, as Gustie would be busy with her own family and shouldn't be expected to devote her time looking after a young girl. Lena didn't know till after they were gone, when she opened Mary's letter to her, what the real story was. She handed that letter to Will, pulling a long face over the memory of Gustie and Alvinia and Lena composing it and dictating it for Mary to write down. They did the same for the letter that Lena gave to Walter, in which Mary told him why she had to leave, that she would never be back, was filled with shame and remorse, and hoped Walter would start a new life without her. He was free to think of her as dead. He could divorce her. She was sorry. Lena even showed Walter her own letter to prove that she didn't know any more than he did.

Walter, when he got the news, stopped sucking on his cigar and stared dumbly around his house, which was all Mary. Flowered wallpaper. Lace at each window. China glowing in the mahogany hutch. Everything pretty and in perfect order. What would happen now to all of Mary's nice things?

Lena had few such nice things for herself. Why Walter had so much more money than Will was no mystery. He was older and had gotten started sooner. He'd spent more working years single, living with his ma and pa, never having to spend a penny of his own, and Walter didn't lose whole weeks of work to the bottle. Lena had her resentments. Mary always had new clothes and shoes. And a full pantry. But she had never lorded it over Lena. In fact, after the death of her brother, Mary, along with Gustie, had been at her bed-side, taking care of her, her house, Will, and arranging Tori's funeral. And since she had come to Lena, Lena would do everything in her power to help her. Oh, she was aware of Mary's sin, but if Walter had been a proper husband, this wouldn't have happened.

Walter's strutting days were over, that was for sure, and Mary would have no more use of these pretty things. Lena wondered if, when the fuss died down, she could have that rose bowl by the window. She'd always liked it.

So Walter just sat there on the sofa. Will pulled up a chair directly in front of him, sat, leaning in toward his brother, elbows on knees, and lamented, "Well, Walt. You just never know about these things. Boy. You just never know." He ran his hand over his face, again and again, repeating, "You just never know."

What else could these men say? They *didn't* know. They didn't *ever* know. Lena went into the kitchen and washed up Walter's supper dishes. *He'd better learn how to do a few dishes. I'm not doing this every blame night.*

She peered back into the living room. The brothers were as she had left them. Will murmuring his small comforts, Walter nodding like an idiot. Lena would have felt better if Walter had ranted, smashed some of that china. But that wasn't the Kaiser way. He would mull it over in his mind. Over and over. In a month or two, he would take it in. In another month, he'd believe it. Then he would react. By that time, Mary would be far away.

Lena couldn't feel much sympathy for her brother-in-law. A year ago, when she and Will had been destitute and in trouble, Walter had not offered them a dime or a box of groceries. He never offered so much as to finish the well that Will had had to leave when they hauled him off to jail. If it hadn't been for Gustie, Lena would now be scrubbing floors for her keep, the childless widow of a hanged man. Gustie had saved their bacon. That's what Alvinia didn't know about Gustie. Nobody knew, but Pard Batie, Gustie's lawyer. To this day Lena and Will had never properly thanked her, and she had never mentioned it. And in the midst of those troubles, which had fallen upon them mostly due to Will's weakness for the booze, Walter had offered Will a drink! That had been too much even for Ma Kaiser, and she popped Walter a good one. Lena had almost liked her mother-in-law then. Ma. Who would tell her? Not that she would care. She'd want Walter to come back with her in the big house. Even she must be tired by now of Oscar and Nyla.

"Walt, you want us to stay with you? You want to come home with us? We'll make room, won't we, Duchy?"

"Sure. He's welcome." Lena didn't mean it, but she didn't expect Walter would accept the invitation. She was right.

When Will finally took his eyes off the stars and started moving again, he said, "I guess he took it pretty good."

"Not so bad," responded Lena. "I think it's going around in his head and hasn't settled yet."

"I think he feels pretty tough."

"They didn't have much of a marriage, Will. Do I have to tell you that?"

"Naw, I know, Duchy. More than you think I do, sometimes."

She punched his arm. He grinned.

"I think he's not missing a woman," Lena sniffed. "He's missing his housekeeper."

"She's still his wife, Duchy."

"PPfffh! Believe you me, I know she's his wife. The way Ned and Jerry over there—" she cocked her head toward Walter's barn, "are his horses."

"Duchy, you're a corker!"

"You keep an eye on him."

"I will, don't you worry."

Alice Torgerson was home with Gracia. For Lena and Will to be out alone at night, even for something as simple as a starlight walk, was rare. Lena threaded her arm through the crook of Will's elbow, tucked herself as close to him as possible, and enjoyed their walk home.

The next day, when the west-bound train screeched to a stop at the Wheat Lake station, three women, two with veils covering their faces and one with the hood of her cloak pulled up over her head, keeping her face in shadow, got off and slipped quickly and quietly into the station's back room. One of the women beckoned Joe Gruba to come back and speak with them. Dropping his cigarette in the snow, he followed them in. The tall woman closed the door behind him and drew back her hood.

"Miss Augusta! Well, I'll be! Miss Augusta."

"Joe, we need your help."

He could see now that she was accompanied by Mary Kaiser who looked poorly—and the young one had to be one of the Torgersons from Charity. He had helped Miss Augusta board only yesterday. He didn't know where the other two were coming from. "Anything, Miss Augusta. You name it, old Joe'll do it. Old Joe'll do it." Joe Gruba wasn't that old. He just seemed old, with his knotty frame, his toothless smile and his lined and scuffed shoe-leather hide.

"Jordis doesn't know I'm here so we need a ride out to Crow Kills. We need you to forget you saw us, Joe. As far as anyone knows, we are—all three of us—in Philadelphia. It is important that people think that. It's important, Joe." She looked steadily and seriously into his eyes.

Joe had helped her before because she was Will Kaiser's friend. In the past two years she had become his friend, and there wasn't anything Joe Gruba wouldn't do for a friend and do it, no questions asked. He didn't bat an eye or skip a beat. "Nobody hears nothing from old Joe Gruba. Nobody hears nothing from Joe. I'll get the wagon and pull 'er up out back. The team's hitched. You have a biscuit. The Missus makes them fresh every day. Help yourselfs. Give me ten minutes then go out the back door and I'll be there."

Gustie nodded. "Thank you, Joe. This means a lot to us."

Joe was as good as his word. In ten minutes, the three women climbed into Joe Gruba's wagon. Gustie, gathering her hood and cloak around her, sat next to him, and Mary and Betty, pulling their veils down once again, took the second seat behind. Gustie hunched down so as not to appear so tall.

Joe's sturdy team moved ahead willingly at a shake of the reins, trotting the cold road to Crow Kills.

Joe chatted amiably. "I got it figured out, Ma'am. I got it figured. If anybody seen us, and busy-bodies me who was I taking out of town, I'll tell 'em you was some missionary folks. Missionary folks come by here all the time like ticks to a dog. I'll just tell the nosies that you was three of them prissy faced Psalm singers come to convert the Indians." This tickled him and he slapped his thigh and laughed a high-pitched hee hee hee. Gustie smiled. He laughed all the harder.

Gustie squinted against the sun's glare and kept her hood up. She had been sorry to miss these icy, snow swept days, winters that most of the locals claimed they could live without and threatened every year to leave for a warmer climate, and how could God make such a deep freeze and expect god-fearing folks to live in it? But she had always loved the winters. The sleeping land was pristine and heaven felt close. Gustie was not religious in the traditional sense and the word heaven didn't fit her views, but it was the only word she could come up with. Yes, on brilliant, crystalline days like this, heaven was close. So was Jordis. Gustie looked forward to seeing the look on her face when she came back. She didn't have long to wait.

Joe pulled his team to a halt in front of the cabin. It had changed since the last time he had seen it. After Dorcas's death, Jordis and Little Bull had built on an extra room and painted the outside white. It looked like a nice cozy cottage now, instead of the one-room weathered shack it had been. Jordis would have built on to it earlier, but Dorcas had liked it the way it was.

Betty jumped down from the wagon first and helped Mary down. Gustie followed and pulled off their bags.

"I'll come out and look in on you, if that's okay, Miss," said Joe. "Way out here in the winter. You never know. People won't think anything of it. I bring mail out to the reservation sometimes, and chew the rag with old Jimmy Saul. Bring him a plug of tobacco now and then. People won't think twice. Why, they'd have to think twice if I didn't come out once in awhile, so that's how that is, you know."

"That would be fine, Joe. We would like that. Thank you again. Oh, wait. Can you send a telegram for me?" She took a pencil and scrap of paper from her purse, wrote a few lines on it and gave it to Joe. She also handed him a dollar.

"I'll take care of it, Miss Gustie. Old Joe'll take care of it. Well, bye now. Bye now. Okay, Bess, okay, Nattie, we're goin' home. To the barn, old girls." The horses stamped their big front feet, blew steam out their nostrils, and eagerly headed back to town and barn.

Gustie watched him go for a moment. When she turned around, Jordis was standing on the porch, a huge smile on her face. "Short trip," she said.

My dear aunts,

I'm sorry for my short telegram. I hardly know what to tell you except to describe what happened. You know we had planned this trip carefully, and while Mary seemed distressed at times, I thought she

175

was naturally concerned about her condition, but also that she was afraid that she, a stranger, would be imposing upon my family.

I assured her repeatedly, even letting her read your letters for herself, that you and Father were eager to have us visit and that you were especially pleased to think that soon there would be a baby in the house. But when I boarded the train in Wheat Lake I found Mary in a state—so pale I thought she was near to fainting and Betty frightened to death. We both tried talking to Mary, to soothe her, but she seemed almost catatonic. We got into Minnesota and I couldn't let it go on any longer. I feared for her and I feared for her baby. I asked the porter which was the first town that would have a decent hotel where we could get off and spend the night because my friend was ill. We disembarked in a pleasant town called Stanton Grove and checked in to the hotel which fortunately did prove to be very comfortable. When Betty and I went to Mary's room we found her sobbing, saying she was sorry, that she felt like she was dying and she couldn't leave the land where she was born, where her babka was buried. She went on incoherently about her roses and her grandmother's prayer book and how without them she knew her baby would die. I couldn't force her to go on. The only thing we could do was come back here. In fact, as soon as I promised her that we would be on the east-bound train in the morning, she became calm and went to sleep.

So, here we are, four women in a two-room cabin. She says, now that she is calmer and able to express herself more clearly, that her fear was in fact that if she gave birth somewhere else, the baby would die. At any rate, she is at peace now and is happily looking forward to going to Philadelphia after her child is born. Jordis seems to understand this. I don't, but I have to accept it.

Dear Louisa, Margaret, Edith. Thank you again for your readiness to help my friend, and I must ask you for yet more assistance to enable us to keep up our charade until the birth of Mary's child. I'm enclosing envelopes in Betty's hand addressed to her mother and to her fiancé, as well as a few from me to Lena. We must send you our letters for you to resend so they will have the Philadelphia postmark, and ask you to, in turn, forward their letters to us here in Wheat Lake. I know this reeks of childish skullduggery, but I see no other way. You see both Jordis and I have a strong feeling that it is absolutely imperative that Mary's presence here not be known by anyone. There are too many inquisitive people about and, while we trust Alvinia (Betty's mother) and Lena, we don't feel that they need to be burdened with this fantastic construction at this time. Pauly still resides with his parents—they would question many letters coming to him from Wheat Lake, and I doubt that he, full of the fire of youthful ardor, and Alvinia, full of mother-love, would be able to keep themselves long away from Betty, knowing she was so close. However good their intentions, our secret would be at risk. So I ask for your indulgence and help.

Express my deep apologies to Oksana for having put her to extra trouble, preparing for guests that won't arrive till summer.

Thank you dear aunts, and give my love to Father.
Your affectionate
Gustie

Chapter 12: March 1901

FEATHER HAUNTED THE BARN LIKE a sleek, gray, luminous-green-eyed phantom. His favorite perch was the high crossbeam from which he could detect the slightest movement under the hay, the merest rustle of straw, the swift, tiny shadow against the wall where a mouse skirted the open floor, trying to make its living between the grain bin and the water buckets. The cat was as devoid of mercy as was the winter that had swept upon them like a furious arctic bear leaning heavily against the buildings, snapping the treetops with silent paws. In the last few days, the bear had begun to howl, disgorging a belly-full of snow.

The mice who had ventured from their holes, attracted to the barn by the oats, impelled by the cold and the famine of the frozen ground, did not long survive the cat. His prowess was such that today there was no movement, no rustling, not a single shadow. He was content to wait. There would be more. There were always more mice. Life was an extremely satisfying affair. In the summer there were juicy frogs, ground squirrels, birds and small rabbits to slaughter and devour from whisker to tail. In winter, only mice. But mice were good.

Feather was distracted from his meditations by the opening of the barn door and a rush of fresh, biting air carried on a shaft of cold white light.

Jordis came in with a bucket of snow-melt in one hand and a plate of cooked food in the other, followed closely by Mary who held a lantern and another plate of something nearly as tasty as fresh mouse—the raw entrails of a couple of perch. Feather didn't need an invitation. He leapt from his crossbeam to the top of the tallest stack of hay bales, skimmed down its side to the floor where he braided himself around Jordis's soft, moccasined legs.

"Ho, little warrior," Jordis said, putting down her bucket and balancing her plate on the top rail of Moon's stall. She removed her shawl and poncho and draped them over the stall gate. The blanketed horses welcomed her with pricked ears and soft equine snuffles. She took the lantern from Mary and hung it on a hook protruding high on the wall.

Mary sat on a hay bale and put her plate on the floor at her feet. The cat streaked to the dish and began to devour the shiny red, blue, and yellow fish guts. Mary let the blanket she had wrapped herself in drop down, revealing her burgeoning form. She had had to remake the dresses she had brought with her, taking the bodices off and cutting pieces from one to add extra gores of material to the others so the skirts could fit over her expanding waist. Over them she now wore some of Jordis's wool shirts for warmth, and because they were so large, they draped nicely over her middle. When the road was cleared to town, Jordis promised to get her some material so she could make something more to her liking. In the meantime, she was happy to be warm and comfortable.

"I can't get over this cat!" Mary laughed. Feather had been the pampered lap cat of Gertrude Kaiser's sister Julia. His paws had rarely touched the floor, let alone the out-of-doors. He had lapped cream from a china saucer and was hand fed choice morsels of cooked meat. At Julia's death, Lena had given the cat to Jordis.

"He got a taste of the wild life," said Jordis, "and it seems to agree with him. He is blood-thirsty really."

"Julia loved this cat. I'm glad he's doing so well." Once Mary's eyes adjusted from the outside snow-glare, the interior of the barn did not seem so dark. The single glass window shone like milk, with nothing visible through it but a bottomless white. The lantern's soft glow brought out a golden shine to the straw. "When did you build this barn? It wasn't here in October, was it?"

"No, we put it up right after we added to the cabin." Jordis had mixed feelings about this barn. Gustie had insisted, gently, that if she was going to be out here in the winter at all she needed a place for Biddie who, unlike the reservation horses, was not used to spending the cold winter months with only a sparse stand of cottonwoods for shelter, or if they were lucky, a three-sided shed. This barn was small, but sound and snug. Grain filled a bin in one corner and a pile of straw took up another. Hay bales were stacked in varying formations against the walls to provide winter fodder and further insulation. With pieces of scrap wood, Jordis had made a platform a few inches off the dirt floor to keep the hay dry.

She liked this place because she had constructed it herself, with help from Little Bull and Leonard, of poles cut from young cottonwoods and the lumber left over from what Gustie had purchased for the house. It was a simple rectangular structure with doors at either end built on a rise so the dirt floor wouldn't hold water, and it was sheltered on the north side by trees. But because it was also a better structure than many of the flimsy cabins that most of the people on the reservation lived in, she felt it was... inappropriate. Tipis, of course, were snug and warm if they were constructed properly, but in the absence of buffalo, those who still preferred tipis had to make do with steer hides, government issue blankets, and pelts of small animals—all poor substitutes for the warm buffalo hides of their grandparents.

Jordis put these thoughts aside as she knelt before the tripod that stood under the window. Suspended from leather straps in the center was a shabby blanket roll fastened at each end with leather thongs.

On the floor beneath the bundle in the triangular space created by the tripod legs was an empty dish. Jordis replaced it with her plate of cooked food: small portions of the fish, potatoes, and fry bread they had just had for their noon meal. She paused just a moment before the tripod and then went back to the bucket of snow-melt.

Mary said, "You take a plate of food out every day. *This* is what you do with it?"

"Yes." Jordis poured half the bucket of water into Moon's drinking bucket and moved to Biddie's stall. Both horses were blanketed and in their stalls, side by side. "When a person dies, you cut off a lock of his hair and put it among sacred objects. There are certain rituals you do for a year. That way, the person's soul stays with you and you honor it. One way is by bringing food offerings. That blanket roll was Dorcas's. She called it her memory bundle. It contains all the things that were most precious to her. When she died, I cut a lock of her hair and put it in there. Since the missionaries got here, people don't do this much anymore." Jordis had taken Moon's blanket off and was now brushing her with long strokes.

Mary peered at the frayed old blanket roll with interest. "Do you really think Dorcas's soul is in that bundle?"

"I behave as though it is. So does the cat."

"What do you mean?"

"When I first brought him out here to Crow Kills he attached himself to Dorcas. He would disappear on his hunting trips, but he always came back to her. Then after she died, he came back to that." She nodded her head toward the tripod. "Wherever it was, that's where he would be. After we built the barn, I decided to keep it out here. She always wanted to be outside more than in, so in the winter this seems like the place. And he stays out here now. I think they are both happy here." Jordis cast a glance at Mary. "Everude used to preach that the devil was in such practices."

182

"Is he the one who hurt you?" Mary had been shocked to tears when she first saw Jordis's scars rising across her back like twisted vines, scars from a beating she received at the hands of Reverend Obed Everude at the mission school. "He was an evil man, Jordis. He should have looked for the devil in himself. That's where he'd have found him. To hurt a child like that..." She shook her head unable to understand cruelty. "Anyway, it was not for him to say how other people should respect their dead." She had kept her attention on the tripod. "But, what happens to the food?"

"I assume the cat eats it, eventually. Maybe the mice. But Feather has never even sniffed it in my presence." She stared at the tripod as if contemplating the implications of that. Seated next to Mary, Feather washed himself meticulously.

They enjoyed the silence for a while. Mary stroked the cat while Jordis brushed the white mare. Mary said, "The wind is coming up again. You hear that?"

Jordis nodded. "I think we are in for more snow."

"Oh. You and Betty worked so hard clearing our paths." With some help from Gustie, they had shoveled paths, one to the barn, one to the woods, where they emptied their refuse, and one to the lake, where Jordis fished through the ice.

"I think this time we will be digging tunnels, not just paths. Anyway, with the snow banked up against the house and barn, it'll be warmer inside than it is now."

"May I stay out here with you for awhile?"

"Of course."

"It's nice here, isn't it? This barn is a good place. It's kind of like church. A small church, with hay bales for pews. Actually, that was the first church, wasn't it? A stable."

"I suppose it was," said Jordis, replacing the blanket on Moon's back.

"I think a soul would want to rest here for a while."

The wind whipped the rope that was strung from the house to the barn door hard against the front of the barn. The horses whickered softly and shifted in their stalls but were not unduly alarmed. Mary stroked the cat who was lulled into a drowsy, trancelike state. Jordis prepared Moon's manger with fresh hay and gave her some oats.

"Thank you."

"For what?"

"For letting me stay here."

Jordis stopped to look at Mary who sat, small and grateful on her hay bale and realized she didn't mean staying with her in the barn while she took care of the horses. Mary pulled the blanket back up over her shoulders. The cat curled next to her enjoying his full stomach and warm back. "I haven't had a chance to speak to you just by ourselves. I've thanked Gustie of course, but this is your home..."

"It is also Gustie's home."

"I know... I know you are doing this for Gustie..."

"I'm not doing anything for Gustie."

"You're not?"

"Gustie isn't your only friend, Mary."

"Thank you, Jordis."

Jordis smiled.

"Gustie asked me once if I was happy. I wasn't then, but I am now. I like our suppers together around the table in the lantern light, and hearing Gustie tell us about Philadelphia. I feel like I already know her wonderful aunts and Oksana. And Michael. Her beautiful garden. I feel like I'll recognize Market Street and find my own way to Wanamaker's! I like listening to Gustie and Betty reading to us in the morning. Gustie has such marvelous books. I like my new moccasins! Before I met Gustie, I never had a friend. And now, I'm surrounded by friends."

Jordis said, "I know just how you feel. Except for the..." Jordis mimed a rounded belly.

Mary laughed, then became serious. "Do you think it is very hard for Betty? To be here, separated from her family, from her boy, and not being able to go to the concerts and the plays and the stores except in her letters to her mother?"

"I don't think Betty cares much for city adventures. I think she is enjoying putting one over on her mother, and she said to me once over a shovel full of snow that this will be good for Pauly. Make him appreciate her more when she gets back. Besides, nobody is keeping her here. She could have gone back any time. She can leave whenever she wants. Or at least as soon as we shovel our way to the road." Jordis replaced the blanket over the black mare. "Have you thought of names for the baby?"

"I'm going to name her Augusta Rose and call her Rose. Do you think Gustie will mind that?"

"She will be pleased. What if you have a boy?"

"I don't have a name for a boy, so I hope I'm right about its being a girl."

Feather's purring provided a cozy counterpoint to the sound of snow being flailed into the north wall of the barn and the rope slamming against its door. Mighty hunter though he was, he still liked being scratched behind the ears.

"I think we better go in before it gets any darker." Jordis put the two empty plates in her snow bucket, slipped on her poncho, and wrapped the shawl around her head and neck. "You'll need both hands getting back," she said as Mary wrapped herself in her blanket. Jordis took a coil of twine from off a knob on the wall and tied it in a crisscross fashion over Mary's shoulders and then fastened it around her waist.

"Now you hold the bucket with one hand and me with the other. I'll go ahead." Jordis took the lantern and blew it out. Its feeble light would do them no good in the raging wind and snow. "Ready?"

Looking like a child getting ready for an adventure, Mary nodded, took the bucket, and linked arms with Jordis.

Feather watched them go. A cloud of snow swirled into the barn as the door opened and the two women disappeared into it. Snow crystals hung tenuously in the air until the door closed. The sound of the blowing wind was muted and the crystals, in their thousands, fell one by one softly to the floor. He got up, extended his claws and pulled at the hay half-heartedly, then bounded over to the stalls and walked gingerly along on the top rails around each horse. He made his usual round of the barn, sniffing out corners, traversing crossbeams. When he was satisfied that all was as it should be, he curled up inside the box that Jordis had lined with a piece of blanket and some straw and placed next to the tripod and the memory bundle, and *her*.

His reason for getting out of bed was boredom with being horizontal. Jack Frye swung his feet over the side of the cot. Through the holes in his grimy socks, the icy floor shocked him and he recoiled with a curse. For instant warmth he reached for the whiskey bottle on the floor by his bed. Empty. He stared at it. Goddamn! His mind worked slowly. He looked down at himself. He was fully dressed except for his boots. He put down the bottle and picked up a boot and grunted pulling it on. He repeated the process with his other foot. With his feet on the floor, his bleary focus fell on the lump on the cot on the other side of the cold stove. It came back to him. Snuce had kicked them out of the saloon. "You're not spending the night in here, if that's what you think," he had growled as the snow began blowing past his greasy window. "You boys get on home."

They had reluctantly paid for their drinks and for two bottles to take with them. The alcohol had probably kept them from freezing to death after the stove went out.

The lump stirred. Jack Frye and Gleeve Pruitt had been snowed in here for two days, mostly drinking and sleeping. Jack looked again at his empty bottle. He knew he hadn't finished it. He was always clear about one thing: the level of whiskey left in his bottle.

It was too cold to sit here and stew. Shivering and cursing, he got up and went to the back of the bunkhouse where he opened the door to the shed.

Even colder air, if that were possible, drifted in. He filled the coal pail, hauled it in and tossed the coal into the empty belly of the stove. Then he squashed up a handful of newspaper from the pile on the floor and threw that in. He had to try several times to light it, shivering and cursing in an ever more strident pitch till the coals caught fire. He slammed the stove door shut and went back to his cot to wait under his blanket until the stove kicked out some heat. When it did, the lump stirred again. This time Gleeve's head emerged. He got up and staggered to the bucket in the corner and urinated.

Jack's vision was clearer now. The bunkhouse was filled with a cold white light, none of it filtering through the front window. He went to the door and tried to open it. He couldn't. Some genius had made the bunkhouse door open out instead of in, and the bank of snow that covered the window also blocked the door. He cursed again and stomped out to the shed. There, the door to outside opened in. The snow was up to his shoulder blades, but at least they could get at it. They could dig out. A dozen cans of beans remained on the shelves, but Jack Frye was tired of pissing in a bucket and eating beans out of a can.

"Grab a shovel," he croaked. His throat felt like sand.

"What for?" Gleeve had returned to his cot and was about to crawl under his blanket.

"We gotta get out of here."

"What's the rush?"

"Cuz I'm fuckin' stir crazy that's what." In fact, he needed to get out worse than he needed a smoke, and that was saying something.

"We can't get the door open. How we gonna shovel if we can't get out? We just wait, Reuben'll shovel us out. It's his bunkhouse."

"Yeah, and if we wait long enough, he won't have to cuz it'll be spring. We can get out through the shed. Put yer boots on."

They shoveled till they hit a cleared patch that ran to the stable. Reuben Stavig and his boys had been shoveling since daybreak to clear the way to the street. All able-bodied men and boys and a few women were out with shovels; Main Street and some side streets were already clear enough for one horse.

In the clear patch, Jack threw down his shovel. Gleevie grinned and did the same. Still squinting against the dazzle of white snow and winter sun, Gleeve didn't see Jack's fist swinging toward him. The impact knocked him into the snow bank.

"Oooww! What was that for?"

"For drinking my whiskey, ya little piss-ant!"

"Well you wadn't drinkin' it! You was out cold and I was freezing, man."

"Wasn't yours! Now we're going to Snuce's and you're going to buy me another half a bottle."

"I can't." Weaving, Gleeve got to his feet.

"We can get there. They've pretty much got the whole place cleared enough to walk. We just have to shovel a few feet east."

"No. I ain't got any money left."

"What?"

"I ain't..."

Jack heard him the first time and hit him again. Gleeve went sprawling again. "Well, you better hire yourself out and get some money and buy me that

189

whiskey and pay your nickel to Reuben for your cot and his beans we been eatin' and all that coal we been burning cuz I ain't paying for more'n my share."

"You'd ha burnt that coal anyway, whether I was here or not," Gleevie whined, rubbing his jaw.

"No matter. You was here. You got the benefit. You pay half."

Gleevie slogged to the general store and asked if they needed help with shoveling. He was told he had to get up earlier, they got their shoveling done already. He was met with the same answer at the post office, the blacksmith's, the Blue Bird Café, and Mattie Olsen's hotel. He went back and checked at the Indian Agency. Owen Braaten didn't need any help either. That left only the saloon. Snuce eyed him, spat into the spittoon at his feet, and said he didn't need any shoveling, but since Eddie Hansmeier hadn't shown up, Gleevie could sweep the place out and wash glasses for a couple days till Eddie shoveled his way out and made it in to town.

Gleevie was humiliated by such work, a smart man like himself, but he had no choice. He had to pay for his cot and replace Jack's whiskey, because if he didn't, if the cold didn't kill him, Jack Frye would.

With hat in hand, he asked Snuce to advance him twenty-five cents and half a bottle of whiskey. Snuce's arteries did not pulse with sentimental feeling for his fellow man, but he knew a man had to live, and he knew that with the snow piled up to the rooftops, Gleevie couldn't go anywhere. So he gave him fifty cents and told him to get a bath. "You got a change of clothes?" he asked.

190

Gleevie thought a minute and remembered he had some clothes, probably cleaner than what he had on, in a paper bag under his cot. He nodded.

"Well, change 'em then and get those washed. Come back in forty-five minutes and start work."

Gleevie went to Mattie Olsen's and paid her to wash his clothes and let him use her bath shed. He came back, cold to his bones because her shed was only heated by a tiny tin stove, the place was drafty and the water lukewarm.

Fortunately for Gleevie, two days later Eddie Hansmeier's mother came in to town to tell Snuce that Eddie had fallen out of their hayloft. Fortunately for Eddie, he'd missed the tines of the plough and only broke his shoulder, but he would be laid up for the rest of the winter. Now Gleevie could earn enough money sweeping and washing up at the Spittoon to pay for his cot and one meal a day at the cafe. It was time spent fermenting his hatred of the squaw who got him thrown out of Charity, where he could have worked on a threshing crew and made good money and been gone before the snow flew.

Slow nights at the Spittoon, Gleeve and Jack played cards. They never played for money. Gleeve never stole any more whiskey, and they got along.

Chapter 13: April 1901

DOLLY WAS BIG, STRONG, AND stubborn, and drove Lena's gentle-spoken pa to fits of cursing in Norwegian when, mid-field row, she would stop. Why—no one could ever tell. She was well cared for, never overworked or worked when it was too hot—Baathor Halverson was a deeply kind man—so her stops were described by his amiably mocking friends as pauses for personal meditation. When Baathor's closest neighbor hollered at him across the pasture... *Hey, Bottle... Why don't you sell her—get another horse?* Baathor, as angry at the nickname that stuck to him in this new country as at fate for sticking him with such a maddening and willful beast, would mutter, "Because nobody else would put up with it!" meaning, of course, that someone else might beat her, or simply have her slaughtered. So, "Nothing moves Dolly" was Baathor's continuing lament.

Lena had no memory of the event; nevertheless, it had attained mythical status in her imagination. She could see herself as a toddler following Pa to the corral, stopping in the middle of it as he went on to the far end to pump water for the stock. The prairie languished in a cloud of August dust. The sloughs and creek beds were dry, the coulees just dips in the scorched land. The only source of water was the well. When the trough was filled, Baathor whistled and the thirsty cattle, knowing that sound heralded abundant cool water, overcame the inertia of the heat and of their own great ruminating bodies to stampede back to the corral for their nightly drink.

Lena could see her pa that evening—how he whistled and *then* he turned and saw his child happily playing in the dirt in the middle of the corral, the cattle already almost surging through the gate, their russet backs heaving together like a muddy river flooding its banks to engulf and destroy everything in its inexorable rush forward. He felt their hooves jar the earth, and he thought, *How can they run so fast?* He could feel their breathing, their beating hearts... and he was paralyzed. Dolly had been grazing in the same pasture. She had looked up when she heard the whistle and with equine wisdom took it all in, and then this willful draft horse, broad in back and heavy of leg, transformed herself in blood and bone and ran like a Thoroughbred. She slipped through the corral gate one horse tail ahead of the cattle and planted herself like the cedars of Lebanon around Lena, who watched with curious glee as the pounding red river of cattle parted and flowed around them.

"Oh, ja," Baathor would say, his Norwegian brogue thickening, to anyone who stopped by to wonder why he no longer cursed at his horse. Then he would tell the story of Dolly who saved his little girl. And at the end of his story, his voice breaking, he'd say, "Oh ja, they bumped her good then, but, you know—nothing moves Dolly."

Lena had her life because of a horse, and that's why she stopped the Chicago, Milwaukee, St. Paul & Pacific on its tracks this cold April morning.

A chilly wind swirled down the rails between the granary and the depot. Lena pulled the pink crocheted cap securely over her daughter's ears and smoothed her own hair down. *We look like a bunch of mud hens crossing Dryback Grade,* Lena thought as she glanced over her shoulder at her sisters and their children, all following behind her. Ella and Ragna, their combined seven children in tow, had arrived earlier on the east-bound passenger train and left their bags at the depot while they ate breakfast at Olna's Kitchen. Now, as they were returning to reclaim their things, the east-bound freight rolled in. Lena waited for her sisters on the platform outside. Before the conductor had swung the mail bag down to Willie Mohs, Lena sniffed the air—Willie said later—"like a prairie dog."

"What in Sam Hill?"

Ella was the first to emerge from the depot with her carpet bag. Lena handed Gracia to her with the command to "Wait here a minute" and sniffed her way down to the fourth boxcar. The conductor was getting up steam to pull out when Lena came running back, slapping the sides of the cars and yelling, "No you don't! No you don't!"

Ella and Ragna, tired from their previous day of visiting cousins and shopping in Argus, rolled their eyes, not in the least surprised that Lena could stop a train. They were resigned to wait while their younger sister carried through to the end whatever disturbance of the peace she had in mind.

"What's the matter?" Ella asked wearily. Her plump cheeks sagged, deepening the crease that drew down the corners of her mouth.

Lena snapped, "Don't you smell it?"

"I smell something," replied Ragna, making her nasty face. "What is it?"

Lena's sisters grew up on the same dirt farm she did, and yet, sometimes they acted so town-bred that she couldn't decide if they were putting on airs, or, if during their childhood, they just hadn't paid attention. Either way, they irritated her. "Horses!" she said. "In a bad way."

She pointed to the conductor and swung her finger to the car in question. "Open that car—down there where that stink is coming from."

"I can't—"

"Open it! I want to see in there."

Willie shook his head with amazement as the conductor lowered all three hundred pounds of himself to the ground. The station manager had seen it before—tiny Lena Kaiser bullying big men into doing what she wanted. He trailed behind them, curious himself to see inside the boxcar.

When the conductor rolled back the doors, Lena uttered a guttural cry, Willie's face fell, and the conductor broke out in a sweat. On the slimy floor of the boxcar lay horses, starved, sick, covered with open sores and jagged wounds, some already dead, some barely hanging on to life, their eyes rolled back.

She turned to the conductor, accusation stark on her face.

The fat man squirmed. "I came on a few miles ago. I wasn't driving when they were loaded. I didn't know—"

"This train isn't going anywhere," she said flatly. "Willie, who's the nearest with a gun?"

"The sheriff, for sure, and Gudierian keeps his Winchester in back of the tack shop."

At Harlan Gudierian's name, Lena shuddered. "Go get Dennis, then. Tell him to bring his pistol."

"Jack, you heard the lady," Willie said to his son who had returned from his run to the post office with the mail bag. The thirteen-year-old turned around and sprinted up Main Street again.

Lena walked back to where her sisters stood, surrounded by children beginning to shiver in the cold. Ella still held Lena's daughter. "You go on to the house," Lena said. "The beds are all made up for you upstairs if anybody wants a nap. I'm going to stay here and make sure this is seen to. Take Gracia with you. I don't want her around here."

Ragna's perpetual frown deepened and she hoisted her own youngest child higher on her hip. "Why don't you let the men see to it?"

"I'll stick around to make sure they do," Lena said.

Ragna knew it was futile to argue. She turned and headed south to Lena's house. Ella, Gracia held tightly to her bosom with one hand, reached down and took the hand of her own three-year old. The rest of the children trudged behind them weighted down with their travel bags.

196

She watched them go with some regret. They had stopped in Charity on their way home to Wheat Lake. It was the only time they had ever made a special effort to visit with their younger sister. She hardly knew her nieces and nephews, and now this. Well, she couldn't help it. She would follow them home as soon as she saw to it that Dennis did the right thing.

She heard panting behind her. "Mrs. Kaiser." Jack was breathless from his run. "Don't know where the sheriff is. Deputy Mulkey said he'd send him down as soon as he finds him. So I went and told Mr. Gudierian and he's coming." The boy saw Lena's face darken. "I thought—"

"No, Jack, you did the right thing. You're a fast runner."

Harlan Gudierian was already shuffling toward them, rifle in hand.

"I think we should wait for the sheriff, then," Willie advised.

The conductor jammed his cap down on his head. "Now, I can't sit here all day. Your sheriff could be anywhere. I gotta shut things up and get going."

He turned away from them to walk back to the open car.

"You can't go on with those horses lying there like that!" Lena said, trotting behind him.

He ignored her and just raised a hand in a dismissive gesture. He dropped it when he felt a hard poke in his buttocks. He swung around. Lena was behind him, raising Harlan Gudierian's rifle to her shoulder, her sights squarely on the conductor's abdomen. She saw the man's face register surprise and then a good natured, albeit condescending, amusement, an expression she had seen before on the faces of those who did not know her well.

"I don't have to be a good shot. You're a big fella." She cocked the rifle, startling the men around her— especially the conductor—and lowered her sights to his groin. "I'll bet you'd miss *that.*"

Willie, a few feet away, witnessed the conductor change his opinion about this small auburn-haired woman and took a step in. "Maybe we should wait for the sheriff, though, Mrs.—"

"It could be a month of Sundays before Dennis shows up. Those horses aren't going to lay there and suffer! Not while I can do something about it. Harlan, give me some more bullets." He didn't respond. "Well, you brought a box with you didn't you? What in blazes use is a gun if you don't have bullets?" Harlan fished in his overalls for the box and laid it in her outstretched palm. She dumped its contents into the pocket of her dress, gave him back the empty box and turned her back on them all. "Help me up there, Jack," she said over her shoulder as she walked briskly toward the open car.

"Yes, Ma'am." Jack caught up with her, leaving his father worried and Harlan limp, his mind working slowly trying to figure out why Lena had grabbed his gun away from him.

She laid the Winchester down on the edge of the boxcar floor, took off her coat and gave it to Jack, then he gave her a leg up. Shafts of cold sun through the slats of the car and the open door behind her gave her plenty of light to do what she had to do. She could still hardly believe what she saw. In the ten-by-thirty-foot boxcar lay about fifteen horses.

She picked up the gun and stared at it. She had never pointed a gun at a human being before. She would live with that later. Her breathing was shallow, only partly because of the stench of manure, sickness, and rotting wounds inside the car.

Closest to her a dying mare lay quietly, patiently. The outline of the horse on her side resembled the curves of a woman's back. Lena felt a pain in her heart. Maggots squirmed in the sores on the mare's flank. Lena tucked the rifle into her shoulder and sighted down the barrel to the mare's head. Her throat hurt like she had swallowed a pen knife sideways. Her hands trembled. She stepped closer and fired at point blank range. She absorbed the kick of the rifle; the sound of the shot pierced her eardrums with pain, and the mare almost imperceptibly relaxed into the floor.

She stepped over the mare's neck to the next living horse, a brown gelding, all bones and ragged hide. She worked the lever action and the shell casing flew out. *There's a place in heaven for horses... Pa said that the day we buried Dolly.* She raised the gun to her shoulder and fired.

Lena wiped her face with the back of her sleeve. She was sweating profusely, though it wasn't warm in the car, and she was crying, but she didn't care. She cried out loud because she couldn't hear herself for the ringing in her ears. Flies crawled over the face of a spotted pony. She cocked, fired. She wiped her eyes again with the back of her other sleeve and moved on to the next horse. Dead already. She stepped around two more dead horses till she found another still breathing. *Cock. Fire.* Another mare, already dead. A

199

burro crumpled in the corner, a mere pile of bones, barely alive. Lena pulled the lever and fired. Tears poured down her face. Her nose ran. The hem of her dress was slick with blood and slime. She killed one more horse, reloaded, and went on till she was finished. She stood at the end and looked down the length of the boxcar. This had to be all. No. At the east end, opposite to where she stood, a horse, terrified by the gunfire, was arching its neck, straining upward but falling back on its side. Lena made her way over and around bodies and through muck toward the struggling animal until she stood over him...a young stallion she could see now—a two-year-old maybe.

"Mrs. Kaiser." A voice in her ear. Sounding far away beyond the ringing of her tortured eardrums. Again, "Mrs. Kaiser—Lena. I'll do it. Go on now."

She looked up. "You here to arrest me, Dennis?"

"No, Ma'am. I'll finish it up."

"It's done." She raised her hand over the dead. "There's nothing to finish."

"What about—"

"Not this one." She yelled out the doors of the boxcar, "Willie!" Her throat still hurt. "I need your wagon."

Willie signaled Jack to bring the team and wagon around.

Out of alarm or curiosity, people who had heard shots instead of the departing train whistle had collected at the depot—Don Grode who'd been at the granary and feed store across the tracks; Carl Torgerson, his son Kermit and two customers from the ice cream parlor; Hank Ackerman, the pig farmer who'd been ambling down Main Street on his way to Leroy's Tavern for beer.

Dennis considered the struggling horse. "I dunno, Missus. He might get up with some help. But even if he does, somebody's gonna have to stay with him. He's in damn poor shape. How you gonna—"

"We need some help in here. Willie!" Lena yelled again. Carl, Kermit, and Jack climbed into the boxcar. They were followed by Don Grode and a couple men she didn't know. She pointed to the horse. "Get him into the wagon. I'm taking him home."

Lena jumped down to the ground by herself. "Willie, send a telegram for me." She lifted the bloodied skirt of her dress and took a handful of clean petticoat beneath it, bent over and wiped her face with it. Hank Ackerman stared at her. "What are you looking at, Hank?" she asked evenly. "You've been in a slaughterhouse before." He nodded gravely and went to help transfer the animal from the boxcar to the wagon. To the station manager, she continued, "Will'll settle up with you later. I don't have any money left on me."

"Don't worry 'bout that. I'll telegraph anywhere you want."

Lena dictated and watched as he wrote it down, word for word, with a stubby pencil into his notebook. Behind her the men had backed the wagon up flush to the boxcar. The wagon bed was lower. The horse was going to have to step down. Someone had also hauled up a bucket of water. They were good men, she thought, giving the horse a drink first.

The conductor, sweating himself even as he stood in the cold wind, looked at his watch and complained loudly to Willie who just shook his head. "The sheriff's in charge now, you'll have to take it up with him." The mention of local law enforcement shut the conductor up and he stood back. Of course, Willie knew that the sheriff wasn't in charge. Lena was.

Coats and jackets came flying out of the boxcar. Lena caught them and piled them in the front of the wagon. There was a moment of stillness and then all hell broke loose. Scuffling and thrashing sounds, and cursing.

"Watch those back hooves, Don!"

"Hell, I'm worried about the front ones!"

She heard a crash against the side of the boxcar and a strangled "sonofabitch!"

"Go easy with him, in there!" Lena called out. She heard more muttered curses.

More thumping, bumping, scraping sounds and Carl yelling, "Look out Kermit!"

"Got it, Daddy!"

One of the boys squealed.

"Pull up on his goddam tail!"

"I wouldn't do that, Carl!"

"Damn!"

That last "damn" was from Carl, who never swore or raised his voice. More grunts and curses, scuffling, thumps and skidding hooves. Another hard slam against the side of the boxcar. Lena was afraid they were going to kill the horse trying to save him, but at last there was quiet except for some very hard breathing, even gasping, which she suspected was coming from Hank, the heaviest of the men.

"Should we give him some more water now, Daddy?" That was Kermit. Good boy.

"Yeah, Son. Not too much."

Through it all the horse hadn't made a sound except for the scrape and scrabble of his hooves trying to support himself and gain purchase on the slippery boxcar floor, and his body slamming into the slat walls. After what was an anxiety-filled long time, Lena saw Carl with his hand on the lead rope and his arm under the horse's head, sort of cradling it, appear in the door opening of the boxcar. Kermit was on the other side, just his hand against the horse's neck, for moral support. Carl let the horse stop and look at the wagon and the step he had to take.

Lena asked, "Did he drink?"

"Yes, ma'am," said Kermit. "He's really thirsty."

"Hand me the bucket, then." She climbed up into the wagon, took the bucket that was still three-quarters full, and let the horse see and smell that she was putting it in the wagon. She hoped he was still thirsty enough to want to get to it and strong enough to try. "There now. Let him come."

The horse stepped down, his knee buckled and Lena stopped breathing while she willed him to stay on his feet. His other leg came down and held. His back legs followed, wobbly, but he stayed up. She let him have another short drink and took the bucket away, handing it down to a very dirty Jack. She watched the men climbing down from the boxcar to the wagon to the ground. Don Grode was limping, but not bad. Hank was rubbing his shoulder and grimacing. They were all covered in muck and slime and smelled godawful, as did the horse. "Tell your wives I'm sorry for the extra washing. But I thank you fellas. The

Lord loves a man who's good to a horse. And that's no lie. I'll drive," Lena said.

Carl and Kermit stayed in the back on either side of the horse, who looked like he could collapse at any moment. Dennis mounted his saddle horse and followed.

They left the conductor muttering to anyone who would listen, "Now what am I going to do with this mess? Out west, there's a drought...somebody was shipping them east to save them. I didn't come on until..." then Lena was out of earshot.

She drove slowly and tried to give the animal as smooth a ride as possible. She heard Kermit ask, "Daddy, how we gonna get him out of the wagon. He can't jump."

Lena thought quickly. Over her shoulder she said, "Carl, you'll have to use the cellar door. Will's tools are in the small shed. Take it off its hinges. It'll hold him."

Lena pulled up in front of her own barn and stopped the team. "Carl, can Kermit stay with him while I clean up?"

"We'll both stay, Mrs. Kaiser. You take care of yourself now."

Lena stayed with the horse while Carl and Dennis removed the door of the cellar. She led the exhausted horse down the ramp with no difficulty and to the barn. Six of Lena's nieces and nephews had gathered around wide-eyed to watch the procedure until they were called in sharply by their mothers.

"I got to get going, Missus," said Dennis, covered from collar to boot-tip with horse manure and ooze. "I got to get me a bath and get back to work."

"Did you get hurt, Dennis?" Lena gave him a worried look. He wasn't limping.

"Well, I'll be black and blue but no where you can see it." He chuckled.

"Thanks, Denny. Thanks a million." She watched him get on his horse, gingerly, she thought, then she got to the business at hand.

There was no time to heat water to fill the washtub for a proper bath. Lena filled a bucket with cold water from the pump and went to the house. Ella met her in the entryway. "Keep the children in the living room and bring me a towel and some clean clothes," Lena instructed. "I can't go take care of that horse smelling like death. And take out some coffee to Carl and Kermit, would you? They must be cold out there. Tell them I'll be as quick as I can." She closed the outside door behind her and locked it so nobody would walk in on her. "Then put some water on to boil and bring it out to the barn with my rag bag. Would you do that for me?"

When Ella brought clean clothes and a towel, Lena was already stripped and scrubbing herself from head to toe. *I won't have to live with this,* she thought dismally, *because I'm going to die of pneumonia.* Her teeth chattered, her ears still rang, and she had a fierce headache. But after drying herself roughly with the towel and dressing in fresh clothes, she was at least warm again. Ella anticipated her next request by handing her a cup of coffee on her way out to bring two cups to the barn. Lena drank it down then emptied the bucket of bath water outside. The coffee relieved the headache somewhat.

Lena didn't go inside her house again. Her sisters would make themselves at home and look after Gracia.

When Carl and Kermit were gone and Lena was alone with the horse in the barn, Ella came with the hot water and rags. Softer-tempered than Ragna, Ella did not berate Lena for her foolishness. She watched as the pitiful animal took more of the fresh water Lena had placed before him. Lena had drunk from it first with the dipper that she still held. Ella could tell by her shaking hands that her little sister had paid hell to do what she had done.

"I don't dare leave him. If he goes down, I sure couldn't get him up again by myself. Would you keep me in boiling water for awhile?"

"Sure, Lena."

"I suppose Ragna's fit to be tied. Wishin' she'd stayed on the train and gone home."

"You know Ragna."

Lena alternately tended the horse's wounds and gave him small amounts of food and water. When Will came home at noon for his dinner—he was working only a mile north of town—his sisters-in-law sent him to the barn.

Lena didn't have to be in the house with them to know that her sisters had clucked and fretted all morning over her craziness—how the colt probably wasn't worth a nickel on a good day and, if it was, the owner would sic the law on her, how one day she was going to lose that nose always putting it where it didn't belong. She could hear them. She could quote them. But her husband only stroked the horse's head and said thoughtfully, "Well, Duchy, he's a pretty sick fella. But you done all right by him so far." No one but

206

Gustie understood why she loved Will Kaiser. In spite of his faults, and she knew better than anyone that they were many, it always came down to this: when he was sober, Will Kaiser was the only truly soft-hearted man, besides her pa, she had ever known.

"I've kept him standing, and he's been taking a little oats and water," she said hopefully.

"Well, give it a go. Are your sisters going to stay and help you out?"

Lena threw a disparaging gesture toward the house. "Nooooo, they won't stay. Not for something like this. Ella might, if she was on her own, but she'll do what Ragna wants. She boiled water for me and brought me my rag bag. She did that much. They think I'm fool-headed." She dipped another cloth into the bucket of hot iodine water, wrung it out and placed it on a particularly nasty wound on the horse's rump. He flinched. The hard one to clean out had been the long gash across his side. She thought that might need some stitching but she wasn't skilled enough for that. "I used up all your iodine."

"I'll pick up some more. Don't you worry."

"We owe Willie for a telegram..." Will's good eye filled with curiosity—Lena was the tight-fisted one in the family, "...and Joe Gruba for a train ticket. I telegraphed for Joe to find Jordis and give her the ticket to Charity. I need help here."

Will shook his head and grinned, "Well, Duchy, I'll be cow-kicked!"

"Do you think she'll come?" Lena allowed a small doubt to creep into her mind, but she shook it out. Of course Jordis would come, because Lena was Gustie's friend. Jordis would come for Gustie's sake, and she would come for the horse.

"Yeah, Duch, I think she will. What about the other horses? Ella said there was a car full."

Lena's voice quavered and her eyes brimmed. "I shot them."

Will regarded his wife steadily then opened his arms. She folded herself into them like a dove to her nest. After a few minutes she pushed herself away and wiped her nose with the back of her hand. "Go on in now and get your dinner. Ragna's fried some chicken, I think. Tell Ella I'm about ready for another bucket of hot water."

When Will left, Lena began to sing. Lena always sang when she was alone. Hymns mostly. It was a lifelong habit. After Gracia was born she sang to her baby. And now, she sang to the injured horse. Through the afternoon he suffered her cleansing soapy water, her warm compresses, and all the verses of "Rock of Ages," "Pass Me Not Oh Gentle Savior," "Jesus Calls Us O'er the Tumult," plus lullabies and Christmas carols in Norwegian. She had done her best. He stood on his own, forlorn and trembling. She saw that, if his scars weren't too bad, he would end up a handsome horse—a brown and white paint. If he lived. Lena covered him with a blanket. There was nothing more she could do.

When Ragna came out with another cup of coffee for her, she asked the time.

"It's 3:30."

"Train's due at 4:00," Lena commented. "Bring Gracia out here, will you?"

"You can't keep a child in the barn."

Tell it to Mary and Joseph, Lena thought but said nothing.

"I've got your dress soaking."

"Thank you."

Ragna nodded.

Lena said, "When Jordis gets here, I'll start supper and we can visit awhile before we go to bed."

"You sent for that...?"

"Oh, shush! Go bring me my little girl. I haven't seen her all afternoon."

Lena was almost asleep, lying curled up on a blanket next to her daughter who was bundled up in two of Lena's crocheted afghans. She heard the door slide open and looked up. Jordis came inside and behind her, the soft-stepping Moon.

Lena almost cried with relief and gratitude. She hadn't been all that sure Jordis would come. She greeted her huskily, "They let you bring the horse on the train?"

Jordis was dressed in a long split skirt, moccasins and a yellow, high-necked blouse. Her hair was brushed neatly into a thick glossy braid that fell down her back. Moon had no saddle, just a small striped blanket on her white back, and no bit, just a halter and lead line.

"We rode with the baggage."

"Both of you?"

"Yes."

"You should have paid half fare then at least."

"No fare. Joe let us ride. Said to tell you he would not take any money."

"That was good of him." Lena was suddenly out of words.

Jordis led Moon to the stall next to Old Tom's. A large bag was slung over her shoulder. She put it down carefully on the floor. Lena watched her approach the paint with the confidence of someone who knows horses and the grace of someone who loves them. She rubbed his forehead and stepped around to his side, and lifted the blanket to examine him. "Did you really threaten to shoot the conductor?"

Lena busied herself smoothing down a lump under her own blanket.

Jordis re-covered the horse and faced Lena squarely. The intensity of her black eyes unnerved Lena, who was seldom unnerved by anything. She said, "You did a good job with him." There was respect in her voice.

Lena relaxed. "Do you think he can make it?"

"We'll see how he does through the night."

Lena nodded and sucked on her forefinger. "I feel bad about leaving those horses to rot on the train."

"They were not left there. Hank Ackerman and Carl Torgerson rounded up some men to unload them. They buried them out in the sand pit."

"Really?" Lena's eyes were wide and moist at this unexpected miracle of human thoughtfulness.

"I asked. Willie Mohs told me."

"Oh. I'm glad they did that. Well, what can I get you? My rag bag is there. All clean cloths. I used up all the iodine. Will said he'd get some more. I'll bring you out some coffee and bread and butter. Then we'll have supper around six. I'll call you and you can wash up..."

"I'll stay out here, if you don't mind bringing it out."

Jordis looked down to pick up her bag and did not see Lena's barely disguised relief that she didn't have to sit Jordis at the same table as her sisters. Her sisters were staying the night. Tomorrow, she could do as she pleased.

Jordis joined Lena on the blanket. From her bag she took out a shabby blanket roll and placed it carefully at her side. She reached in again and drew out a packet of dried leaves. "Boil this in a gallon of water. I won't need any iodine."

"For how long?"

"About forty-five minutes. Then start another one." She handed her another packet. "Boil this one down to half a gallon."

Lena stood up and brushed herself off, then picked up her daughter. "What do you hear from Gustie? I got a letter...let's see...a couple weeks ago now. I don't write. I told her I wouldn't. Not to Gustie. She's an educated person and I am so poor at writing things. I'd be ashamed to have Gustie read anything of mine. But you tell her I always like to hear from her. And Alvinia reads me Betty's letters. She sure sounds like she's having a good time. I'll be right back with some coffee for you. Will'll sure be glad to see you." Lena spoke awkwardly. And yet she was not anxious to leave. "Thank you for coming." She stood at the door. "My sisters think I'm crazy. Will doesn't." She ran a hand lightly across her lips as if brushing something away. "I just can't stand to see an animal suffer."

She slipped out, sliding the door closed behind her.

The cat had remained still and quiet, enjoying the brush of Jordis's hand when she reached in to his dark space for the sweet smelling packages. He stayed where he was till the barn was quiet. He wasn't afraid of people, just particular now about when he made his appearances. Even though the voice he'd heard was familiar, he stayed in his hiding place until the door closed. Then he crawled out onto the blanket and looked around. This was a barn but not his barn. No matter. Jordis was here and She was here. Feather padded over to Jordis and put his paws on her knees. "So, little warrior, you decide to join us?" She stroked his back and thought about Lena. She had a much better understanding now of why Gustie was fond of this woman. *I can't stand to see an animal suffer.* Friendships were built on less.

She got up and went to the horse. Putting her hands on either side of his head, she breathed into his nostrils.

Chapter 14: May 1901

I SPEND MOST OF MY TIME here in the barn, cross-legged on my blanket, wrapped in my poncho, contemplating how I have been brought here to tend this wounded horse. I fan the flame of equine spirit that still dances warily in his eyes.

When I knead his muscles, he leans into my hands. I am coaxing a shine into his coat. Though he will never be seamless, he is knitting himself together. Streaks of lightning across his left shoulder and down his chest and another across his flank will remain as signs of his suffering. By our scars we are made relatives.

Dear Gustie:

I am so glad to hear that Betty has been a help to you. She has always been willing and good at all household chores and will be useful when Mary's time comes. Of course, you have many doctors there and won't need a midwife. My Betty doesn't need a lot of looking after—she is a sensible girl and except to set her heart on this Catholic church mouse, has never done anything foolish—but I am grateful to you for taking her under your wing and showing her something of the world outside of Stone County. It may be her only and last chance as she is still bent on marrying Pauly Wirkus and settling down with him for the rest of her life on that rock patch that the Wirkuses call a farm. Enough said.

Please write to me and Lena and tell us how Mary is and all about you, too, and my Betty—if she misses her boy terribly—if she is homesick for her family. She has never been away from us before.

It is none of my business, but I wonder if you will be back. Now, maybe not my place to ask, but Lena said she thought something happened out at the reservation—something even before that great and awful tragedy which we all know you took to heart—to make you go, but she did not know what it was. For what it may be worth, I am sorry if that is the case and I sure think it was none of your fault whatever it was because I know you care about those people and that is a good Christian thing, but they are not the only people in the world, and neither, for that matter are Axel Kranhold and Mathilda Langager and the rest of that stiff-necked bunch who make such a parade of going to church but Jesus said it was better to say your prayers in a closet and they sure do like bowing their heads in public. You have friends here and don't you think you don't. Lena misses you but won't say so. Will says so, though. "Gustie's a grand girl!" he says and shakes his head the way he does like a big *grinning farm dog. I'm still mad at that man, though he seems to be all right now for a while.*

I do feel for Mary. It is not for me to judge how she came by her predicament. She would have received little kindness here from the Kaisers except for Lena and Will, and she's afraid of her own priest. She told me that much herself. Lena knew you would treat her kindly. You have always been good to everyone, even when they were not being so good to you. Enough said.

Alvinia Torgerson

PS. Jordis is bringing that horse around nice as you please. She walks him outdoors behind Lena and Will's house every day now and she and Lena are great friends and I think it is because she lets Lena do all the talking! Ha Ha. She doesn't mind my chickens visiting him with their treats. My children sure do like her and that horse. She calls him Skydog.

Lena was still in her nightgown, enjoying the quiet and the pale morning light washing her kitchen and the smell of her fresh coffee when she heard a wagon pull up. It was not even six o'clock in the morning. She ran back into the bedroom to get dressed and told Will to answer the door. As soon as she heard Oscar's voice she was mad. *The blame fool doesn't ever visit us. Acts like he doesn't know us most of the time, then when he does show up it's before the first rooster has had time to clear his throat.* She quickly buttoned up her dress, pinned up her hair, and hurried back to the kitchen in time to hear Oscar's woes.

"Gonna have to hire a new man." Oscar was slumped at Lena's kitchen table. His right paw around a cup of coffee, the stump of his left arm hidden underneath his jacket.

"Well that's a rough go," Will commiserated, pouring a cup for himself.

Did Shorty Larson finally get a belly full of Oscar's mean temper and low wages? Did he find something better? She hoped he had. No one should have to put up with Oscar.

Will asked the question. "Did Shorty leave?

"Naw, I fired him."

"What? Why on earth would you fire him? His wife is expecting their first child and you fire him?" Lena poured herself some coffee and leaned against her sink, waiting for an answer.

Oscar was not intimidated by Lena. "For not working," he growled. He took a sip of his coffee, set the cup down and stirred in another couple spoons full of sugar.

That's right. Use up all our sugar, you selfish pig. Lena said, "Shorty is a good worker. You never complained about him before."

"I got a couple jobs south of Wheat Lake as soon as the ground thaws enough. Shorty won't go. We'll have to stay in Wheat Lake till the work's done and he says he won't be gone from home overnight with his wife expecting." He took a good swallow of his coffee and added, "We can stay in the bunk house there."

"You could afford to stay at Mattie Olson's hotel. Wouldn't hurt to give that nice widow-woman some business." Lena glared at Oscar. She wasn't intimidated by him, either. When Oscar and Lena were together, which wasn't often, Will had the same feeling he used to get around Roy Graebner's prize bull when, as kids, they used to dare each other to taunt him through the fence. They'd had more luck than sense because that bull was the most dangerous animal in the county. One day it smashed right through the fence for no reason anybody could think of and went after Molly Graebner who was hanging out the wash. Roy shot two bullets into his head. The first one just slowed him down and the second one dropped him right at Molly's feet.

Will would just as soon they changed the subject, but Lena wouldn't let this go. "You can't expect a man to leave his wife for two weeks when she's getting ready to have a baby."

"Well I can't have a man deciding when he's going to work and when he isn't. I need a man I can count on."

"You've always been able to count on Shorty. This is different. Why can't he work with Will or Walter while you're gone?" She looked at Will. She wasn't sure they could afford to pay an extra man. Maybe for one week they could, and Walter could use him the rest of the time till Oscar came back. Will nodded. "You can find somebody in Wheat Lake to help you out for those two jobs and when you come back you'll still have Shorty and you won't have to train in somebody new."

Oscar took some more of his coffee and stared at her floor. Lena thought he might be considering her suggestion. She pressed her advantage.

"Why don't you go to Snuce's place in Wheat Lake and pick up somebody who's only looking for a couple weeks' work?" Tavern keepers always knew what everybody in town was up to. Especially the men who were down and out enough to work for Oscar Kaiser.

Dearest Jordis,

For heaven's sake! Are you living in Lena's barn? I know she doesn't intend for you to stay out there all the time—you say this arrangement suits because of your soul-keeping duties and Feather, but I don't understand why you can't leave the memory bundle— and the cat—out there the way you do at home. The horse surely doesn't require round-the-clock watching still? You know how this upsets me. And—Yes, even as I write, I can see you smiling and it is most irritating.

How long must you stay there? When will your horse be well enough to go to our house? We have a perfectly good barn there if you must sleep in one.

The three of us are well. Mary looks forward with great happiness to the birth of her child and moving to Philadelphia. I have painted an attractive picture of my aunts to her. Indeed, where Mary is concerned, I am confident they will not disappoint. I believe they will find in her all the qualities they so longed for in me.

She doesn't say as much, but I suspect that Betty is more than ready to go home. Both Mary and I have made it clear she is free to go anytime. She can tell Alvinia the truth or continue the charade and say that between the aunts and the score of physicians they have employed, Mary is well looked after. Frankly, I doubt that Betty would succeed in deceiving her mother in person, and all will be revealed to Alvinia within her first evening at home.

A word more about my aunts. While they used to drive me to distraction, they have participated in our play with enthusiasm. Even Louisa, who is inclined to cool detachment, is sending me warm and amusing letters. She says that Edith has been happy and pleasant for the first time since before Lincoln was shot. Margaret is always Margaret, but in this case, being Margaret is a good thing. You see, they have actually gone out to all the concerts and plays and on all the sight-seeing excursions that they have been describing in detail to us, so that Betty can fill her letters with believable accounts of her activities. Led by Margaret, they have also taken themselves out on Betty's shopping trips, and due to their good efforts, Betty has some lovely dresses. (I instructed them to keep in mind where she lives and to choose things the girl can actually wear in a place like Charity, where she needs good dresses for going to town and to church, but NOT for attending a Philadelphia debutante ball (like the one for which they so carefully outfitted me twenty years ago and to which I refused to go).) They have chosen well, and Betty's new frocks quite become her and will suit her life in Charity. They also supplied her with a new bonnet, matching gloves, a bag and some lovely undergarments and nightgowns that embarrassed as much as pleased her. She was, after all, supposed to be shopping for her trousseau while in Philadelphia.

I also asked Betty to make a list of all the things she would have liked to bring back to her family if she had had the chance, and again, the Weird Sisters succeeded admirably. I was stern with Betty, telling her that if something was not right to say so—we would *send it back or give it to someone else, and my aunts would try again, but their choices were perfect. Bonnet and gloves for Alice, dolls and a miniature porcelain tea set and hair ribbons for her younger sisters, a tie-pin for Severn, warm sweaters and belt buckles for the younger boys, a belt for her father, and a cameo brooch for Alvinia.*

My aunts also acceded to my request to send us my mother's steamer trunk of sheet music, which has occupied the corner of the parlor since her death, with no one to make use of it at all. I didn't think Father would mind parting with it, and Louisa confirmed that he was quite agreeable to sending it to someone who would appreciate it.

So, yesterday when Joe pulled up in front of our cabin, his toothless grin wide and his back seat laden with parcels, Betty was speechless that all of these things were for her, but then she nearly succumbed to tears over the expense of it all, telling me that while her parents had given her spending money, it wouldn't begin to cover even one of her dresses. I assured her that my aunts have more money than they know what to do with, and that they had greater pleasure in spending it than Betty could ever imagine. This is the truth, and that is what she can tell her mother.

But then we speedily arrived at another moment of frustration, when Betty was looking through the trunk full of music, unable to play a note of it for want of an instrument. So I flew out of my chair and said—take what you can carry and let's go! More eager for an outing than any one of us would have admitted, we grabbed our caps and veils and coats, and attired again like Joe's missionaries in case anyone should spot us, we set out for Shoonkatoh, trusting that my poor wagon looks like any other poor wagon and that, at a distance, one black horse is much like another.

The roads are muddy but where the wagon trail was impassable we just drove around it over the prairie grass, which is going to come through rich and green any day now.

What a lovely day for a ride, cool and clear. When we pulled into the mission grounds in the late afternoon, Betty and Mary kept their faces covered and waited in the wagon while I went to find Father Flagstad. I knocked at the rectory first and he answered the door with his usual politeness; then, as I raised my veil, he was all amazement. I told our story briefly. He grasped the situation at once, most surprised that he had suspected nothing and that the many people on the reservation and off who have shared our secret have done so with absolute confidence. Without hesitating to even put on his coat, he rushed out to greet Mary and Betty and invite us in. He was most kind to Mary and served us coffee and bread and butter. Matt and Tim came in (they seem a foot taller than when we last saw them in November), their mouths agape at the sight of us. Father Flagstad took them aside, spoke in low tones, and sent them back out to their chores.

I don't know who is the baker at the rectory, if the good priest bakes his own or if one of his parishioners performs that task for him and I didn't ask. I just relished the taste of oven-baked bread again after all these months.

The time came to explain why we had ventured out. He was again taken by that enthusiasm which animates his whole being, and loping—his shabby frock coat

221

flapping—led us to the church. Betty arranged herself and her music before her on the ancient piano and began to play. The boys came into the church to listen, and so did Leo LaBourteaux who had been doing some handy-work out back. No grand piano in any concert hall ever sounded so fine as did that old battered upright. She played for about forty-five minutes. There was not a dry eye among us—even Matt and Tim tried to suppress a sniffle or two.

Oksana told me that when I was an infant my mother used to park my cradle in the parlor and play her baby grand for me for hours on end. I do not remember this, of course, but I believe it accounts for the feeling of incredible sweetness that comes over me when I hear piano music. I settled there and then on my wedding present for Betty. It means another letter to my aunts and one to my father as well. For this, I do need his permission.

We then returned to the rectory and had dinner with Father Flagstad and his boys. It is Tim, I believe, who plays the piano, and he very hesitantly asked Betty if she would teach him to play better. She agreed wholeheartedly, though how they will actually arrange lessons on a regular basis, I have no idea.

We were all enjoying being out so much that for a few moments we forgot the reasons for our keeping out of sight. When some visitors came to the mission, we all tensed visibly, and Father Flagstad rose from the table and told us not to worry. He would take care of it. Fortunately, it was only some travelers asking for directions and for permission to water their horses. They were soon gone and it was time to don our caps and veils and start back to Crow Kills. Father Flagstad promised to visit us only when he could do so without attracting attention, and he invited us to return any time Betty wished to play. All in all, it was a fine day marred only by your absence.

My dear, I have not thanked you for helping my friend Lena. You will say, no doubt, that thanks are not necessary, but I thank you all the same. I know that you have had more opportunity to see Lena's crustier side, and fewer opportunities to see her finer nature, which runs deep and better than even she knows. I miss you sorely and long for our reunion.

Your loving Gustie

Anything was better than sweeping floors, washing glasses and emptying spittoons. That's why, when the sullen, one-armed man came into Snuce's place that afternoon in early May looking for a hand for a couple week's work, and paying three times what Snuce paid, Gleeve tore off his apron and announced, "I'm your man!" It sounded easy. Drilling a hole in the ground—how hard could that be?

After looking him over the same way a man might eye a horse at auction, the man growled, "You look strong enough. Worked around big machinery before?"

Gleevie admitted that he had not.

"Follow orders?"

"Good as anybody," Gleevie said.

"Okay then. Meet me at the Hanson place on Monday. I'll be pulling out of Charity at sun-up with my rig, and I expect to pull in there before dark. Be there to help me set up."

"Where's the Hanson place?"

"Ask around." The man, who said his name was Oscar Kaiser, threw money on the bar to cover his half-drunk glass of beer and left.

Gleeve left the Spittoon that day and collected his wages for the week. With the new job starting on Monday, he gave himself the weekend off.

He found Jack lying on his cot in his long johns, smoking a cigarette and staring at the ceiling, waiting for the supper hour when he and Gleevie went to the Blue Bird Cafe for their one meal of the day. Gleevie told him the news.

Jack stubbed out his cigarette in a coffee can of dirt by the side of his bed and pulled on his pants. "Well, good luck with that. I've heard that that Oscar Kaiser is a hard man."

Jack was not given to sober pronouncements about anything, but Gleevie shrugged it off. They went to a supper of tough beef and undercooked, greasy potatoes, then back to Snuce's for their bottle of whiskey and game of cards. Snuce was not much put out that Gleevie quit. Help came and went. It was part of the business of running a saloon. In any case, Eddie Hansmeier was due back shortly. If the glasses weren't always so clean that he served his whiskey in, the lights were too dim inside the Spittoon for anyone to notice.

Jack knew where the Hanson place was and gave Gleevie directions. He made sure he was there well before dark, and Mrs. Hanson, a tall woman with large hands and deep lines in her face, kept his coffee cup filled as he sat on her porch waiting for Oscar Kaiser to show up. Mr. Hanson greeted him with a tip of his hat but was busy with his boys finishing chores and didn't stop to talk. The sun was low and a sharp wind was blowing up when the well rig, pulled by a team of four huge draft horses rolled into the yard.

Somehow, Gleevie had gotten through twenty-nine years of life without laying eyes on anything more complicated than a shovel whose sole purpose was to sink a well. What rolled into the yard that cool evening in May was an incomprehensible contraption of large and small wheels, levers, pulleys, shafts and belts and rods and a derrick that was taller than anything Gleeve had seen before. It looked like a cross between a horrible giant insect and a big pile of junk. It did not look like it could do anything but grind up whatever got close enough. How it would drill a well, he couldn't see. And when it was belching hot steam and noise and the derrick was pumping and all those wheels, levers, pulleys, shafts, belts and rods were whirring and pumping, it was his worst nightmare.

My dear Gustie,

It is too ridiculous for me to send my letters to Philadelphia, so I have written a note to Joe—from now on all my letters addressed to Little Bull, Winnie, or Carrie are to be brought to you.

There is no need to scold me. I am taking Skydog home tomorrow. Moon is getting restless. She is used to some freedom, and I want him to have the taste of freedom as well. Tomorrow we will go as far as your house, where they can wander the pasture. When he is well enough, we will come to Crow Kills. I asked Lena if she wanted him, since she is, after all, his savior, but she cannot afford to keep another horse, and Skydog is going to be a handful. He likes her, but she says she would be afraid to ride him. He is high-spirited, even though he is not yet at his full strength.

He is beautiful. White as a cloud with sable brown markings—wide patches, not spots. Where Moon is all the lady, he is a real boy. He will bear his scars forever, but that just makes him more ours. He is terrified of thunder. I believe the sound of the rifle in the boxcar must still be sharp in his ear. When it thunders, no one can get near him but me.

As skittish as he is, the whole town, one by one, has come to see him. I have the feeling that they do not want others to know that they have come, except for the Torgerson children who stop by every day with something for him, a carrot or apple or a piece of sugar candy, and sometimes they bring something for me. Yesterday they brought a whole sack of cookies, all for me, as if I am not getting fat and sleek on Lena's cooking. I have never eaten so much, or so often. I must get away while I can still fit through the barn door. (Even Feather has put on weight, and I have not seen him prowl for mice lately. Lena is stuffing him with cream and chicken. I tell him not to get used to it.)

Anyway, the others who have come around include Mrs. Axel Kranhold saying she came to call on Lena and "while I'm here I thought I'd peek in on you..." Well, she peeked in and did not visit Lena at all, as I suspected she had no intention of doing. Hank and Orville Ackerman came by to tell me they would paint your fence and keep your grass scythed down while you were gone. The O'Gradies brought me a bag of oats. Said it was on the house. I have even seen all

the members of the school board except Axel...he must
have felt his wife's coming was the same as his coming
himself—and in a way it is, as one is as odious as
the other—and one was enough. Even Lena's minister
came by. I think the only one who has not is the
Catholic priest, Father Nicolay.

It did not take me long to realize that neither I nor
Skydog were the object of all this attention, but you
and Mary. They will not come right out and ask all the
questions that must be on their minds, and I will not
help them by volunteering anything. I say only that
you are both well and enjoying Philadelphia in spite
of the rain.

Your Jordis

PS. Tell Betty that her brothers and sisters miss
her. Especially Alice. Though Alice has perked up of
late due to the regular visits from Dr. Llewellyn. Alvinia
had invited him to dinner some time ago, hoping, I
believe, to spark something between him and Betty.
He took to Alice instead and she to him, though Alvinia
frets that Alice is not serious or even tempered enough
to be a doctor's wife. Lena has told her that that will
be his problem!

Are Jimmy Saul and Leonard still bringing you fish
and game? I told Joe to make sure to let them know
I would not be there for a while. I know you can fish
but, my dear, when will you let me teach you to shoot?
Then I do not have to worry about your starving to
death. You cannot live on fry bread and potatoes.

I asked Father Flagstad about the Lesnars, the
poor family who unwittingly brought the plague upon

*the Red Sand. He said they suffered with the disease
for a long time but were lovingly cared for by Mrs.
Tollefson at Doctor Llewellyn's place. The children
died first, then Ina, and last, Reuben. Father Gregory
buried them in the Catholic graveyard in Wheat Lake.*

The first night that Gleevie worked for Oscar Kaiser,
he did what he was told without understanding what
he was doing or why. Laying lengths of pipe here,
moving the derrick, adjusting the ropes, putting a
huge tub in place that Oscar said was for the mud.
What mud? Gleevie would find out. He nearly got his
hand smashed under a heavy plank. Oscar slid it off
the back of the rig. He'd tossed it really, and Gleevie
moved his hand just in time so only the tip of his
middle finger got caught. Tears stung his eyes, it hurt
so bad. Oscar said, "Pay attention. You'll get hurt."
When Gleevie, wincing against the pain of his finger,
picked up the plank to move it into position, he was
amazed that Oscar had lifted and threw it with one
hand. Gleevie could hardly lift it with two.

They broke no ground that night but, as it was
after dark, Mrs. Hanson invited them in for supper.
They washed up at the old well, which provided only
a mean trickle, and went into the house for the best
meal Gleevie had eaten since he was kicked off the
threshing crew. Mrs. Hanson apologized for serving
them left-overs from dinner, but as Gleevie looked at
the table laid with sliced ham, cold chicken, pickled
herring, potatoes fried brown and crisp with plenty
of onions, fresh-baked bread and butter, and yellow
cake for dessert, he still thought this wasn't going to
be a bad job.

An extra man came with Oscar that first night. A man who resembled him, but even with his white hair, Gleevie could tell the man was younger than Oscar by a couple of years, maybe. He had a wet stogie rammed into the corner of his mouth, and where Oscar's voice was a deep growl, the new man's voice was like sand being swirled in a tin cup. He was not surprised to learn they were brothers.

Walter, for that was the brother's name, stayed for supper, even though once he had handed the reins of the team over to Mr. Hanson's older sons, except to add sugar to his coffee, he didn't lift a finger. He must have figured that, brother or not, driving the team was work enough for one who wasn't on the payroll.

Gleevie noticed that Mrs. Hanson had seemed pretty concerned with Oscar's brother. "How are you doin' now, Walter? How's it going?"

Oh, doin' pretty good, was all he'd say. He ate enough of her cooking for two men who'd worked all day. Gleevie just watched, ate his own good share, and kept quiet unless spoken to, which he wasn't.

After supper, Walter rode back with them on a horse borrowed from Mr. Hanson. He left the horse at the livery stable and went to the depot to wait for the midnight train to take him back to Charity. Oscar didn't wait with him. The brothers didn't seem to have much to say to each other.

That first night was also the last night Gleevie shared a bottle and a game with Jack Frye. Thereafter, Gleevie got to the bunkhouse, shed his clothes down to his underwear and fell on his bed like a puppet with its strings cut. No bottle. No game. It was just as well because his whiskey money now went to Mattie

229

Olson for regular washing since he came home filthy every night.

The work was harder than anything he had ever done. His muscles ached from pulling pipe wrenches all day, from hanging on to the handles that with each rise and fall of the derrick rammed the drill bit deeper into the earth. He felt every jolt, every jar. He didn't know if he was pushing it or riding it. Either way, the blisters rose on his hands and broke and burned. His middle finger, where it was smashed by the plank, was black and it looked like he'd lose the nail. Oscar never asked him how it was. Guess he could see how it was.

The well was lubricated with mud and by early afternoon he was usually covered with mud and grease, and then he began to freeze in the chilly May winds. Once, when he was especially soaked through and the wind was especially sharp, Mr. Hanson gave him a dry shirt to go home in. It added to his washing bill with Mattie, but it was worth it.

He got no breakfast because Oscar insisted they be always up and on the road before daybreak in order to be at the farm by dawn. Oscar saved food from his supper the night before to eat in the morning. But Gleevie didn't have money for supper, because Oscar would only pay him by the week. So the only meal Gleevie got was dinner. He was grateful it was a good one. Mrs. Hanson must have noticed, because one afternoon, she came out with something wrapped in a piece of newspaper and handed it to him behind Oscar's back. Gleevie nodded gratefully, slipped the parcel into his pocket and had thick slices of bread and butter that night for his supper. After that, Mrs.

Hanson managed to slip him something—whether bread or a couple boiled eggs—every day.

Oscar and Gleeve didn't talk much. Oscar had no gift of gab and Gleeve was just too tired. It wasn't like farm work, where you could always sneak off and grab a nap in the corner of the hayloft or behind a windbreak. Here he was at the well machine, under Oscar's eye from daybreak to dusk. He ate with the man, slept with the man, and did everything but take his shits with him. Gleevie worked because he was afraid not to. The truth was, something about Oscar Kaiser, one arm or no, scared the bejeezus out of Gleevie. And he couldn't leave because he couldn't collect his pay till the end of the week. There was no other work to be had. Eddie Hansmeier was back with Snuce, and he knew better than to ask Jack for a loan unless he wanted his jaw broken.

They worked on Saturday, and Oscar would have worked through Sunday, if Mr. Hanson had not asked them not to, it being the Sabbath.

Oscar paid him Saturday night. Gleevie had supper at the Blue Bird with Jack, and then he slept most of Sunday. He thought he could get through another week.

Gleevie worked doggedly for four more days and sighed in relief when they struck water. Then they had to move the rig to the Zimmerman place a few miles west of Wheat Lake and begin again. It didn't matter that they had finished a job and were starting a new one, Gleevie still had to wait till Saturday for his wages. So he stayed on.

The day they moved the rig, they returned to the bunkhouse early. No supper had been offered them at the Zimmerman's. Jack, as usual, was lying on his back, smoking his cigarette. "Hi ya," he said.

Gleevie looked at him with envy. Jack had saved money from his time at the Indian agency. Jack Frye was smart all right.

Oscar changed his shirt. He was likely going to the Blue Bird for supper. He didn't invite company, and Gleevie had no desire to go with him. He sat down on the edge of his bunk. He'd wait till Oscar went out before he suggested to Jack a walk to Mattie's, pick up his washing, and then maybe some supper. Gleevie had the money now for a cheap bite at Snuce's if he didn't have more than one glass of beer to wash it down.

"Saw that squaw some weeks ago," Jack drawled.

Gleevie knew who he meant by *that squaw*. "Oh, yeah? You just remembrin it now?"

"No, but when I remembered before, you was sleepin'." Jack took a deep drag of his cigarette and watched the smoke plume from his mouth. "Right after the thaw. Saw her over there at the agency with them other Indians gettin' their annuities, then sashayin' over to the store, big as you please. I followed her over there. She didn't see me, but I kept my eye on her all right. Buying some of that flowery cloth that the ladies make their dresses out of. What's she doing with that stuff? I says to myself. Never seen her wear anything like that. So I just watch her. Puttin' on airs. Now I suppose she's going to dress like a white woman. Maybe she was buyin' for that old maid school teacher. That skinny bitch—I'd like to give her what for."

"Well, you're going to have to wait to give her anything," Oscar rumbled from the corner, making Gleevie jump. He'd forgotten for a minute that Oscar was there.

Jack propped himself up on his elbow and took another puff, then delicately tapped the ash of his cigarette into his dirt can. "Why's that then?"

"She's gone." Oscar tucked in his clean shirt.

"The hell you say." Jack was interested.

"Uh huh." Oscar put on his jacket. Gleeve noticed how Oscar performed his tasks, with more method than a two-handed person; nothing was fumbled. Nothing was missed.

"Gone where?" Jack narrowed his eyes against the stream of smoke rising from his cigarette.

"Back east. Visiting her people in Philadelphia. Took my sister-in-law with her and one of the Torgerson kids." Oscar put his hat on and went out.

That Saturday, when Oscar paid Gleevie for the week, Gleevie thought seriously about taking the money and running. He could go to the next county where nobody knew him and get some farm work, working his way west to the gold mine. But Oscar said he would add an extra dollar to Gleevie's wages if, after the Zimmerman well was sunk, he would help him drive the rig back to Charity. Gleevie, with some foot-shuffling, told Oscar that he wouldn't mind at all, but he had orders from Sheriff Sully not to show up in Charity, ever again. He explained how he had just been talking to that squaw and the Sheriff had misunderstood and warned him off. He didn't mention that the Sheriff had shot him. Oscar laughed. It was the first time Gleeve had seen Oscar even crack a smile.

"I can handle Dennis Sully if it comes to that. Just drive the rig till we meet up with my regular man and you can go your own way."

Gleevie agreed. But before they could do that, they had to find water on the Zimmerman place. After hitting rock and having to start a new hole, he was in despair it would happen.

Ed and Martha Zimmerman weren't like the Hansons. The food was not as plentiful or as good. They weren't pleasant family people. They had kids all right, a bunch of them, but they were sort of a ragtag outfit with bad teeth and sour looks. And unlike the Hansons, they did not make Oscar's hard nature easier to chew.

When he didn't do something the right way or fast enough, Oscar didn't get mad. It was worse. He got a look—like he really didn't expect Gleeve to do any better. *Hire a fool. Get a fool.* That was Oscar's motto. Even in silence, he made it clear that he only bore with the situation because he knew it was temporary and because he enjoyed watching Gleevie wilt, little by little, more and more, each passing day. Every night, Gleevie dreamed the same dream with minor variations: he was a fly in a web; the spider fed off him and when he opened his eyes and peered through the filmy stuff that bound him he saw the hungry face of Oscar Kaiser.

There was one particularly bad day. Oscar had a pipe in the vise and was tightening a fitting, coupling it to another pipe, and he demanded a certain type of wrench to finish the job. Gleevie still had trouble distinguishing one wrench from another; but for size, they all looked pretty much the same to him. He looked at the pipes Oscar was working on and bent over the tool tray to try to find the wrench he thought would best fit. But he was taking too long and he knew it. He began to sweat and then he felt a boot in his backside and heard a familiar grumble, "I can't wait all day." Oscar had kicked him, not hard enough to push him over, just enough to make him lurch forward and stumble to keep his footing. Oscar grabbed the right wrench and laughed. Ed Zimmerman laughed, too. Gleevie burned. It gave a man a bad feeling to be treated the way you'd treat a colored man, or an Indian, or a dog. It wasn't right.

The next day, his hands wet and freezing, he fumbled his grip on a screwdriver and dropped it right down the drill shaft. Oscar just grunted, took another screwdriver from the tool tray, said, "Wipe your hands," and handed it to him.

Lena found Jordis in the barn. The barn had already been cleaned. Jordis was sitting on a hay bale oiling the leather horse tack. No stiff piece of hide ever touched a horse in Jordis's care. Lena smiled approvingly. While Jordis stayed with them, she had oiled Old Tom's bridles and halters till they were soft as velvet.

Lena had walked all the way out to Gustie's place with a pillowcase slung over her shoulder and carrying her daughter most of the way. She'd done this walk before. She liked it in good weather. She could sort of let her mind wander away from her own troubles. Today the air was crisp and dry. Good day for planting, she mused. Everyone hoped for good weather. If the farmers failed, everybody failed. Even though she lived in town now, she had been a poor farmer's daughter. She never got over her feeling of being directly connected to the seasons, to the weather. Out here, that connection meant life or death.

Jordis got up when she saw Lena in the open barn door. She put down the halter she was working on and held her arms out for Gracia. "Whooo, little one," she said softly. Gracia toddled forward and allowed herself to be held up in the air and kissed. Jordis put her down gently again. Gracia was not a smiling child, not like Deborah, Winnie's girl, but she did seem to like Jordis.

Lena sat herself down on an empty cream can and let Gracia toddle around the barn. "I think Skydog still knows me. He came up to the fence and nodded his head. Do you think he remembers me?"

"He does. And if he hadn't, he'd have let me know there was a stranger around. He does that."

"That's a good thing. So he's doing all right, then. And you look fine, too. I wasn't sure you'd still be out here. But I thought, if you were gone, I could just stay here awhile. Gustie always said I could. I don't mean to barge in on you."

"Lena, you are welcome here. Whether Gustie is here or not."

"Really?"

"Really." Jordis returned to her seat and picked up the halter. "Is there anything bothering you, Lena?"

"Oh, no. I just wanted to see how you were getting along and bring you this." She pointed to the pillowcase.

Jordis said, "Do you want to go in the house and have some coffee?"

"No, I'll have some water from the bucket." Lena got up and helped herself. "It's nice out here. And Gracia can't hurt anything. I can let her be without fussing at her."

She sat down again and with two fingers wiped away the water dribbling down the corners of her mouth. A whippoorwill called in the distance. Her eyes wandered the inside of the barn and rested on the memory bundle and its tripod in front of the south window. "What *is* that?"

"It used to belong to Dorcas."

"Oh. I saw it in the barn at home... I just thought it was some of your things that you liked to keep off the floor. Why do you keep it out here?"

"I think Dorcas would like it out here."

Lena thought for a minute. "Yes. She probably would. I like barns myself. Especially where there are horses. Before I got married, I always worked in houses where there was a baby, and I always liked visiting a barn where there's a horse. The smell of horses makes me feel comforted. Safe, like. When I was a little girl, we had a horse that wouldn't let anything happen to me. I didn't have to be afraid of anything when Dolly was by. Too bad she didn't fit in our kitchen! The only one I ever had to be afraid of was Ma."

"Your mother?"

"Oh, yes. 'Spare the rod and spoil the child.' She believed in that like one of the commandments."

Lena kept talking, keeping one eye on Gracia who was quietly amusing herself in a pile of straw. "I felt those whippings, I can tell you! My sisters, now...Ella and Ragna...they never got whipped. They were such goodie goodies. They never took my part in anything. Even when they knew I hadn't done something, whatever it was, and that they'd been the ones to do a thing, they always stood by and let me get the whipping. I got my own back though, once. I was too young at the time to think it, but I sure have had a lot of satisfaction ever since. Ragna's always been mad at me for it, too." Lena chuckled.

"What did you do?" Jordis was genuinely curious.

"Bit her toe off." Lena's blue eyes snapped with glee. "We never had shoes to wear till there was snow on the ground. Ma and my sisters were sitting at the table. I was—oh, about four or five. I crawled under the table and bit Raggy's big toe off. That was the only time I never got whipped because Ma was too busy. She slapped the toe back on with a wet towel and ice and took her to the doctor. We lived only a couple miles from town at that time. And Ma must have got it just right or that doctor did something just right, but that toe grew back together. It's crooked and she can't wiggle it. It's kind of deformed looking." Lena crooked her forefinger to illustrate. "But it's there. Nobody sees her blame toe anyway, probably not even Pete, she's such a priss. I don't know how she ever got those children." Lena laughed. "And every time it rains her toe hurts and she thinks of me and gets so blame mad." They both laughed.

238

The gray cat, who had been lounging on a crossbeam leapt down gracefully and took after something only he saw. They watched him streak outside. Gracia tried to follow but gave up as soon as the cat disappeared from sight.

Lena gnawed the tip of her forefinger.

"So how have you been, Lena?"

"Oh, can't complain."

"How is Will?"

"He's fine. Got a lot of work now, which is a blessing. So he's gone before it's light and back after dark. He just has time to eat and sleep and go again. But that's the way the well business is in the summer, you know." She paused and stared a moment at nothing, her mind had wandered. Then she came back. "Heard from Gustie?"

Jordis was so used to the charade by now that she didn't hesitate. "Yes, I got a letter yesterday."

"How's she doing?"

"She is eager to come back. As soon as the baby is born and she sees Mary settled in, she'll be back."

"Well, that won't be till the end of July, probably."

"Yes, but Philadelphia is lovely in the spring and she will be able to leave before the worst heat of the summer."

"You've been to Philadelphia, haven't you."

"Yes."

"You went to school there. To college."

"Near there."

"Nnn hmm." Changing the subject, Lena reached for her pillowcase. "I baked bread this morning." She held out a loaf wrapped in a clean, flour-sack dish towel. "And I brought you some rhubarb sauce. You like rhubarb, don't you?"

"If there is sugar on it."

"Oh, my sauce is nice and sweet." She held up a jar of sauce that glowed pink in the soft light of the barn. She put it back in the pillowcase. "You've got two loaves of bread here and three jars of sauce." She closed up the bag and looked out the barn door. "Iver's late today because he's got the oxen pulling the cream wagon. They're slower than molasses in January, but with all the rain we had yesterday, some of the roads are too muddy to get by on with his heavy wagon. The horses would have a heck of a time, but the oxen pull through anything."

They stared down the empty road that lay flat and straight till it curved over the rim of the earth. Jordis asked, "Can you tell me why his oxen have women's names?"

"Oh, that's a good one!" The locals no longer thought anything of three of Iver's oxen bearing feminine names unless a new arrival questioned it. Then they sometimes told the story, but more often did not. Old timers especially liked for people to wonder, like they wondered about snipes down south and jackalopes farther west, so they could wonder why Iver's oxen, by definition male, were called Sally, Kate, and Daisy.

"Kind of a cute story...when I heard it, it made me like Iver a lot more. You know he's quiet. I like a man that has something to say for himself so you know what he's thinking, but Iver seldom says a word. Anyway, it was right after Ruby came to town and they weren't married yet. Her family were distant cousins to Iver's family. They lived in Chicago and were poor as dirt. They sent her out here hoping to marry her off to Iver. She wasn't forced, as I understand it. She had a return ticket in her pocket if she didn't like him. Lena paused to swat at a fly that buzzed too close to her face. "Well, she was a sweet little thing—just sixteen years old—had never been out of the city before. She was staying at Koenig's... Iver paid for that...and he was kind of courting her. So, one day she went with him to the livestock auction at the fairgrounds because at that time he had only one yearling bull—that was Joe—and he was looking to build a good team. So he bid on some calves and bought three that he liked and when they went to get them, they looked so cute in their pen, and Ruby had never seen a calf before and let them suck on her fingers the way they do and was so tickled, she asked Iver if she could name them. Of course, he must have been happy to hear that, because everyone could tell he was head over heels for her but she hadn't said much, so this kind of let him know that she might stay. So, he says sure you can name them...anything you want. And she says, well this one looks like a Kate, and she went down the line, naming them Kate, Sally, and Daisy, and the men standing around began to snicker. One mean old fool there said Iver better be careful of marrying a girl who couldn't tell a bull calf from a heifer...he'd never get any children, and they all snickered and hooted and Ruby started to cry. But Iver said it made no difference...she'd named them what she wanted and that's what they'd be called. And by jinx, don't you know Ruby and Iver got married the next week, and she helped him hand raise those oxen so they are the best, gentlest team and will do anything for him. They're still called by their maiden names as you might say, and Iver and Ruby have three nice boys so I guess it didn't matter what she missed seeing on those calves." Lena laughed.

"Lena, you tell a good story. Indians are good story tellers, so I know."

Lena had to think a moment to accept this as a compliment. But she did and said with a smile, "Well, thank you. Iver's really late today. I planned on riding back with him and not bothering you all day."

"You don't bother me, Lena. I like the company."

"Really? I might take you up on that cup of coffee then."

"If you don't mind making it, you can go up to the house and I'll just finish out here."

"I don't mind. I'll open a jar of this sauce. It'll go good."

Lena left and Jordis hung up the leather tack she had finished. She took her knife out of her boot and cut the twine around a bale of hay and filled the mangers. She heard the horses in the corral snort, and then Skydog made a sound peculiar to him. A low-pitched whicker that held both anxiety and warning. It couldn't be Iver. Skydog had gotten used to him and the familiar rattle of the cream wagon. He hadn't made that sound for Iver in weeks.

She walked out into the sun and greeted Orville and Hank Ackerman. They had come to keep their promise to scythe down the tall grasses around Gustie's house. Gustie liked Orville and didn't seem to mind Hank. Jordis thought they were both dull-witted, mean-eyed white men. Maybe not Orville, not

242

yet. Jordis knew a lot of white men. Only a few did she refer to as "white men." The term encompassed all that was stereotypically bad about the European colonizers. Once she even referred to a full-blood Dakotah as a white man because she didn't like him. She never spoke that part of her mind to anyone but Gustie and Little Bull.

Jordis greeted them with a smile and told them they were just in time for coffee and Lena's good rhubarb sauce. The scything could wait a few minutes.

Hank was getting heavier and heavier. His middle had expanded to barrel proportions and yet he climbed down off the wagon with almost as much agility as his eighteen-year old son.

Orville, once he was on the ground, looked toward the corral where Skydog was pacing back and forth nervously. Moon stood quietly in the shade of the lean-to Jordis had put up since there were no trees in the pasture. "He's lookin' good, isn't he?"

Jordis nodded.

Hank said, "Well, there's that fella...Cloudhound... what is it you call him?"

Jordis said between her teeth, "Skydog."

"Oh, that's right." Hank smiled mischievously at his son. "Why don't you go over there and pet that horse?"

Orville grinned back, "Because I'm not tired of livin'."

They both laughed.

"His staying behind that fence is just being polite." Hank nodded to Jordis. "That crazy horse could sail over that top rail like nothing if he wanted to."

"Then I guess you'd better not give him a reason. Go on up to the house. Lena's making coffee. I'll be right behind you."

She turned to finish up in the barn and heard Hank tell Orville, "She better castrate that sonofabitch before somebody has to shoot him."

Her thoughts about castration at that moment did not apply to her horse.

They had been more than two weeks at the Zimmerman place. It felt like two months. But it was finally over. Gleevie helped shut down the rig, hitched the team, and drove them back, silently—Oscar didn't seem to notice—for several hours. They had started before sun-up and were met about noon at a crossroads some way from Charity by a pleasant enough fellow who introduced himself as Shorty Larson. He tied his horse to the side of the rig and changed places with Gleevie on the seat.

Oscar got down and walked out from the rig and fished in his pocket. There was no farewell glad-to-know you handshake. Not even a thank you. He handed him his pay, fifty cents short. "Where's the rest?" Gleevie asked looking at the bills in his hand, a pitiful sum for the week he'd just spent, freezing and starving and being laughed at and kicked like a dog.

"You gotta pay for that screw driver," said Oscar.

"But it was old. It had rust on it. It wadn't worth no half dollar!"

"But now I still gotta buy me a new one and take an afternoon off to go get it. Take it or leave it."

Gleeve just looked at the money in his hand, and Oscar turned his back on him.

Gleevie got on his horse and took the road north to Charity. The rig, with Oscar and Shorty, kept going east. Gleeve felt like he had never felt before. Oh, Jack Frye had gotten pissed and punched him a couple of times. But there was something man-to-man about that. A good square punch in the head. A punch you could return, or not, and no hard feelings. But this was a slow drip of sarcasm, of making you feel bad; the slow drip drip drip of disregard. He felt like a bug. No. Worse. He felt like a woman. That woman on the Arkansas border who he saw a couple of times. When she had served her purpose you threw your money on the table or the bed and left without a backward glance. Gleevie felt like that, and the feelings churned as he got closer to Charity. Maybe Oscar wasn't afraid of Sully, but Gleevie didn't want to get locked up or worse, so, even though the straightest shot to the road west and the easy pickings of the gold mine was up Main Street, he didn't want to push his luck. The thought of Sully taking the side of that squaw only added to the fires burning in his gut. Gleeve angled around the town on the east side. The detour took him right past Gustie's house.

Iver never did show up, so it turned out to be a good thing for Lena that Orville and Hank had. After they had drunk most of the coffee she'd brewed and ate all of her rhubarb sauce, they took a few whacks at the weeds around Gustie's house and offered to take Lena home. Now Jordis was alone again in the barn and settling her horses in for the evening.

She heard his first footfall into the barn. Skydog had nickered and stamped his feet restlessly at his approach, so she was not surprised that someone stepped through the side door, only surprised by who it was. Gleeve Pruitt.

He held a gun and it was pointed at her. "Don't reach for your knife or I'll shoot your hand off and then by god we'll see what you'll be reachin' for."

She took him in as if a poisonous snake had just risen in front of her—she became suddenly, deeply still.

He was just inside the door and he moved in a little closer. "I asked last time, and I was willin' to pay. Now I ain't askin' and I ain't payin'. Now you can reach down, ginger-like, and take that knife out of your boot slow and lay it down on the floor."

He took another step forward, keeping his gun level, pointed at her. "I will shoot you by god."

Jordis said softly, "You look hungry. I will bring you something to eat."

"I'm tellin' *you* what to do! Put the knife on the floor or I'll pull the trigger."

She had no doubt that he would shoot her. She had survived a bullet once before. Maybe she wasn't supposed to, and now that bullet had finally caught up with her again. This wasn't how she expected it would end. But she was not going to give up her knife just because he had a gun pointed at her. He might kill her but he couldn't tell her what to do. "You will not get what you want while I am alive," she said.

For a moment, she thought that he might drop his aim slightly, relax slightly, but he didn't. "You're brave, I'll give you that," he said.

246

She said with less softness, "You can walk out of here with nothing on your head, or you can kill me. Those are your two choices."

He snorted softly. "Shit. I'll shoot you."

Her mind slipped into a higher, more perfect plane of stillness, where she felt Dorcas's presence strongly. So, she would end not as the keeper of her soul, but as its companion. The irony was not unpleasing. All her thoughts rose and fell in less than a heartbeat.

"Now lose the knife."

"No."

"I'll kill you."

"You will have to."

"I ain't particular. I can take you with a bullet in you as well as not. I ain't the sort who needs the fight to get it up."

"Kill me then." She was bored with him now.

He took another step forward, placing himself in the shaft of light coming through the small west window directly in front of Skydog's stall. Jordis saw the light suddenly flash off the barrel of the gun at the same time as she heard the soft *chink* of the hammer as Gleeve cocked it. She didn't have time to begin her next breath or think *Dorcas* before Skydog screamed and smashed through the stall-gate.

She saw Gleevie pause in mid-breath in the first infinitely small fraction of a second when the edge of that scream hit his eardrums. Just his eyes moved toward the sound to behold a horse. Just a horse. Now on top of him. And for Gleevie, by the time he realized it was the horse whose blast of rage was directed at him, there was nothing more.

In the same moment, she saw Skydog make one hop forward, his hooves striking Pruitt, knocking the gun out of his hand, probably breaking his rib cage and bringing him down. The gun went off with a *crack!* as it hit the floor, firing the bullet harmlessly into the north wall, and Skydog, half kneeling over the man, grabbed him by the neck with his teeth and lifted him and shook him.

Quick as a snake, inexorable and crushing as an avalanche, Skydog had struck, and even she, who could have slipped her knife between Gleevie's ribs without losing her smile, was stunned.

She had heard stories from tribal elders, those who remembered the tales of their grandfathers who, as boys, saw the wild herds—how a stallion was capable of grabbing a sick or injured colt and killing it like this. But she never thought to see it herself. And never like this. From the time he burst out of his stall to when he stood over the lifeless broken body of Gleeve Pruitt, it was less than eight seconds.

She had been calm as the bottom of Shoonkatoh. Now she had to control her own trembling to find her voice. "Skydog!" she commanded raggedly. "Back." The horse stepped back. She was vibrating from head to foot but managed to grasp his halter and lead him out of the barn. She stood for a time, her arm over his neck, leaning against him, her forehead pressed into his white mane. He trembled and blew out through his nostrils. They remained so until their breathing and heart rates had slowed. Then she lifted her head and looked around her. Moon was nervously pacing the perimeter of the corral. She heard the swallows under the eaves of the barn cheeping, and she wondered for

248

the first time how they escaped the claws of the cat. The sun shone down soft and warm. She heard the far-off bark of a dog.

She knew what she had to do. She could not put Skydog back in the barn. In his current state he could jump the corral fence as easily as he had broken his stall gate. She had only ridden him once. She pulled herself onto his back for the second time and galloped him in to Charity.

In front of the sheriff's office she did not dismount. The door was open. She called, "Sheriff Sully!"

He came to the door, his tin coffee cup in his hand.

"Hello, Jordis."

"Come with me."

The sheriff looked at her face and the sweating horse. He tossed the dregs of his coffee in the weeds beside the wooden walk, left the cup on the windowsill, and reached inside the door for his hat.

Chapter 15: June 1901

"COULD ONE OF YOUR BOYS take me out to Gustie's place?"

Alvinia, her hands deep in dishwater, took a long look at Lena standing in her kitchen doorway and gave a yell, "Kermit!"

Gracia leaned in to Lena, clutching her skirt.

Alvinia's gangly sixteen-year-old, clad in too-big hand-me down overalls, sloped around the corner.

"Take Mrs. Kaiser out to Miss Roemer's place and then come right back. Daddy needs you at the locker this afternoon."

"Yeah, Ma, but Miss Roemer ain't there..."

"*Isn't* there," Alvinia corrected sharply as she wiped her hands on a towel.

Lena said to the boy, "I know. I want to speak to Jordis. She's still there, I believe."

"Sure. Team's hitched."

"Wait a minute. These are still warm from the oven." Alvinia dumped a plate of breakfast rolls into a bag and added a loaf of bread. "For Jordis. Help yourself, too." She brought the bag over to Lena and gave it to her, and with the other hand, which she took from behind her back, gave Gracia a cookie. The girl took it and stuck it in her mouth. "Say 'thank you,' honey," Lena instructed. The child made an inarticulate squeak through the mouthful of cookie and Alvinia said, "You're welcome."

Skydog raised his head, and the new light in his eyes lifted Lena's heart, if only for a moment. He shared the corral with another horse—a small brown gelding that Lena didn't recognize.

"Thank you, Kermit. And thank your mama for me again. Here, hang on to Gracia." She clambered down from the wagon and reached up for her daughter.

"Sure, Mrs. Kaiser. Want me to come get you later?"

"No. I don't know when I'm going back, exactly."

Lena went into the house. Fresh flowers sprouted from a mason jar of water on the table by the window. She could tell Gustie was not the one living here now. It was too tidy. Gustie had a tendency to leave books and papers about and dishes in the sink. Lena left Alvinia's rolls and bread on the table and dropped her own small bundle on the chair. Gracia's face was flushed, so she removed the child's sweater and draped it over the chair back.

Shifting Gracia from one hip to the other, Lena walked a mile east on a back road that was little more than a wagon path. The deepest ruts were filled with muddy water. She stepped or, when she had to, jumped over them. She arrived at water's edge, removed her shoes, tied the laces together and slung them around her neck, and waded north until she came to a smooth sandy patch, a beach artificially constructed by fishermen who needed a place to launch their boats, otherwise impossible through the weeds and cattails, mud and tangled rushes that hugged Dryback Lake. Lena sat on a skinny log, what was left of a cottonwood that had snapped off in the wind and had been either hauled or blown here. There were no trees growing around Dryback.

The sun was high and warm. Gracia in only her diaper and a shirt played in the shallow water as it lapped around her in gentle waves. Followed by their harems of smaller brown females, drake mallards turned their shiny blue-green heads to look at them and kept swimming. A long-legged killdeer picked through the sand at a distance from them, cautious but not deterred from pursuing its livelihood. Farther away, rounded piles of brown twigs and moss and leaves marked the industry of muskrats. Clam bubbles rose through the clear water from tiny holes in the sand. Seagulls mewed above her.

Clutching her prayer like a life rope, Lena tucked her head down and leaned her forehead into her tightly clasped hands, her body clenched in bitter tears before her God. Her world, today, had come to an end.

When Jack Frye first got the news, he was in his corner of the Spittoon, slow-nursing a bottle of whiskey and hoping somebody would come in who was willing to lose money at poker. So far he'd had no takers.

He only half listened to the talk around him, but pricked up his ears at something Harold Bjordahl at the bar said to Snuce: "Hey, I think that guy worked for you for awhile, last winter, didn't he? That guy—Puckett or Parker or—"

"Pruitt. The guy worked for me was Gleeve Pruitt."

"Yeah. Him."

"What about him?" Snuce, not much interested, was gathering up dirty glasses into his wash pan.

"He got himself killed a couple weeks ago."

Snuce paused in his bar-keeping duties to look at Harold.

"Ja. Got killed by a horse." Harold took a deep satisfying drink of his beer and wiped his mouth with his sleeve.

Jack got up from his chair. "What?"

Harold Bjordahl turned around and addressed Jack, happy to have someone more interested in conversation than was the barkeep. "You know him?"

"Yeah. Gleevie. If that's the one you're talking about. Used to play cards with him."

"Got killed by a horse." Harold lifted his glass again. It was a warm day and the beer was cool.

Jack shook his head and chuckled. "Well, by God! That damn kid couldn't find his way out of a snow bank with a shovel and a blowtorch. He gets himself kilt by a horse. How'd it happen? He fall off'n it?"

"No. The horse belongs to that squaw. The one that—"

"I know the one." Jack suddenly did not think it was so funny. "That white horse she always rides?"

"Different one. Anyway, she's in her barn there, see? And the horse is there, and this Pruitt fella goes after her. With a gun. Sheriff ruled it self-defense. Or—whatever you'd call it. Ja. They found just enough money in his pocket to bury him." Harold Bjordahl chugged the rest of his beer. "Well, I better go see if the missus is through at the store. We've got to be getting back for chores." He belched grandly, put a coin on the bar and left the Spittoon.

"I never knew he had a gun," mused Jack, returning to his seat in the corner. He didn't feel much like talking any more or playing cards. He poured himself another drink. The more he thought about what Harold Bjordahl had just told him, the madder he got. The more whiskey he drank, the sadder he got. By the end of the afternoon, he was crying into his last glass of sour mash, vowing to avenge the death of the best goddam friend he ever had at the hands of that murdering savage bitch.

Snuce threw him out.

Jordis found bread and rolls on the table, a pillowcase and a baby sweater on the chair. She checked the barn. It was empty. In the middle of the yard between house, barn, and pasture, she stopped. Then she mounted the white horse again and took the rutted trail to Dryback.

As she approached the lake, she heard what sounded like a wounded animal. When she got closer, she realized it was the sound of a woman crying. Jordis slid off Moon's back letting the reins drag, and padded in soft moccasins toward the sound. She saw

Gracia first. Jordis stopped a few feet away from her. Neither mother nor child was aware of her presence. Gracia stood up and tottered forward, following the line of suds that headed the lapping waves. Then, she wailed and turned to her mother who, self-absorbed, was slow to react. In two bounds, Jordis was at Gracia's side. She picked her up around her waist. Lena, startled, asked, "Is she all right?"

Jordis examined the child's foot. "She stepped on a piece of shell and cut herself. It is not deep. Just scared her."

"Come here, Precious. Mommy'll kiss it."

Jordis placed the child in Lena's outstretched arms. Lena lifted the foot and kissed it. Gracia reduced her volume to a whimper. "There, there, you're all right now." The youngster forgot her hurt and squirmed. Lena let her go and she toddled back to the undulating line of foam. She ran after it, and back again, squealing as it chased her.

Jordis sat down next to Lena on the log and watched Gracia play. *All our hurts should be so easily forgotten,* she thought. She watched the flapping of some ducks taking flight, some chasing others away. A melee of squawking and quacking and flapping ensued over territorial or nuptial rights, and then the water was peaceful again.

She knew enough of Lena's history to suspect the cause of her tears. Jordis had lost a brother to whiskey. She had nothing but sympathy for Lena. She let some time pass before she asked, "Will drinking again?"

Lena's shoes were still slung around her neck. She raised them over her head and thrust them at Jordis saying, "Look at my shoes!" and started to cry again. Jordis took the shoes and turned them over in her hands. They had holes in the sides, the heels were worn thin and they were lined with stiff paper.

"I said to Will I need new shoes and he told me he would get paid for the well he just finished last night and I should go to O'Grady's and pick out what I wanted—that was yesterday—and he'd pay for them this morning on his way out to his next job." Lena wiped her nose with a handkerchief she took from her sleeve. "We don't have any more credit. There was only one pair Kenneth had that I liked and that fit me and I told him to keep them, and Will would come in and pay for them this morning. Fine. That was fine." She gestured emphatically with her wadded up handkerchief. "So, this morning as soon as I got the baby fed and dressed, I went to O'Grady's to get my new shoes and Kenneth looked at me so funny. And I said, 'What's the matter, didn't Will pay for the shoes?' And he said, 'Yes but Will took the shoes with him.' And then I went out on the street, just going to walk over to Alvinia's thinking maybe Will brought them back to the house and I saw *her*. That widow woman. You know her. Widow my eye! The town *whore*..." Lena cried so hard she almost choked on the words, "She was wearing my shoes!"

Jordis knew about Stella Ronshagen. She had appeared in Charity about a year ago, rented a house on the western outskirts of town and soon after, the whispers began to swell. She didn't take in washing or sewing but appeared to do well enough on favors extended to her by men who visited her after dark and left before daybreak.

A few local men, some married, were rumored to visit her when they left Leroy's Tavern with too much whiskey heating up their blood, but the rumors had not reached the amplitude of naming names. Jordis was heartsick at the thought of Will being one of these unnamed men.

"After Gracia was born I was in pretty bad shape for a long time...you know... I couldn't..." Lena stopped to wipe her eyes. "...so I began to wonder if sometimes when Will was drinking he didn't go see her. But I thought, no it couldn't be. Will would never do such a thing. Not even drunk. And in that condition, what woman—even a whore—would want him? But he's been drinking a lot lately. Oh, not the falling down kind of drunk this time—staying sober to go to work, and drinking after work and coming home later and later. But no, he's been there with that whore and he's bought her things when we pretty near don't have enough to eat sometimes. Where's all the money for the last two jobs I asked him and he says, 'Oh I had to buy more pipe or the price of acid went up or I lost a wrench.' Well he didn't lose any blame wrench and she got my shoes!"

"Are you sure he didn't take them to bring them home to you?"

"They were the only pair Kenneth had that I liked that fit!" Lena repeated angrily. "And you don't see me wearing them, do you?" She cried again, and Jordis listened with her eyes on the bank of clouds building up on the far side of Dryback.

"I have forgiven that man for everything—you have no idea. But not this! I'll keep his house and do his washing..." Lena shook her head in a *no no no* to

257

everything else that married life implied, "but he has soiled himself with that woman... I'll never have any more children."

Lena sobbed piteously. Her right fist was tucked hard and tight into her breast bone as if to stop the bleeding. Jordis no longer felt heartsick over Will Kaiser—she wanted to horsewhip him.

"Thank the Lord I've got my baby. But now, even if I wanted to go and clean other people's houses—and that's all I'm fit for—it'd be hard to find somebody to take me in with a baby. He's good to her and she loves her daddy. I can't take her off somewhere to grow up with strangers looking down their noses at her."

A wind had picked up. "Lena, there's a storm coming. You and Gracia ride Moon back to the house. I will follow you."

"What are you going to do?"

"Shoot our supper."

"That's fine." Lena got to her feet with resolve. "I can clean a duck as nice as anything. Give me something to do. I need something to do."

Jordis slapped her thigh. Moon came to her. She gave Lena a boost up on the mare's back, lifted Gracia up to her, and slid her rifle out of the soft pack strapped to Moon's back.

When Lena was well on the trail to the house, Jordis made her way back through the marsh grass and got a big drake in her sights. She never shot females.

Chapter 16: July 1901

*D*EAR GUSTIE,

 I thought I was beyond such anger, but I am not. I am so terribly angry.

 They have robbed us of everything. I thought, "What is there left for them to take?" But they have thought of something. The last thing we had of our own. Our names.

 The government has now ruled that Indians must have surnames.

 Indians must have surnames. I have been repeating that to myself all day. It makes me laugh and cry and want to paw the ground.

 Some of us, of course, mostly those who were baptized and entered into the church registries already had two names. But they had some choice.

 Now it is the law of the land.

 To Owen's credit, he was not happy bringing us this news. He left the papers with Little Bull at the Red

Sand and then rode to Charity to tell me himself, and also give himself an opportunity to visit the Torgersons while he was in town. I think he is sweet on Lavonne, who is turning sixteen sometime soon. Alvinia likes him well enough, but Lena says (because of his small size, his buck teeth, and his unfortunate, high-pitched voice) that she always feels like chasing him with a broom. I hope she never says that in front of Alvinia.

I can use the law to my advantage. I was given one white name at school, and I can now add an Indian one. I chose Manyroads, but am making it one word so they will accept it. Red Standing Horse is now James Redhorse. He took the name James to honor old Jimmy Saul. My heart fell for our chief. Adding a wasichu name to Little Bull is a loss in stature. Two nights ago, the chief appeared at my door and we pored over your books. If he has to have an Anglo name, he thought it should be a good one. He found one in Shakespeare— he liked Duncan, so he is now Duncan Little Bull. Owen says he will fill out the papers Duncan Little Bull and will add a note that Little Bull is the important family name of a chief and should not be shortened. We will see how far we get with that.

We have another horse. I took in Gleeve Pruitt's gelding. Found him wandering along the road after Dennis and Fritz took away the body. I call him Whisper. It fits him. He is a shy horse who has heard few kind words.

By now, I wanted to be at Crow Kills with you, but Dennis says I should stay around till the circuit judge comes through. It would look bad if I took off. So, here I am still, and there you are. How life conspires to keep us apart.

A note about Lena. As I wrote last time, she went back with Will, and I have since heard that Stella Ronshagen moved on west. Lena has come to visit me a few times since and never again mentioned the subject of her unhappiness. I want to warn you to expect a change in her, for I know you will, unlike some, be acutely aware of it. She is older, and there is a stiffness around her mouth. Some light has gone out of her. A softness, or pliancy, is gone. She lives now only for child and church. I think she still does not like me, although she likes me better with uncropped hair. All I would need to do to ease her discomfort is join the Lutheran church, then she would not mind me so much. It would not matter that I have not changed inside, because she now lives a life all of appearances. To the world, she is still a respectable married woman, and to Lena, being respectable is more important than being happy.

She would be surprised to know that I know precisely what she feels about me, and yet, I like her more and more. I should have trusted you. You see value where it exists. Where I see a lump of coal, you see a warm house or a diamond. Will stops by at times. They are seldom ever seen together anymore, and he is much the same as ever. I think he understands what he has done, but is at a loss as to how it happened. He comes to see the horses. I see these two people locked in a kind of misery that neither wished for, and for which they have no escape.

I hear the rattling of Iver's cream wagon. Will close and give this to him to post.

Love,

Jordis

Dear Mama,

Gustie and I are worried about Mary. It's nothing we can quite put a finger on. But she is always saying the Rosary. She always did pray a lot, but now she is in her own small world. If it were not that the three of us traveled together and share the same house, we probably would not notice. I don't know how to describe her exactly, but while being sweet and friendly as ever, she is withdrawn. It is more than what I have ever seen before in a woman this near her time. One day, she was sitting out in the fresh air, looking so sad, and I asked her if she was afraid of giving birth. She said no. I thought she would say no more, so I was getting ready to leave her to her praying when she said (to the best of my memory) "You know, Betty, the Blessed Mother intercedes with her Son to forgive. But Father Nicolay told us that there has to be repentance and restitution. If you knock a hole in your neighbor's wall, and he forgives you, that is all very well, but there is still that hole that must be filled in. There must be restitution! When he says that, his hand always comes down flat, with a crack on the pulpit. He always makes people jump." She laughed, but I'm afraid, Mama, she is worried about things that are beyond the skills of a friend or a midwife. We don't know what to do.

Tell Alice I think Dr. Llewellyn is very handsome!
Love to all,
Your affectionate,
Betty

My dear Betty,

A long time ago, Mary said something to me about that priest, Nicolay. That man walks around like he just stepped off the cross. As far as I'm concerned he's just making a show, but Mary puts great stock in what these priests say. Not that we don't listen to our pastor, but you know if he gets too far-fetched or high-horsed we can get a new one. The Catholics don't work that way, apparently. That man has put the fear of hell into his whole parish, and to no good end I say.

Mary's grandmother was something peculiar, too. I heard from Helen Czmosky's mother who knew the Waldowskis back when the old grandma was still alive and Mary was still running back and forth across that slough like a little muskrat to take care of her since her father wouldn't have the old lady under the same roof with him because she had been against him marrying her daughter. He never forgave her and that's why she had to live alone in that shack across the way there and the only good thing about it was that it was usually upwind of his pigs and him too. I heard that he was a filthy nasty coot and not too nice to Mary either which might explain a lot of things. Enough said. And I heard from I don't remember who that the old lady was a gypsy. Or at least back in the old country, that's what she was. I wouldn't be surprised—they say she had pierced ears! And her name was Hajas. I never heard a name like that before. So who knows what she filled Mary's head with, and then on top of that whatever it was Mary had to take from the mouth of this hell-fire priest. No good comes from all that popery, if you ask me. But what you and Gustie can do about it, I don't know. Wait and see, I guess. When she holds her baby *in her arms, all this popish-gypsy nonsense may drop away.*

We miss you, dear. Both you and Severn gone leaves this house with some hollow spaces. The chicks talk about you all the time and want to know when you are coming home. Daddy and I wonder too, of course, although I know it will take Mary some time to adjust once the baby is born.

Do you have enough money? Daddy is worried.
Love,
Your mama

Gertrude Kaiser lived seventy-nine years. According to Lena, it was too long. The Kaisers were a long-lived family. She had no doubt that Pa Kaiser would be alive today if someone hadn't killed him. *Drank like a fish. Healthy as an ox. No justice in this life.*

The funeral wouldn't be till the day after tomorrow. Lena would help the Ruth and Esther Circle prepare a lunch in Ma's house where the mourners, if there were any, could come after the service. In the meantime, Will and his brothers could see to the arrangements. If the three of them couldn't handle burying their own mother then it was just too bad. Mary was the only one in the family who had ever cared a fig for the old bat, and Lena never could understand why. Ma wasn't especially kind to her. Ma hadn't been especially kind to anybody.

So Lena wanted to enjoy her one day away from all things Kaiser. Months ago she had offered to help at the Fourth of July picnic. The last two years she hadn't contributed but a few pies. This year, she brought her pies, of course, but she also wanted to be there, in the thick of things.

The Fourth of July was a big day in Charity, a time when the whole town got together, played baseball, and ate; entertainments of various kinds were staged on the bandstand, but mostly people just took the opportunity to visit until dark; then there were fireworks and a dance. Lena had missed a lot of it last year. She didn't want to miss it again. She wanted to be out and about and have a bit of fun. Lena liked fireworks and she loved to dance. Will would be back from Molvik's long before the dance started. He wouldn't miss the fireworks.

Alvinia picked her up in the morning, saying, "You look nice, Lena." Alvinia was always good about paying a compliment, even though she had seen Lena's one good dress a hundred times or more.

"Where's Carl?" Lena inquired as she lifted Gracia up for Lavonne to hold in the back and clambered up to the wagon seat beside Alvinia.

"Oh, he went out early with Kermit to lay the bases for the baseball game. He closed early today."

"Well, it's just noon now, I expect everybody else has closed up shop too. Will used to be good at baseball."

Alvinia nodded but said nothing.

When they got to the fairgrounds, which lay just outside the city limits west of Charity, Alvinia took Gracia with her and her children to the Bierschback house, while Lena brought her pies out to the tables and looked for something to do.

She surveyed the southwest quarter of the fairgrounds where the tables were arranged under a canopy; there had been a light shower that morning. The green and gold smell of fresh-cut hay filled the air. Hay that would now have to be dried before it could be stored. She inhaled deeply. Some enterprising souls had erected a few smaller tents with tables and chairs if the grass remained too wet to spread a blanket on. She hoped the cloudy haze would burn off by nightfall. But, if it didn't, they could still gather under the tents and have themselves a good time. A little weather never stopped anything. The children would be disappointed without the fireworks, and so would Lena, for that matter, but plenty of cake and ice cream would make the disappointment go down easier.

The tables were gradually filling up with bowls of creamed herring, platters of sliced ham and cold chicken, lefse, boiled eggs and potato salad. There were also the pig roasts, sauerkraut and pickled pigs' feet that the Germans were so everlastingly fond of, but she didn't have to eat what she didn't like. There were pickles, sauces and jams, several kinds of bread and rolls, and buckets of lemonade. One table was all desserts: her pies and the pies of other women, apple, and rhubarb mostly; kringle, cookies, donuts, cobblers, krumkake, rosettes, and cakes of all shapes, sizes, and flavors. By the steam rising from the spout, Lena judged this was a fresh pot of coffee. She took the potholder and picked it up to walk it around before it got cold.

People were settling into small groups. The yelling and cheering from the baseball game that had started at the east end of the fairgrounds drifted over to her and she smiled. It was her first real smile in a long time.

The pot was heavy so she headed for the closest group of people. Porter Vogel and his wife and their five children were nesting on a spread of blankets. Porter smiled up at her from under a wide-brimmed black hat. "Hello, Lena," he said.

Before she could respond, he continued, "How's your little girl? What is she now...?"

"Fifteen months." She got it out quickly before he went on.

"They grow like sprouts, don't they?"

"They sure do. Would you like some...?"

"What do you think of this weather? Mother thought we should stay home this morning. Isn't that right, Mother? But I said, Mother, now these children have worked hard all week and a few drops of rain shouldn't stop them from having a good time and in we came. Isn't that right, Mother?"

Lena thought that "mother" probably was never really included in any of their conversations except in their retelling.

But Mrs. Vogel did speak. "Sorry to hear about Gertrude, Lena."

Before Lena could acknowledge her sympathy, Porter interjected, "Fine old pioneer lady. You know I was just saying to Mother that Gertrude Kaiser was one of the last of the original people to settle here, even before Charity was officially a township. Her husband, old Frederick, drilled the first wells for the homesteaders when he came out here...from where?"

"From around Pierre, I believe," said Lena.

"Yes, she had a lot of sorrows in this life, as we all do. Losing a son and a husband and a sister in the same year. Many sorrows. Now she's at peace. It's a blessing."

"Probably," said Lena. She eyed his coffee cup. "Warm that up for you?"

"But you children were good to her."

"We tried."

"Especially Mary. Now how is Mary, these days? I hear she went east with the oldest Torgerson girl and that Augusta Roemer. They've been gone a good while now, haven't they?"

Lena was getting fidgety. "Have some coffee here before it gets cold now, Porter."

He held out his cup and then his wife's. "Thank you, Lena, you know I..."

"Nice talking to you. I've got to get this coffee around before I have to go in and heat it up. It's never as good heated up the second time, you know. You have a good time now," she directed her last wish to the children who sat quietly around their parents. Lena added a thought, *and try to get away from your father for a few hours at least.*

Lena switched the pot to her left hand and moved on. She saw Harlan Gudierian playing cards with some men at the next nearest table. If he waited for Lena to serve him coffee he would die of thirst. She couldn't help it. She felt sick inside just looking at him.

The next table was populated by Don Grode and his wife and their son who had been born about the same time as Gracia. She hadn't seen Don since he'd had the stuffing knocked out of him by Skydog. "Hello, Don. Loretta. Can I give you some hot coffee?"

Don shook out the dregs from his cup and held it out. As Lena filled it, she asked, "How's that shoulder?"

He grinned and rubbed it for emphasis. "It only hurts when I hear a train whistle or a horse whinny."

Lena laughed sheepishly. "You've got a good man here, Loretta. He helped me out that day, I'll tell you."

"I know he's a good man, but it goes to his head if I tell him too often," Loretta smiled at her husband.

"How's this little boy?" Lena reached out and patted the head of the chubby child sitting in his mother's lap. "He sure is handsome. Has his mother's eyes, doesn't he?"

The compliments were exchanged about both their youngsters, Don and Loretta expressed their condolences over Gertrude while Lena rested the pot on the table. Then she took it up again and went on her way.

At every table people accepted refills, offered condolences about the death of her mother-in-law and speculations on the weather. Death and the weather—the two staples of conversation out here. The weather was the great equalizer. No one ever got tired of it; it was always changing, and all were subject to its whims. People could remember winters from their childhoods, and the droughts described to them by their grandfathers; they could recall the way the sky looked back in '68 before THAT hailstorm, and everybody who was old enough would know what they were talking about and add details of their own. Their memories were histories of weather and the good or bad times that resulted.

At the Gunderson table, Maimie Gunderson, a sturdy, red-faced widow who ran her farm with her sons, was no different. "Well it's hard when the old folks leave us, that's for sure. Now, when did you lose your ma and pa, Lena?"

People sure did like talking about misery. Especially, other people's. "Pa passed on when I was sixteen, and Ma died about eight years ago now."

"Take a look at that sky," Maimie looked up and launched into all the possibilities inherent in such a sky.

Lena longed to get on with it and with less conversation. The sky was overcast and her mother-in-law was dead. It was enough. She still had about a quarter of the pot left. She saw Nemil Glasrud sitting by himself and she headed over there. "Happy Fourth of July, Nemil. Fill that up for you?"

"Don't mind if you do, Lena. Thanks." People made fun of Nemil, still a bachelor in his mid-forties. He cleaned up pretty well, even though you couldn't say he ever dressed up. He was in his Sunday best shirt and overalls, his shirt pressed and his shoes had a spit polish on them. The worst that could be said about him was that he was homely and didn't have much to say for himself. For a while, people thought he had his eye on Gustie but she firmly and kindly had put an end to that. He had had his eye on every unmarried female at one time or another, but no one ever was interested in Nemil.

"Well, bye, Nemil. Enjoy yourself today. You going to the dance tonight?"

"Naw, I'll stay for the fireworks but I gotta lot of work to do. Gotta get home so I can get up early."

Lena supposed he'd given up looking for a wife. She felt sorry for him. "I hear that Ike Thorson is going to get his fiddle out later and Magna Nilsen is going to sing—that is if they ever get that bandstand up." Hammering could still be heard from the middle of the fairgrounds.

He nodded and smiled and seemed content to say no more.

There wasn't much coffee left and it was lukewarm so Lena dumped it out.

She spied Leroy unloading a keg. People wouldn't want more coffee now. They'd likely switch to drinking lemonade and Leroy's sarsaparilla.

With the empty pot swinging over her arm, Lena wandered over to where they were nailing in the last boards on the bandstand. The men of the city council were there. No doubt they were anxious about getting the bandstand sturdy enough so they could ascend and take their places above the rest of the common citizens of Charity. Behind their backs, these men were often referred to as The Twelve, because they gave themselves airs of the Apostles, or more often, in Lena's opinion, a jury passing judgments on everyone and everything around them. Except Lester Evenson. He was the one level head in this gaggle of ganders. They were the same twelve as sat on the school boards for the city and the section schools, and the same, excepting Lester, who had fired Gustie. And except for Lester, she didn't have much use for any of them.

Axel Kranhold nodded in her direction and Sighurd Dahl, a huge-bellied man waved benevolently. She gave him a half-hearted wave back. *Hypocrites,* she hissed to herself.

On her way back to the Bierschback house, Lena passed Kenneth O'Grady setting out a tub of hard candies. "Hi, Kenny," she said. "I'd offer you some coffee but I'm all out. There's probably a fresh pot ready if you want me to bring you some."

"No, I think I'll have a glass of Leroy's sarsaparilla."

"Sounds good," Lena said. She eyed the colorful candies. They wouldn't last long, and she popped one into her mouth. "Where's Morgan?"

"He's at the baseball game. I gave him the day off."

Lena moved on and spied a plump woman leaning back in her chair with her feet up on another chair. Someone had just brought her a full plate and a glass of lemonade and she was smiling broadly.

"Hello, Olna! I almost didn't recognize you without your apron!"

"Hi, Lena. This is the only day of the year I get to eat other people's cooking. It sure tastes good."

Betty Torgerson had been her best help. Lena didn't think she had hired anybody since Betty left. She deserved to put her feet up.

"Well, you enjoy yourself now. I'll be walking around here. You holler if you need anything."

"I sure will," Olna said, her mouth already full of potato salad.

Lillian Bierschback and Ethel Sauer, their houses being closest to the fairgrounds, though some distance apart from each other, had opened their homes for use the whole day. Both families had large ice houses to keep the lemonade and ice cream. Lillian also kept her stove going for a constant supply of coffee. She had the larger kitchen of the two, so Alvinia set up her ice cream making operation there. It was time Lena returned the pot and checked on Gracia.

The sky was overcast, still. The early shower had lightened it somewhat, but the tents and canopy stayed up. Lena, who had a good eye for weather, thought there had been a slight change. "I don't know. It looks yellow to me. The air, it's all kind of yellow like. Do you think there's a twister brewing out there? What do you think, Percy?" Percy Bierschback was keeping a game of checkers afloat in his back yard for anyone he could snag into playing for a few minutes. His current game partner was Barney Fossum who studied the board and ignored the weather. Percy took the toothpick from his mouth, gave the sky a sweeping look. "No. There won't be a tornado."

"Why not?" Lena demanded. He was always so blame sure of himself. That was the one thing that got her goat about Percy Bierschback.

"Because there's no hail. No hail, no twister. That's the rule. You can count on it. We got a fraidy hole over there if you're worried." He pointed the toothpick toward the Bierschback's storm cellar. "It's your move, Barney."

"Don't rush me, Percy. Don't rush me," Barney's eyes never left the board.

Maybe Percy was right. They'd had sprinkles all morning. Here was another one. She ducked into the house.

Alvinia was cranking the ice cream maker with vigor. Her forehead gleamed with perspiration and she dabbed it off with her apron and continued to crank. "Kermit promised to come by and do the next batch. He's got younger arms than I do. Then we'll round up all the boys over ten to do this. They are going to eat most of it. They can do the cranking."

"Where's Gracia?"

"In the living room. Kirstin is playing with her and Lavonne is watching them. They're all right. Sit down for a minute. Speak of the devil."

Kermit appeared behind Lena with a bag in his hand. His wheat-stalk hair was slicked back and he had on a white shirt and a pair of pants instead of his usual uniform of Carl's hand-me-down overalls. "Here's more salt, Ma."

"Thank you, Son. Just put it down there and remember where it is. You told your friends, and they are all taking turns?"

"Sure, Ma, they'll be here."

Alvinia quit cranking and pushed the ice cream maker toward him with her foot. "You can finish this batch. Your mother's tired. Take it out on the front porch. It's cooler out there."

He picked up the tub.

Lena asked, "You need help with that?"

"Nope. I got it." He lugged the tub to the front of the house.

Alvinia said to Lena, "The coffee's fresh."

"Oh, good." Lena had given everyone a cup of coffee but herself. "Want one?"

"No. I'm going to float away."

"What happened to Alice?" Lena took her coffee and sat at Lillian's kitchen table. She reached for the sugar bowl.

"She's out with Clark. He came in on the train last night and Doc Moody and Edwina put him up for the night. I told her to enjoy herself today. She's been
274

taking over Betty's chores. Laverne is pitching in." Alvinia handed Lena a spoon.

"Your children are all good, Alvinia. Every one of them."

Alvinia smiled, fully convinced. She fanned herself with a dish towel. "Will still at the funeral home?"

Lena nodded. "I told him he better go if he wanted to see his mother buried decently." Lena put a spoonful of sugar in her mouth and followed it with a sip of coffee. "Oscar would be too cheap to buy her anything more than a pine box, and he would lower her into the ground without an aye, yes or no. And Walter without Mary is useless."

Alvinia looked casually through the door to the next room. It seemed they were the only adults in the house. The children in the living room were all noisily involved in a game of some sort. She lowered her voice. "What's Walter going to do? Has he said?"

"No. And I haven't asked him. I don't know why he doesn't just divorce her. She told him in her letter she isn't coming back. It's like he hasn't taken it in." She paused a moment to reflect. "We can never tell anybody where she is, you know that, don't you Alvinia?"

"Well, yes, we all..."

"I mean, Walter is not a Kaiser for nothing. They are a mean bunch. I don't know if he is planning something..."

"What could he be planning?" Alvinia stopped fanning.

"Maybe nothing. Sometimes he seems too dumb to plan his next cigar, but I'm telling you...the Kaisers have a mean streak...and I know it's in Will too, but only when he's drunk. I've never seen a speck of meanness in him when he's sober. But those others. The whole family, every last one of them, had a meanness that would just curl your toes. And Walter is a Kaiser. That's all I'm saying."

"Enough said, then." Alvinia couldn't sit idle for long. She went back to her work at the stove, breaking eggs into a pan, adding cream and sugar to mix up the custard for the next batch of ice cream. "Do you think Mary will stay in Philadelphia?"

"Where else has she got to go? Gustie's people will take care of her, and they've got the money to do it. Seems odd like, Gustie leaving her own family like she did, doesn't it?"

"She never told you why?"

Lena just shook her head.

"Well, you never know what happens in families, Lena."

"You said a mouthful! What do you hear from Betty?" Lena sipped more coffee, this time without sugar.

"Oh, the usual. She's..." Alvinia stirred her custard and turned away from Lena.

"She'll be home soon." Lena knew that Alvinia missed her oldest daughter something fierce—more than she missed Severn. It was only natural. The first born. The oldest girl. The one who had been going along with Alvinia on her mid-wifery since she was a youngster. "Then you'll be planning a wedding."

Alvinia lightened. "Don't remind me!"

"You promised the girl."

"I know and I'll keep my promise." Alvinia shook her head at the mysteries of the world, which mostly were the things she couldn't control. "Well, this custard looks about right. Lavonne!"

Alvinia's fourteen-year old daughter came into the kitchen. Lavonne was looking more and more like Betty, although she probably wouldn't be as tall. She nodded politely to Lena and said, "Yes, Mama?"

Alvinia transferred the custard from her pan to a large mixing bowl. "Take this out to your brother and put the batch he's working on in the ice house. Now do it like I showed you, honey, so it doesn't melt. Then you can go out with your friends. I'll look after the little ones." Lavonne's face transformed like prairie sky from clouds to sun. "Okay, Mama!"

Lena finished her coffee and put the cup in the sink. "Well, I'll go back out and see what I can do out there."

"I'll go check on Kermit. I don't want him stuck all day in here, either. The chickens should have some fun." Lena found Gracia and Kirstin still happily occupied with some rubber blocks.

The shower had passed but the sky was still as thick as Alvinia's custard. A tent had gone up and Percy and Barney were under it, still nagging each other over whose turn it was.

Alvinia followed Lena out the door and said, "Percy, you've been sitting in front of that checker board long enough. Come in here and take a turn at this ice cream. We all know you're going to eat your share."

Percy gave his ample stomach a good-natured pat. "You're right about that, Alvinia. Just give me two moves to beat this fella and I'll be right there."

Barney winked at Alvinia, made a move and Percy made his next move. Then Barney with a quiet smile, picked up a black checker and hopped over a string of red ones and triumphantly swept the board clean.

Percy looked dumb-founded. "Well, maybe I'll have better luck with the ice cream. Good game, Barney, good game. Come back later and give me a chance to beat you again!" Both men laughed and Barney headed toward the fairgrounds and the food tables, and Percy obediently followed Alvinia into his house. Lena didn't know where Lillian was but she was probably, now that she thought of it, watching her sons play baseball.

Lena liked baseball herself. She used to watch Will play, but since he lost his eye, he couldn't see the ball, either to hit it or catch it. Still, she liked to watch other people play. She decided she had better use the outhouse first. The closest one was the Bierschback's at the end of a narrow stone path back of the house. Percy had planted some bushes around it, but they weren't tall enough yet to be much of a windbreak. She went in and settled herself in the semidarkness.

After a moment, she heard some laughter and the voices of two men approaching from the back. She recognized the voices of Bud Hedke, the barber and Arnold Prieb, who with his wife Janelle, ran the post office.

"Here, you want another snort?" That was Bud, and if his wife Dorothy found out he was drinking, he'd be in for it.

"Don't mind if I do. Don't let the missus catch you with that." Arnold, it seemed, had been thinking Lena's thoughts and she smiled.

"Don't intend to."

Lena's thoughts wandered and she tuned out the voices of the men until she heard Arnold say, "Wonder who's going to take it over now she's gone."

"Don't know."

"Who owns it? She was only renting as far as I heard."

Lena knew at once what house they were referring to. The house, which was more like a shack, could be seen from across the fairgrounds to the west on the other side of the road. It was the only empty house around Charity that she knew of. She had heard that Stella Ronshagen had left town. Lena didn't know and didn't care why or where she went.

"Maybe Lester Evenson and his bank own it."

"Well," it was Arnold talking now, "It's a loss in community entertainment."

Both men chuckled.

"I'll tell you, the Kaisers'll sure miss that one." Bud had had too much to drink. His words were slurring.

Arnold snickered, which encouraged Bud to go on, "You know what they're saying—it's the first time the Kaiser brothers ever drilled the same hole!"

Barely restrained laughter.

"You mean Walter and—"

"No. The other two." The voices were coming around the side of the outhouse. "Not Walter, far as I heard." One of the men rattled the door. Lena was frozen on her seat.

"And I always say," Bud's mouth ran more than when he was sober, "I always say, if they go out for it, it generally means they don't get it at home."

Arnold Prieb said, "Well, whoever is in there ain't coming out soon enough for me. I'll just go back over there and take a leak. Thanks for the snort."

"You bet."

The men went their separate ways.

Lena's eyes, accustomed now to the dim interior of the outhouse saw with perfect clarity the slats barely joined so that the wind drifted through the seams and chinks. Light seeped around the door that drooped slightly on its hinges. Holes carved high in the two front corners allowed entrance to two more thin streams of light. In the far upper right corner was a spider web. Lena did not see the spider. No doubt she was waiting in the dark of the deep corner for her next victim. A gust of air came through the hole and sent a tremor through the web.

Lena's feet didn't even touch the rough hewn floor. *Like a child on a throne,* she always said of herself in the toilet. The air was saturated with the familiar smell of human excrement. Lena felt the appropriateness of her seat now, hearing what she had heard. A single board with a hole carved out of it was all that kept her suspended over a shit hole as she added her own shit to the pile.

Lena rose, cleaned herself with a sheet from the stack of papers in the corner and arranged her clothing. She came out into the daylight that wasn't bright enough to make her blink. The hazy air lay over the land like a veil. She felt like her insides had been rearranged. She felt...she didn't have a word for it. What word covered so much ground? What word covered friends and neighbors speaking of her humiliation as a joke and blaming her for it to boot?

What word covered the ground of hurt, of wounded pride, and betrayal by people she had thought of as friends since she had come to live in Charity as a new bride? She wasn't part of Charity any more. She'd live here, but except for going to church she would keep to herself. She would never forgive them. Not one of them. Never in this world. And she knew that she would be called to answer for that someday, too.

Riding Moon with Gracia in her arms, after she had cried so bitterly, first by herself, and then to Jordis, she had resolved that never in her life would she shed another tear for Will Kaiser, and now that promise kept itself. Her eyes were dry stones. She felt a bleak sense of loss, of groundlessness. She remembered the white horse, her gentle step, her smooth gait. She had a good name, that horse. Lena wished now for her wide back to rest upon and her white mane to hang on to. To ride her forever to the moon and beyond.

If she weren't a mother she would leave. She'd leave Will. She'd leave this town. She would just disappear. Mary had done it. Lena would have done it too. But not with a child. She could go hungry, but she wouldn't make Gracia want for anything.

She would never tell anyone what she had heard, and no one would ever know why she hated Bud Hedke even more than she hated Harlan Gudierian.

She walked west to the Sauer house. She had spotted Granville and Ethel Sauer on the fairgrounds earlier. She doubted that anybody would be there, and she needed to be alone.

She entered through the back door. Her feet moved and she moved with them, feeling heavy and a hundred years old. She passed through the kitchen

281

and in the dining room, pulled out a chair and sat down at the table, running her hand absently back and forth over the creamy linen table cloth. On any other day she would have admired this cloth, and Ethel's blue and white china shining softly through the glass of her china hutch, Ethel's wine colored carpets, her furnishings. But not today. Today, in one of the finest homes in Charity, Lena sat amidst ashes.

She felt alone, and resolved to be so. She already had her understanding with Will. She didn't have to go over that bridge again. She would never look at any of these people the same again, except Alvinia and of course Gustie. She knew enough of them to know that they would never allow such talk in their presence, as she herself had silenced the pious ladies of the Ruth and Esther Circle when they aired their views once about the new school teacher, Augusta Roemer. Lena had told them off good that day.

She would keep herself upright and make sure that Gracia would have the best she could offer and never be ashamed of her mother at least, and protect her from the nastiness of this town called Charity.

She raised her head to have one look at Ethel's china before leaving this house. She didn't expect to ever set foot inside it again. She did not long so much for the things Ethel had that she could display and polish—her dishes and her furniture—but for what these things represented to Lena. A home full of love and laughter. Granville and Ethel were a happy couple with happy children. They seemed always to have a house full of people, and on Christmas, this house was always brightly lit and full of music, even though they were Methodists.

She would see if Alvinia needed help, then gather up Gracia and go home. She had to strain her eyes to see the pattern on the china plates. It was awfully dim in this room. It shouldn't be, not with that big window—the double window with its curtains drawn back so nothing obstructed the light or the view across the fields. Lena stood and turned slowly toward that window. Through it she saw clearly, against the greenish-yellow sky—a huge funnel cloud, its tail whipping the ground like an angry snake. Gray and brown with bits of stuff swirling around in it, like chunks of dirt in dirty milk. The thing was indescribably huge and coming fast.

Lena had no time to run. She dropped to the floor, rolled under the table and covered her head with her arms. She felt a rumbling, and a roar, like the sound of a train, filled her ears, except instead of hearing it from the depot platform, she was face down on the tracks. She squeezed her eyes shut, gritted her teeth against the fearful howling and tried to remember the Lord's Prayer. The house tipped. She stretched out her arms and grabbed the table legs and held on, keeping her head down and her eyes shut. She smelt something gassy and then had trouble breathing at all.

She had no idea how long she lived inside that roar, gripping the table legs. One corner of the house was lifted up enough so she felt the slant but not enough so that the oak table moved. She hung on anyway to keep from sliding out from under it. She didn't want to be left uncovered to be hit by falling glass and God knew what. Within that eternity, she began to find, one at a time, the words of the Lord's

Prayer. By the time she got to *Hallowed be*, the roar ceased, leaving silence rushing in her ears.

At the same time the house settled gently, as if a big child had picked it up to look under it and then been scolded and told to put it back down so as not to break anything. She could breathe easily again. That was the good thing, she thought, about a big sturdy house like this—it could withstand almost anything. She relaxed her grip on the table and drew in her hands. They were numb. She flexed them to get the feeling back in and the stiffness out. She crawled out from under the table and tried to get to her feet. She had to use the table to pull herself up. Her legs felt weak. As she did so, panic hit her like another storm, almost bringing her to her knees again. A tornado could pass by one house, leaving it unscathed, and take another standing right next to it. Gracia was next door at the Bierschback's. *Oh, please God, please God let that house still be there. Please...*

Her dread was engulfed in pure amazement at the sight outside the big dining room window. Rather, the opening that had been a glass-paned window. The glass was gone. Nothing looked the same. The two small trees that were in the Sauer's back yard were not there. The fields beyond were blue. She staggered through the kitchen to the back door. The door itself was gone and so were the steps leading up to it.

She hung on to the door frame and looked out and saw the long bodies of a dead tiger and a dead lion. They were being moved, or rather arranged, side by side, with care by a bunch of men. A half a dozen large, scrawny dogs, all varying shades of yellow and gold mulled around and just as many lay dead on the ground. Besides the men who were arranging the big cats, strange people were huddled together, crying, and some picked through the rubble. There was something odd about all these people. Two children in red, shabby coats turned to look at her. She gasped. They had terrifyingly old faces.

She lowered herself to the ground, wandered out a few paces, and stood taking in a landscape in which nothing made sense. "Am I dead?" she asked no one in particular.

"No." The answer came in a woman's voice from her left. Lena turned and saw her sitting on a crate. Her yellow hair frizzed around her face and lay down her back in a mat like a beaver tail. She was wearing only a bustier and some frothy petticoats, tattered and dirty, in faded pink and yellow. She was smoking a cigarette and blood formed a trail down the side of her head.

Lena stared at the woman. *I must be dead.* But this sure wasn't anything like she expected to find in heaven or in hell. Maybe the Catholics were right all along. This was purgatory.

"You're in Cleremont." The woman spoke dully, without inflection, but in an accent that sounded familiar.

"Cleremont?" Lena had been born on a sodbuster's farm not five miles outside of Cleremont. This couldn't be Cleremont. Cleremont was a whistle stop seven miles east of Wheat Lake.

The woman dropped her cigarette on the ground and watched it smolder. "The twister just set your house down like a cherry on a cake right there five minutes ago. Anybody else in there with ya?" Now

Lena placed the accent. It was similar to Dennis Sully's, but more drawn out somehow.

"No, I..." Lena turned to look at the house. The second story was gone, neatly sliced off. She turned back to the woman. If she wasn't dead she must be having a very bad dream. "What is all...this?"

"Shadrack's Circus and Novelty Acts. What's left. I'm Maizie."

"Oh!" She wasn't crazy. She wasn't dead. Lena remembered now an ad in the paper for the circus that was coming through Stone County all the way from somewhere in the south like Louisiana or Tennessee. At the bottom of the ad, in bolder type had been *Maizie Boggs and Her Amazing Dogs*. It looked like their chief attractions, the tiger and the lion and the dog act were gone.

"These your dogs?" asked Lena.

"What's left of 'em," Maizie said dully.

Lena's fear about Gracia suddenly rose like a wave, held back behind her eyes by the thinnest transparency of will. A rivulet of that fear broke through, ran down her throat and swirled inside her chest. It wouldn't do to lose herself to hysterics here. Not now. She had to think. If this was Cleremont she should be able to find her way to the telegraph office, if it was still standing. Ahead of her there was rubble of blue and red striped canvas and splintered wood where tents and wagons had been destroyed. Beyond that, the flax fields looked serenely blue, glittering with fresh rain under a sunny new sky.

Lena walked around the Sauer house and saw where Main Street began, and still was, all three blocks of it, intact. If she remembered correctly, the

286

telegraph was in the post office and that was the last building on the west side. She picked up her skirts and forced her legs to run. She passed a man sweeping up the glass from a store window. He said "hello" but Lena was too full of fear to answer. She kept running.

The door to the post office was open. Behind the counter, an elderly man sorted mail as though nothing had happened. In here, not a piece of paper looked disturbed. He peered over his glasses and hooked a thumb under one of his suspenders.

Lena's knees felt as if they would give way and she held on to the edge of the counter. "My name is Lena Kaiser," she panted. "I have no money with me. You see I was carried here, just now..." she pointed south. "I was carried here from Charity in a house by the tornado. I landed in the middle of the circus. I need to telegraph home and find out if my little girl...tell them I'm all right. I'll see that you get your money back. My two sisters live in Wheat Lake and my husband and his family live in Charity. My people started here. We were the Halversons. My pa—"

The man held up his hand and said, "I'll send your telegram, Missus. Just tell me what and to who."

"I'll get your money to you, don't worry."

"I'm not worried." He unhooked his thumb, reached for a pencil and licked the tip, and leaned on the counter with his elbows, pencil ready to write.

"Let's see." Lena trembled from head to foot. "What should I say? Oh, say...say...Oh...send it to Alvinia Torgerson in Charity." She didn't want to send it to Will. If he was sober, he'd come and get her, but she never knew, any more, if he was going to be sober.

"Say, 'Blown to Cleremont. Is Gracia all right? Waiting answer. Lena.' Does that sound all right?"

"That should do it. Glass of water or some coffee while you wait?"

"No."

Lena staggered outside and collapsed on the edge of the wooden sidewalk. She heard his keys tapping out her message. Then, quiet.

The fear and panic that rode high in her chest began to spin like a ball. She had to contain it. She almost fainted from it. She put her head down on her knees and encircled them with her arms. She didn't care about anybody or anything except Gracia. She didn't care about Will. The whole town of Charity could be just a smudge on the way to the Rockies if only Gracia was still alive. She herself could explode and die and it didn't matter as long as she knew Gracia was well. *Don't you dare take my child and leave me! Don't you dare! Please God*, she prayed and threatened and made promises till her mind was exhausted. Finally when she was certain she couldn't bear another moment, the telegraph clicked.

She jumped up and ran back inside. The man was scribbling on a small piece of paper. When he finished, he handed the paper to her. *Gracia well. We are all well. Stop. Only house and outhouse gone. How are you? Stop. Alvinia.* She nodded her thanks, took it outside, resumed her seat on the sidewalk and wept. As she dried her eyes on her skirt she thought for the first time with annoyance, *Wait till I see Percy, the big dumb cluck. 'No hail, no twister.'* She found a handkerchief in her pocket and wiped her face and blew her nose. *I hope the house didn't land on*

*anybody. Oh! Ethel! Poor Ethel! Her whole house cut
in two and gone.*

Lena remembered now the crying circus people,
the blood on Maizie's head. She spotted an old straw
hat lying on the ground. She picked it up. "Is this
anybody's?" There was no one to hear her question
except the telegraph operator and he didn't answer.
*There's no use in getting a sunburn on top of everything
else.* She put it on and went to make herself useful.

If Gracia had been killed, there would have been
no reason to go home. No reason at all. But knowing
she was well and safe in Alvinia's care, Lena could
take her time. She wasn't one to leave a mess.

She tucked her precious message into her pocket
and walked briskly back to the scene of the circus
carnage. She was grateful for the hat. With the haze
swept away, the sun was beating down strongly. She
found Maizie where she had left her. "Here, let's find
something to clean you up with and see how bad your
head is. Cleremont doesn't have a doctor. Someone
would have sent to Wheat Lake for one by now." No,
she reminded herself. Dr. Llewellyn was in Charity.
They would have to send to Ft. Gifford.

One man in a blue outfit that looked like dyed long
underwear was crying over the bodies of the big cats.
She felt sorry for him and them. As Lena took charge
of Maizie Boggs, she noticed others were coming out
to help the circus folk.

The townspeople were gathering or carrying those
who were hurt into the church. Lena took Maizie by
the elbow and followed along. The inside of the square,
one-room church already hummed with low moaning
and weeping, and other quiet, soothing voices.

Lena found Maizie a place to sit at the end of a middle pew and told her to wait. Blankets, bandages, food, and buckets of water were appearing in the back of the church and Lena collected what she needed. She draped a blanket around Maizie's shoulders and put a cup of hot coffee in her hands. Then she bathed her head. Maizie accepted Lena's help numbly. The wound didn't look bad, but you couldn't tell with head wounds. Lena said, "When a doctor gets here, you'll have to have him look at this. Are you hungry? There's a lot of food here. Let me bring you something."

Maizie shook her head and began to weep copiously. "My dogs! My dogs!"

"They're not all dead." Lena patted her shoulder. "Let's go take care of them. Can you stand up all right?"

Maizie nodded, and Lena walked her to the back of the church.

At the door, they were met by the tallest man Lena had ever seen. Seven feet tall, at least, she estimated. "Amos!" Maizie cried. "My dogs! My dogs!"

"It's all right, Maizie. I was looking for you." He had a foreign accent Lena couldn't place. "I got them rounded up."

Maizie went to him and he took her hand tenderly. She stopped and looked back at Lena. "I hope you get home all right."

Lena waved and thought, *I hope so too.*

There now seemed to be as many people from Cleremont in the church as there were injured. Everyone was being looked after. Lena was hungry. She hadn't had anything all day except a piece of candy and a cup of coffee. From the food stuffs being brought into the church, Lena took for herself the heel of a loaf of bread and dipped a bowl into a shiny pail of milk still warm and frothy from the cow. In a corner seat out of the way she sopped the bread in the milk and ate it hungrily, then she drank what was left. She left her bowl in a basket of dirty dishes and looked around for the minister. He wasn't hard to spot—a roly-poly, thin-haired man in a worn black suit and clerical collar. He was hauling out a bucket of dirty water and she caught up to him just outside the church. "Excuse me, Reverend..."

"Mickelson." He put his bucket down, wiped his brow with a handkerchief and smiled. "Are you with the circus?"

"Oh, no. I was blown here from Charity. See that house over there? What's left of it? I rode in on that."

He stared at the bottom half of the house and back at Lena in her blue dress and battered straw hat. His amazement dissolved into a chuckle. "My my my. So you need to get home, then."

"Yes, pastor, I do. But I only need to get to Wheat Lake from here. I have people there."

"Well, now, let's see." He mopped his face all over again, appearing glad for a moment to catch his breath. "Come with me," he said. He left the bucket where it stood.

He took her along Main Street to the same windowless store she had passed on her way to the telegraph office. The Rev. Mickelson said, "Wait here now. Don't worry." He went inside and in a few minutes was out again, accompanied by the man who had been sweeping glass off the sidewalk. "Mrs..."

"Kaiser. Lena Kaiser."

"Mrs. Kaiser, this is Otto Ditmanson. He owns our general store."

"Hello there." Lena adjusted her hat. "I'm sorry I ran by you before. I was worried about my little girl, you see, and I had to get to the telegraph..."

Otto Ditmanson just smiled and waved away her apology.

The minister's brow wrinkled in concern. "Is your child all right?"

"Yes." Lena nodded for emphasis.

"Thank heaven for that."

Otto Ditmanson said, "My boy can take you in his wagon."

She heard a harness jingle and shifted her gaze to see a pretty gray pony come around the corner pulling a big-wheeled cart. There was just room for two people on the seat, Lena was small and the boy driving the pony wasn't too big either.

"Thanks a million. And you take care of these poor circus folks, now."

"We sure will," said the minister.

Lena thanked them both again and climbed up into the seat of the cart.

The boy grinned broadly. His hair was red. His face was freckled. "I'm Rusty," he said.

"You must take after your mother."

"Yes, ma'am."

"I'm Lena Kaiser. You can call me Lena."

His father said, "Get her to where she wants to go now and come right back. No dawdling."

"Right, Pa." Rusty seemed pleased with his responsibility and his unexpected adventure. He clucked loudly and the pony started forward, his head high.

292

"So, Pa said you were carried here in the twister!"

"That's right."

"Jiminy! What was that like?"

Lena thought for a minute. "It was like having a train run over you. Very loud. And hard to breathe."

"Jiminy! And it sawed that house right in half and you're okay?"

"Not a scratch."

"Jiminy!"

"Yes, that about covers it. That's a real nice pony you got there, Rusty."

"Yes ma'am," the boy said with some pride. "Pa and Ma gave him to me for my birthday."

"What's his name?"

"Bob. Bobby."

"Good name for a pony," Lena said.

Rusty was a talkative young man and Lena listened, interposing a brief question here and there. She learned that he was thirteen years old. He went to school and helped out in his father's store. He had one younger sister and his mother kept chickens out back of the store so they sold eggs in addition to their other goods. Lena put her head back and breathed in the fresh air. The atmosphere had been scoured clean. The few trees around Cleremont had bent and broken branches. The crops still leaned. Rusty worked in his father's store now but he didn't plan to do that forever. When he was old enough he wanted to go west or east, he didn't care which, to see an ocean. The birds were coming out singing up a storm—little bird *glory hallelujahs* that they survived. Where do the poor birds go, she wondered, when the wind and hail come? Somehow, they survive, or most of them

293

do, anyway. She saw a snake slither off the road into the grass, and a ground squirrel disappeared into the roadside wildflowers. A hawk circled overhead, getting a bead on some small animal whose misfortune meant the hawk and his family lived another day. God's world was not kind, but somehow it worked. Rusty continued to muse on how he would get the money to go to an ocean, maybe he would work his way along.

With her fear lifted, Lena enjoyed herself. She felt bad for the people in the circus. She felt sorry for the animals and for Ethel Sauer. But she and those she loved were unscathed. It was a glorious day to be riding in a cart with a strapping lad named Rusty behind a pony named Bob.

As they rolled past a field, Lena checked the corn. *Knee high by the Fourth of July.* Right on schedule. The twister had cut a narrow swath. She was out of its track now and didn't see any damage anywhere.

"I really appreciate your giving me a lift, Rusty. You know, I know somebody who has seen the ocean."

"Yeah? Which one?" Rusty asked eagerly.

"She's from the east."

"That would be the Atlantic then, Ma'am."

"She could tell you a lot about it and how to get there, too, I'll bet."

"Really?"

"Oh, yes. I'll have her write to you. It won't be right away because she is away visiting. But when she gets back, I'll ask her to write you a letter and you can take it from there."

"Gee, Mrs. Kaiser, that would be swell! Jiminy!"

The cart rolled along. The sun was lowering itself in the west. Lena pulled the brim of her straw hat down in the front to keep the sun out of her eyes. She was lulled by the rhythm of the cart, the repetitive jingle of the harness and felt more relaxed and at ease than she had for months. Rusty broke the spell.

"Here we are, Missus." He was about to turn them to the left to go into Wheat Lake when Lena put her hand on his arm. He pulled Bob to a stop. "Town's up that way, Ma'am."

Lena swatted at a mosquito and considered. "I'm too late for the train." She could go into town and stay with Ella or Ragna. They would take her in because they had to, not because they were glad to see her. But they were stingy with food and had no space. She wouldn't be comfortable there. She didn't feel like bunking in Joe Gruba's back room at the depot, either.

"No, go that way." She pointed right, to the south. "I know a place I can stay right down by the lake."

He turned Bob to the right, and they followed the trail until they mounted the crest of a slight rise and just ahead of them, Crow Kills appeared like a prairie mirage, blue and glistening.

"If you go in just a little farther, Bob can turn around easy where the grass isn't so high. Right here, see? I can walk from here."

"Okay, Ma'am."

"There won't be anybody there now but they won't mind if I bunk in overnight." Lena thought there might be some coffee, maybe a little flour to stir up a pancake for supper. Or she could go fishing. That would be fun. She could cook out under the stars. Maybe even take a dip in the lake. It had been ages since she'd been for a swim. She'd wash her clothes and wrap up in a blanket till they dried and watch the sun set while her fish cooked, relish her good fortune, thank God for His deliverance, and apologize for being mad at Him. She would go to bed, and in the morning before it got too hot, walk back to Wheat Lake. Joe Gruba would give her a ticket to Charity. She'd be home in time to pick up Gracia and put the supper on for Will.

"Thanks, Rusty. And thank your Pa for me again." As he disappeared over the rise she called, "I won't forget to tell my friend to write to you."

When she turned back to the cabin, the pipe that poked slantwise through its roof coughed out a wisp of smoke. Either she hadn't noticed it before or someone just lit a fire. Fiddlesticks! Some Indian was squatting there while Jordis and Gustie were gone. Lena almost turned around and headed back to town and Joe Gruba's back room, but she was so close. She might as well take a look. Maybe whoever it was just stopped to make some coffee and would be on their way. If it was a woman, it might be all right, even if she had to share the cabin for the night. The Indians were hospitable. Nobody ever had a bad thing to say about them in that way. She would at least check it out. If she had to, she could make it back up to Joe's before dark if she stepped on it.

This place had clearly seen only a small amount of rain. The wagon trail was muddy, and Lena didn't want to do any more damage to her shoes than she had to. Will had promised her a new pair in a week when he got paid for his well at Ackerman's. Hank always paid on time. But in the meantime, the ones she had on were still lined with cardboard and she didn't need to get them wet. She picked her way through the lumpy prairie grass where it was cut down by the side of the trail. The evening sun was bringing out the mosquitoes and she kept her hands waving in front of her so they wouldn't land. Large green grasshoppers bounced high away from her with each step. One, confused perhaps, landed on her skirt and stuck there. She shook it off. A red winged blackbird a yard or two away, eyed her with malevolence. "What are you looking at," Lena asked, pulling the hem of her dress out of some prickly weeds. She was either going to do damage to her shoes or her dress. She shook her head, and then got a whiff of something delicious. With all her attention focused on avoiding insects and prickly plants, she hadn't noticed the steam rising from the black kettle on the tripod out front of the cabin. *Well, it's more than coffee they're making.* But Lena was so hungry that she was relieved not to have to wait till she caught a fish and cleaned it to eat.

When she was within a few yards of the cabin, the door opened. Lena emitted a squeak and stopped. Betty Torgerson stood stock still on the porch that fronted the cabin, her eyes the size of pie plates. "Mrs. Kaiser!"

"Betty!"

"What are you doing here?" They spoke in unison. Actually, Lena said, "What in Sam Hill are you doing here?"

Betty opened her mouth but nothing came out, so Lena said, "Well I got blown to Kingdom Come in the twister and now I'm going home. When did you get back from Philadelphia?"

Betty remained speechless. Behind her, Gustie appeared in the doorway. She stepped out beside Betty. A little smile appeared on her face. "Hello, Lena."

"Gustie! What in Sam Hill? Where's Mary?"

"She's here. She's lying down now."

"When did you get back? Did she have the baby already? It's early. Is she all right? She didn't leave the baby..."

"No, she hasn't given birth, yet."

"Then..."

"We never went to Philadelphia."

"Oh. I thought you were going to Philadelphia."

"That was the plan."

"But... I got a letter from you from Philadelphia! So did Alvinia. She showed me a lot of letters from Betty from Philadelphia."

"Lena, come up here out of the sun and sit down." Gustie offered her the rocking chair that still held its place where Dorcas used to sit and rock. "You look tired. As a matter of fact, you look absolutely horrible. What happened to you?"

"Well, I'm not sure anymore." Lena climbed up the steps and sat down gratefully, fanning herself with her hat. "First, there's dead tigers and dogs all over the place and a woman with orange hair in a tutu, and then there's this. I'm not sure I'm not dead."

"You're not dead, Lena. I'll get you some water. Supper will be ready before too long."

Jack Frye woke up, startled out of a deep sleep by something. Where the hell was he? Had he gotten drunk and fallen asleep...no, he hadn't been drunk for days. Not since he got down to his last two dollars. He ached all over, he was wet. And there was a sharp pain in his left shoulder. He raised himself up and looked. He'd been lying on a rock. He tossed it.

He scratched at his neck, already swollen from something that had bitten him. Running his hand along the back of his neck and then behind his ear, he felt something, a growth which he pulled at, swearing. He looked at it. A fat tick, swollen with Jack Frye's own blood. Bastards! Little buggers! He smashed it between two rocks. He knew he'd be covered with them, because he now remembered where he was and what he was doing here.

In the night, he had bellied through the sparse brush that sprouted along the bank of Crow Kills. Waiting for daylight, he'd fallen asleep.

Jack Frye had fallen on hard times. Through no fault of his own. He'd been frugal. He'd lived in the bunkhouse summer and winter. He'd fished and caught frogs and cooked them up as often as he could. The frogs were only good in the fall, when they were fat and the legs were good eating then. A little frog, there wasn't enough meat on the legs to justify the time and energy that went into catching it. He had fished the southern loop of Crow Kills where he could hunker down, not attracting the attention of the Indians, and watch his pole. He fried up his fish outside or sometimes, in the winter, on the stove in the bunker.

He had kept himself in tobacco and whiskey. A man had to have his smokes and a drink now and then. But when he opened his coffee can that he hid under his cot and saw there were only two dollars left he had to have a plan. Oscar Kaiser had told him that the old maid was gone. That meant, there would only be the squaw out at the lake, and maybe not. He hadn't seen her in town in awhile. Maybe she was gone too. He walked out of Wheat Lake in the middle of the night so he wouldn't be seen leaving town, and just before dawn he had come to the southern loop where he knew the cottonwoods and underbrush would give him a little cover. From there he walked east till he got in sight of the cabin and then he crawled. The brush wasn't thick enough to hide him if he didn't approach it like a weasel. His plan had been simple. Wait and watch till he was sure the cabin was empty and then go in and steal what he could. It wasn't like they didn't owe him. They surely did. Maybe there would be money in there. Maybe things he could sell or trade. Blankets, clothes, food. He would take whatever he found. But he'd fallen asleep and slept almost all day. The sun was already behind him. He was only about 15 yards away, looking up at the cabin. He saw people there and he didn't dare move so he squinted and tried to clear his vision. His mouth was dry, but until they went inside or left, he didn't even dare elbow his way down to the lake for a drink.

The evening sunshine settled over the land like a benediction. Stories were passed back and forth while Betty stirred the pot over the fire, and Gustie kept the coffee cups filled and supplied Lena with bread and butter to tide her over till the stew was served. When

Mary joined them, Lena went over her story again, leaving out, as she had in the first telling, the reason she had gone off by herself to the Sauer house.

Lena didn't know whether to be more amazed at her own flight in a twisted-airborne house that took her over thirty miles in fifteen minutes or her friends being right here at Crow Kills all winter and nobody finding out about it. Nobody, that is, except Joe Gruba, Clark Llewellyn, Fathers Gregory and Flagstad and, it seemed, every Indian on the reservation. Lena sniffed, "All of these people knew you were out here, all this time?"

"More coffee, Lena?"

"Yes. Thank you."

All these people had known, had helped them, and had kept quiet. Father Flagstad, whenever he could get away from the mission, brought them loaves of his fine white bread. "He is a good baker," said Gustie. "You're eating his bread right now." Lena had to agree, it was very good bread. One night when Mary had complained of stomach pains, Gustie had ridden for Clark Llewellyn who diagnosed indigestion from eating too many of Minnie Gruba's homemade sausages. After that he checked on Mary regularly. Father Gregory had been asked to come and had become a weekly visitor, because Mary longed to hear the Mass, and Betty wanted to continue her instruction in Catholicism. Carrie Red Horse (Lena learned about the Dakotah having to change their names and wondered what the fuss was about) had brought Gustie her new winter moccasins and saw Mary suffering with cold and swollen feet. She returned the next day with a pair of fur-lined moccasins for Mary, who almost cried in relief even as she told Lena about it. Little Bull and Jimmy Saul provided them with rabbits and fish and sometimes kindling to start their coal fires. "We'd have been a lot colder and hungrier without them," Gustie said.

"Well, that's sure something," Lena said when the whole story had been told, and still taking in the strangeness of it all, stared across the lake, darkening under the passage of a stray cloud. She brought herself out of her deep mood and turned to Betty. "Your mother is going to have a fit!"

Betty cast her a wry look of agreement.

"What's in the pot?" Lena, who was getting hungrier by the minute in spite of the bread, got up to join Betty at the tripod.

"Rabbit stew. With turnips and carrots and wild onions."

Lena peered into the steaming kettle and decided that, although it smelled good, it looked undressed. "No potatoes?"

"We are all out."

"Do you have eggs?"

"Yes, plenty of those. Joe brought us a pail yesterday."

"Get me a couple then and some flour."

Lena demonstrated the fine art of making a decent dumpling. She believed that with Betty getting married soon, she should know, and she wouldn't learn it from her mother. "You crack your eggs into a bowl, like this. Give them a few beats with a fork till they get cloudy. See? Not foamy. Then you add your flour. I like to add it a little at a time. It's easier to keep the lumps out that way and also you'll never add too much if you add it slow like. You can add a little salt, too, if you want. Now here's where you don't add the baking powder. (Lena was sure Alvinia added baking powder.) Baking powder makes them all airy. Cakes should be airy. Dumplings should be a little chewy. Otherwise they get soggy and nasty in a stew and ruin the whole thing. Now you add enough flour so it's sticky, like this, see? It's thicker than cake batter, and a lot stickier than bread dough. Then you add it to the hot stew a teaspoon at a time. When they rise to the top, they're done."

Betty had watched politely, suppressing a smile, but when she bit into one of them for the first time, she said with obvious surprise, her mouth still full, "These are good!" Lena nodded in satisfaction.

When the bowls were filled all around, Gustie took some green leaves and twigs and put them on the fire. Smoke drifted in their direction. "Discouragement for the mosquitoes," she said. She took her bowl and sat on the bottom step to the porch. "How's Jordis?"

"She's something!" Lena shook her head. "I'll tell you. I thought I was good with a horse, and Will is good too, but Jordis—that horse just perked up and decided to live when she put her hands on him. I swear I saw the decision go through him like a tickled muscle. And Dennis isn't going to do anything to him for killing that crazy Gleeve Pruitt. Dennis always acts sensible. He doesn't look for trouble or make more or less of a thing than it is."

Gustie's face got grim. "She didn't write too much about that."

"Well, he came after her, don't you see? This Pruitt fella, and the horse killed him." Lena helped herself to another slice of Episcopalian bread, which she dipped into her stew and brought dripping to her mouth. She continued to talk and eat at the same time. "I guess it wasn't pretty, but for crying out loud, the man was coming after her with a gun and evil on his mind. I say the horse should get a medal.

"He won't tolerate anybody coming too near him but Jordis and me—and Will, and he doesn't mind children. Hank walked into the barn one day and the colt made such an uproar, and he wasn't that strong yet, we thought he'd give himself a heart attack. So, for awhile, the barn was off-limits to everybody but immediate family." Lena swabbed the inside of her bowl with her bread, not realizing she had just included Jordis in her immediate family.

Gustie smiled.

"What's so funny?"

"Nothing. Go ahead, Lena."

"Well, something was done to that horse even before he was put in the stock car, believe me. She's going to have to keep a tight rein on him, that's for sure, but if anybody can do it, she can. She's gone out to your place now. I miss both of 'em. I even miss the blame cat." Lena contemplated her empty bowl and decided to let her stomach settle before getting any more. She leaned back against the support pole of the porch where she sat with her feet dangling over the edge. She had relinquished the rocker to Mary.

Without turning around to look at her, Lena asked, "What are you going to do now, Mary?"

"After the baby is born, I'm going to Philadelphia. I just couldn't go before. I don't know why. I know it would have been easier on everyone if I could have..."

"Don't be feeling that way, Mary." Gustie reached up across the space between them and touched her hand lightly. "We had a good time out here, didn't we?"

From the other side of Lena, Betty was quick to add, "We sewed and read and fished on the ice—and played cards like loose gambling women!" She waved a big green fly away from her food. "Mary owes me three hundred thousand dollars!"

Gustie aimed her gray eyes at Betty. "If we had known we were harboring a card shark, we'd never have started playing."

Betty said, "I play at home with my dad and my brothers."

"What do you play for?" asked Lena, who was not opposed to a good poker game if no money was exchanged. There was a line between fun and something that smacked faintly of the devil and money was usually on it.

"Chores. When I win, they have to do my share of the cleaning and washing up. That's how I buy more time to practice the piano."

"Even your dad?"

"He's a good sport. Yes, he's done a dish now and then for me. I used to think he let me win just so Mama would let me have more practice time. But I've never been sure of that."

"For a good cause." Mary beamed. "Lena, have you heard Betty play?"

"Yes, in church. She's better than Mrs. Happy but don't tell the old goose I said so."

Mary changed the subject. "Lena, what were you doing in the path of the twister when nobody else was?"

"We were at the fairgrounds for the Fourth of July picnic." Lena answered vaguely.

"I know, but you said you were at the Sauer house by yourself...where were Will and Walter? Are they...?"

"They're fine. They weren't even at the fairgrounds. They were at the funeral home. Ma died yesterday."

"What?"

"She just keeled over at her kitchen window. Boom! Gone. Funeral is the day after tomorrow."

"Oh. Ma is dead?"

Lena turned and looked at Mary. She saw tears in her eyes. "She was nearly eighty, Mary. That's a good long life."

"I don't know how good it was." Mary put her spoon back into her unfinished bowl of stew.

"You may have a point there." Lena hopped off the side of the porch and went to the kettle to ladle herself more stew. "Anybody else?" Betty nodded but came to get her own.

"I have to pay my respects."

"Now, how are you going to do that?" Lena just stood by the tripod, her bowl in her hands, looking at Mary, and wishing she had never mentioned Ma's death.

No one spoke. Gustie set down her bowl in the grass and watched ants find it and crawl into it.

Mary said, "I know I can't go to the funeral, but I could go to the grave after they all leave. No one who cared for her will be there to say a prayer, or say good-bye."

"You can pray here." Lena took another mouthful of stew. She ate it standing up.

"I know, but it's not the same, is it?"

"I suppose not." She went back and sat on the steps next to Gustie.

"She was just so alone always, and now she will be alone. I can't bear for her to be put in the ground without anyone to say one sincere word over her grave. It isn't right. Nobody loved her, Lena. I feel so bad for Ma."

"She wouldn't feel bad for you."

Mary said nothing, just stared at the smoke still coming up in thin clouds from the fire.

Lena put her bowl down and took a deep breath. "Well, all right. I feel bad for her too—in a way. And I expect she's with the Savior now. She lived with a Kaiser all those years. The Lord would not require any person to go to hell twice." Lena swatted a mosquito against the side of her neck. "Nasty thing!"

Gustie took her eyes off the busy ants and looked at Mary carefully. "What is it you want to do, Mary?"

"I want to go back. I can get my things while Walter is at the funeral—it is the only way I could be really sure of him not walking in on me. He wouldn't miss his mother's funeral, no matter what."

"What things do you need, Mary? I could get them for you," Lena offered.

"Babka's prayer book. I don't know how I could have left it behind. But I did, and that shawl you knitted for me, Lena. I want that. I don't know how I could have forgotten it."

"For Pete's sake, Mary, I'll knit you another one. And I can get those things for you. Just tell me where they are. I'll send them to you."

"I want to see my house again. Just once more. And my roses. Are they all right? My roses?"

"They're blooming nice as you please. Will is looking after them." Lena softened. "We won't let your roses die, Mary. I promise you that."

Gustie picked up her bowl and shook out the ants. They disappeared into the grass. "We should be able to manage this. If we leave tonight after dark, we would be at my house by daybreak. Mary will have a whole day and night to rest, and the next day, during the funeral, we'll go to her house." She turned to Mary. "You can get your things, and in the evening, you can stop at the grave, and then we'll come back here during the night. No one will see us come and no one will see us go."

"You're really going to go to Philadelphia this time?" Lena asked prying out some strings of rabbit from her teeth.

"Yes. I don't really know why I couldn't go before, but I can go now. I'm even looking forward to it. That is if your aunts haven't changed their minds."

"My aunts are very excited to have you and to have a baby in the house. So is my father."

"Will they like me, do you think?"

"Mary, they will adore you. You will be to them everything I never could be. They will suffocate you with kindness if you let them." Gustie paused a moment before she added, "Now, Betty. What shall we do about you?"

"What do you mean?" Betty did not look at Gustie.

"I think it is high time you went home."

Lena, sitting closest to Betty, thought she heard Betty sigh. A sigh of relief, perhaps?

"I think we just make it simple. You and I took the train back from Philadelphia as far as Wheat Lake so

I could pick up my horse and wagon. You stayed with me to keep me company."

"Gustie, you have the mind of a schemer and a conniver!"

"Why, thank you, Lena."

When even Lena had finally eaten her fill and given up her bowl to Gustie to wash, the crying of the circling gulls caught their attention at the same time as a strong wave of wind lifted their skirts and blew their hair. They saw the humped backs of black clouds rushing toward them from the south. Betty and Gustie hauled the pot up under the porch roof, and Betty pulled the tarp down on the southern side. They brought more chairs out and sat on the porch.

The sky over the lake remained blue with only wisps of white cloud. They gazed at it through the curtains of rain that poured down upon them. Being at the physical edge of a rainstorm was like being in a dream. Lena just shook her head and said nothing. This had been a peculiar day all the way around.

Once the herd of angry bull clouds had stampeded past them, the land was wet, but softly sunny again.

The light remained diffused over the land and stayed that way till after ten o'clock. Saying that they had to use up their bottle of milk before they left, Gustie put the kettle on, and they sipped milky tea and watched the light fade over the lake and turn Crow Kills' mated pair of pelicans to silhouettes.

Their conversation, along with the prairie sounds, became more subdued. People would be going home late after the Fourth of July celebration in Wheat Lake. They hoped they would be on the road late enough so they wouldn't meet anyone. But in case they did encounter other travelers on the dark road, they decided that Lena would tell the truth about how she had ended up in Cleremont and now was getting a ride with some Hutterites who were traveling at night as a favor to her who was so anxious to get home to her baby. Hutterites who only spoke German. If Gustie, Betty, and Mary wore black, and took along black bonnets and veils to cover their faces, in the dark no one would recognize them.

Gustie felt sadness every time she left Crow Kills. She had always thought that it was because she was leaving Dorcas, then because she was so often leaving Jordis. But tonight, even though she was going to be with Jordis, she felt a sadness trail across her heart like the silver train of the moon, which lay like silk on the water.

She wanted not to go. But she couldn't forbid Mary to return to Charity. Mary would grieve for Gertrude Kaiser, for her prayer book, for her last look at her beautiful house. She needed these things to store in her heart in order to go on. She needed things to be finished in one place before going to another.

Gustie hadn't finished anything with any of the people she loved in Philadelphia. She had just left. Her mother she had never known, and yet she had always felt there was something there that needed to be done. And it had to be done with and through her father, or through her aunts, or even through Oksana and Michael. All these people had known Philippa Caine, the woman she couldn't remember but who haunted her in small ever present ways. Gustie had left things unfinished and unsaid between herself and her father. The few letters they had exchanged in the last year had been welcome but superficial...there was so much else.

Maybe Mary was the wise one. You never left anything behind. You always took it with you. But at least you had to tie off an end, close a book before you could put it back on the shelf. Or at least end a chapter. Even if that meant only one last look at some roses and collecting a book of Polish prayers. Gustie wished she had had more courage, more patience to stay in Philadelphia just a little longer. And yet, she did not look forward to going back. She heard Lena's voice calling from the wagon. "We're ready, Gustie." She splashed her face with cold lake water and walked back up the bank to take the reins. Fireflies blinked in the weeds around the cabin and in the brush under the cottonwoods. She thought she saw something stir there. Probably a badger, maybe a raccoon. By dawn they would be tucked in safely at Gustie's house in Charity. A big surprise for Jordis. Mary and Betty could rest in the bedroom, Lena could have the trundle bed, and Gustie and Jordis could spread a blanket in the barn. They had done it before.

Jack Frye hadn't been to Charity in a long time. It was too high brow for him. But this was the place to go to collect a payment for something he figured would be important enough for a certain somebody to pay for.

So he'd just strolled down to the last boxcar of the west-bound train and as it started up, when nobody, especially Joe Gruba, was looking, he grabbed onto the moving train and swung himself on board. At the curve that headed into Charity, the train slowed down. He jumped off into a weedy patch at the side of the tracks before the tail of the train got in seeing distance of the depot. He brushed himself off, picked up his hat, and nonchalantly walked into town.

He asked the first person he met where the saloon was. That was the place to go for information. He was directed to Leroy's Tavern. Even Charity's saloon was high brow. It didn't smell of anything but beer.

"Where might I find a fella named Walter Kaiser?"

"Today you'll find him either at the church or the graveyard."

"What'd he die?"

"No, his mother died. If you have business with him, you might want to wait till another day."

"Uh huh. Thank you."

Jack couldn't wait another day. He needed money now. He nodded to Leroy and left the saloon.

Out on the street again, Jack asked a tall thin man in black with a broad black hat. "Where is the church?"

"Now which church would you be looking for?"

"How many churches you got?"

"We've got a Lutheran church, a Catholic church, the Methodists and the Episcopalians. And I think there is some church down over the hill there and I don't know what they call themselves. I and my family are Methodists. You're always welcome..."

"There's a funeral today for Walter Kaiser's mother."

"That would be the Lutheran Church then. You go right up Main Street. It's the white church with the steeple at the far end. Can't miss it."

Jack thrust his hands deep in his empty pockets and walked north. He passed Olna's Kitchen. The smells coming from there were delicious and made his stomach rumble. He'd only had a can of beans while he waited for the train back in Wheat Lake. His last can of beans. After he got his money, he'd come back and have hot roast beef and potatoes and gravy. And all the black coffee he could drink. His mouth watered. He'd throw in some biscuits and apple pie.

But when he got to the church, he wasn't sure how to go about what he was there to do. A few people were going in. He couldn't tell if they were late or early. Either way, Walter Kaiser was most likely already in there. Jack was pondering whether or not to go in when he saw someone familiar. It wasn't that he recognized the face as much as the missing left arm and the bear-like walk.

Oscar Kaiser stopped when he saw Jack Frye. Jack took a step forward. "I'm looking for your brother."

"Which brother?"

"The one you said his wife was in Philadelphia. That one."

"Walter. What are you looking for him for?"

The left sleeve of Oscar's black suit was folded and pinned to his shoulder. He wore a white shirt buttoned to the neck and no tie. He gazed at Jack with an intensity that sucked all the cockiness out of him. He tried to gather his purpose together again. "I got some information for him."

"Like what?"

"Well, it is news he might find valuable."

"Valuable?"

"Well, if I could speak to him he might..."

"You want money?"

"Well, a man goes out on a limb, you know. Puts himself at a certain risk to his own wellbeing and I just thought that might be worth something to your brother. Maybe not."

"What would be worth money to my brother?"

Oscar's ghost of a smile was so demeaning it got Jack's back up. He said, "It's about that wife of his. He might be interested to know she ain't in Philly delphia. That's what."

There was some alteration in the atmosphere. Jack suddenly wished he were someplace else. He forgot why he had come here. To tell a man—yes, for the money. He needed money. Yes, but now...

Oscar readily reached into his pocket and took out a five dollar bill. Jack took it.

Yes, money was what he'd come for. But now he was unsure. He felt confused and didn't know why.

Oscar misunderstood Jack's hesitation and dropped another dollar into his hand.

Jack swallowed. "She never was in Philly delphia. She's been layin' up there on the rez with them Indians." *Don't spill it all at once.* "That ain't all."

Oscar read the sly look on Jack's face and handed over three more dollars.

"She's got a bun in the oven!"

"What?"

"Big as a house. I guess she let some buck get on her when she was out on the rez when they all was sick that time."

Oscar looked skeptical.

Jack was afraid he'd take the money back. "Why else would she be layin' up at the reservation with that old maid with a bun in the oven and ready to pop? You tell your brother that."

"I will."

"But there's one more thing."

The look on Oscar's face told him he shouldn't push it.

Jack said, "You can tell him he don't have to go to Wheat Lake for her either. She's comin' here."

"When?"

"Today. Right now. Well, I don't know how long it'll take to get here. They all piled into a wagon night before last and headed this way. He could just ride out on the road east and he'd sure run into them."

"How do you know so much about my brother's wife's business?"

Jack had his story ready. "Well, I go down there fishing every now and again. I was down there day before yesterday, and thinkin' the cabin was empty I just set my line a little closer to it than I usually do. The fish weren't biting so I just kept moving over to see if I could get a bite and pretty soon I heard voices. I've had some trouble with the Indians, so I just stay down, see, till they go on by and hope nobody sees me. But then I hear women's voices—they sound like white women so I peeks through the underbrush and I see em. The school teacher, a young one—you said something about a kid being with em, right? And the one in the family way. I can't hear em but I see em all right. Then I fall asleep and when I wake up they're getting in their wagon and I followed em and see them take the road to Charity."

"How do you know they're coming here?"

"Don't think they'll head cross country. Not with a woman in a family way bouncing around in the wagon. No place else to go on that road between there and here but here."

Oscar put two more dollar bills in Jack Frye's hands. "This is for keeping it to yourself. You know, Walter would like his business between his wife and himself to stay there."

"You betcha. Nobody'll hear it from me."

Jack had his pocket full of money. He spun around and headed back to Olna's to take care of his empty stomach.

Gertrude Kaiser's funeral was at eleven o'clock. At five minutes after, Gustie with Mary beside her, pulled up in back of Mary's house. Both women were veiled. There was no one on the street that they could see.

Gustie climbed down first and helped Mary out of the wagon. Saying she knew right where her things were—she would go upstairs, get them out of her dresser drawer, come right back out—Mary disappeared into her house.

Gustie leaned against the wagon wheel to wait for her and keep an eye on the street. Most people in Charity, she imagined, were at the funeral. They'd go out of respect for one of the earliest homesteaders in Stone County rather than fondness for the woman herself. Gustie also imagined the scene this morning when Betty appeared on Alvinia's doorstep. Her homecoming must have gone all right since the girl hadn't come back seeking sanctuary. Gustie smiled. Alvinia would have had her back up, like Lena had, but like Lena, she would have gotten over it quickly. Betty planned to go with her family to the funeral. She promised Mary she would say a special prayer for the old lady. Jordis had agreed to go as well. Jordis didn't care much for churches but Mary felt better knowing that there would be at least a couple of genuinely sympathetic people there. Jordis wanted to make Mary happy.

A minute passed. Not yet noon and it was warm enough so that the black dress Gustie wore was too hot and her hat and veil were stifling. She puffed the veil out away from her face with a sharp exhalation and tried to endure it for a minute more. Through the black netting, Gustie saw Lena and Jordis running toward her. Lena was waving her hands. Gustie waved back.

"Where's Mary?" Jordis's voice carried down the block. So much for keeping this a secret.

"She's inside. Why?" She saw Alvinia coming behind them in her wagon.

Lena panted as she called, "Oscar isn't at the funeral. I asked Nyla where he was and she didn't know."

Alvinia reined in her team and hit the ground running as Gustie tore off her hat and ran for the door. Right behind her, Alvinia said, "I sent Betty for the sheriff just to be on the safe side."

No longer caring about quiet or secrecy, Gustie banged open the door and yelled, "Mary, Mary, we have to go. Now!" They ran through the kitchen and entering the living room they saw her. Mary lay at the foot of the stairs, on her side. One arm was twisted underneath her and the other lay across her face.

Gustie almost stopped, but Alvinia kept moving and Gustie was carried in her wake, dropping to her knees beside Alvinia who took Mary's wrist, seeking a pulse as she lifted Mary's arm away from her face.

Mary's eyes were closed. There was blood on her lips. She was already going gray. Alvinia concentrated on finding a pulse as Jordis knelt beside her and Lena knelt on the other side of Gustie. Lena grabbed for Gustie's hand but no one said a word.

They heard the front door open and Dennis and Betty rushed into the room at the same time as Oscar Kaiser appeared on the landing at the top of the stairs.

Betty knelt with them, closing the circle. They all looked up. The question in each of their minds never made it to anyone's lips, because a sly smile crept over his thick features. He covered it with a look of feigned surprise, but not soon enough. They all saw it and knew what he had done.

With deliberation, Dennis drew his gun out of its holster, aimed and fired, shooting Oscar in the heart. Oscar crumpled where he stood, in a heap on the landing, the look of real surprise, the last look he had in life, became his mask in death.

The gunshot left a hush in the house. Nothing was heard outside. Alvinia said, "Dennis, you better go."

Dennis gazed at Mary, pain chiseled deeply across his face.

Gustie at last found her voice. "Go on, Dennis. You weren't here. We'll take care of her."

318

Dennis Sully's eyes finally left Mary and took in the faces of the five women looking up at him. He didn't see one tear. He holstered his pistol. He took a last look at the form on the floor, turned and walked out of the house.

"She's dying," said Alvinia.

Jordis unsheathed the knife from her boot and held it out to Alvinia who hesitated only a second. As Mary's heart fluttered its last, Alvinia cut through her dress.

Chapter 17: August 1901

O SCAR KAISER DIDN'T HAVE A funeral, just a graveside service poorly attended. Pastor Erickson said a few words over the coffin before it was lowered into the ground. Shorty Larson and his wife were there, and Will and Nyla. No tears fell. Shorty was now going to work for Walter Kaiser, at increased wages, so those who thought of it at all imagined that Shorty was not mourning so much as giving thanks. Oscar was laid to rest next to his mother in the Kaiser family plot. Pa Kaiser had thought ahead, purchasing enough ground to bury himself, his wife, his sons and their wives. There would be one plot left over because Mary was to be buried at Crow Kills, where she had been happy.

Mary's funeral was held under the sky. Alvinia had insisted that it not be held in the Catholic church in Charity. "Mary was always afraid of that priest, why would we let him have a final say over her?" Lena and Gustie agreed and Walter went along with it. They spoke to Father Gregory. He agreed to have a Catholic funeral for her with one stipulation, that she be buried in consecrated ground. That meant that he had to come out and consecrate the spot where she was to be buried next to Clare and Dorcas. Jordis didn't mind but asked Little Bull for his permission. He gave it.

The service was attended by most of the people of the Red Sand as well as Owen Braaten, Lena and Will and Gracia, Alvinia and Carl and all their children. Pauly Wirkus came out of respect for Betty and also out of curiosity to see where his sweetheart had spent most of the winter, in secret. He was having a hard time getting used to the idea. Clark Llewellyn held Alice's hand during the Mass. Joe Gruba and his wife Minnie were there, and, to Lena's surprise, so was Nyla. She had taken the train to Wheat Lake and ridden out with Joe and Minnie. Her face had changed since Oscar's death. She no longer had that pinched, sullen look. She said to Lena, "I'm going to miss her. She was always so nice to me."

"Me too, Nyla. Me too."

A number of people had ridden that train to attend Mary's funeral: Doc Moody and Lester Evenson and their wives, Kenneth and Morgan O'Grady, Axel and Harriet Kranhold, Hank and Orville Ackerman. Olna had closed her café for the afternoon to attend. Lena never expected them to make the trip out here to the Indian reservation to attend the funeral of a quiet woman no one had paid much attention to, but there they were. And Walter, who seemed more bewildered than grief stricken.

As the service began, Betty, Lena, and Alvinia subtly eased themselves away from their men and joined Gustie and Jordis at the front, forming a crescent around the coffin and, unaccountably to all who noticed, holding hands. Jordis, at the far right, held Mary's child. Gustie grasped her free hand.

Even when the five women weren't holding hands, which they never did again, it seemed as though they formed a wall around Mary's life and death. Mathilda Langager was the only one to try to breach the wall and she tried it with Betty, thinking perhaps as the youngest, Betty would be the weakest. Mathilda had stopped her on the street coming out of O'Grady's the day before the funeral. She asked, her mouth smiling, but her eyes hard, "How was Philadelphia, Betty?"

"It's a beautiful city," Betty smiled back. Then she said with a seriousness that took the smile off Mathilda's face. "They call it the City of Brotherly Love, did you know that?"

Mathilda shut up and no one ever asked Betty another thing about Philadelphia.

No one had been told exactly what happened that day in Mary's house, but people talked, and because the stories they told each other were vague, they had to color in the details themselves. Folks added a bit here, embellished there, and surmises soon became undisputed facts. The thing took shape and solidified into a story that was not quite right and not altogether wrong. They had put one and two together and come up with about four and a half. The story went something like this: Gustie had taken Mary in
322

when it was discovered she was expecting. A Christian thing to do, no matter how you looked at it. Before Gustie sent her off to Philadelphia, Mary wanted one more visit with her lover and had arranged to meet him in her house. They had been confronted by Oscar Kaiser, and there had been violence. The unknown man had left before Gustie and Alvinia discovered the bodies.

There were as many theories as to how and why Oscar Kaiser had come to be in Mary's house that day as there were storytellers. That was one part of the story that had never jelled. And how Betty played in all of this, nobody could figure out. She had to have gone to Philadelphia. How else could you account for the fancy belt buckles and hair ribbons being sported by her brothers and sisters?

People also remembered a stranger in town asking questions and eating his dinner at Olna's Kitchen. Could he have been the father of Mary's baby? *That little geezer?* others scoffed. No, it had to be the tall dark fella that some folks remembered seeing ride out of town at a gallop on a big black horse. Had to be him, that's for sure.

Whenever Walter Kaiser's name came up, which it had to, people stopped talking and sucked their teeth and shook their heads. *Poor Walter.* What else could be said? In his presence they talked about the weather and the price of feed and seed.

Walter himself hadn't changed much. He was quieter perhaps, but he still went to work—work was going to pick up for both Walter and Will now that their elder brother was no longer a competitor—he still did his shopping at O'Grady's and had dinner from time to time at Olna's. People wondered what he was going to do and it appeared he wasn't going to do anything.

After the story of Mary's death was told, tongues more or less stopped wagging. The birth of an out-of-wedlock child would have caused considerably more comment if Mary were alive and well. But she had paid the ultimate price for her indiscretion, and most people had the decency to let it go at that.

Folks wondered about the fate of the child, but no one stepped forward to offer a home, assuming that Alvinia or Lena would take the child in.

People worried about Sheriff Sully who had become withdrawn, almost sullen, frustrated perhaps by not being able to apprehend the killer. Just a year ago, he hadn't solved the murder of old man Kaiser either. No one blamed him, but the sheriff was apparently taking it to heart. There was talk that he had mentioned going west.

Gustie and Jordis, Lena, Alvinia and Betty never discussed that day among themselves. They didn't have to. They knew that they had, each one of them, fired that gun. Dennis had only happened to be holding it at the time.

Under a cloudless sky with a breeze fluttering the cassocks and vestments of the priests and mitigating the heat of the August sun, Father Flagstad said a few words about Mary, how she had come to the Red Sand to help in their time of need, Little Bull added a few words of his own, and Father Gregory said a Mass. Then, Alvinia stepped out of the crescent of women and faced the assembly. Alvinia wasn't used to speaking up in front of gatherings of people but "somebody besides a priest has to say something," she had said. "Mary wanted someone to say a sincere word over Gertrude and she deserves nothing less from us. One of us has to do it." Lena answered for them all, "Well, looks like it's you then, Alvinia."

She stood before them all, her voluminous blue striped dress billowing around her, her hands clasped tightly before her. "Alive or dead, you are in the hand of God." She relaxed her hands somewhat. "I never knew anyone who seemed to be more in His hand than Mary." She brushed a stray wisp of yellow hair off her forehead. "I'm going to speak plainly. I've delivered more babies in and around this town than Doc Moody." She looked at him with a no-offense-meant-but-it's-the-truth kind of look. He nodded back in acknowledgement. "I've delivered the deformed who in God's mercy flew to the arms of Jesus in a few hours of drawing their first troubled breaths; I've taken the still-born from their sorrowing mothers' wombs directly to their tiny graves. Every time I think I've done it all, I learn you've never done it all till you're dead and past doing anything." Her eyes rested on Rose, sleeping in Jordis's arms.

"Mary was a child in a woman's body. I don't mean she was not smart, or that she was mentally off in the way, like...say... Lena's poor brother Tori, who fell off a wagon when he was four and knocked his head and was never all there for the rest of his too short life, God bless him." Lena nodded as well, a blessing on her brother Tori. "No, Mary was childlike in the way little ones are before they learn any kind of meanness, before they learn to pass judgments on things—what Jesus meant when he said you have to enter the Kingdom of Heaven as a child, and that is why I know that no matter what—Mary is in heaven now because she entered it as a child. And I know that when we are born, God shifts us from His right hand to His left. And when we die, we just go back to His good right hand. That's all."

The day after Mary's funeral, Nyla surprised Will by giving him Oscar's well machine and his team of horses.

Will's machine was, as he had often said, a pile of junk being held together by spit and good intentions. His work horses were getting old and hadn't been prime stock to begin with. He had never even had room to stable them in his own barn. But now with the new rig, and the new team, and selling off his old machine for parts, he was going to enlarge his barn. Old Tom would now have regular stable mates.

Jordis saw him coming, riding Old Tom and leading four brown, heavy footed draft horses. He dismounted and she walked out to meet him. "Hello, Will. What have you got here?" She'd never been to one of his drill sites so she had never seen his team.

"Well, these are my old team. They're just about ready for slaughter, but Lena won't have it. She threw a fit, by golly, so I was just wondering." He took off his hat, smoothed his hair and replaced the hat. "I was just thinking, maybe you could turn em loose with those others." He indicated Biddy and Moon and Whisper grazing in the pasture. "They're easy keepers. I'll bring you out some oats and a little sour mash now and then. I'll help you add on to your barn."

"What are their names?"

"Sonny. He's the oldest. Dan, here—you gotta watch his front left leg. He gets kinda stiff in the winter. I just rub it at night with liniment. It does the trick.

"Bonnie's a good old girl. Never gives any trouble at all. Jumper likes a cookie now and then. She has a real sweet tooth."

Jordis just pointed with her chin to the pasture and smiled. He led them to the gate, opened it and unhooked their lead ropes. He patted them on the rumps as they went through. They stood for a moment to assess their new situation, then ambled toward the water trough. Biddie, Moon, and Whisper gazed at them with interest, without welcome or hostility. "They'll be fine here," Jordis assured him, fastening the gate.

"I know they will. They'll be fine with you. Lena will be mighty glad."

"You can come and see them any time, Will. Any time at all."

Never before had such wedding preparations been seen in Charity, South Dakota. Alvinia had swallowed all her objections to Betty marrying a Catholic boy in a Catholic church, because she had promised Betty she would. And she was so relieved to have her girl back home, her converting to Catholicism no longer seemed like such a terrible thing.

Alvinia's mother had sent her own wedding dress made of yards of heavy satin and lace she had brought from Norway. "This is what I should have given you, now it should go to Betty," she had written. "Do what you will to make it wearable for her, if she wants it."

Betty wanted it, with alterations, which Alvinia did not know how to accomplish, so she went to Lena with her problem and the dress.

"Well, now isn't this a beautiful mess of stuff?" Lena's eyes shone as she let the satin flow over her hands. Alvinia produced a picture that Betty had cut out of a magazine of an elegant gown, lace and satin, but without the Old Country look of the one Lena was holding.

"I don't know what to do," moaned Alvinia.

"It's the simplest thing in the world," Lena assured her. "I've been doctoring patterns and making things up and fixing things up my whole life. Sewed my first dress when I was nine. Now...let's see what we've got here." Lena spread a sheet on her living room floor and laid the dress on it. She knelt and examined it front and back, comparing it to the dress in the picture. Then she looked to see what seam width she had. Gracia toddled into the middle of the dress in her stocking feet and sat down among its multitudinous folds and frills. The mothers smiled at her indulgently. Lena said, "Well, it won't come out exactly, but, I can get it pretty close." She looked up at Alvinia. "You say Betty likes this material all right?"

"Oh, yes, she likes it. But—"

"—it's old fashioned. Young girls don't want to look like their grandmas, and I don't blame them. Why should they? Now, you bring Betty over here this afternoon so I can take her measurements. This'll be easy because she's smaller than the dress. I can see that. I did this for Eunice Peterson, you know, but her

328

grandmother was a little bit of a thing when she got married and Eunice, well...you know she's a big girl. I had a heck of a time! So I'll be taking away, not trying to add. That's always easier."

Alvinia said, "We can pay you in..." she was about to say *a lifetime of free freezer space*, when Lena interrupted her vehemently.

"Alvinia Torgerson, now you listen to me! I'd have died right there on that dining room table if it hadn't been for you and Betty and Alice." Lena turned back to the dress, muttering, "There aren't enough dresses from here to Kingdom Come to make up for that."

Alvinia quietly backed out of the living room leaving Lena to fuss by herself.

Wherever they went, the Torgersons were met with a similar reaction, though none so outspoken as Lena's. Alvinia had indeed delivered more babies than Doc Moody, but unlike the doctor, she had never accepted a penny for her services. Carl had performed many kindnesses as well...handing over an extra pound of meat to a poor family, allowing extended credit to someone in hard times, making a delivery when someone was sick.

The Mothers and Daughters of the Holy Rosary, which Alvinia concluded was the rough equivalent in the Catholic Church of the Ruth and Esther Circle in the Lutheran, made beautiful arrangements for the sanctuary out of autumn flowers and small sheaves of wheat.

Every woman in town cooked or baked something for the reception. Carl cleared out the dining and living rooms to provide space for borrowed tables, and the night before Betty's wedding, the tables were resplendent with the finest linens and china and silver that Charity had to offer. The town had given up its treasures, including Edwina Moody's sterling silver coffee service and Mrs. Lester Evenson's crystal punch bowl.

Gifts for the young couple came from all over Stone County. Because of her tenure as waitress in Olna's Kitchen and her travels with her mother as midwife, Betty was known even by people she did not remember. Carl set up another long table in the back of the house to hold these many gifts until the bride and groom should open them. All gifts, that is, but one.

The afternoon before the wedding, Jack Mohs ran to the Torgerson house to tell them they better get to the depot and bring their wagon, because Betty just got a jim-dandy present to beat all.

"Well, for heaven's sake, Jack, tell us what it is!" demanded Alvinia.

"No, Ma'am. Pa'd kill me. He said it should be a surprise!"

The entire Torgerson family arrived just as the men that Willie Mohs recruited from the granary, Leroy's Tavern, and O'Grady's General Store were straining under the weight of Betty's present as they unloaded it from the train. When Betty saw it, she gasped and clapped her hands on the top of her head, as if she needed to keep it from flying off. From Gustie's descriptions, she knew exactly what she had just gotten as a wedding present: Philippa Caine's baby grand piano, which had, until three days ago, sat for over forty years in the parlor of Gustie's house in Philadelphia.

Dear Betty,

I want to give you a wedding present. Alvinia said that fixing up your dress is enough, but that's just ripping out and sewing up a seam or two. After all that you and your mama have done for me, and this being a special and blessed occasion, I want to give you something special. So I'm giving you my pie recipe. So here it is.

It's easier to make good pie in the winter because you can let your lard and your pastry dough cool outside. But if you make pie in the summer, just make sure you've got ice in your ice box. Otherwise it's a big waste of time and you'll just be making a mess.

So you take some nice apples and peel them and slice them pretty thin and you can let them sit just covered in cold water till you have your pastry ready. Now if you do that, you can add just a scant tsp. of whiskey to the water but you don't have to. Then you take two cups of nice white flour, add a little salt and a little sugar, and sift it. I always sift my flour. Then I sift it again. But you don't have to sift it twice. It's just nice if you do.

Now your lard has to be fresh and cold. You can add a little butter too, and that has to be cold. You slice up the lard and the butter into small cubes and you add a few cubes at a time while you cut them into the flour. You do this as fast as you can so it doesn't warm up and get gooey. You add enough lard so that your flour makes pea-sized balls. If you let the balls get bigger, you're going to have tough pastry. I'm telling you.

Now you have to add a few sprinkles of cold water as you toss your pastry with a fork. Just enough to make it all stick together. Then, you divide the dough into two balls and wrap them up and put them in your ice box or outside in the winter. Let them sit there for about half an hour. If you haven't already peeled your apples you can do it now. You have to get the steps right as you go along. Some women think that it doesn't matter so much. If you add too much water you can just add more flour and work it in to the right consistency. But you do that, your pastry will be like tree bark or shoe leather and that's fine if that's what you want.

Don't overwork it. You're not making bread. You're making a pie. So now you have two nice round shapes of dough. Put one on a lightly floured board and you start to roll it out. Just sprinkle flour over it so the rolling pin doesn't stick to it and roll it out nice and easy in all directions. You turn it around, you see, on the board, and you roll in all different directions equally so it stays round. Don't bear down on it hard. Roll it with a light hand. It takes longer that way but it rolls out nicer and thinner. If you roll it with a heavy hand, you are not really rolling it out, you're just flattening it. That's why they call it a rolling pin and not a hammer. When it is the right size, you just fold it in half. Use a wide spatula so you don't rip the edges. You pick it up, again help yourself with the spatula so you don't rip it and put the fold side in the middle of your pie pan and open it, and press the pastry down snug in the pan. Well, everybody knows this so I'll skip on to the apples.

Now you have to go back and drain the apples and blot them with a clean dishtowel. You put a layer of apples in your pastry, and sprinkle with sugar and cinnamon, a spot or two of butter. Not too much butter. Then another layer. I like to make three layers. Here is where you have to know your apples. If they are sweet or tart. You want enough sugar but not too much. Tart apples—you'll need a couple cups of sugar. Sweet, not so much. You're probably going to have tart apples for baking because if it's a sweet apple you'll just eat it raw. Now the pie is filled and over your top layer of sugar you sprinkle as much cinnamon as you like, and just a little bit of nutmeg. If you put in too much cinnamon and nutmeg your pie will smell and taste like a pomander ball and nobody likes pomander ball pie. If you can't do just a little, better not add it at all. I'm telling you. Then you take a teaspoon of whiskey and sprinkle it lightly over the top of everything. Or you can wait and brush it on the top of the crust before you sprinkle that with sugar. Try it both ways and see how you like it. I go back and forth. Can't make up my mind. Now everybody knows how to close up a pie so I won't bother to write that down. Your oven should be hot enough to slow-bake a chicken. Hotter than that and you're in for trouble. And you have to pay attention to the weather, because in different weather it takes longer to bake. I don't know why. But you have to watch it.

Well, that's my recipe. With a little practice, you can make a nice pie.

Lena Kaiser

Gustie did not stir at the sound of the soft knocking at the door.

Jordis was reading in the main room. She gathered her shawl around her and went to the door. The time was after midnight. "Dennis," she said softly, stepped outside and closed the door quietly behind her. "I thought you had gone." The fragrance of a fresh cut hayfield was carried on a wave of night air.

"I'm on my way. Koenig owed me a favor and tonight I collected." He took his hat off and pointed with it to the two horses whose reins were draped over the corral fence. Jordis peered into the night and by moon and starlight saw Fever and an animal she didn't recognize, about a hand higher than Dennis's little saddle horse.

"Always been a quiet horse. He won't be no trouble. I was wondering if you'd let him pasture out with your mares. He does good on grass and little oats. Likes a carrot once in awhile." Dennis went silent. Then he resumed. "He won't make it where I'm going. He's too old now. You're the only one I know who'd let him be," he paused, "if you wouldn't mind Ma'am."

"I'll take good care of him, Dennis."

"Here's some money for his oats." Dennis reached into his pocket, and Jordis put her hand on his arm.

"That's not necessary. Do you know where you're going?"

"Always wanted to see the wild country up in Canada."

"Keep in touch. We'll write to you, Dennis, if you let us know where you are."

He nodded. His eyes darted to the house and back to the space around him, not focusing on anything in particular.

334

"You want to see her, Dennis?"

He rubbed his hand across his mouth and then over the back of his neck. Then he nodded.

Silently, Jordis led him into the house. She picked up her reading lamp and lit his way into the bedroom where Gustie lay sleeping. Beside the bed was a cradle. Jordis held the lamp so Dennis could look down and see his and Mary's child sleeping peacefully, covered in a pink crocheted blanket and a square of soft, embroidered leather. He just looked. She held the lamp until he looked away, then she left the bedroom. He came out a moment later. She left the lamp on the table and followed him outside. Neither of them said a word. He gave Fever a light pat on his neck, then walked around him and mounted the other horse.

Jordis raised her hand—a gesture of farewell that she wasn't sure he'd see. He gave a little salute against his hat and disappeared into the night.

She heard soft steps behind her, then Gustie's voice. "I knew he'd come."

"How long have you been awake?"

Gustie stood behind her in her nightgown. "Since he knocked on the door."

"Why didn't you get up?"

"I thought it would be easier if he only had to deal with you. I think this was hard for him. I can't imagine how hard, actually."

"Here." Jordis placed half of her shawl around Gustie's shoulders. They stood together gazing up at the stars.

Epilogue: November 1901

AN HOUR BEFORE SUNRISE, I am at the grave to greet the morning star; to begin the ceremony.

I am too warm under this poncho and the shawl that Gustie wrapped about my head and neck. I drop the shawl and face the southeast, holding the memory bundle close to me, the year-long abiding place of the soul of Dorcas Many Roads.

I do not want to let it go. I know, alone here in the starry dark, that my year of soul keeping has been more for me than for grandmother. The old ones were wise. The loss of those we love is beyond bearing. Yet we must bear it. They knew that to keep a soul, performing all attendant tasks with devotion, eases the way to parting. At the end of the year, when the rites have been fulfilled, grief is transformed, and the parting can be endured. Perhaps even celebrated. Still, can I bear it to end?

I have not performed to the letter of the tradition because I have had no one to teach me, but in this I know my own heart; I have been true to the spirit. For this morning's ceremony, I have fasted and purified myself in the sweat lodge. This last thing is not usually done by a woman, but neither is the keeping of souls.

The star appears, bright and glowing in the winter sky, and climbs steadily in the dark until it fades into the pale light of dawn. It is time.

I feel Gustie's approach behind me. She has Rose in her arms. I must let the ending come.

I lower the bundle to the ground and unroll it across the top of Dorcas's grave. I see her precious things once more: the turtle shell, tobacco bundle, two stones, the decorated leather in the shape of the lizard, the stone spear point, the small piece of buffalo bone, the bundle of porcupine quills, the eagle bone whistle, and the lock of Dorcas's hair.

A strong gust of wind, as if summoned, lifts the hair, scattering it over the prairie, leaving the heavier items behind on the blanket.

I speak the words in Dakotah. I have had to practice and practice them. My tongue does not fit smoothly around my mother's language, but Jimmy Saul taught them to me. He says this is the right way to end.

About Paulette Callen

Paulette Callen's first novel *Charity* was published by Simon and Schuster in 1997. Since then, she has written three other novels: *Command of Silence*, *Death Can Be Murder*, and *Fervent Charity*.

Her poems, articles, and short stories have appeared in small journals, magazines, and anthologies. The poem "See, Nadia!" was included *in Beyond Lament, Poets of the World Bearing Witness to the Holocaust* (Northwestern University Press) and was subsequently selected by artist Carol Rosen for inclusion in her *Holocaust Series*, an eight-book collection of photo/text collages housed in the Whitney Museum, the Simon Wiesenthal Center, and the University of Tel Aviv.

Paulette's employment history includes the Communications Department of a large corporation, a movie theatre, a bank, the gift industry, the ASPCA, the insurance sector, as well as summer stock theatres and a year-long stint with a comedy improvisation company. For nearly four years, she served as a volunteer staff member for POWARS (Pet Owners with Aids Resource Services) in New York City.

After many years as a resident of Manhattan's Upper West Side, she has returned, with her rescued blind Shih Tzu Lily, to her hometown in South Dakota.

Visit her website:
www.paulettecallen.com

OTHER BOOKS FROM
YLVA PUBLISHING

http://www.ylva-publishing.com

CHARITY
(revised edition)

Paulette Callen
ISBN 978-3-95533-075-0 (paperback)
364 pages

The friendship between Lena Kaiser, a sodbuster's daughter, and Gustie Roemer, an educated Easterner, is unlikely in any other circumstance but post-frontier Charity, South Dakota. Gustie is considered an outsider, and Lena is too proud to share her problems (which include a hard-drinking husband) with anyone else.

On the nearby Sioux reservation, Gustie also finds love and family with two Dakotah women: Dorcas Many Roads, an old medicine woman, and her adopted granddaughter, Jordis, who bears the scars of the white man's education.

When Lena's husband is arrested for murdering his father and the secrets of Gustie's past follow her to Charity, Lena, Gustie, and Jordis stand together. As buried horrors are unearthed and present tragedies unfold, they discover the strength and beauty of love and friendship that blossom like wild flowers in the tough prairie soil.

BACKWARDS TO OREGON
(revised and expanded edition)

Jae
ISBN: 978-3-95533-026-2 (paperback)
521 pages

"Luke" Hamilton has always been sure that she'd never marry. She accepted that she would spend her life alone when she chose to live her life disguised as a man.

After working in a brothel for three years, Nora Macauley has lost all illusions about love. She no longer hopes for a man who will sweep her off her feet and take her away to begin a new, respectable life.

But now they find themselves married and on the way to Oregon in a covered wagon, with two thousand miles ahead of them.

BEYOND THE TRAIL

Jae

ISBN: 978-3-95533-083-5 (paperback)
136 pages

"Luke" Hamilton has always been sure that she'd never marry. She accepted that she would spend her life alone when she chose to live her life disguised as a man.

After working in a brothel for three years, Nora Macauley has lost all illusions about love. She no longer hopes for a man who will sweep her off her feet and take her away to begin a new, respectable life.

But now they find themselves married and on the way to Oregon in a covered wagon, with two thousand miles ahead of them.

KICKER'S JOURNEY
(second edition)

Lois Cloarec Hart
ISBN: 978-3-95533-060-6 (paperback)
485 pages

In 1899, two women from very different backgrounds are about to embark on a journey together—one that will take them from the Old World to the New, from the 19th century into the 20th, and from the comfort and familiarity of England to the rigours of Western Canada, where challenges await at every turn.

The journey begins simply for Kicker Stuart when she leaves her home village to take employment as hostler and farrier at Grindleshire Academy for Young Ladies. But when Kicker falls in love with a teacher, Madelyn Bristow, it radically alters the course of her tranquil life.

Together, the lovers flee the brutality of Madelyn's father and the prejudices of upper crust England in search of freedom to live, and love, as they choose. A journey as much of the heart and soul as of the body, it will find the lovers struggling against the expectations of gender, the oppression of class, and even, at times, each other.

What they find at the end of their journey is not a new Eden, but a land of hope and opportunity that offers them the chance to live out their most cherished dream—a life together.

COMING FROM YLVA
PUBLISHING IN SPRING 2014

http://www.ylva-publishing.com

HIDDEN TRUTHS
(revised edition)

Jae

"Luke" Hamilton has been living as a husband and father for the past seventeen years. No one but her wife, Nora, knows she is not the man she appears to be. They have raised their daughters to become honest and hard-working young women, but even with their loving foundation, Amy and Nattie are hiding their own secrets.

Just as Luke sets out on a dangerous trip to Fort Boise, a newcomer arrives on the ranch—Rika Aaldenberg, who traveled to Oregon as a mail-order bride, hiding that she's not the woman in the letters.

When hidden truths are revealed, will their lives and their family fall apart or will love keep them together?